D0605011

Also by Adam Thorpe

MORNINGS IN THE BALTIC

MEETING MONTAIGNE

ULVERTON

ULVE

FOR JO

1650

RETURN

He appeared on the hill at first light. The scarp was dark against a greening sky and there was the bump of the barrow and then the figure, and it shocked. I thought perhaps the warrior buried there had stood up again to haunt us. I thought this as I blew out the lanterns one by one around the pen. The sheep jostled and I was glad of their bells.

He came down towards me, stumbling down over the tussocks of the scarp's slope that was cold and wet still with the night, and I could see he was a soldier from the red tunic that all the army now wore, it was said. He stopped at a distance. He had that wary look of one used to killing. His face was dark with dirt, and stubbled.

Deserters had been known to kill. I went on blowing.

He watched me all the time. Then as I turned towards him, he looked away and down into the valley where the village was beginning to smoke.

I saw him side on and I recognised him.

'Gabby,' I said.

He turned.

'I wondered when,' he murmured, so I could hardly hear. He was the tiredest man I have ever seen.

He sat. He draped his arms over his knees and buried his face in them. Then he looked up at me, smiling.

'I've shook hands with him,' he said.

'With who?'

'General Cromwell. I've shook hands with him.'

'With the General?'

'Aye.' He said this with defiance, but I had no cause not to believe him. Whether a man has done a thing or no, I know when he believes he has, and that is all the same in the end.

'That is a fine thing,' I said. I sat down next to him and wondered if it was right to tell him. And he looked at me so smiling that I hadn't the heart. Of course, I wish now I had, but it might not have saved anything. Sorrow is a water that flows however you try to dam it, that is my thought. It will find a way.

'At Drogheda,' he said. And do you know, I remember this man as a boy at my table, come in to tell me of some carriage he had seen along the main road, of the white glove that had waved to him, and cast him a penny. And other stories I forget now.

'At Drogheda,' he said again.

He wiped his lips that were sore, I noticed.

'Drogheda?'

'Across the water,' he said, pointing at the clouds. He shivered, and I offered him my coat.

He took it. I hoped the sun would strike us soon. Down in the houses smoke broke through mist, piled higher and higher until it whitened with the sun. Up there the larks were warm.

He huddled in the coat. Some taut thing had gone. You could smell his tiredness.

'At Drogheda,' he said, 'in Ireland. I shook his hand, like this.'

He clasped at air and moved his hand up and down. I could see it. I could see the General in this place and I could see Gabby be taken by the hand and have it shook.

The dogs pawed him, and I whistled them off. I reached into my basket and broke a piece of bread and a corner of cheese and handed it to him.

Did he scoff them!

I passed him the firkin and he tipped it back so that the ale runnelled either side of his mouth and down onto his leggings. He coughed and wiped his mouth and I confess I took back the ale double-quick for I had another twelve hours to thirst by. I lived the other side of Ulverton then.

'Was he a big man?' I said.

He sighed and licked his sore lips and picked at crumbs. He was thinking.

'No,' he said.

I was surprised at this, though Gabby was never a small man himself.

Soldiering made him more crookbacked, not less. He looked no different to you nor I.

He turned surly then, and asked why should he be? And I kept out of it because Gabby seemed changed and I was alone, and my dogs then were soft. I fancied he might own a gun under his tunic.

So I said nothing either about the other matter, even when he asked.

'Anne,' he said, 'my Anne.'

He was asking, in his own way. He'd been off so long and all of us thought him dead though I didn't tell him.

'You'd best go and see,' I said.

I stood and fiddled with something—I think a lantern door or maybe a yoke or maybe both, one after the other—anyway, something to show I was busy and maybe I couldn't talk. I also sent the dogs scurrying after a big ewe on the scarp who was doing no harm there. I am a cowardly man.

I could hear him rubbing his chin, like a saw on a horn.

'She's not dead then,' he said.

'No.'

'Not poorly then,' he said.

I said no, and whistled, and said he'd best go and see. My heart was thumping, I'll say, like I was a guilty man.

He stood up.

'I know why you're sore,' he said. 'I know why. I'll thank you for the food and drink, and the talking, but I need no judgements, William.'

His voice was hoarse.

I shrugged. Then I spoke not looking at him.

'Best go and see, that's all I'll say. I knowed you as a boy, Gabby. You used to sit out sometimes. We looked at the words in our heads and seed if they were God's words or no, remember? Then you've gone out fighting for God's word on earth and I don't know if matters have changed, only that the King has lost his head and after Newberry old Joshua Swiffen's field was smashed and sodden with blood and nothing's altered as I can see. That's all.'

I made this little speech much like the parson's because my heart was thumping and I wished to divert his thoughts from Anne his wife. I think now whether it mightn't have been better to tell him outright, but I was frighted.

'You know the farm was broke. Soldiering was how I would set it right.'

'In heaven or on earth?' I said.

He smiled at that.

'What I have sewn into my tunic will see us through,' he said. 'I fought for God and Anne so she might have a son that lives and no parish nor more working for Swiffen nor Hort nor Stiff nor any of them. I've come right back,' he said.

He reached into his breeches and pulled out something I thought was gold but when he oped his hand it was a ball of old ribbons that had long ago been red.

'She were allus dreaming of it,' he said. 'She were allus dreaming of her hair all up in silks. Hair black as a raven and all up in red silks, like a lady. And rings on her fingers! Aye. She were allus dreaming of it!'

Those ribbons looked so tattered and pale and torn it was sad, like he had pulled out his own heart. Even his fierceness was not that of love but, as I think it, of anguish.

I paused in my whittling of the yoke (for that's what I was doing) and nodded my head neither knowingly nor as judgement. I could see the heads he had torn the ribbons from and all the fingers he had maybe cut for rings, if he were telling the truth, and prayed without moving my lips. He smiled and put the clump of ribbons back into his breeches carefully like it was a live thing and not to be hurt. The cocks were hollering from the thatch down there but else all you could hear were the cluckets ringing all over the coomb as the flock grazed. I thought. I thought how quiet we were compared to the noise of soldiering. The business at Newberry had set my sheep off in a canter, miles off.

He took my hand all of a sudden, that had a knife in it, so I dropped the yoke and threw the knife down and took his hand. Then we hugged, and kissed, as old friends, and I smelt the liquor on his skin that was a deep part of him and not just for jollity, and I wondered to myself how he reconciled this with God's word.

He was crying.

He was a little boy again. There were stains on his tunic, that smelt of guns, and he took out a little leather belt with powder cases hanging from it, and threw it towards the scarp, so as it fell it twisted out, spilling bitterness into the wind.

'Wexford and Drogheda,' he said, choking a little on the last, 'we did for all of them at Wexford and Drogheda. That was God's word. Women and kiddies, William. God's word. A flaming minister. A shining sword.'

'Yes, yes. I heard of this,' I said, then whistling back my dogs who had gone after the bandolier.

'You had?' he said, looking up.

I nodded, and turned away, and went down the slope a little. He followed.

I stopped at a bush and hooked out a small skull with my crook and showed it to him.

'She was lambing. Dog. It's in the nature of things, Gabby.'

The skull still smelt somewhat so I cast it back.

'Until the Last Day when the Kingdom comes,' I said.

'Then I'm a dog, no better nor worse.' He grinned, and I knew he thought I was a simple old man for my parables.

'I thought you were needing forgiveness,' I said.

'That's for me to decide,' he said, 'though we were blessed by the parson after. We were all black with the smoke. Now you have God's kingdom. I don't need no powder. All men will be equal in the common weal. Shepherds and kings.'

'No kings,' I said. I was a little angered, that's true.

'No. No kings.'

He grinned again and clapped me on the shoulder and then was off down the slope, where he tumbled and came up again laughing, down towards the thatch where the mist still clung and the cocks and dogs were hollering as if to warn him, for I wasn't. I just stared, angered somewhat, and worrited more than a man can say by what he would do when he found his Anne with her husband, that wasn't Gabby, for we had all thought him dead these five years.

I had my ewes folded for it was into February, and I spent that day thatching the hurdles. I remember it as a bright day, the warmest so far that year, save for a bitterness when the wind got up. I was struck into deep thought while the needle and twine did their work. Save for my page or a passing vagrant without his certificate cadging a day's work (which I always refused) few were the times I had someone to talk with out on the sheep-walks. It were pure chance that Gabby had happened on that way back, I said to myself, over and over.

Or was it?

Maybe so, still, but now I'm thinking hard that Gabby knew I would be folding by the barrow, for that's where we would sit when he was a boy, and his little arms pulling out the lambs in a slither.

It was for news of Anne he had passed this way. It was a preparation for sorrow, or gladness, from an old friend he might trust to tell him gently, and not stir the village. His farm was hid behind a hill on the other side and I saw him skirt the thatch and take the walk that goes up through the coppice. And the thing is, I had not told him. This preyed on my mind that much so I thought, well, I will go and see. For I half-expected Gabby to return running helter-skelter up the slope towards us, scattering the flock with his howls.

But he never did.

My good Ruth had rolled a dumpling of barley-flour that I cut into more from need than liking: it was another coat in warmth. I did so and sat the dogs and hollered the page over to bide with the ewes (though none had lambed yet) and took my lantern, it being dusk or thereabouts, and walked up through the coppice to the crest above Gabby Cobbold's farm—for I still thought of it as his, a little mean thing shuffled round a yard with five great elms casting most of it into shade.

It was smoking. I could make that out even in the dark and it all looked peaceful. There was no reason why the fire shouldn't have been lit excepting they were poor and it was late in the winter but maybe I thought his return would have put all out, like a cold gust my lantern if the door is not shut or the horn come away from the window.

It was a guilty man that wound his way down between the furze into business that was none of his. The Lord forgive me, I said, for it is my conscience that drives me to this. I knew where the dogs were and came up against the other side where a chalk wall had let in one window shuttered against the cold. There was an old cart-wheel all rotten and split leant up nearby and I rolled it to the window and stood up on the nave and set my eye against a crack in the shutter.

This was the parlour.

There were stools and a bed and ropes and tools but no Gabby nor anyone. The nave jiggled. There was frost in the air. I thought what a strange man to be pressed against a farmhouse wall like a fox-skin, white-haired and all.

Then I thought to see better I had best ope the shutter, maybe hear them in the next room. It was either rats in the thatch just above my head or voices, I couldn't be sure. Or my own breathing, which in all my fifty years had never been so short and loud.

Over the night came the thump of the cows in the stable, and their decent smell. There was a calf, too, which Anne had prayed for but, so they told me, had gone sick, as everything went since Gabby's father had been taken years before. The very earth had killed him.

I oped the shutter so slow its noise became a tree in the wind.

I could see them through the parlour door, which was latched back.

Gabby's arm, its red cloth and buttons, his hand round a cup. Anne's face with the hair like Mary Mother of God's in the church before the soldiers came to burn her. Thomas Walters opposite, looking hard at the table, still with his hat on. Thomas Walters was the spit of his father, also Thomas, a shepherd from the next valley who I would meet at the fairs and did not like for his drinking.

They sat in silence. I wished to see Gabby's face and tried to tell his thoughts from the hand tight round the cup. Thomas Walters was sullen. He had a clean jaw. His hat was twenty years old. He was thirty-four. Anne had the sad look of Mary in that old painting.

Well, no one had killed anyone, I thought. And there were Gabby's old ribbons on the table, like they had always been there. Though no one had spread them out.

They would come to some arrangement. It was the property that was the issue as much as the sin of two husbands. Anne had been that keen to marry, the old parson had done something clever with the parchments. Gabby was dead or as good as, we all agreed. Anne had wanted kiddies like food and drink. The farm was no good to anyone. Thomas Walters had happened along and helped her out on both accounts, it seemed. Although she had lost each babby as it came.

I held the shutter hard against my cheek so it would not flap about and stir them. I was afraid of Thomas Walters. He was a big man with a big nose and drank. His bottom teeth closed over his top. His hat covered his forehead. He had five brothers. He laughed at the Execution when we heard of it. There's still respect.

But no one spoke, that was true. It was like they were listening for the right way, like in church over the rustle of skirts and a child's coughing and the babbies. Listening for the Word that would tell them the right way. As I was listening with the wood of the shutter dark with soot against my cheek. And I think now that over the cold and the wind came the voice that told them, but it was not God's voice, and Gabby never heard it.

My page was on nightwatch but Ruth was asleep when I came back. We slept apart. She had it in her head that it was a sin to sleep together after child-bearing was over. Even in winter. I am a pious man and nodded when she told me. That night I cried. That was twenty years before I spied on the day Gabby came back.

Why I say this is that my thoughts then were running on marriage, and how it is only for child-bearing in the eyes of God, but in my mind it is working out a love that is caught like a ram in brambles and must be cut free only by the hand of Death. Or it will tear something from you.

And while I lay rustling around in my wakefulness staring at the thatch or my dreams (to close my eyes is always to see the same as when they are open on the downland) I thought how Gabby was paying for his tearing away into soldiering, despite the fact of its love for God, and fighting for the kingdom of God on earth.

But I was lonely as Gabby. I cried that night, too. Ruth breathed through her nose in her sleep and I thought she didn't care for me save to bring the master's coins and have a roof over our heads. I thought of all the times we tried to make children together and I could remember each time, and how it was good.

She was afeared of bearing. I delivered our girl when old Win Oadam called out to me and it came out legs first like a lamb but not with the head between the legs so I was worrited but the babby was a good one. Ruth on all fours like a ewe and my hand warm inside her. Our girl lived three years.

I was not like some men and agreed to touch her no more and turned my thoughts stronger to God and to the flock and lambing and so on. The fashion began about then to breed new types and my master made me observe the fashion. His sheep, I might say, are some of the strongest in the county.

I remembered how warm she was in the nakedness of Eve. Would Gabby be thinking now of Anne in the same way and her under the same roof with Thomas Walters next to her flesh? Would she be praying for forgiveness? Would Gabby claim the farm for his own? Would Thomas Walters leave as he ought in the eyes of God, that always watch from the clouds or the stars?

No wonder I never slept that night!

Now it happened that a shepherd belonging to the Hall had an accident and was laid up all that week and a boy ran up to ask if I could go over and see to a ewe who had slinked and was in trouble, the first lamb of that year and dead. I left my page to watch the flock with one of the dogs and took the upper road to the fold that was a little past Gabby's farm (as I thought of it). The road across Frum took me in sight of the place I had spied into two days back. No one had seen Gabby, though everyone in the village knew he had returned. Gabby's farm was far enough out that no one dared have a look lest bad things were afoot and they would be party to it. Some said Anne had taken both men into her bed because after the third bearing she would not be churched until the magistrates fined her into it, and then she entered in her farm boots that stank the place out. Others said that all this proved she was sickly in her mind after the babby died.

/ 12

I pulled the lamb out but the ewe was torn and I used a knife on her windpipe and they gave me a side of pork for my trouble. On the way back I stopped on the crest where the upper road runs between the sarsens and gives a good view of the farm. It was bitter up there, and the ewe's blood was still under my nails. The smoke from the farm swung across the coomb over the five elms that seemed to be hiding the thatch like a secret. Then I thought, why not go in and call on Gabby.

Why I thought this was because I would not be out that way for a long time and I could say in honesty I was passing. I could even share a slice of pork as I knew for a fact that two mouths to feed were two too many on that farm and three were famine, as Thomas Walters had lost his ploughing at Stiff's.

My heart beat bad as I walked down and the tussocks were hard with frost. The snowdrops were half-closed, I remember, so it was well after noon, but not yet dark.

The dogs fretted at their chains. They were thin as empty sacks and slavered terrible. The yard was hard as rock. Anne was at the door looking out with a face in a storm. I tapped my hat with my crook at some distance and said how I was passing on the way back from lambing for the Hall. She said nothing but tightened her shawl and nodded me inside.

It was hardly warmer in there as I remember. The wood was damp I suppose and it was all smoke. At first I saw nothing but the window with the sacking over it but then I made out the trestle and behind the trestle Thomas Walters, chewing bread.

He was always a lazy man.

I swung the pork onto a stool and stood in front of the fire, such as it was. I could see then the parlour window and wondered if I had moved the wheel and prayed for forgiveness in my thoughts.

'Pork?' said Thomas Walters.

Anne was patting butter so the cows feed well, I thought. She patted and put her hair back as it swung down from under her shawl. She was a handsome woman, even then.

'Been up at the Hall. Ewe were slinking. I thought as you would like some.'

No sign of Gabby.

'Spirit of the Commonwealth, shepherd?' said Thomas Walters, chewing his bread like a cud. You could hear his top teeth hitting the back of his bottom teeth, like fire-irons.

'Don't know as it's that,' I said, smiling all the way.

Thomas Walters grunted, and mopped his bowl.

Anne spoke.

'We have enough,' she said. 'Thank'ee.'

As more of the room lightened with accustoming it felt as if Gabby had never been there. No red tunic, no laugh, no smell of powder. No bag.

'I thought as you had more now to feed, perhaps,' I said, as best I could.

Anne looked up smartly. Thomas Walters stopped his bread at his mouth and it stayed there.

The fire went on coughing like a sick child.

'How do you mean?' Anne said.

'He met me coming down. When was it . . . two days, first light. Hadn't seen a fighting man since they cleared our church of idolatry last spring. Don't seem a year ago do it? You can smoke that pork like they did the Virgin. Didn't see no wrong in her.'

The teeth began clacking again, but slowly.

'Seems you be talking about deserters,' said Thomas Walters.

Pat, pat went the butter, but faster.

'Wars are over,' I said. 'The kingdom of God on earth is at hand. Though it can't save an early lamb or its mother. Bitter, bitter.'

'William,' she said, 'you are taking the heat.'

I shifted myself to the side and sat on a log, which was indeed damp, with all the cold of the woods still in it.

Thomas Walters looked at the log as if it were the very throne of Charles.

'Look sharpish, Thomas, and get the man a cup,' Anne said.

Thomas Walters was not happy.

'He's here on prying business,' he said.

I sniffed hard, and rubbed my hands with the blood still under the nails, and the gloves frayed at the big knuckles, that now hang from a nail by my hearth as a remembrance of those times and my work. I can see them now, about the cup in that cold mean place, after Thomas Walters had tipped the pot of ale and handed one to me.

It was well nigh water, in fact. But warm.

'He's gone,' she said.

Thomas Walters's hand shook so as the pot rattled on the hook as he put it back over the smoke.

I wiped my mouth and thought a bit.

'That's as I thought,' I said. Though it wasn't.

'Indeed?' said Thomas Walters.

He stood in front of the fire picking his teeth.

'Poor lad,' I said, and drank.

'Well, he's gone, and that's an end on it,' said Anne. I thought the butter might be patted to nothing, she went at it so quick.

'We were friends once,' I said.

'Indeed?' said Thomas Walters. 'Then you might have knocked the sense out of him p'raps. You shepherds.'

'I knew your father,' said I.

'I know.'

'Droving the flock with that great stick of his. Great hazel stick he'd near poke your eye out with.'

Thomas Walters smiled, without his eyes. He was the spit of his father. But his father had decent eyes, saving the drink swilling around in them. Neglect, as I reckon, made the son Thomas Walters was. The man that stood there, smiling.

'Well,' I said, 'you won't be needing so much pork then.'

'I know what you're about, shepherd. You'll go get chilblains sitting where you oughtn't. He had no right to assume.'

Anne looked at him as one claps up a dog that's growling out on the steal.

The question is, was I the deer or the keeper?

I chuckled to myself at the thought, and both looked fit to hang me.

Well, I wasn't staying. Gabby had gone and that was a fact. He might never have returned. I stood up and wiped my mouth and lifted the pork onto my shoulder.

'Thank'ee for the ale,' I said. 'These are mean times. Maybe we'll have a bit more sharing out of things now the church is whitewashed and the King in his coffin. Though I'll miss the dancing myself. Keeps a man warm.'

Thomas Walters nodded the smallest nod I have ever seen. Anne bit her lip fit to bleed. Some said she was growing to be a witch. Well, since Maud had gone head first into the chalk by the north yew they had to have someone to blame all on.

At the door I said:

'With them rings from Ireland he'll set hisself up alright, and that's a fact.'

'Rings?' said Thomas Walters, sharpish.

I knew that would hook him. I turned to look at the yard. The thatch was touching the cows' backs off the shelter, it was that sagged.

'That's what he counted his love with. Pillaging. He shook the General's hand. We all took him for dead. And all the time he were thinking of us waiting, and how he'd afford new thatch for the shelter, and the barn. But he'll set hisself up alright, I shouldn't wonder.'

I left then as one leaves a night on the downs full of its silence, that is pushing something terrible at your back which you don't turn round to for fear of seeing it.

I heard steps behind me and I was halfway across the yard.

It was Anne. She was panting. The cows followed her, nudging. She held herself tight and looked up at me, fierce but frighted.

'What rings?' she said.

Thomas Walters was in the door, in the shadows.

I shrugged as a man does when he is at the fair and offered a low price.

'What rings?' she said, real fierce.

The poor cows were nudging her but she was stone, like.

'I'd say he brought them back for you and the farm. He'll be a sad man but it's no one's doing. He was a boy. He fought for the kingdom of God on earth, and shook General Cromwell's hand. He'll set hisself up.'

'He had nothing,' she said.

'Maybe,' I said.

'Nothing. And he never did. He was never good for anything but what he went and done. He left me,' she said, and she was shivering.

'He did,' I said. I made to move but she held my arm like a jaw round a bone.

'Nothing,' she said, between her teeth, that were half of them gone already, and she only thirty or so.

She was nevertheless a handsome woman.

I thought of telling Ruth but I didn't. She would only grumble that it was none of my business and there would be trouble. So I watched her go to sleep that night after prayers without talking, as we sometimes did, both staring at the thatch above our beds and wondering in between the words how we would fare when the other went under and there was only the rats rustling, not a body you had touched. We never talked that night and I didn't tell her.

Then the lambing started and I were sleeping out, but I thought of Gabby all through the lambing. He had left a silence where I heard my own whispering, that was many things going round and round in my head. I took up a Bible and heard the parson's words as I read because I couldn't read the letters, but always the whispering came on the wind and the taste of bitterness like the smoke that would blow sometimes out of the coomb across my scarp. And I shook my head but the whispering grew louder. I thought I might be going mad like half the old shepherds went up there all on their own.

I thought of how he had shook hands with General Cromwell in all the smoke and all the women and children of Drogheda spilled like empty sacks that Gabby had helped empty. And I saw Ruth among them, I don't know why. She had her legs wide open like the times we made a babby or like a ewe ready for a ram. And there was General Cromwell shaking hands with Gabby and both smiling while Thomas

Walters clacked his teeth together next to them and turned round and saw me looking on my damp log, and shot me.

These were dreams but I was awake. I shook my head free of them and took to making dolls out of straw but always they had their legs wide open and they smiled like General Cromwell or Thomas Walters. And sometimes as I was lifting out a lamb I thought of Anne with my hand inside her which was really Ruth and the ewe kicking out its legs as the lamb came out in a slither, all new.

It was on account of guilt, I reckoned, and one day in April I went to the church and left the boy with the flock and the church was empty. It still smelt of whitewash where all the old paintings had been covered over by the soldiers and the parson looking on nodding all the time, though he cried that night as I remember. I must say that I could remember all the paintings and when I looked at the white walls they were there anyway, particularly Noah and the funny old sheep that were clambering up in a pair to the only ship I had ever seen, rocking on those little blue waves that was the beginnings of the Flood, I suppose.

I stood in the middle of the church and looked round slowly at the walls and saw all the paintings from Creation to Judgement Day, and in my mind heard the parson's words, and the rim on my hat was fair crumpled up I was that nervous of talking with God in His house.

But I knelt and the stone was cold and I thought of Gabby with my coat on him, shivering, I don't know why. And I told God of my thoughts and fears and that if I was going mad to spare me with a quick dying. And I asked God if He could whitewash all my thoughts like the soldiers had covered over the old paintings that I had known as a boy and a man. But thoughts were not on walls but ran like deer and the smell of whitewash mocked me.

The church whispered back my mumblings, and I was afraid lest someone might hear, and looked all about me. But it was deathly empty. I wished idolatrously for the statues and pictures still to be there, and the coloured glass they had broken through with poles and stones and their guns.

All in one day, with the parson and some of the village cheering in the graveyard. But my thoughts would not be smashed and covered so easy. They were deer running through the forest, and I prayed hard that God might save me.

For I never thought of Gabby as leaving that farm. In all my thoughts I could not see him crossing the yard and knocking the noses of the cattle and striding up the hill with his rings sewn into his pocket, jingling. To set hisself up. I could not see that, however hard I furrowed my brows and bit my lip and sat silent with the bells and the wind all round me out on the scarp. And even in the empty church with its whitewash smell like old rivers I could not see him leaving the farm.

And when I saw him there it was only through the parlour door with me shaky on a broken wheel and his arm shining with buttons in its red cloth. And the cloth would always run with blood as the arms did on that field after the business at Newberry when to walk across it was to lift clouds of flies from the arms.

And there was Anne and Thomas Walters in the shadows, and Anne's crumbling teeth round my arm like a dog's that is mad, that was really her hand.

So I shook my head and said that if there was blood that it should come out so as I could know my guilt in sending him down there into his judgement. And the church whispered back exactly my own words that I had said loud when there was a footstep behind me at the door and it was Anne, staring at me turned round to look at her.

I shook my head but she didn't go. There was mud on her boots from the rains. She walked into the middle and I stood with my heart swallowing itself.

She was like the Virgin statue, with the hair all about her neck, and her hair crow-black and wet from the rains.

She stood as still.

'I'll be going,' I said, as best I could.

'Not on account of me,' she said. 'You called me, did you know that?'

She was a witch.

'I was talking to God,' I said, and made the sign of the cross.

'Talk to me,' she said, and she held my arm, but softly.

'This is the house of God,' I said, but didn't take my arm away. I was afraid, and a little mad. She was panting and her coat was open.

'William,' she said.

She began to cry.

Frankly, she had a smell about her that was not healthy.

'God will forgive thee,' I said, 'if you confess and you don't need no parson to do it with the church an open house for sinner and saint alike.' She hadn't gone to the sermon last week for that was it, as I remembered.

'He done nothing for me,' she said.

'That were no reason to kill him,' I said, before I'd thought it.

She went as white as the statue then, before it was burnt.

She pushed her hair back into her shawl, for it had dropped right in front of her eyes.

She walked away and nodded me to follow. I was afraid. I had my knife in my belt and I asked forgiveness for thinking of it. We walked up behind the church onto the downland and up into Bailey's Wood from where you could see my grazing, the other side of our river, rising up against the sky. The rains had stopped. My thoughts were shouting in my head and I held it but then she stopped in a little clearing where there had been a hut once. It was grass and stones.

'William,' she said.

I remembered her as a little chit and how sometimes she'd sell at the door and she had the same look then. At the end of the clearing a woodman's shelter or it might have been part of the hut dripped from its thatch that sagged and was all looped about with bedwine as no one tended it now and she took my hand and we went in.

She looked at me first and then wiped my brow and I thought of the Virgin and Christ, and Mary Magdalen that tended Him and wiped His feet, and all my thoughts were whitewashed over, for the deer running through the forest had become a painting on a wall, that her hand brushed over and over. She took my arm and it stroked her legs with its hand where the skirt had been lifted so the white skin was open to the air.

I felt inside her like a ewe and she was the same warmth. I was pleased, somehow, that Ruth and the ewe and Anne were the same warmth. There were no more pictures. I went inside her as a man does and her skin was open to the air and was soft and full where I touched it. She was happy.

The rain began again and dripped on us through the thatch and I buried my loneliness inside her.

Then I went back up to the fold and saw the boy off with a penny. I had no more pictures nor whisperings. Only the voice in my ear that was a woman's and was warm as my own fleece that I sat there in thinking of the next time she had said when I might return to the wood and only a penny for the page and his silence.

And the next time we lay on bluebells and it were sticky, and in the autumn the bedwine dropped his old man's beard into her black hair and I said it was her crown of silver, but she said nothing. In the winter I brought a fleece with me and wrapped her in it so she wouldn't shiver. For it snowed some of the times.

And this went on, oh, for years, until I couldn't see the bedwine plumes in her hair no longer before I blew them off. Then she sickened and died one winter. Sometimes she would whisper the name of Gabby in my ear. And I an old man!

She was the last witch I ever knew.

I was a little mad, probably.

That's the story.

[Reprinted by kind permission of *The Wessex Nave*.]

1689

FRIENDS

It was not snowing when we set out. The barest places can look heavenly under a bright moon and it was so then. If it had been in any way otherwise I can assure you we would not have set out.

The funeral of good Reverend Josiah Flaw had been fitting but full of sorrow. His assiduousness did cause his death: one stormy evening had him out to administer his flock, whereupon a chill came upon him and he forthwith sunk into the lap of our Lord.

Though his living was as mine and bore barely a roof yet he too was at every beck of those 'twas his ill fortune to mediate for betwixt the ire of the Lord and their gaming and fornication and drinking and covetousness and all the customary excesses, my children. O horrible oaths likewise do our ploughmen bellow, our sowers bark, our reapers bawl at every interposing stone. But when I have flung up my hands at their wantonness, Josiah Flaw was ever zealous for their betterment, that every peasant in his parish might praise the Lord as they delved and not scandalise the very corn.

His being the parish of Bursop.

It too does have its gaggle of ranters. It too does have its precious life-blood sucked, a cheating zeal that sups up as the east wind among the rabble, and leaves our churches hollow.

You shalt see how deep to the heart hath this poison entered, my children, when this true history is wound up.

'Twas not snowing nor in any ways foul when we set out. We thought to foot it back in no more than two hours, the said parish not being unknown to most of you as lying on the northerly edge of our chalkland yet, alas, without a convenient road between us on account of I know not what but those customary reasons that come betwixt convenience and human kind.

The snow already fallen the yesternight was soft no more than a thumb deep. Thereafter was iron.

Then we three left without foreboding. Our curate, our clerk, and thy minister.

Without foreboding did we set out illumined by a round moon which made the snow all abouts gleam and our hearts exult so virgin did the world seem and blameless.

And upon that vast blamelessness of snow the Lord espied us and craved to mantle us in His safekeeping for some have maintained He did abandon us or that He was full of ire for none other reason than mine own inadequacies.

I have heard the whisperings.

What presumption.

As if those small faults, those thinnest fissures from which we are none of us caulked lest stopped up by death, were worthy of God's ire whilst all about be poxed and gaping.

My children.

The draught be about your legs. My voice cries out of the stone. List, list, we are empty and void. Our walls are smitten with breaches, and little clefts, and our roof is as the furrows of the field, and the stink of neglect doth come up unto our nostrils. Doth the Lord sift us in these days of famine, that is not a famine of bread, nor a thirst for water, but of hearing the words of the Lord, that good grain only doth fall upon the earth?

And the seed is rotten under our clods.

And the drunkard is with drink. And the ploughman is with his oxen. And the inhabitant of Ulverton doth loll fleshly abed. And thus saith the Lord, I will send a fire on the wall of Gaza, and of Ashdod, and of Tyrus, and of Edom, and of Rabbah. I shall smite you with blastings and mildew. For ye have turned judgement into gall, and the fruit of righteousness into hemlock.

Rejoicing in a thing of nought.

Woe.

That our piety is no longer snug with companions.

That we are spaced so, like scattered candles in the dark.
That we are cold.
Woe.
Woe.

For a zealous wind doth blow amongst us, withering the vine.

And the armies of the flashing mind devour the poor secretly.

Then beware, my children.

And that no conjecture further rot amongst you into malice, I shall relate the true history. Not a false whisper upon a filthy wind.

Beginning upon that track that runs higgledy-piggledy worn by shepherds and their more manageable flocks between Bursop and this habitation but rarely by folk making betwixt the two, for it runs along the crests and is not the crow's way, and trusting in the fine light, and William Scablehorne having the way well, being once a shepherd's boy, we soon took to the maiden downs, and were not troubled in any wise by having at our feet but immaculate snow.

For one happy hour we proceeded, my children, across that waste, fortified by our faith, by reflections on the good character of the late lamented and instances of this, and by my fine brandy which, though it was partook of eagerly by William Scablehorne, did barely wet the lips of Simon Kistle our late curate. And even merrily did we proceed, like true pilgrims, towards our holy harbour, for we could mount any drifted incline without sunken shins, and our swift pace hindered the cold from entering our bones. Even merrily, despite our mourning robes, did we proceed across that white waste.

So it was that Adam awoke in the garden that fateful morning teeming with light, unaware of the leadenness which was to befall that very noon.

There is a shame which bringeth sin, and there is a shame which bringeth glory and grace.

Cast a stone into snow and you shall hark no sound. Whip petty Vice and he shall howl but pettily.

Purge, purge, my children.

Purge those false whispers from the foul wind that have set your ears to tingle and your eyes to crowd with base lying images that rise like dust betwixt us. Rather feel inly that rawness of the very first morning of the very first day of Creation before the zephyrous balm had blown through the avenues of the universe and scatter the dust that lies upon your judgement like a filthy cloud and freeze the canker-worm that eats thee up unto the last hair and make white, my children. Make white and bruise not. Do not cast a stone to bruise the snow, do not welt the innocent back nor slaughter the lamb.

Do not presume to judge from a dung-hill of ignorance a ragged stinking deformed beggar, let alone thy minister!

Or is the hour come with toleration that the basest scum can judge the appointed, can lift on the heap of great waters of this modish freedom, and engulf all?

If so, woe.

O how virgin lay the snow, how darkly across those bald flanks that no ploughblade has yet delved and but the lips of sheep crop we three light hearts and easy minds of the sure in faith, forgetful of the inward rottenness, the hidden of the land, the blistering poison that thrives unseen, progressed. How uncomplainingly did we our bread that I had in my pocket from the funeral feast chew upon the empty scarp at Goosey Hill. With what heartiness did we slap William Scablehorne off of snow after he did tumble, and set his wide crown back upon his head, and slow descend from the high crest onto Furzecombe Down.

O how pure are the eyes of the unknowing, when iniquity lies all about them!

One fact let me make plain.

Our Adversary has many subtle devices at his disposal.

But that which was not expected but which so suddenly approached and overwhelmed us in that vale was in no wise owing to his actions.

God, but God, controls the seasons and the winds, my children.

The seemingly unreasonable changes therein.

He maketh his sun rise on the evil and on the good and sendeth rain on the just and on the unjust.

Nay.

Stealthily, stealthily, doth our Adversary work.

Inly he thrives, breeding in our corruption the filthy spots that shall consume us, threshing from our sins the rotten stinking putrefying heap of our damnation, fattening upon the smallest waywardness that he might belch forth its sourness at our last breath and plunge us without stop unto the ovens of Hell.

Trust, then, in divine grace.

For may we remember the agonies of Mary Brinn late of our parish whose ague did cleanse her unclean stomach and did pour forth upon the pillow the sweat of her redemption that she did embrace with a fearful and devout mind unclouded of drink's affections. And may we remember the sufferings of Thomas Walters late of our parish whose scall was endured as Job's and whom I visited in his humble abode not a stone's throw from this our holy house at his moment of release and whose ancient visage, ravaged though it was, bore upon it a smile sweeter than any I have ever beheld because he had had broken upon him the light of our Lord. O wicked are the ways of the flesh and the disease therein yet blessed is the state of the soul in bliss as I did witness only last week in this our habitation God rest their souls amen.

Yea, out of the whirlwind comes the still small voice.

Out of the howling wind.

Thou didst cleave the earth. Thou didst walk with burning coals before Thee, and the clouds were the dust of Thy feet. Thou didst break asunder and scatter the mountains and Thy wrath was terrible, O Lord.

O my children.

On Furzecombe Down I tasted of despair.

Yea, on Furzecombe Down the whirlwind came and filled my mouth and the snow stopped up mine ears and I chewed on ashes and was blind.

O my children.

In mine own parish. In mine own parish far from succour I did grow weak in faith. In that sudden tempest so small and feeble I did feel bowed down before the wrath of the Lord I called as Our Saviour Himself did upon the Cross, I lapsed into the greatest most horrible sin of all yea as if I had never once known Him or ever entered into the house of our Lord or as if my attire was but so much stage costume or rags as it did feel like in that ferocious cold and as my companions did appear to resemble whipped by the wind that made their cloaks blow before them and their hats to come off.

And Hell is but a single tiny thought away, my children.

You may well shift.

But you are looking agog at one who has felt the hot rasp and icy nip at once in his bowels and on his cheeks.

The fires and frosts of Hell's perpetual kingdom.

Whatsoever be the talk of holy frauds. Whatsoever be the modish jabber of those inly lit up, as by some angelic taper. As by some luminous blossom.

Now this, my children, hear closely.

At the very moment of my despair and numbness in which the sudden inclement weather and its great gloominess all but obliterated my senses my Reason like our single shielded lanthorn swung by my hand endured and I reckoned that one amongst us was not feeling his suffering as he ought.

Nay, hear me out.

For it is in this point that the nub even the fruit of my sermon lies. For in these moments of extremity our greatest challenge comes and I do not speak of bodily challenge though that be severe. I speak of those challenges to our intellect and to our faith more subtle than the momentary clouding of that faith in despair which has doubtless chilled each one of you at some time in grief or in melancholy or in sickness and which is overcome when the light of Reason is restored or not at all. Indeed, I might add that those momentary nights of the soul are as limberings up that exercise and stiffen faith and our resolve. They imitate the night of our Lord. But our Adversary has subtler ways still.

Nay, let me proceed.

One amongst us namely Simon Kistle our late curate, God rest his soul, who came to us on very tender pinions out of his ordination and was barely fledged and had as you recall but a downy beard, was beckoning out of the foul wind that blew our cloaks about our heads for Mr Scablehorne and myself to shelter in the lee of a small hummock.

This hummock being but the sole swelling on a waste of snowy furze.

And Mr Scablehorne and myself did make for the hummock with our hoods held tight to our faces that we might not be blinded by the snow and did crouch there, it affording in the lee some shelter from the blasts.

Then think, my children, what degree of horror came upon your minister when poor Mr Scablehorne did lean across to me and did part my hood from mine ear and did whisper that our comforting protuberance was none other than that place where certain of the spiritually distracted in our grandparents' time fell into unspeakable depravity and cavorted lustfully in nakedness upon its flanks and that is called thereby the Devil's Knob.

Yea, and how often have I cried out for these heathen spots, like that great mound high upon our own southerly flank, called by some filthy name, that I shall not blister my lips with repeating, but that flaunts itself at this our humble house of God—how often have I cried out for these to be removed as a black wen from a face, that no canker might work unseen within, to pollute and foul the rabble? Yea, who was it but he whom ye now see stood before you that rooted up and broke upon a great fire the seven stones of Noon's Hill?

Think what degree of horror coursed through my frozen joints. And I bid immediately Mr Scablehorne and Mr Kistle to pray aloud, that though our words might be obscured by the loudness of the blasts, we might scatter this wickedness. And I bid to cease from his sniggering poor William Scablehorne, whose wits were already turning in that exceeding discomfort.

My children.

William Scablehorne our clerk for forty years, whose rod was ever vigilant amongst thee for the smallest yawn, whose pitch-pipe did clothe the poverty of our singing with its asseveratory flourishes, whose hand remains in our register as a meticulous record of his attention I perceived was already slipping, my children.

Yet when I did turn to Mr Kistle who was clad in his customary hat and coat that you might recall as being as threadbare as the times, and out at one elbow, and wholly inadequate for the present great cold, I did perceive that in spite of his shuddering exceedingly every limb, he bore upon his face an expression I had never previously viewed upon his attenuated countenance, but which I swiftly ascertained was one of a comfortable elation.

List, my children.

I had indeed been amiss in not keeping a more eager watch on my curate. The dull chafe of our duties oft wears us to forgetfulness. Yea, my despair at the scandalous practices of this parish was all but consuming my will and my attention. Even on that very day not more than one month past when my curate returned from London with an excitable air I discovered, upon entering our vestry, a certain lackey of this village pissing upon the floor. And having with my heaviest candle-bearer cudgelled him out he did swear at me and declaim that it was the action of no Christian to strike a poor man who has Christ seeded inside him. That no fellow, however ragged and mean, might be contemned by those set up above him by riches. And that I was a dunce.

Nay.

Snigger not, my children.

Weep, rather.

Weep that you have sunk this far.

This thine holy house become a piss-pot.

List, list.

Mr Scablehorne being of a sudden flung into a fit of coughing that did spray me with its bloody phlegm, my attention was drawn from my curate. But holding Mr Scablehorne close to me, cradled in mine arm, with a handkercher to his mouth, and the lanthorn up in mine other hand that I might view the sick man and his eructations more proficiently, I was able to turn my head once more towards my curate.

And I did dimly see him staring outwards, with a smile upon his face as of one latterly taken, and I thought he had indeed been taken but that his limbs were still shuddering, and I bid him turn up his collar, and come close, that we might endure together until this wrathfulness had blown itself out.

But he was as the dumb stone, laid over with the gold of my lanthorn. As if there was no breath at all in the midst of him.

I clamoured to him, and putting the lanthorn beside me I shook his arm. And he then did turn to me, moving his lips as if in supplication, that were very blue.

But at that moment Mr Scablehorne being vexed exceedingly with coughing, erubescing the virgin mantle before us with his fluids, and quite sopping my handkercher, I was otherwise preoccupied.

Though putting the bottle of fiery brandy to my poor clerk's lips, and leaving it there in his ebbing grasp, that he might relieve his agony, I could turn again to my curate. And lo, he was moving his lips.

And leaning closer towards him, I did feel his cold mouth chafing upon mine ear, and the rasp of his collar upon my cheek, and did have the following words deposited in a whisper, but clear as a bell, from my curate:

'I have Perfection.'

And somewhat startled by this curious yet in these teemingly blasphemous days familiar eruption, I did bid him repeat it.

And again he deposited in mine ear-hole this drop of venom that blistereth as it touches:

'I have Perfection.'

And putting my mouth to his ear likewise I returned the following:

'Mr Kistle. Pray tell me what Perfection it is that you are having.'

And he did smile broader, and did say, from Matthew 5, Verse 48, that I did recognise straightway:

'Be perfect, as your Heavenly Father is perfect.'

And put his chill hand upon my shoulder. Like a father might do to a son.

Too well in our own humble parish of Ulverton, my children, know we this chill hand upon the shoulder. This eructation of Perfection.

Of the Light within. Of the Seed of Infinite Wisdom.

Being once the rantings of fools and madmen who are now the quiet of the land, blighting.

Too well. Ah, too well.

Too well know we the enemies of the cloth and of the steeple, of our Church and of our God, my children, that draw the ploughmen from their ploughs and the clerks from their offices. Too well know we the filth glossed over with a semblance of our raiments, breathed forth sourly in every meeting house, that is open to every Revelation of any lying Enthusiast e'en as ridiculous as that of Mahomet, as a broken roof is ope to every drop of rain. The fig tree shall not blossom, and the labour of the olive shall fail.

Yet I will rejoice in the Lord.

Yea, in that day sing ye unto her a vineyard of red wine. I the Lord do keep it. I will water it every moment. Lest any hurt it, I will keep it night and day.

Think, my children, of what horror there was within me when I heard Simon Kistle speak into mine ear of Perfection as to a dunce. Think how near to the quick has come this blight that mine own curate was breathing it over me and turning it in my bowels who had trodden in my house, and prayed with me, and performed numerous services in my name upon mine own horse when I lay afflicted with the headache, and whom I had trusted as one might a son. Think of my horror.

But ever regardful of the vexed state of our situation, that the blasts or the evil nature of that afflicted place might have deceived mine hearing, after administering to myself some heat from the bottle poor Mr

Scablehorne would barely relinquish to me I did turn to Mr Kistle and say to him, in a loud voice, though his nose was but inches from mine own:

'What is it you mean, that which you uttered but a few minutes past?'

And through the scouring of the wind that was having at us still in the lee of that wicked place he did set his glimmering face up to mine and his whole body shaking or should I say quaking he of a sudden grinned and stroked my arm and answered:

'My fruit is being brought forth to Perfection. I am ripe in Christ. For Truth requires Plainness and Simplicity and my seed is sown. For the sorrowful nights of affliction are over, and the sun is burst upon us.'

Imagine my children what astonishment I received this with, I that was almost stuck fast with cold and could barely see my hand before me in the extremest danger of death and no allaying of the storm in sight with the words of the late service ashen as it were in my mouth and the wind whipping my hood almost threadbare and poor Mr Scablehorne's span almost up beside me. Imagine my astonishment—nay, even fear—at those fateful words that appeared to me familiar and awful, except that I could not bring myself to imagine that the quaking habit had fallen upon mine own curate and rather imagined that this extremity of exposure had bred in him a kind of despair, or foolishness, and that he was not in his right mind.

And so, not wishing to break the truth of our situation too quick upon him, I put my hand upon his that was without glove upon mine arm and said:

'It is meet that your thoughts should be filled with sunshine, Mr Kistle, for the inward man is the vital, and is fed by the Scriptures, which are the very Light of life.'

And I reached into mine pocket which was already sodden and bringing out mine holy Book laid his hand upon it and sought the lanthorn and did hold it above the holy Book, that the feeble rays might illumine sufficient to bring my curate out of his distraction.

And I did call out, through the great noise, 'Herein are all things necessary to the eternal life. Though we cannot read we can lay our hands upon this Truth and think on our sins, and on the Day of Judgement. This shall be as the bread for the hungry, and the wine for the thirsty, and our mantle for the cold, Mr Kistle.'

But he then straightway seized hold of the Book that is the Light of our Lord and the Word of God and the path to our salvation if rightfully understood and inwardly digested, and did pull it violently out of my hands, and did hurl it from me, into the blackness and misery of the night, so that for a moment I was stonied into silence and could utter no word but a sort of gargling.

Bereft as it were of the Word itself, viciously cast into darkness.

And so astonied was I that my fingers let hold of the lanthorn, that straightway rolled across the snow throwing out its light as a wheel till snuffed by that motion.

And all was as blind as in the beginning before the Spirit of our God moved upon the face of the waters.

And despite my poor clerk being seized at that moment with a most severe coughing that did send his bloody gob forcefully against my cheek I could not turn to him in mine own extremity, but instantly did hurl myself forward into the night's blasts, searching upon my knees for our holy Book. But so forcefully buffeted was I by that horrid tempest, that I was cast to the ground and did thereupon weep in the snow for my staff and our salvation. And when I rose again I was as the seed thrown upon the wind hurled hither and thither till my hand alighted upon a cloak of wool, being manna in that desert fastness, which did thereupon crumble to ashes in my mouth when I did handle it further and understand that it was but the frozen carcass of a sheep, withered almost to fleece and bone. Yet so distracted was I that I dragged it towards our poor shelter, and laid the sheep upon Mr Scablehorne's legs, that had but the thinnest of leggings about them otherwise.

And still in that severe cold the beast did have a smell about it. O let us pray the Day of Judgement doth swiftly come, that our corrupt bodies may put on the mantle of innocence and our black and unwholesome bile be scoured and the blown flies fall away that our flesh and bones may walk cleanly into the house of our Lord.

Then instantly turning and fumbling in that blackness for Mr Kistle's collar, that I soon found, I tugged him, as it were, out of his exultations.

For wrath is oft just.

'Mr Kistle,' cried I, 'what mean you in throwing from us our holy Book, that is our Staff of Life, we being in such extremity and so near to death as it may be we are?'

And he did shout out, in a high voice:

'Welcome the Resurrection! The Scriptures are but the way not the means!'

And I replied, in a trembling voice:

'They are the Word of God, Mr Kistle!'

And he cried out again:

'Worms might have God's Word for supper, I say! Welcome the Resurrection!'

'What are they then, Mr Kistle, if not the Word of God?'

'Christ is within us! Open thyself and be free! Cast off! Cast off! Welcome the Resurrection!'

And other such roarings.

Then hanging though he was from my grip upon his collar, he did bring his mouth to mine ear, so that I could smell the sourness of his feeble breath, and uttered, quite certain of his wits, the following:

'The Scriptures are but the declaration of the stipulations of the Saints, Mr Brazier. Let the worm now have them. Open thyself and be free.'

And at that moment the clouds tore asunder before the moon and a brilliant light was cast through the rent and indeed Mr Kistle's collar choosing to tear at that same moment he fell from me onto the snow, so that I was delivered of the frightful vision of his glimmering face that the moon had illumined.

But still disbelieving of the filthy stinking blasphemies that had pierced the blasts, and fearful lest the wicked nature of the hummock had infected us with its fumes, I lifted up Mr Kistle from where he lay upon the snow upon his face, and asked him what need the Scriptures, and my ministry, and his curate's post, and the Communion of the

Church of England, if he had the Word of Christ within him and naught else needed. And raising his arms on high and shaking in his error so that I well nigh lost my grip upon his hair he did shout out that naught else was needed, that he had Perfection inwardly and God was in his conscience and that if I were to understand this I would cast aside my vestments and blossom. And the moon shone upon a sheet of snow that had adhered to his face within which his eyes and his mouth shifted constantly and so filled with horror was I by this vision that I stepped back and tripped upon William Scablehorne or rather the sheep about which his arms were held for he had evidently derived comfort therefrom. And sprawled beside him I saw that the bottle was drained at his lips, and that a mess of his fluids lay upon his cheek, and that he was no more in the living realm than the withered beast bound by his arms, against whose poor flayed skull his own face did nestle with a like grin.

I see in your own faces, my children, a mingling of horror and sorrow. We know not when the sickle of God will sweep deeply into us. His harvest obeys not summer. Mr Scablehorne now rests, my children, in the quietest of sleeps, sure of having performed his small round. And having filled his narrow way with an abundance of song and inward rejoicing and general diligence most especially witnessed in the white cleanliness of this surplice of which only having one, such is the thinness of my living, it must needs be cared for mightily, in all this lies the reward of a greater life, a peck to weigh in the scales and naught to scoff at.

And having ascertained his state I speedily administered the appropriate rites and fervently prayed for him even in mine own extremity of cold that was beginning to seize me like a vice. And I would indeed have covered his face with his own coat, but his limbs were exceeding stiff and I could not prise them from about the aforesaid sheep.

And so left him, alas, uncovered.

As ye have no doubt known of.

As ye have no doubt known of, and lamented thereof, from out of a whisper on the filthy wind, though not the worst that hath carried its poison amongst thee! A whisper carried calumniously against thy minister who did through his own trembling lay that soul to sleep nevertheless, my children, with the words that are ever fit.

That I must utter when your time comes. Without a slip in the utterance. Such are my responsibilities.

The business with the deceased complete, I turned towards Mr Kistle who had gone.

And just then the moon again was lost and a great gloominess once more compassed me about as if I had been cast into the deep as Jonah in the midst of seas, for all thy billows and thy waves passed over me, O Lord.

And though I did shout none heard me in that infinite desolation, save the Lord.

For on climbing the declivity with slow and labouring steps, so feeble did I feel, that I might view round about to better vantage should the clouds once more rend themselves and light be let out, my hand did seize by chance the heel of a boot, as Jacob took his brother by the heel in the womb.

And when I looked up, lo, I did see my curate by moonlight again with arms outspread above me, vexed by the buffets and blasts of the storm upon that chalky top but stuck fast, as it were, to their exceeding cold as if upon a cross.

And after I had reached beside him and urged him in his ear to descend, he only cried out, through a numbed mouth, that which was at first hard to comprehend, but on the third repeat had blasted mine own ear more than the snow upon the whirlwind, and was the following:

'I am set free from the burden of sin!'

And seeing that his cloak was more out behind him wildly than about him, and that beneath his cloak his shirt was loose, I made the latter fast with the utmost difficulty, my fingers being chilled to the bone, and wrapped my arms about him and might have brought him down but that we slipped and fell and in this tumble I placed my hand upon a small furze bush concealed beneath the snow and did give myself great hurt from the thorns thereon.

And Mr Kistle did remain upon his back in the snow, and did shout to me many things through the blasts. He did shout that the spirit of Christ was rising within me. That I must put off all worldly things and taste the sweetness of a humbled life and this mortification of the flesh that was sent by God to prove our inclinations and set the seed within us to leaf and blossom, and that the perfume of His ointment was all about us for we both dwelt under His canopy and were bathing in a river of unspeakable joy.

O my children.

Never was our miserable state of sinfulness and wretchedness more clear to me than on that chalky summit, bowed down beside my ranting giddy blasphemous curate whose stinking spewings forth I had not the strength of body to smother or e'en answer, my lips being quite helpless with the cold, that a burning firebrand might not have melted them.

Simon Kistle is no more, my children. But what you will be asking in your hearts is more to the matter than his end. It is the after-life that is the pith. Whether his gross and obnoxious Enthusiasm was intact at the moment of his passing, he being taken with all his infirmities and downright blasphemies ripe in the husk as it were but incorrigibly poisoned and rotten. What didst thou our minister do to save his soul to cling to he who was your pillar nay your companion in extremity?

List, my children.

The scuttling of mice in our poor thatch or the wind under the door or the squeaking of thy boots shall in that other life of happiness be transported into harmonious music the like of which we cannot imagine, save were we to come of a sudden out of a city's huff and clamour and stink by chance into a vast nave filled with the loveliness of a choir dropping from the sweetness of their mouths such songs as might move our bowels and make us walk upon the high places. For the other life be perpetual music, my children.

And in these vain and jesting times we must tune ourselves to that which is harmonious and lovely for in Hell all is grating, and freakish, and loud with misery, like a knife upon a whetstone perpetually pressed betwixt the grindings of teeth in torment.

And now imagine how similarly vexatious to my ears was that blasphemy of my curate mingled with the fearful clamour of the storm. And fiercely in my soul did I desire to stop up the sluice from which his hope of salvation was already flooding, that he might though he be taken be raised into life everlasting, when the Last Day comes and the trumpet be blown.

So I rose and went to him still upon the summit of that desolate slope blasted by the storm and bent to him and with my left hand under his head I did plead with him to leave off his ramblings and this Enthusiasm that had come upon him so suddenly no doubt owing to the touch of this infamous place and to come down into the shelter of our Lord, into the lee of the Scriptures, to throw himself upon the mercy of the Lord and His Word. And I shouted to him those words of David in the Psalm:

'Thou art he that tookest me out of the womb, thou madest me to hope when I was upon my mother's breasts. I was cast upon thee from the womb, thou art my God from my mother's belly. Be not far from me for trouble is near.'

And I also recalled to him the words that did begin my peroration this morning, my children:

'When our heart fails God is the strength of our hearts and our portion for ever.'

He was shivering and his teeth chattering and his face and hands were exceeding cold, but he raised himself upon one elbow and shouted loud unto me:

'You are mistaken. This blessed state has not come upon me suddenly, but has been growing within me for several months, since God led me to a certain book I saw in a window and took home, that was the Christian Epistle to Friends writ by George Whitehead. And Barclay and Fox I also read, and others, that persuaded me of my own state of ignorance and blindness and it was as if the sun had burst upon me and the scales fallen from my sight, and all that I had thought mad and foolish I saw might not be, but I was fearful of telling anyone

anyone though I found no satisfaction in my employment and in the shapes and shadows of religion, flaunting words that are so much dust to the lascivious people, who nevertheless doff their hats to the steeple and enter in to the ceremonies, but have never tasted the banquet that lies within themselves, but only stuff their mouths with the serpent's food.'

I was much astonied to hear this Enthusiasm had been on him so long, and called tremblingly into his ear:

'What am I, then, that feeds them this dust that is the serpent's food, and has command of the steeple, or rather tower, under which they do doff their hats, Mr Kistle?'

And he made reply, with an obnoxious sigh, so that my ear grew exceeding hot, the following:

'Thou art the fat and wanton smotherer of their souls, Mr Brazier.'

My children.

Snigger not.

For this Mr Brazier is the very same Reverend Crispin Brazier of His Majesty's Church of England that doth stand before ye now, and hath command of this parish, and maintenance of all its souls, and is our Lord's minister on this base earth. O wherefore lookest thou upon them that deal treacherously, and holdest thy tongue when the wicked devoureth the man that is more righteous than he? O what thick and palpable clouds have descended upon this our land, that our anointed guardians of the Faith must rail against the revelations of blockheads and the wisdom of creeping things, yet be mocked!

O Thou didst walk through the sea with thine horses.

O Thou didst slay the nations.

Give them, O Lord. What wilt Thou give? Give them a miscarrying womb. Give them dry breasts.

Woe.

List, list.

To touch the very marrow of the matter now.

I ask thee: is not that man that runs toward Death willingly more culpable than those poor Gadarene swine, for he does it in full knowledge of his trespass? We are weighed in the balance and are found wanting and if the grapes be not fine the wine-press cannot be trodden into sweetness. The Lord it is who decides when the tender grape shall be gathered, when the reaper shall bow with his hook and the ears of the barley fall. To cut ourselves untimely off is to wither on the vine, to foul the streams of Lebanon, to worm the apple and bring frost to the garden of our souls and the chafe of despair upon our necks, O my children.

For Mr Kistle did then rise stiffly and took off his coat and gave it to me, saying, 'Take this. I wish to embrace the Power of my Lord. To come into his presence as naked as the babe and as helpless and as innocent, washed of all my sins. For my soul is one with God and my seed blossoms.'

My children, he did take off his garments one by one and I was helpless to interject.

He it was, he alone it was who rended his garments from himself.

Not as the foulest whisper on the filthy wind hath dropped it amongst you, infecting with its calumnious poison.

Against thy healing minister.

Who was so near death or so I felt and not able to stand and my heart hard against him for I saw he was foolish and drunken, but not with wine, that I could not interpose myself betwixt his foolishness and his action.

Meaning our late curate.

And he did toss his garments to me, calling them after Isaiah but filthy rags of righteousnesses, and did thereupon halfway out of his worsted stockings fall heavily and nakedly upon the snow. And did not tremble.

My children, whither his soul went I cannot say, but his breath did not melt the snow at his mouth.

And on perceiving he was no more, I besought myself to seek succour, but on stumbling out for but a few moments I was so cruelly whipped by the storm that I returned, and laid myself at the mercy of our Lord, huddled in the lee of His compassion whose comfort is ever nigh e'en in the most fearful of times, and that did, thanks be to God, did come with dawn in the bodily guise of a shepherd and his dog, as ye well know.

And if I had indeed swaddled myself in the garments so venially cast to me, so foolishly cast off, who says I did evil?

Seeking life.

As the reasoning soul must.

Yet the ear of jealousy heareth all things, my children.

Though he that toucheth pitch shall be defiled therewith.

1712

IMPROVEMENTS

I have near on sixty acres, most being white land. My great-grandfather enclosed it to sheep some hundred years ago but I till the greater part of it now, with no recourse to the Manor Court. Commoners are the harrow-rest to improved husbandry, is my opinion. I have hedged about my lower fields, and that land is a piece of beauty, in right order. To dung it, I have used all sorts. Pigeons'-dung I have found to be most advantageous on cold land, where the clay makes it spewy underfoot. A neighbour has sown his cold land with hay-dust straight after burning and ploughing. This, he says, kills the acid-juice most effectively, but I have yet to try it. I have for the rest of my land, being white and dry, applied the yield from my hogs-yard. I have found eight pigs to be sufficient for trampling of the garbage and weeds and Cornish muskings to make sixty or so loads of fine manure.

This last week it was recommended to me by my cousin, who husbands the other side of Ulverdon, towards Effley, that I apply on my white land human ordure, being the product of a suitably-placed house of office, not too near the dwelling—if I were to cast in also, every two days, straw, or suchlike, to clot it. Once broken down, it may be carried to a furthest field and heaped up for putrefaction. He has shown me a crop further advanced and fatter than mine which, he claims, is advantaged by said application of his own manure. I reckon this to be more owing to the said field being well sheltered from the easterly winds by a tall quick-thorn hedge all along one side. My own land is much unsheltered and I propose to enclose my upper fields from the violent winds of cold springs and the scorching winds we sometimes have when the corn is just fattening.

I have this day, being a nipping January, carried out to the fields my horse-piss and hogs'-piss, these being frozen and thus facilitating carriage, the motion of the cart being otherwise too great to enable the filling to the brim of the buckets. Piss, I have been told, is most beneficial to white land in wet seasons. It must, like other soils, sit for a suitable time, as the making of vinegar from beer, or else its properties will not be forthcoming, and possibly be injurious to the roots.

My wife, hitting her head on the door into the cow-stall, this room being dark and the day being so overcast it was almost resembling night, lay in her bed for the afternoon and complained of a headache. The maid cooked my dinner but let the fire out. I myself scoured the pots. I found the buttery to be in a filthy state, with much garbage and even a dead rat tucked into the corners. Today was mild for winter.

My spring-corn field is in good tillage. I rose early and walked it the length around as the church bell gave out the early service. It is my highest field and faces the village, which affords a view but is injurious to the crop as I am southerly to Ulverdon. I lost my hat when a gust blew, and chased it. It was very raw. I also met a vagrant dressed in nothing more than a shirt and a ragged pair of skin breeches, no doubt his father's. He was holed up in the lee of the corner oak. I gave him a quarter of the bread I had taken up with me and the milk from my bottle, and sent him on his way. I pray that some of the gentlemen who berate our Chapel might try to live as this vagrant, more like Christ than they. This field had been of rye when I ploughed it with a narrow furrow before the first frost. I perceive that the winter has already shattered the furrows, these being narrow, and mellowed them out finely for the first harrowing. I received great pleasure from this observation of good practice.

It has been noted that women, if crossed, go pinched and silent, which is the healing-in of their womanly agitations, or they turn shrewish and bellow as if in labour. My wife does neither. She goes ill and lies abed. This causes much distress to our maid, who must redouble her efforts. We cannot afford to pay her more. Today she neglected to scour the pots when my wife had lain already three hours on her bed owing to our rupture at midday. This concerned nothing more than the small matter of the dairy's cleanliness. The first day of February was clear and the thatch smoked from the frost as if on fire.

Last night she hit me with the stick we keep for this purpose beside the bed. Flesh obeys not the cooling of the mind but pain only. We prayed together afterwards.

I have begun, being now February, to spread the dung on the field which I grassed last year. The two labourers who joined me in the summer were somewhat put out by this practice, being somewhat earlier than was the practice on their common, and it took some little time to explain to them that with this method the spring rains might wash the goodness of the dung down to the roots of the grass (which is St Foin) before it is dried to dust by the sun and blown off. They scratched their heads and maintained it was a queer thing. The smell of the hogs'-dung was lessened by the cold, I noticed.

This has been a dry February. I am hoping for rain in March, or my method will be put to question.

A waggon, left out of shelter in the small bennets lea for convenience, has split along the sideboards: Farmer Barr, passing by, informed me that it was the action of the night's frost on the wet wood. I must shelter the waggon forthwith, although it is an old one, and loose in the hubs.

A storm last night has put out many of the greater trees and scattered the heaps of dung I took to the upper fields a week ago. A calf came out seeming well but died an hour or so later, whether to the effects of the storm I cannot conjecture. There is undoubtedly some kind of magnetic activity at work when the wind is very strong. The parlour is still full of smoke where it was blown down the chimney, having no opportunity of egress. The door was blown out in the still-room, and several pickle jars were lost—namely, the violets, the cowslips, the flowers of broom. My wife took this sight somewhat poorly.

A fire, this end of February, reduced two cottages to ashes on the edge of the village. One of my labourers spent the day building another for the poor widow whose wretched abode one of these was. In total the goods lost were two stools, two tables, a candlestick, and three truckle beds. The rest were carried out before the fire properly took hold but amounted to less than half the loss. Our Chapel will provide a proportion. The smell of the burning is sharp even here.

The habit of folding sheep on the fields to be sown is much taken up in these parts: I have hired fifty ewes (wethers are not so beneficial) and their lambs, whose dung in particular is rich, partaking as it does of the mother's milk. This has cost me 7d for each night, but I am certain that it will gain me profit from the greater yield this summer. My labourers claim I am making shepherds out of them, although they too have sheep on their commons. They do not fancy the moving of the fences, I fear. This day my wife was found by the maid, with a straw doll hung about her neck.

How to avoid the spalting of dry land when it is ploughed took up the bulk of my conversation with Mr Lisle, Esquire, whom I encountered on the Ulverdon road, past the ash-copse, early this morning. He was on his way to inspect a spongy ground he had pared off and burnt the summer last, and sown with hay-dust. Mr Lisle reckoned on ploughing lightly therefore, or not at all, because the bad ground that is turned up beneath the good makes the effort worthless. Mr Lisle's horse was made jittery by a crow that swooped very close, but he was in no danger. This led us swiftly to a second observation: Pliny's remark that good soil can be told by the flocking of crows and other birds to its turning-up, stirring the air about the ploughman like gulls about a ship. This is due to the abundance of certain types of insects who are particular about the soil they choose to abide in. Mr Lisle is a great expert on these matters and an hour spent in his company furnishes a good crop of information. He has much land hereabouts but I believe he comes from Crux Easton, to the South. He reckons on there being another month of dry weather, the last year being so moist. He has the Queen's ear, it is said, but that is only from the fusty-minded of Ulverdon to whom any man that hails from afar and bears the title of Esq. is worthy of awe.

My wife has not eaten for two days. Yesterday I placed before her some white meat with bread but she scarcely looked. Our maid swept and stoked the fire all the while talking of her sick father who aids in the smithy but is no decent church man, and not making allowance for my wife's situation. I am resolved to be rid of her. She wears her bodice loose and will not tie up her hair as is seemly. She beats the coverlets like a mad woman, or a soldier his drum. It scares the poultry across the yard. There was no butter churned this week, as I was busy with the ploughing of the fallow, which I have resolved to turn to wheat and not let it lie idle, my wife was abed, and the maid was in the herb garden (it being a new moon this Tuesday), and planting chervil and coriander on my wife's instructions. I saw the market from the top field and reflected that this was the first day we had not sent to it with butter. I prayed then and there in the field and, being on my knees, noticed the brashiness of the new-turned-up soil more keenly than heretofore. The stones are very light, but enough to rest the harrow, I fear. My knees have remained cold, which is curious. They have retained the winter in them as the soil does. I heated some water and washed before the fire this day.

This morning early I smelt spring.

Of the inestimable advantages of enclosing land: despite the clovering of the fallow that is taken up by many neighbouring villages, the fusty gents of Ulverdon, hid in this valley from the outer world as they are, have decreed that fallow remain naked for fear of wearying of the soil. Some men I know, seeing my and others' clover and St Foin, and the health of the winter cattle, and the goodness of the soil so pastured, chafe at this regulation, and would fence their strips if it were affordable. They might, at ploughing, remove the fences and thereby gain still the common advantages of the shared plough and oxen. However, to such degree are the stones of tradition buried deep that no man might lift them alone, or stub up the shrubs of complacency. The bare widenesses of the commons around Ulverdon, that are not to sheep, suffer considerably, in places, from the winds, and I have seen a score of strips with the meagre corn quite flattened each summer.

I have spent this day constructing a dry hedge for the protection of my young trees that I am to plant about my top field. I hired a lad to help me, as my servants were dunging. The lad was amused by this artificial thing, but I explained to him that the winds up here would nip the tender trees and he nodded sagely. If we are to Improve effectively, the young must be instructed forthwith in the new ways.

I was paused in my tawing of the harness by a shriek from the upper window of the house. My wife had taken it into her head to batter the poor maid with a pan for tearing a hole in the linen for the flock-bed. The hole was but a finger's width where already the linen was worn almost out. The maid was somewhat bruised about the face but otherwise unharmed. I gave her a jug of beer for which she was exceeding grateful. My wife lay abed. I myself bathed the afflicted places with a tincture of camomile, and was reminded of Our Lord's feet.

On tawing of harness: it is to be recommended that, if cracks in bending from over-dryness are to be avoided, a proper dressing of allum and salt must be applied to halters, cruppers, belly-bands etc., and especially where the leather is horny, or has a seam of black running through.

Today I caught the maid at her offices. She was pissing within the dairy and not, as instructed, upon the dung-heap which is hidden from general view. Being midway through her passing of urine she made no effort to hide herself and I was afflicted with a view of her private place, which, unlike my wife's, is crow-black. Her skirts were too far up about her waist to shield any particular from me and I remonstrated with her, but am recognisant of the fact that my prayers have gone unanswered. The Lord works in mysterious ways.

My wife beat me, on my instructions, again this night. I am much disturbed, at present, by appearances in my sleep of our youngest, who has not been gone from this world more than a year now. I woke deeply troubled by this. I was about the yard early overseeing the oxen and a coulter was badly nipped, I noticed. If the Lord has not granted me a son, and only sickly daughters who do not live, my cousin must take hold of this land when I am gone, and the thought weakens my resolve. This morning was deadly cold, and the foddering barton was stone-hard in white heaps. Despite the decent feed, the cows are milking thinly at present. Their racks are halfway full and little is trodden that is not straw. My servant says it is the inclemency of the weather. Some of the udders are, indeed, cracked. Everything steams.

The advantages of the turnwrest cannot be over-estimated. When combined with a draught of horses it is incomparable. My own draught remains of oxen but Mr King's I have seen in action and his horses are easy of manoeuvre and appear faster, particularly at the headland turn, which in my lower fields is altogether too narrow for my heavy beasts. We replaced three shares in one morning, the soil being so brashy. The coulter cut deep, it being a dry month of March so far, and a drier February, this year 1712, but the crows and rooks and gulls followed close on our heels, which bodes well for the soil, which I have meliorated with much dung since the wheat harvest. The land's chockiness was never so obvious as this morning, when the share was bone-white after the first furrow. I pray for a dripping summer which always spreads its juices easily in our dry chalk land. In dry summers the barley ears tend to blight and a shrivelled look.

My uncle having made me of a bookish mind, despite it being viliorated with matters such as dung and mouldiness, I have on my shelves several volumes, of which the most-thumbed is Bunyan's. His is the pilgrim who names the world a 'wilderness', and visits the valley of Humiliation. Perched before the fireside, reading by the glow (as we are low with candles, and my wife had settled early, not wishing to worsen her headache with drawing-up of old holes in old stockings), and still aching from the stilts of the turnwrest which I held for more than an hour while my ploughman rested, and the share too blunt already, and the tilth deep, I noted that, far from being a source of contentment, the pilgrim's woes matched mine too greatly, and I likened my life to the handling of an oxen team on a chocky, declivous field, with the rooks so loud about me that I could not hear my own breath, or the ploughman shouting from the hedge that the coulter was loose, and but shallow cutting.

Today I went to market and on my return, upon the scarp above Five Elms Farm, that was once old Anne Cobbold's the witch, I noted one elm to be down, most likely in the January storm, and it being old, and wondered about the name, and that my own farm, being simply Plumm's, which is my own family title, might lose that title when I pass on, which upset me greatly.

Today we ploughed the last acre. There is much debate at present, among my neighbouring farmers who have come by, over the number of earths that is desirable after naked fallow. I have one field that has lain still for two summers, with only camomile and redweed upon it, being fallowed before I tried the clover and St Foin, and being a field much reduced in richness by my forefathers, who rested it not. It is a loose, spongy ground, and Farmer Barr was of the mind that, were I to plough it up and sow it to one earth, as I had considered, I would have much trouble with the redweed, or poppy. If the land is settled and fast, as it may be after three summers or more, the redweed seed is choked where it is turned under. I told him that I thought it better, then, to wait for rain, which might impact the soil, and render it suitable for one or two earths. Farmer Barr is cursed himself by redweed and is sore on the subject. I left the ploughman to clean and oil this dusk and went inside to ask after my wife, who is again poorly, and to relate to her the advice of Farmer Barr, only to encounter my maid sobbing in the still-room. When asked for the reason of her distress I was met with no answer. Hearing the noise of the bed above I knew my wife was not deceased, which had passed through my mind, and sat down. Her hands were as ice. I took to rubbing them and, seeing her face lighten its load, asked her again. She being a very young girl, and a simple one at that, laid her head in my lap, which was redolent still of the field, and thus we remained for at least a half-hour. What happened following this attempt of comfort I will relate as best my troubled hand can put it down. She arose, closed the door to the kitchen, which rendered it very dark in the still-room, so that I was afraid for the bottles, whereupon I heard a rustling, like the prickles of barley in a wind, and felt a body that was unclothed from the waist down upon my lap, and my breeches unlaced with a dexterous hand before I could render a note of complaint or astonishment. I saw in my mind only the turn of the furrow, the coulter slicing, and the crows with their baleful cries. The Lord forgive me. We broke five bottles: of sallets, of gillyflowers, and three of white lilies.

The aftermass of clover I mowed October last, being kept suitably dry, we thrashed this day, it being clear and warm in the sun, though still middest March, and, after beating the husks again that were separated from the straw, got a goodly seed, fat and rounded, and five bushels of it from the first acre. That field being of seven acres, the whole should be thrashed before the week is out. I flailed for three hours, which eased my thoughts, and gave me much satisfaction.

My wife, it appears, suffers from nothing more than fear, or trepidation. It is plain to me that her last bearing, where she screamed for more than twenty hours, and lost much blood, and the child too, rendered her an invalid in the mind, if not the body: this being the reason she will not have me so much as stroke a hair upon her head. The stick she uses against me at my request, when I am driven to desire for procreation, is now guardian of this aforesaid fear. She is a weak vessel, then, and God has granted me a stronger. This day, being late March, and my seeds-man out in the field already, I am driven to these wild thoughts, that both please and distress me.

This day the cattle have been turned out.

In the dairy, this afternoon, with the door closed, I sought to seed my heir, against a full churn, her hands still ripe with butter, as a ram tups a ewe, but praying all the while I cast. Lord forgive me. A little rain this first week of April. I do not think anyone heard, although the girl's cries (of pleasure) were hard to silence. We tipped over the churn, and lost, I reckon, a half of our butter.

The nails in the sideboards of the dung-waggon having loosened, and some lost, through the hard motion of the cart on the frozen ruts and also on the declivities of the road likewise stony with frost, I have taken up the advice of Mr Nash and thonged with leather, well greased, the sideboards to the raths and found these to be fast after a week of use. The dung spread in January has not, owing to the dry weather, and only a little rain the first week of April, done much goodness to the soil, by my reckoning, which is owing to the generally dry nature of white land that is not easily taken to drinking up the dung's juices.

My seeds-man is advanced in years, and I have noted, that having a weakness of the wrist owing to his years, he is apt to back-drop much of the seed, which as he advances is plain to see, and will lead to a thicker run of corn where he broadcasts, and a thinner elsewhere. This seeds-man, having been my labourer at this season for twenty years, must soon be replaced, if an even spread of corn is to be realised henceforward. My cousin at Effley has pointed out the advantages of a seeds-man pacing against the incline of a field, if the field be so out of level, that uphill and downhill he must take short steps, whereas on the level his steps are apt to be lengthened, and so, broadcasting at every step, the seed be spread too thin. Also, if the seeds-man get tired, as he is apt to going up and downhill, his steps will thereby be shorter. The danger, as I did then remark, with both of us watching my seeds-man who did once or twice stumble, and did cover his beard in soil, is that of casting too thick, as with a weak wrist. My cousin agreed, and, doffing his hat that he did then use as a seed-lip, demonstrated to me the correct measurement of the stride, which he had arrived at after much observation on the commons at sowing-time, where are to be seen many seeds-men at once.

On Mr Tull's seed-drill: this last ten years has seen a score of attempts at the introduction of this invention, which by all accounts is far superior to any seeds-man, and might, it is said, sow three tons of seed at one session. However, the former seeds-men and their companions in labour have withdrawn their labours completely at each attempt, and so simple fear of Improvement, which might increase general profit and feed our nation the better, which in time of war is seen to be more necessary, has miscarried this robust child of science, and so we must suffer weak wrists and wheezing old men.

This day, again, within the cow-house, up amongst the hay, when all the men were harrowing, and the cows at pasture on the leas, the grass being fat enough, I did apply my member to the use it is best made for, which is the making of an heir. The maid did keep her silence, and afterwards spent much time taking hay from her hair, which she wears still loose, and plucking off my shoulders lengths of the hair which had attached themselves to my coat, and which my wife, who is at market, might be made ill-thinking by. I note that upon her left dug, that is the maid's, a small indentation is to be seen which, when questioned after, she did relate how she was bitten thereupon by a mongrel, who are a curse through the winter months, and most particularly to shepherds. The cow-house tallet, being generally dark at the rear, and we obscured by hay, has several parts in its wall where the sun alights through holes and cracks, and one of these illuminated us quite suddenly and made her cry out when the sun did come and go, as it did, this being a windy April. It was by this light that I examined her more particularly, and spied the bite-mark. It is remarkable how the hay has sufficed overmuch for the winter, much still lying about in heaps, and we deep within it, and the cattle already out to grass. This is owing to the richness of hay from clover, one acre equivalent to six acres of other, wilder, sourer grass, and it being our practice to feed only the oxen with hay beyond January, fearing a harsh winter. I explained as much to the girl, when she had let herself down into the foddering barton, and was picking her way through the dung therein, there being no one about in the yard at that hour, but such husbandry matters do ill please her.

I have thought, this night, before the fire, after a day of harrowing, and casting clover-seed upon the tinings that it might grow with the barley-seed already cast, how God approves, in his Majesty, the lowliest act of procreation, whether in the starky, stiff soil of husbandry or the moistness of woman. Because all coupling is in His image, if it be to belly, and further improve Creation by begetting, and not after lust only, or for craving of it. If my seed chitts within her, and within the soil of my land, then there is merely profit, and no waste. My wife did spin all day, but is now abed. I did read before the hearth but nodded off for a half-hour and bent the page on Leviticus.

I note, on my top field, the slow progress of the harrow, this being the brashy field, with a multiplicity of small stones that rest the tines. My labourer was of the mind to remove them before the next year, which would bear little profit for me owing to the requirement of much labour to achieve a clean field. I answered, that the stones, being on white land, and that land being dry and light, make an additional weight much needed by the soil. My man grunted only, which is always the response of the simple-minded. Still no rain.

Mr Philip Swiffen, of Speen, whose land abuts on the old castle at Donnington, and who I have been visiting this day to enquire after malt-dust, and to view his winnowing machine, which is the first to be acquired in these parts, and which unnecessitates a reliance on wind, its sacking sails providing a goodly breeze which blew my hat off, showed me a field which was the place of the battle between King and Roundhead, and he boasted that it yielded wheat whose ears numbered a regular five to seven, and some at fourteen! This, he explained, was owing, most like, to the blood spilt on that land, whose juices were thereby more nutritious. I have heard this before, but not at first-hand.

My dreams are at present troubled: of dogs, and paps, and my wife's face under the harrow, which comes of the accident up at Farmer Garrard's, where a man was drawn under the tines when the horse (for he uses no oxen) took fright at a boy's bird-clapper being sudden operated. A dose of brandy aids my sleep each night. My wife watches me.

My bile being bad I took white lily. Two sheep slinked their lambs in one night this week, and that is the last, though we have four pur-lambs, who will make fine tupps. There was a rime on the thatch today, and my breath never went from the air. The maid's warmth was welcome.

I note that, in my field that was sown to St Foin a year past, and on which I suffered the cows to go after the oats were cut, the grass is much injured by their feet and the cropping of their mouths, and is still not recovered, this being due, no doubt, to its youth and the dryness of these latter months. I will hayn it up from the cattle for the remainder of the year, lest further injury be suffered by the young shoots.

My maid is not well.

The manure passage in the cow-house was deepened this day.

The clover between the barley is already a good sward. I applied pigeons'-dung after the seed, this being a cold and clay field, and the manure of my poultry. It has worked to pleasing effect. May 12th, and still no rain. Today was hotter than any before in my memory. The maid is creamy about the face. On enquiry, she pushed me off, and ran to the houses of office, where I heard her retch. She is undoubtedly bellied. I informed my wife that she (the maid) had eaten of pork poorly-salted. My wife considered it owing to the habit of steeping fish in the common well in the square. I was at a loss for an answer, for she said this strangely. She tends the herbs from six until half-past seven every morning, which I think excessive, but she will not hear of it. There is hardly time to bake, and our bread is too chock with bran, and heavy.

My wife enquired, this night, why the stick had not been put to recent use. I was at a loss for an answer at first, but took out my small Bible, that I carry always, and laid my hand upon it. A wind got up and I had to rise in the middest of the night with a lanthorn to shut fast a door into the barn that was banging with much distress to the cattle. I found the latch broken, and tied it up with rope, and was much tired by this exertion, and the wind, and the hour. The wind was warm, being a westerly, but the yard appeared rimed with the moon full out, and I retired swiftly.

Although my writing is not smooth, and my tongue thick, I wish one day to write a book of husbandry, as Mr Fitzherbert's that wrote formerly, and Mr Worlidge's that my uncle, though only a parson, had upon his shelf, and lent me. There is in this latter the likeness of a patent seed-drill, which I believe never to have been tried.

I did, it seems, overfeed my St Foin, according to Farmer Barr, which made it sweet and so the cattle cropped it too close. All our timber is now stored. I am fashioning new flails from the thorn, and two new forks from the hazel. My ploughman reckons on there being the need for a new mouldboard, the wood somewhat scuffed and dented, and on indicating this to Farmer Barr, the latter postulated a greater use of iron in the plough's parts, which would enable a lengthier service, but the ploughman, who was with us, readying to plough the fallow for the wheat crop that day, maintained that an over-use of iron would be evil to the soil, whereas wood is of the soil and so is not pernicious. Why then, I asked, is it not evil to have the share and coulter of iron, when they and they only touch the soil deeply? He was at a loss to answer, but maintained simply that, the less iron the better. I asked why should the iron poison the soil. He said it was common knowledge. Ah, how common knowledge vitiates all attempts at individual Improvement of husbandry, and of the science of its betters!

I was much relieved today, May 17th, by a thunder-shower which the roots of the corn must be glad of. On riding into Ulverdon, afterwards,

I noted how the earth that was cracked and white on the road was now brim with water, but not yet soft. The fields around exhaled an odour which was most pleasing. The commons were full of folk for the strips are abundant with pernicious weeds, but once pulled they will no doubt burn them, whereas if they were to cover them with dung, or soil, they will compress into a substance like butter, and cut easily for application on the fields the next year. I met Mr King in the square, and we entered the ale-house called the New Inn (although it is by no means new), and he told me there of rags that might be bought in London for 2s per hundred-weight, and chopped by widows and suchlike for circa 6d per hundred-weight, and so chopped to an inch square then scattered at the second ploughing, which cloth turning fusty underneath would procure nourishment for the seed at winter sowing. I was much taken by this, and he promised to provide me at a decent rate, whereupon I would try it upon the second earth in July. He would fetch me the cloth within the month. I have noted the mouldiness of cloth on vagrants, and on buried cast-offs within the yard or fields, but have never considered its use as a manure. We were much disturbed, in our discussion, by rowdy fellows one of whom slipped on the straw, where he had sent his spittle, and cracked his nose. The evil usage of the grain that is now ripening in my field is the Vice of the age, although in moderation essential to good health. The crop that my labourers sow and harvest is frequently too much within them, so that their breath continually smells of barley, as it were, and their minds fuddled by it. Mr King agreed, and stated that one seeds-man addicted to this tincture before us on the table witnessed the evidence of his sickness at harvest, when the field resembled a harlequin in the prints, all patches, and he vowed to Mr King never to touch a drop again, which is remarkable testimony to God's working.

May 25th. When told of the maid's state, and the necessity of saving a girl's reputation, by adoption of the child, my wife took it ill.

This beginning of June, was the clover lea cut for hay. The weather being doubtful the second day, we enlarged the cocks and did not turn them, but left a hollow within to allow air to penetrate and dry. A steady rain for half a day did little damage therefore, and the weather is dry once more. As experiment, I left at least three cocks'-worth tedded over the field at nightfall, and on returning in the dewy morning found that the moisture had penetrated and expelled some of the juices, mixing with the sap, and so expelling also the smell of the grass, which in the cocks was exhaled much stronger: these having not been in contact, excepting their bases, with the nitrous properties of dew. I indicated this to the mowers and even the gatherers, but they seemed not to understand. The women and children laughed at my talk, indeed. One hay-rake broke upon a stone the last day, its brace having come loose, but not spotted in time. The grass having been mown at the time it began to knot, this crop should be exceeding rich, whereas if left longer, so that the stems are showing, it will be thinner and sourer. The crop has not suffered overmuch from the dry, although the barley amongst it is somewhat thin and brownish.

The maid has taken to a fuller skirt. She appears robust. I have put aside already the cost of her carrying, which she agreed at 7s, which is indeed a princely sum for a natural task, involving as it did her pleasure, which I have asked the Lord His forgiveness for.

June 20th: a hard rainfall, that left the barley ears dripping, and the thatch-runnel to go down my neck, and the corn to lose its thirst by, for it fell for two hours without cease.

I found this day, upon entering the hogs-yard, my wife seated amidst the peelings with a clout about her head, looking exceeding merry. My brandy bottle lay broken upon the ground, and I feared for the animals that their feet may be penetrated by the pieces of glass, and rendered maim. She allowed me to take her back into her bed, and I noted that she had clarted her hands and face with hogs'-dung, and washed her in silence, for I was angered by this display which was injurious to all our reputations, since it was seen by several of the servants gathered for their payment that evening, this being the close of the month, and no doubt chosen by her for that very reason. I have spoken to Dr Kemp, after the

Meeting yesterday, who advises rest, and a medicament of some tincture with a Latin name that smells of camomile underfoot in autumn, but is not. My wife is going mad, owing, no doubt, to the confinement and its subsequent effects some time ago referred to. I prayed with her that God might meliorate her condition, and render her fit. Today was very hot. The sun has already undone the wetness of the recent rain, and the earth cracks and is friable underfoot. The odours of the aforesaid hogs'-dung are not displeasing, however, within these walls, as they turn my mind to Improvements.

The peas in the top field are somewhat thinnish. The new trees I planted thereabout to fend off the northerly winds have a blighted look owing to the lack of rain, but they have life in them yet, and should serve. My bird-boy bagged two ravens this morning with a sling-shot, and hung them out to smell off the others. On close inspection, the raven resembles Jewry, with its beak, that is larger than an ordinary crow's, and its feathers, that are loose about the neck, like a Jew's scarf in the illustrations. This same bird-boy, however, killed a rook last week, which no more resembles the ordinary crow than I resemble a common thief. He is no more than nine, but has an exceeding lack of teeth, which I put to his habit of chewing on sticks, which he does without cease from dawn to nightfall, as well as a certain tendency to brawls with his elders in the village. Despite the heat, he wears a coat of the thickest hide. I dwell upon this boy because he is the same age as my own would have been, had the good Lord seen fit to let him be so. How strange divine Justice appears to us mortals below, when one sees this boy hollering from his station by the oak on the headland, brought into this world only to scare off or slaughter scavengers such as himself, if of a lower order!

On my return from market this day, I made way for a shearing team of twenty or so, who were white from head to foot from the dust of the road, on the way to Squire Norcoat's, and who resembled the fleeces they were to relieve the sheep of.

This day, July 1st, I made the girl lift her dress so that I might feel the belly. She is well filled, and ripe in the cheeks. She asks now for 8s, but I have remained firm. My wife has gone flueish, and remains abed. Dr Kemp inspected her stool this day, and pronounced it of a better colour than before. She is much disturbed this night by strains of music, which she believes to be of angelic origin, but which I have informed her (to no avail) has been carried by the breeze, this being south-easterly, from the concert at the Hall, that Lord and Lady Chalmers are giving for their heir's coming-of-age, and is said to be very grand. I have seen lights moving in the trees, that are afar, yet there being no moon the merriment may be thus glimpsed, as well as heard.

I write this late, and unsteadily. The rags from London arrived midday, in two carts, and I hesitated where to store them. I chose a cart-shed built before my grandfather's time and half stoved-in by weather and time, but great enough for the purpose. The rags smelt strong, of vagrants, sweat and suchlike, and I was chary of touching them, fearing pox and so on, but the carter was keen for a 1d to unload, and did so. Hearing a noise, like that of an animal in distress, from the rear of the shed, where the wood abuts us, and is much given over to bramble and bedwine and pernicious shrubs, and is generally wild, some of it clinging to the shed wall, and pulling at the old bricks, I ventured round with a mattock, and saw between the leafy growth into an unexpected clearing, wherein my maid and a newish labourer taken on for the harvest were coupled, he crouched behind like a bull, she on her fours with her belly and dugs suspended, tupping as the beasts do. I stood fixed to my station, and they continued unawares, half-concealed by the wild growth, while the carter unloaded nearby, whistling. I confess I cried, and the noise disturbing them, they uncoupled, and grinned foolishly, and I drove off the labourer, by the name of Griffin, with my mattock, and he was much torn, it appeared, by the wild growth he fled through. I seized the maid by the shoulders, and shook her vigorously, whereupon she turned pale, and I left off. On enquiring why she should risk 7s and the child by bathing its head in another man's seed, this being pernicious in the extreme to its health, even its life, she gave me notice of her intent to tell Parson Brazier (old fool though he be) of the true declination of the bellying, that her conscience might be appeased, and she might enter into the Kingdom of Heaven anywise. We agreed, therefore, to 9s. I am employing twelve old people from the village to chop up the rags upon a block set out for the purpose, which will cost circa 7d per hundred pieces. My head is full of pence and shillings this day, and the wet-heading of my heir by a common labourer hurts me greatly, but I must proceed gently. The stink of the rags is still about my person, much of it of smoke from the city, as well as of general poverty. I noted one shirt to have the stain of blood all down its front, whether from illness or some heinous action I will never fathom. I am keen to bury them, that they might go finnowy the quicker.

Viewing all of my fields in turn, I note how the riper corn (or grass) lies at the headland, though the soil there be often poorer. This, says my cousin, who has come to inspect my rags, that are this day being chopped, is owing to the easier start the corn had under the lee of the hedge at the headlands, where the earth is warmer, because sheltered. The ears there lie full in the hull, where the rest of the field's are not yet swollen. The advantages of enclosure are obvious, therefore, to even the stubbornest commoner.

My wife has not talked to me one word for two weeks now. I continue, however, to read her passages from the Epistles. Her bed-linen is stained with her sweat, although she has no fever to speak of. She does not appear much in distress, but now and again will walk to the window, open wide the shutters, and mutter into the yard upon her herbs. She will not be parted from her straw doll, that she lies with. This day, being my birthday, we turned a roast upon the spit, and my cousin and the servants who live with us (this being three) drank too much berry wine. My wife remained abed.

More rain, for a half hour, this July 17th, but not sufficient to meliorate the barley. I meditated in my bed upon ways of irrigation in times of drought, and conceived of a pump with several mouths, that might be carried upon a cart, if the cart be watertight and very large. This just before I slept and dreamed of a son delivered from a raven, which disturbed me greatly in the middest night.

The maid this morning ran to me crying whilst I was overseeing the loading of the rag pieces onto the waggon for carriage down to the fallow. She had a cut upon her arm, where my wife had lashed her with a waggon-thong from the shed. An old ploughman called Perry, who was up to view the rags, recalled how the witch Anne Cobbold could cure these fevers of the mind by mumbling and staring and various doings with animal bones laid in the river at night. He it was who as a boy kept the sheep watched over while the old shepherd sinned with her, when she was turned into a ewe: there being little doubt of the truth thereof, as I have heard this from the mouth of a most reliable witness, and also from one who delivered Anne Cobbold of a dead child, that was covered over with a silky fleece throughout, and had a blunt snout very like a sheep's. Yet I remonstrated with the man to keep the Devil's work out of it, and he kept his silence then. He is full of stories and no teeth. I sent the maid home. I fetched an old dame from the village to scour, wash et cetera and ring up the cheese clout, while my wife lay abed. I found the waggon-thong upon a hook in the still-room, in the shape of a noose. We scattered the rag pieces evenly upon the naked fallow, each seed-lip taking a goodly number when packed in, and earthed them in with the coulter. My cousin says they might warm the ground through the winter, as they once warmed poor fellows. I said I preferred not to recall from whence they derived. The two seeds-men thought the whole affair the work of madness. I said that when they saw the crop chissum despite this spongy ground they would heal their words with the tines of Reason and Progress. They said, nay, it would only give the ground pox.

My eight swine have yielded, in one year, fifty-two loads of fine manure. I am glad to have kept such close account of this, the first year I have done so. I have a book wherein I vouch to record all possible numbers of yields, loads etc., that a proper reckoning might be made of methods of Improvement, and the exact profit thereby pertainable.

In order to meliorate my wife's illness, I have given over the sum of £5 to the building of a new Chapel upon the site of the old, in Bew's Lane, this one to be of brick, not wood, and my name to be enscribed with the other contributors within, upon a small stone.

The field of St Foin that I hayned up from the cattle is well filled, and ready for cutting: the kernel is of a purplish hue, and the husk brown. Being thus not quite full in general, excepting at the headlands, the seed will not shed overmuch at mowing. It being extremely hot in the day, the mowers will start in the middest night, at three of the morning, and cease cutting when the sun shining causes the seed to shatter. They may then proceed again in the cool of the evening.

Our pond is quite dried out, and cracked. It is exceeding hot, and the river is full of children these days. The field is almost mown. The moon is at its fullest and by its light the mowers can see as well as in the day. They say it is still too hot, even in the night, and the owls make them fearful, because they are a superstitious breed of people here, and would rather be abed. One, by the name of Shail, claims to have witnessed a dance of fairies on his way to the field, this occurring in the ash-copse, and filling him with much wonder, but I scolded him severely for his softness. The roads at this early hour are very white indeed under the moonlight, and it is indeed surprising warm, and odorous. I insist upon the swarths being turned in the early hours, when the moistness in the ground sticks the seed to the ear, and not when the sun is hot. I demonstrated to the mowers the efficacy of this rule by shaking lightly a rakeful in the midday and shaking out well nigh all the seed. The swarths are turned by the handle of the rake, ears first, as advised to me by Farmer Barr. The seed is not ripe enough to cock straightway.

My wife has spoken to me, but names me the Duke, as in the latterly-dismissed Marlborough, I presume. I cannot fathom to what this refers, or whether in her madness it means but nonsense. Over what have I gained victory? What armies can I lead in her befuddled head?

The servants giggle in corners of the yard, which distresses me greatly. The maid is very full for her time. All the St Foin is reeked and they are to be thatched forthwith. I noted that when the cocks were built up, the bulk of each shook all over when struck by the rake, that striking the top sent a shiver, as it were, all the way to the bottom, as if the mown grass had turned into a jelly. So the action on one part of a body affects the whole. The reeks are too large for this effect to be easily noticed.

The maid took me into the still-room very early, at six, and we coupled, which made me anxious for the child, but she had hold of my member and it was exceeding hard to desist, as I had not lain with her for a month or more. We coupled like beasts.

The wheel upon a waggon returning over the St Foin stubble and striking an indentation cracked and split suddenly, and threw a labourer from his seat atop the hay. His head in turn striking a flint upon the ground, was cracked wide open, and he was carried into the village by his fellow harvesters, to the inn, where he died forthwith. His name was James Pyke. He was a good man, a member of our Chapel, an excellent labourer and servant, and left a large family. I had only been talking to him, about the dryness of the reeked hay, and the possibility of thunder, an hour before. I fear the hard frosts of the winter acting upon the damp wood weakened the wheel within. It was the same waggon I found split before, having lain abroad, and took in, but too late, it seems. The other fellows returned greatly upset by this misfortune, and resumed thatching with unwilling limbs, or so it appeared. The bell rang out and we took off our hats and stood for a moment and I read a short prayer. The wainwright stated the wheel to be too far split to be mended, and I have perforce to pay for a new one, which being of a large and heavy type, will prove costly. The split occurred along two of the spokes, these being of cleft oak, but nevertheless weakened as stated before, which led to the general collapse of the felloes, and the weight of the waggon falling cracked the nave. So might a small error lead to the greater, and to fatality. The way is harsh and uneven for the true pilgrim.

A horse that is kittle may be so owing to temperament or mischance or ill-breeding or ill-treatment. However it be so, it will prove a danger for its master. So it is with wives. This day I found the straw doll hung from the beam in the cow-house by its neck. I burnt it forthwith. It was indicated to me by one of the servants, who was paid 6d for his silence. The Chapel was knocked down this day, it being only a flimsy structure of wood, and the new to be begun forthwith. Farmer Garrard was over this day, and averred, on surveying my new clover crop, that he might adopt this method of seeding, viz.: to sow the seed in the husk, that it might prove to crop more evenly and thicker, whereas to sow clover-seed on its own, pure, milled from the husk, perforce proves too light a cast in the March winds. I said, that it might be advantageous, then, to mix the seed with sand, or sifted coal, or wood-ash, to give the half-pecks weight, that it might fill the seeds-man's hand, and not prove too buoyant. He stated, that this was good advice, if the seed were milled, as oatmeal is, but that effort might be spared in the first place by retaining the husk anyways. Farmer Garrard's own clover field, mixed with Polish oats, that shadows it from this summer heat, is exceeding thin in places, owing to the blustery days in which the pure seed was cast, and scattered errantly. I averred that I would use this digression in my Sunday speech in the Chapel, as a parable fitting to the times. The seed being the soul, and the husk being the body, or flesh. We are cast into this life with the trappings of our flesh, that gives us weight, whereas if we deny the flesh, we are too light, and buoyant, like a cloud of bedwine seed, and know not where we go, as a man who denies himself meat grows thin, and lassitudinous. United in the flesh, our soul grows a goodly crop of virtue, the winds and rains our sufferings, that gives us exercise and greenness, and not to be shirked. Farmer Garrard, who is a Church man, said that the sermon for him mentioned flesh overmuch, although he is himself fleshy, and we laughed.

Being in the town this day, I viewed the new Corn Exchange, which is exceeding large, and pretty, and built after the manner of a Roman temple. I did good business with a corn merchant from Salisbury, and got a price for a winnowing machine which I must consider, and bought two barley hummellers of improved design. I avoided the new toll-gate by crossing a pasture, which amused my servant greatly. Returning through Ulverdon, I met Mr Webb, the wainwright, who was cutting a mortice into the nave of my new wheel, and who stated he would dish the wheel, it being large enough, at little extra cost. He demonstrated to me his new bruzz, this being a chisel of the shape of a V for the mortice-corners, and much neater in action than his previous tool. It is of much concern to him that a man died owing to the splitting of a wheel he had made, and fears for his reputation. I told him, that I thought it more my doing than his, because I did not cover the waggon through the storms of December, and that the frostiness and dryness of the later winter was all to blame. At the bridge over the river, a vagrant with a mongrel begged for harvest work, but he had no passport. On stating that passports, certificates and suchlike were not required for harvest work, he placed me at a disadvantage as a Christian man, and I had resort to the truth, which was that I did not approve of his face, this being sharpish, and of a gingery stubble cut through by a white scar. He cursed me then and there, which was discomfiting, as his curse was that of the magic arts, and spoke of progeny to be blasted et cetera, et cetera. My servant and a passing neighbour, Mr Hobbs, threw the man into the river, and Mr Hobbs went to tell the warden, that the Justice might be informed of a needed removal.

Harebells thick upon the waysides and pastures. Larkspur, buttercups, and the ramping fumitory amongst the arable. Hoeing does not coerce these into submission, but they are not sufficiently tall or thick to be a veritable nuisance to the crop, as redweed is, or dead-nettle. The advantage of clover, St Foin etc.: to reduce pernicious weeds. The naked fallow, that I dunged with rags at the second earth, and which Farmer Barr prophesied an abundance of redweed for, has grown up again thickly with that cursed flower, and being a dry, hot year, has turned friable and loose, so that any rain that it receives will run through, without benefit to the wheat I am to sow there. If I were to have left it fallow for a third year, then it might have proved fast and good.

But by our errors we learn, and prosper, as much as by our virtues. I might leave it as a fallows-stale for a further year.

During the harvest, which began Monday last, despite threatening weather, my maid aided the gatherers, which concerned me, but it is the practice amongst the commoners to labour until the final week. She raked together the gleanings, and did not bend to sheave, as this is arduous for one large in belly. The barley is not good, but sufficient. The oils are taller, the husks thicker, than is customary in a wetter year. My sickles are smooth-edged, as the custom of grasping the corn in bunches to cut seems to me to hold up progress, and the smooth edge cuts straight through without the requirement to bunch. However, barley being of a thicker stalk than other crops, the sickles must be sharpened more frequently, their edges taken off by the stalks, and so my cousin at Effley is insistent on using the serrated blade, which requires no strickle to keep it keen. For a proper comparison, one must try both types, and keep careful time on the acres, that one may be seen to be advantageous over the other, although, for an exact, scientific comparison, reapers of the same strength, age, and application must be used, which is a near impossibility, as every labourer appears, these days, to have his own peculiarities of temperament. But the harvest progresses, anyways, and the weather holds off, it still being exceedingly hot, and one labourer already overcome, though he had no shirt. The air is very dusty, and I have my sneezes, but the sound of the cut corn, like unto the rustling skirt of Nature herself, pleases me as greatly as usual. We have caught twenty-three rabbits and a stoat.

My wife walks at night.

The practice of mowing corn with a scythe is not common in these parts, as women find the effort too arduous, and there are not the men to go round. I have heard it to be three to four times as speedier, with one acre per man mown in a day, compared to but a quarter with the sickle. However, it is possible only with an abundance of strong men, despite the amelioration of time, and in this instance I am content to wait until English genius has conjured a suitable machine that will necessitate no rows of dogged reapers, gatherers, bandsters and whatnot, although I fear that time will be long a-coming. I have this day, walking about the top field with my stick, lifted fifty-five docks, and an abundance of bindweed, and almost as much shepherd's purse. I watch my maid from a distance, whom I have replaced part of the day in the house with the old dame named Trevick. This old dame reeks terribly from the armpits, and has the most sour piss, which makes the houses of office stink long after she has visited, and makes me concerned for the ordure beneath, that it prove to make injurious manure. My maid consorts with the other harvesters most loosely, and they make much fun of her condition. I fear for the child in this heat. The price of the winnowing machine is too high, I have decided. My new throw-crook, of improved design, having its spindle caged and the handle cranked, has been taken to with some reluctance, but it now proves a most efficient and speedy maker of straw-rope, despite its old-fashioned mortal operators, who would still be berry-picking like children for their sustenance if society had been left to their charge.

My insistence that a furrow be drawn at harrowing time, now allows the reapers a measure in the wheat-field, whose heads are otherwise buried in the stalks and unable to guide them. Thus small Improvements might yield much greater, and foresight be the loadstone of husbandry.

This day being the last of harvest, and thunder in the air, and the sky heavy, we brought the last load home with much rejoicing, and, alas, much ale in the downing. Our festive meal was sobered only by my wife's appearance, at the door, during the songs, like a ghost of winter past, berating the labourers, and myself, for our luxury, and snatching [away?] from the midst of us the corn Doll, which action upset the labourers greatly. I said nay, she would not harm it, to appease them, for they were somewhat inflamed with drink, and might have pursued her, had I not promised them what I could not in truth [be certain of]. How halting the progress of Improvements, as long as this talk of corn spirits, and fear of suchlike, continues to clot our tines! I left the meal early, as is my wont, before the songs become lewd and what is [permissible?] in the eyes of God after hard work oversteps the boundaries and grows rash. It was my grandfather's custom, in the time of the Commonwealth, to gather the harvesters in common prayer, and to allow only one tankard of ale apiece, and no songs, and but small fare upon the table. This I cannot hold by, and think it a mistake [not] to reward our brethren placed lower than us on the human scale for their unstinting efforts, or they might deem it [rotten?] that they labour in their sweat for other men, and not themselves, and break the chain of bonds and service that retains us [in] contentment, and themselves in peace. In truth, my wife appeared again before I left, and her countenance was such as to strike a chill in the proceedings, and to still the song, but I begged the assembled company to pursue their merriment, to strike up once more, and [not] allow present ills to frost over their reward. I could find my wife nowhere, but only the corn Doll, torn into a thousand pieces, as if chewed and spat out, upon our marital bed. I must make another the same forthwith, or the men will be exceeding anxious, and fearful of this place, [maintaining] the Shadow of the corn, as they call it, has been set free, to pollute us, as no doubt was my wife's [desire?]. I must seek God's forgiveness for adopting such heathen practices, as making a [corn] Doll. I write this in my room, with the merriment exceeding loud downstairs, the squeals of the maid louder than all others. I have touched too much of the wretched tincture, and must perforce [vomit?] though I am heartily pleased at the weight of corn now rested upon the straddle-stones, neatly thatched, that [is] exceeding odorous across the night air.

I write this with an [unsteady?] hand. The company snoring across the benches, sprawled like Balthazar's Feast over table, straw, and even out in the yard, some coupled together in the first sin, though clothed, mercifully, I stepped out in the middest night, and [crushed?] a fiddle underfoot, that was left [in] a rut, and took myself to the furthest rick, that I might take some corn in secret for the Doll, tho' it be not from the last [sheaf], and my lanthorn casting its light by chance into the cow-stall as I passed, and seeing there a shape hanging like a sack, entered in, and held the lanthorn up, and met of a sudden the eyes of my wife lo[o]king wide-eyed at me, as if to berate [. . .] but on reaching my hand out, she did turn at my touch [and] look likewise past my head [. . . ?] dangled by the neck above the manure passage, with a straw-rope the instrument of her [undoing?], and cut her down with much difficulty by [means of] a hay knife, and saw that she was expired, blue in the skin, and puffed, and [broken-necked?], and cried out, that God might take her into His arms, anyways, though I know where she is fast bound, and could [wake up] no one, cursed be that tincture! [except] the old dame, whose body [reeked of piss?], coming up the path at dawn, for so [long] had I lain with my wife in the cow-stall, amongst the straw and dung, stricken as [I] was, and vomiting.

God rest her soul.

I have been unable to write observations for a month. It is time already for the fallow to be sown with wheat. The heat of summer is gone, mercifully. A slight frost last night. The flails sound from the barn all day. My wife has been buried out of sacred ground, near the new Chapel, three weeks to the day. My maid talks of marriage.

I have sown my spewy field, a small one of three acres only, with hay-dust, that the acid-juice might be killed, after paring the turf and burning it.

The fallow was sown with wheat this day, October 12th. No gusts, and the new seeds-man has a fine cast.

My new hummellers stamp well, are lighter in action, and so less effortful. This year, I have tied a sheet across the door to prevent poultry from pecking the grain thrashed, low enough to retain the chaff-wind.

Today we riddled with a bamboo mesh, but I noticed no difference from the split willow. The barley seed is good, in spite of the inclement weather. The wheat grain is full from the application of dung, I believe, in the late winter.

I saw my wife last night, at the window. I do not believe in spirits. My men will [not?] venture into the cow-stall alone.

Today I found a cross marked in chalk upon the tree in the yard. My maid talks of marriage, too loud.

My cousin, over from Bursop [i.e. Effley], is to proceed with turnips this next year, he says. I say, let the men of Surrey and Kent do what they will, I am for grass.

This November begins with much rain. The soil [. . .]

Last night, again, my wife appeared at the upper window, though she outside, and I within alone. Her face was white, as chalk is, and [gleaming?]. Her expression was of an inmost [. . .] I pray heartily every morn and eve, and in the night. The wind is high and doors blow about the yard, open[ing].

I have rebuked my maid for impropriety. To marry her, as is her suggestion, will annul the charitable nature of my adoption, while making the child no more my own in the eyes of the world, and will give rise to rumour. This angered her. I am paying £1 for her confinement, and the child. She is unruly. However, she retains her strength, and I think only of my son, and that the farm will remain Plumm's, and [not] fall into my cousin's hands, who is not of my name.

The trees about my upper field are almost all withered. The artificial hedge has budded. It is the northerly nature of the winds this last month of December that has killed them finally, coupled with the dryness of the past year, sufficient to viliorate the roots. The peas proved parched here, and this field is scarcely worth the toil and expense. I looked down upon the village, and at the market in progress, and considered how content the folk amongst those buildings were, to labour for others, and see only hobgoblins, and not their dec[e]ased. The two ravens hung up here are quite bleached of feather and flesh, without odour, and the crows are too numerous, owing to the previous [. . .]

The crows are too loud. This is owing [. . .]

This day my maid, entering the parlour, fell down upon the ground, and cried out, and was taken to the upper room, to the flock-bed, and was visited by the old dame, who will see her through, and at my insistence by Dr Ke[m]p, who pronounced her ready. She cries out very loud through this night, as I write this, and pray.

I have a daughter.

This New Year, my field that was fallow, and is now to wheat, has suffered somewhat from the harsh frosts of the past week, its soil being of a [spongy?] nature, and I fear the effect of the rags might be impoverished by the inclemency [of the weather].

The threshing is finished.

My wife continues [to appear] at the window. The maid threatens me and I must silence her with 6d a week. The infant grows apace, well in health. I have considered allowing the maid to retain it after [suckle?] but she will have none of [this]. The Chapel is roofed, and the stone in place. My cousin came by and he has hired a winnowing machine at cheaper rate, the threshing finished, [for] the next year.

I have sketched my pump for the irrigation of dry fields, and am well [pleased?] with its design. The Chapel members wish to enscribe my charitable action upon a further stone, but I have desisted. This day I counted my profits, [which] have come to £40 and 5s. I walked about the yard, and propose to replace the cow-stall and barn with new [buildings in] brick.

This day I smelt [spring?]

1743

—no, do not think me unhappy. I scratch by candle tho' 'tis sunlight outside—but this endurance is for benefit. I hear the rooks loud as in that poem by Mr Pope. Old aunts not yet. O William, return quick and halloo under my window. Your position with Norcoat is secure, I hope. I do not have the stomach for your loss of a few days—more would kill me. Charles does well. He suckles regular, the wet-nurse tells me, and his swaddle is ripe with healthy excretions. You shall see him anon.

'Tis cold here too—my fireplace is not built for coal—I prefer the blazing faggot tho' they have fallen for coal.

My husband is in London also. If you should pass him, and he should recognise your appearance, do not flinch. Be open. Rub your hands and laugh for he will be witty at someone's expense, if not your own, my love. 'Tis strange, but my knowledge that he is visiting women goes hard with me. I think this is because 'tis the fashion to think a man that is married can lack fidelity without scandal, yet a wife must be quartered for it. I bear the weight of this house upon my meagre shoulders—I am its reputation.

I cough from the puffs of my fireplace. 'Tis a veritable vapour in here, but not the medicinal sort. There is no egress for the poor smoke. We are prisoners both.

My mind starts then grows weary: 'tis the effect of the delivery—

Nurse Fieldhouse has been in here a minute past. I concealed this letter 'neath another, part written, to mine uncle at Stagley. She has eyes very small but sharp as diamonds. Ten to one she will recover our secret from its hiding place or I be less careless.

I give this to the maid tight-sealed as usual, but I daresay thumbs will at it. Check the seal is not broke. I spread powder on my desk so fingers may not fiddle.

Our love is a well—'twill draw forever.

Dearest, I am,
yr eternally loving,
A.C.

March 8th.

Most dearest William,—

The clock pit-a-pats or it may be my heart, but 'tis certain there is no pebbles upon my window-glass yet. I waited upon my canapé half the night. Owls—my mantel clock—a single horse upon the lane that took my heart up to my lips—but no signal. I turn the pages of Crébillon but with half an eye for it. Come across the lawn, my stag, your doe weeps bitter tears. 'Tis half of February you were gone, and you said you were certain back yesternight. I will wake the neighbourhood and set the swans flapping out of the lake if you don't come.

Charles is a dear sweet little thing. He is brought twice a day and I know he has your eyes. My husband returned and handled him like a book, opening and shutting his limbs. Charles gave a tiny sneeze at the snuff. My husband's nose is Chalmers beaked, and it seems my Lord is a little outrageous that his son is not the picture of those ranged along the gallery, with such dismal looks, and so severe a snout to every one. My own *retroussée* has escaped capture also. He has such a dear sweet little nose, that is all his own. Blue blue eyes—tho' they tell me that will change—'twill be your mahogany brown, dearest love, for he has your chin, exact as if he had stole it. 'Tis certain he is yours.

This room grows so tedious and fusty. Because I have a slightest of fevers I am to be confined a further week upon the end of the month. I tie this with a red ribband that is the bleeding of my passion. Real blood flowed when I was delivered of our son. Did I say before that Dr Mackernes was caught in the mud on his way from town, and 'twas a woman still odorous from the field that served me? Her hands were large and chapped and red, she had come straight from her delving. Bint it was who called her. Bint is the man you encountered at the wall that night. He would kill his own mother if enough guineas were rubbed in front of him, but my Lord will have none other as a valet.

I did not like the poem you sent. 'Twas too indecorous for my taste, tho' I daresay my dreams shall tease me more if you do not arrive quick.

I grip my bed-post and think only of your member, tho' I still hurt under from the birthing.

I am, sweetest love,
thy sweetly loving,
A.C.

March 25th.

Dearest William,—

Your letter came with others from aunts. I am sorry to hear of young Norcoat's scarlet but more sorry that it means your absence still. Scarlet is in the village this month very severe, Oadam tells me, and Charles is not taken the village side of the house, for tho' we be high up and the village below, the wind does now prevail this way—it is east and bitter. I always hear the clock strike from the church as if it is ours, and malodorous tendencies must be borne likewise upon the wind. Tho' my constitution is not as delicate as my sister's, yet I am surely prone. Charles will be inoculated against the pock soon as he is ready—after two years. I could not bear his loss. My sister has borne four and all have lived. I pray it is the family way.

The fat angels above me vex with their smug smiling. 'Tis the painted ceiling I talk of, that looked down upon our lovemaking that night, tho' 'twas screened from their innocence by the bed. I will forget what constitutes daylight soon. Do not drop a word about me with your friends in London. Show no interest if anyone serves you a question concerning Ulverton Hall, for all are ears and wicked tongues.

I would like to hold your tongue with my lips. Press it ever so gentle. Take liberties with it.

My Lord sat upon my canapé and held forth this morning upon the Election. He will be chose, of course, but he must brag like all men. He is showing an uncommon tenderness to me, and I fear he will be fiddling my buttons before long.

I hold myself in the nights and think of you. I have no secrets from you.

Dearest,
I am,
thine ever loving,
A.C.

April 4th.

Dearest sweetest William,—

The woods bloom & the fogs cluster upon the river. I have a cold that clings, for I let the breeze at my bare shoulders when I let slip my nightdress and think of you.

How is this? I am not out from Confinement, my love—no. Let me tell. I have, in the middle night, taken the liberty to fold aside the coverings upon the east window and laid my cheek against the glass. I see naught of course of the moon or Nature for they have shuttered me in. But I felt the window loose and a nail was out. Two minutes it was lifted, and the shutter squeaked ope an inch. Thus it is that mine only hindrance is removed and I see the world through a chink. I dare not ope any further for the stable boys are always clattering about early morning beneath—you recall the stables are to one side—they will be telling on me or expostulate and thus give all away to the grooms who are honest but eager men and do anything for a crown in the palm. 'Tis very early morning I let the light in. I wish the shutter had been oiled. Nurse Fieldhouse is two floors direct above but I am certain her ears are the best.

Can you not return and find a bed in the village? There is an inn, you must have supped there sometime. I have seen it from the carriage—in the square—it don't look too filthy. Then you might rustle over the lawn all in black when the owl is out and all of them here slumbering fast and call to me, or scatter your pebbles on the glass—but I will be waiting—it will be like before—tho' you may not climb up as you have been in Town. To see your face, and we might talk.

I am out of sorts not only from the cold I have but by Mr Golding our country lawyer who was allowed in here would you believe to show me my Lord's will—he has drawn up anew and most is left to his brother if Charles should not live, & my jointure is £1,500. His brother has so small an estate in Huntingdonshire that ours must of necessity become his, for this brother is now made Earl and his land can hardly bear such title. Our own is not reckoned above £3,000 a year. We might spread to the very wall of the Manor and then you might run to me without muddying. If we were to inclose the Commons (my Lord has ventured this) then Charles might stride with his title, not feel pinched as he must if we do not knock in a few fences. What vexes me most is that £1,500 is hardly sufficient to keep in silver and support a London house, lest I dust it myself. Tho' if I have your love in perpetuity that is worth more than any cash.

The rains have been severe this week and Mrs Price was bogged in on her way from Slough up to the handles, she told me. Lady Montagu came to visit in sedan chair and the poor creatures carrying her had mud from the road up to their chins. She is fearful of all horses after her accident many years past, and will only stand for human legs to bear her considerable weight. She lives five miles away. I daresay it is tremendous inconvenient for Lord M. to have a wife with such an obsession.

I run on. Do not be unfaithful in London. I could not support the knowledge of your handling any other flesh but mine own. If you feel the heat then do as Onan, and spill your seed in the dust. My brother learnt this from a footman he told me and 'twas that discovery had him leave off me.

I cannot think of you but as mine. When my Lord touches me I must clear my mind of those greasy women 'tis told me he visits in London, or I would perforce vomit on the instant, so jealous do I feel, tho' there is not a spark of love for him in me. Is this not strange? I am healed under and crave your member. I wish to talk baldly but fear this will be discovered. Burn it on the instant, do not fasten it up in a drawer for the servants will always be meddling, tho' you say you have only a cook in London. I hear from Mrs S. that there are books from France that would make a libertine blush. Old aunts and rooks—and Nurse

Fieldhouse—and Wall the housekeeper (who has graffito scribbled upon her face for features)—these are the sum of my fare here. Our last lovemaking I forbade your request, but now I shall be willing to drink you, my sweet love, till you are dry as bone. I run on and on. I pant like the hart for the stream. It is close in here and the clock ticks to madden me—there is no other sound but sometimes feet passing overhead—everything squeaks here tho' it is only built the twenty year. I am swaddled till I breathe no more, or hardly. I sneeze. Are you in good health? Never will I abide cinnamon again, or the smell of it. My caudle has so much of cinnamon I cannot taste the wine. I ask for beer but caudle it is until I sweat it. I am so weary of aunts and neighbours.

I have asked how the Norcoat boy is and he mends, thank God. I hope he is slow at his Latin that you might remain longer with him, as long as my life.

I am,
yr deepest loving,
A.C.

April 12th, 1743.

My sweet W.,—

I am at my bureau that you admired so, inlaid with the ivory herons you told were your soul's five desires, and touch your letter with my cheek as I write this. Its perfume is yours—how long in your pocket?

My head aches to read of your delay in returning. The boy is mended. Can you not be contracted for his Latin on the instant? I cannot think the scarlet tires the brain so that one must remain without schooling for a month after. I have your ribband in my hair. I say to Nurse that 'tis from my childhood. It is indeed true that as an infant I and my sister crept up to the top of the tower at Stagley, and forced the window ope, and let our ribbands fall to the lawn, tiny red things—mischief was ever in our nature. I have kept it since. It binds the hair of my dear Phoebe, you remember her—who smiles always shyly from my mantelshelf, tho' she have one eye all cracks, & her dress be torn—my anger once—I am capable of anger. Dear Stagley! Yours plucked from your letter smells, I fancy, of your powder. When you come we must loosen our ribbands and let fall our hair, and play the savages.

Each morning I sit at the window—and lift it—and peep till I am blinded, for the light in here otherwise—only of candles—is so dim even by day I grow suited to it, and the sun rising above the rim of our estate (it is all furze and sheep-bells there) quite takes my sight from me. The smells of the garden soothe me, and blow the fustiness away for a period. This morning was all dewy, and they have cut the grass and rolled it, and the perfume was exemplary. You worry that my cold will worsen by the window, but it has not done yet. Yesterday a fox (I saw it clear) ran along the wood-edge for a good minute. I felt tenderness and esteem for its cunning.

I dream of raspberries and mutton. Also of you: those are bold dreams indeed! I cannot help my dreams. Our Chaplain came in this afternoon, to talk of my being churched at the month's end, and of Charles's baptism: he has a scratchy, fussy manner, and smells of cupboards. I could not help but think, as he went on, of what perdurable state he would consign me to did he but know the half! I do not like him—he was my father-in-law's man—he looks at you over the top of his spectacles, but at one's forelocks, never at the eyes. How few of the family of this great house do I feel anything for but a quiet despising—doors are ever opening and shutting, I hear them, but I do not care a fig for those who turn the handles. This whole house is rooms of India paper and woodenness and fuss.

Our baby does well. I feel such affection for the creature it cannot but be yours, tho' it screams. He is fat now, like a cushion. The wet-nurse has such plump breasts I cannot fear that he lacks but rather has excess. When I held him yesterday he clasped my breast through the silk within his tiny lips—it was quite paining. I don't think my breasts, being sharp, will ever be likely to support such mettle, if I were to choose to feed, which Lady Osborn tells me is the talk of the most fashionable at present. One is so in the rear here—of the mode. My Lord would not support any change in my dugs, so that is that.

Pray write soonest—

I am,
ever loving yrs,
A.C.

April 31st '43.

Dearest William,

Tore your letter open at the harpsichord—I told you 'twas to be delivered—they chipped a leg upon the stairs but 'tis tuned—I press it without consolation, the sound muffled in this swaddling tightness, but I play to chase Time faster before me. Wall entered with a bundle and it was but a breath before the rest were scattered upon the keys when I espied your hand: your curls and extravagances.

They are blotched by my tears—religiously spilt. You were amiss to pause in penning a reply and more amiss, double amiss, to write so curt. Do you not know how thin I have become? I look in the glass and see how tiresome I am, poor pale thing, to vex you with my sentiments and my passions. 'Tis the pier-glass with the cupids. Alas, one has a wing chipped. Is that hurt yours or mine? I cannot bear to see it. I will have it took down to the breakfast room, where it will serve my husband's vanity. He is always at his neckerchiefs.

Why can you not come earlier? You must be burning for me but I daresay London does not lack a dousing. Lady Mortlake has cut a pretty figure of fun in the papers. A monstrous fortune she is—but she has scattered her favours as monstrously. They say there is not a dawn has passed this last year she has not combed her hair of a fresh entanglement. We have the *Gazetteer* brought here by chaise—I do not rust overmuch from lack of scandal.

My candle gutters now.

There—it is out. They let me only three—it is to rest me—I live and breathe in a kind of wavering gloominess that throws awful spectres upon this brown paper—it is the ugliest—his father's taste was all for buff—'tis like living in a jug.

Alas! this will not move you, I know it. You don't in the least care for me. The female sex are all cloth to be cut anywise. My dress for the Christening was thought for you to gaze on—you are invited with the Squire—nothing more natural than his boy's tutor should be invited next him. White sattin—with about the bosom: hibiscus and China oranges in yellow chenille—and rough sheaves of corn between—& twining stuff in gold threaded along the arms—that are puffed so light the whole may impart a pleasing effect of breeze and motion, that you say you favour in nature, when the trees are not stiff and artificial but fanned by gales. It is all done for below £100. I will be Diana, but not chaste.

I shall make you laugh—that will bring you. You laugh in the throatiest manner. How I stifled it that night upon yon bed! When you are returned and I am out we shall seek some mossy glade—and under the moon languish with our sickness. But laugh at this: I have had the Chaplain sent away to the London house for a month. There is no Chapel there—he will be bored as a mouse without a pantry. 'Tis I did it: he came in last week with his fuss in his fingertips and his greasy collar grating upon his bony neck and sermoned me 'till I near wept. When he had departed I ventured to say to Miss Fieldhouse (who was ever present, dull crow) that the Chaplain's cheek was high-flushed—and his voice had a tubercule clatter to it—and I was fearful. I said this in the silliest manner, as one lightly throws a crust to a beggar at the gate, without consequence or thought, but she devoured it as the beggar and on the instant was gone to see. She reported back forthwith that she had come upon him in the Chapel clearing his throat—but I know he has always had this habit, it is as my husband's blowing air through the nose, a sign of nervous tendency—and she informed Wall, who did the right things—has had the man sent packing, for a while. A new Chaplain is ordered: some mouldy curate, I suppose, out of some dusty shelf.

Did you make merry noises at that? I fear not. I am deep out of spirits with melancholia and my cold. My son does hardly cheer me: he screeches like a big door, tho' he is ever tiny and round. Talking on screeches, there was a concert party held in the Dining Room, three nights past—& held to be very agreeable to all—most my husband's gaming friends. I heard it in snatches through my door. The flutes did play my heart.

My sister at Stagley has had sent me a curious present: a black. He was part of my poor Aunt Eliza's affairs, that being a sorry clutch of old fashion jewels—horses—parcels of yellow gloves—fire-forks—a Hudson that caught her to the like—a mothy Felletin—six chairs that were more scuff than velvet: this the whole left us. My sister did not know I am still confined. He is named Leeward after his natural abode tho' I have not heard of it. He is about eleven. I thought Leeward the windless side of ship—that is what I recall my brother told me, the one that is in Barbados and always at ropes. I would not wish to go on the sea. I have not seen the boy but Wall tells he is eager tho' she is no lover of blacks. I have to change his collar, it has Aunt Eliza's name inscribed. My husband thinks him to have evil tendencies—he saw three blacks on the gibbet at Crowthorne from the carriage, the coachman told him they had robbed the inn there and sent the lady into a vapour from which she is not recovered. But I will be rid of him the moment the man in him cracks his voice.

Alack that is the bell for tea—I can just hear—I shall miss the post: I must write three letters for your one or there is no bundle to muffle yours in.

My husband behaves exceeding well, tho' his complaint makes him tear at the servants.

I prattle only to conceal my anguish—nay, my want to see you—it don't ease with this scribbling.

Pray return soonest.

My love,
I am,
yr desirous,
A.C.

May 3rd '43.

My dearest only William,—

Alack how blustery this May began—I espied on it from my chink and saw the poor hinds with their herds upon the ridge quite blown about. Did I tell you—no I think not—how I saw a village maid and her swain in a field at our perimeter ply their love—she sporting with him—all turfy dalliance, he bashful—each gathering flowers then scattering them over one another—dark-hued but a kind of native prettiness she had, tho' the light was still wan and they were far. Perhaps I painted the scene with innocent colours, but such melancholy pangs did this sylvan lovemaking bring into my heart I near fainted at the window, and sought my salts.

Your letter did not cheer me. You cannot think of going to Italy yet. This Pompey—is it near Florence? It is insupportable, the thought of you preferring to wield a spade in the dim ancients' rubbish than to lying with me. Has life become quite so umbrageous that the long-dead are become more dear to you than she who muses on little else but upon your appearance below my window? I feel almost angered, 'tis true. But you know your own affairs best.

No, I cannot think but that London has tempted you from your greener pangs. You would say to me how you dreamed of these simpler charms—of Virgil's shepherd lads piping on their reeds, and did sing to me once a pastoral song, and that summer night we did gaze upon the swans from my Dressing Room—there was a moon—they had a radiance from their wings that stopped our hearts—O I have writ a poem on that night—and rent it to shreds and cast it upon the fire—and writ another—and folded it in my bosom, where it pricks me still.

O William.

Perhaps 'tis among the olive groves you will find your nymph. You did admire ours upon the plinth by the temple, the one that holds herself, startled—in marble. You have forgot already. You murmured in my ear in the Dressing Room—do you recall—how its silver brilliance on the lawn was a famished soul yearning for love, and then folded me in your arms. You said your only fortune was yourself—and your books—& your cat. When you weary of the heat & the fevers and the pots and pans of Rome, you will blubber back to me, smelling of thymy shores no doubt. And then I will close my window tight upon you, even if it may catch your knuckles.

I am angry at you.

A knock at my door—it is my husband—he was sober—he kissed me upon the neck—he leaves his paint upon my cheek—a red bruise—and departs to Bath. So. This is how men serve. It was always thus. I hid this paper—he enquired what letter I was writing—I tickled him beneath the nose with my pen—I told him it was my lover, but the aunt's was uppermost—he did laugh at my feint—we laughed together—his breath on my ear—his house is scrubbed thrice a fortnight, but his mouth all neglected—my nostrils quiver at its stench—bacco and spirits and gaming—it is old cabbages and burnt milk in the scullery. He is hardly decent tho' clouded in powder. I am too severe. 'Tis he brought back from London last week figs and pomegranates of jewels that he laid upon my table himself—for he does love his nymph.

I must cease immediate—I am too choked. Italy! Our native haunts, our soft lawns mean nothing to you, tho' they enfold your truest heart—

A.C.

May 25th, '43.

Dear William,—

You profess love to me, but this prisoner is yet unlocked. My cold has worsened—I am hoarse—perhaps sweet Charlie will have no mother to caress him but a ruddy nurse only—do I frighten you?

Forgive me. I am well, hale as you are. But I am still Confined. My cold has been chased off by the caudle, or by the evacuations Dr Mackernes did me last week. You say the seal upon my letter to you was broke. I give my bundles to a dull-witted maid—she dusts my room, no other—who is not the prying kind. But mayhap another of the great family has smelt a plot and means to rub cash from me. Once Wall did ask who Mr W. S. was and I told her—'twas a solicitor of my brother's affairs in Barbados, that lives in London. But I blushed. I did not tell you earlier, I was too fearful what you might think. I cannot tell of Wall's thoughts—she has no features to speak of, she is scribbled in chalk. She is a broiling hen.

I am to remain in this wretched room another fortnight. Why, I cannot rightly say. The doctor will have it. The orchard blossoms are all dashed, I hear, in the nipping gales of last week. How I miss their sweet fragrance, tho' the earliest mornings at my chink are sweeter than any dream of paradise. The lawn is greener sure, in its dewy state. I wish the stables were farther off: their odours mingle if the wind is southerly. The woods are verdant now. I saw the vixen again, she is not yet caught. A redbreast took pity on me and perched at the sill, and warbled his tiny heart near to bursting—this only yesterday. I have put my rose oils on the hinges, and the shutter is silent. But you are not come. All about me the house tumbles like a muffled drum. No, it is mostly shut from me, the noise. Silent as the Stygian pool. I read little now. I am moroser. Why do I not fade away, like the night shadows in the woods? I am hearty well—in body. This gloomy room frets out of me any inkling of comfort. I know every inch of the stucco: it goes about and about my head. It is old fashion, that makes it more insupportable—my head aches from it. All shields, warlike in a lady's room. I stitch wearily, tho' my boldest yet: the Four Seasons, at my Lord's request, for his settee in the Dressing Room, that is worn black & greasy from his too much sitting. 'Tis all husbandry, took straight out the freshest pattern book—got from Mrs Price—but so slow do I dip and tug that the wretched ploughman must eternally plod, it seems, 'pon my lap—'till either he or his maker drop. I have sent for new silk for the bed. The old is too blue. I am sick of the oils—but for one—a Fête-Champêtre—for Fools—they make merry above my canapé—I dance with them in the gloom.

Take the note enclosed to Hapgood's in the Strand and buy a waistcoat, if as you say yours is threadbare. Don't mention who you are. I like crimson sattin the best, tho' you might not favour me with a view of it. I have sent invitations for the Christening. You are bound to it—the Squire, wretched man, will not dare keep you away, he don't care for bad form. Do not come too showy. Dress your hair careful, in a half-bob. Don't wink at me.

You are bound to it, William.

I don't care if they read this. Do what they will.

Here is half your ribband.

Lady Oxford was here. She is out of mourning. I have no other news.

I am,
yr forlorn,
A.C.

June 5th.

Dearest W.,—

Send no more post here. I smell a plot, or a discovery. Each week they lengthen my confinement—I cannot see or know why. Dr Mackernes I think to be in on it. He would purge his liver for a fee. He has bled me thrice since we last wrote—I feel weak and dismal—Mrs Danvers they evacuated till she was a husk, for her distraction after her delivery. I shall burst in this confine. Likewise, and for this reason, I would wish our dear sweet little baby unwrapped of his swaddling, but Nurse Fieldhouse will not hear of it—calls it new-fangled liberties—so he may only wave his arms about from yesterday. I held his hand—'tis like ivory, only warm—his arteries beat with our blood in the wrist—he does just exist but already how favourable I feel towards him, more than to other little creatures I have encountered, such as the daughter of Mrs Danvers, whom I felt nothing for at Christmas.

I tell you this that you might beat with a fatherly devotion.

I would wish my ink watered—my glass is empty, I have run out of sand also—but I fear any interruption—I will blow on this 'till it not blot and I have the seal-wax from this morning—shall hand it to the maid with a coin that she be persuaded to give it to the black boy—he combs my Pekes but they will not let him in—they will never think to address their suspicions to him. Before it was Hodgetts the groom of chambers 'twas handed to by the maid—she is called Hambling—she is devoted to me and has too dull wits for intrigue, but Hodgetts wears gold garters and is insufferably proud—he has ambitions—Hambling has a wart the size of a guinea upon her forehead, but Hodgetts has told Wall that Bint has taken a great fancy to her, for otherwise she is shapely—Wall told me, and I told her I did not care if they married, or did not, I was so weary. Hambling must tell the black boy to conceal it—I have named him Scipio, and then again Leeward, for Scipio is my husband's stallion—Leeward is then to give it to Mabberley—he being the hoary-headed gardener brought with me from Stagley, who cut roses for me when I was merely babbling, twenty year past, kind old soul—he will hang for me if I wished it. He takes it to the chaise. There—I have it in a nutshell they shall never crack.

Address your letters to Elijah Mabberley, of Maddle Lane.

I write in haste, lest you write too quick again (tho' that be not likely)—your resumption of the Latin next month fills me with cheer and expectation my poor vessel of a heart can hardly bear—how each day drags itself to the moon—I spin patience with ropes of sand—there! I have blotted with my tears—imagine how I crouch trembling at every noise and knock—no great house has more quivering a caged bird. I have my fan ready to spread upon my desk, for the air lies like treacle and this early heat would have me faint—but my fan is as well my cunning concealer, it is so large when spread, and the herons painted upon it fly.

I would have you lie between me on the instant, but I must long more. Your expressions of affection were received as mine were—O ill-defined joys, that groan as they are cherished, and strew boughs of blossom as they sting our feet with longing!

I am,

ever yours—

A.C.

I plant this finger upon thy lips, and write my love upon them.

June 20th, '43.

Dearest William,—

I am joyous our plot passed off without mishap, and our love spun itself happily over the distance, so strewn with traps and spies. I hope you are burning the letters. Leeward conducted himself with propriety—he is told to speak nothing of this task—lest he feel the deck beneath him that returns him to sugar-cane. Hambling told me he flinched at that, as at a whipping—he has welts upon his back, she says, from the smart of a cart-whip (not Aunt Eliza's, I think). If only all our servants were so, and in no need of wages, that make them so hard on us, and intrusive.

The danger is in the passing of the letter from Mabberley to the boy, but he walks the Pekes, and Mabberley clips a great laurel that utterly conceals him from the house, that is on the way. If you had come before, we had no need of this.

Your poem I have read a hundred times, by night, and by the window at dawn, as I feel the perfumed air of morning upon my cheek. I have been in here near three months—I have wept to be released—my husband is officious on my health, speaks highly of Dr Mackernes, and has not fiddled my buttons. I do feel weak, and nauseous, but 'tis the heat. Nurse Fieldhouse has been severe on the rocker for standing at my door (we are opposite to the nursery) when she oped it. Perhaps my thin, pale countenance persuades them I am to be shut from ills. I flush so easily. I am wan only from your absence. They anger me. I would like to beat them all with my cane—they gave me a cane to walk from bed to canapé—I have only one use for it, if it were to come to that.

The fourth stanza pleased me best. But how does it sound with 'vernal' and 'umbrageous', favouring 'sylvan' & 'silvery'—and the chime 'lawns' & 'fawns' in the stead of 'hay' and 'tea'?

> So rears the golden face of this great house
> Through th'unnumbered leaves, that trembling start
> At your fair hand, when like a vernal breeze
> You brush aside their hues, to fleet o'er lawns
> Towards umbrageous glades, small cots, and fawns.

'Tea' was too thin for the swelling passion in your lines. Forgive my meddling. Do not be upset. It is a woman's way to stitch up and mend.

We have forty deer now, if you think 'fawns' a conceit. Twenty are bucks, that will be stags in three years. At Blenheim, where they have more than a hundred, their antlers were loud and like posts being struck with the echoes, when they fought. It woke me very early, but I saw nothing for the mist. This was last summer, when you were a figure only glimpsed from my carriage, but nearer my thoughts.

I sat on the terrace on my return then, and let my coffee cool—I was so distracted by your scarce-seen face on the way.

Here is more money. I cannot give further without my husband knowing. Our mortgage has been raised to pay for the new improvements—there are to be curves introduced to the lake—'tis tedious the number of times my Lord has rustled his plans before me—Mr Kent has measured and tutted over the straight lines—'tis all to be wild—some cottages to be razed where he has marked 'Wilderness' very flowery upon the plan, tho' it shall be naught but birch and bindweed—& brings to mind that tedious Bunyan my childish locks brushed slumberously too many times, at dear Stagley—yet all the better for us to sport within!—and cool glades to spring up, and an hermitage built from stone and turf—we might use it for other than study, quoth I. My husband games too much away—he says money is like powder sugar, it soaks away so quick, but not if the purse is lined with scruples. To pay the improvements and the new damask hangings I have ordered for the house ('tis all to be lined in crimson & green, and new stucco of ivy and wild clymatis and lilies etc., and chimney-pieces in Drawing Room and Library wholly replaced with Italian marble—inlay of pink & white roses, tho' these alone are £400) he is to use the cash that was formerly to pay back the mortgage, and so forth. He tells me he has bonds from his nephew that his nephew's widow wishes to settle—she requires cash, having a meagre jointure, and wishes to lay out £3,000 in land for her son. Our tenants are in arrears with low prices but all their stock, that we have seized from them, is not sufficient to discharge more than half the rent. We are to purchase an adjoining estate—'tis a farm by the name of Plumm, we are to pluck it out from the pie, and then have the next valley to our own—'tis a farm well handled but poor—there is a woman husbands it, a little proud—there is some scandal attached to her birth, but I forget what now. Then our estate will be reckoned more, but still not sufficient, for my husband's family sank much into the South Sea with the Bubble, and our hold is still perilous, tho' he don't tell me that when I was hitched into my bridal apparel by my dear Papa.

But you find such talk tedious, I know. Do not send me books. Tho' the Watts was small, 'tis trying for Mabberley and the boy to conceal beneath their coats. Have you a date for your return? I cannot bear this talk of 'soon'. You don't mention Italy. I hope it is forgotten. 'Tis feverish hot there.

Each blotch is a kiss.

Do not spend on Claret and Sherry, or maids by the belly.

I am,

yr ever loving & longing,

A.C.

July 4th. In confine still.

My only William,—

You say you shall unlock me. Why do you not? I cannot fear but that your being out at elbows—and staying thus in London—means you have lost your position—or you would fleet back on the instant to your Grammar, and your Lady. They say the boy is playing hoops in the garden of the Manor House. There is a murmur that he is to go to Eton this year—that is how Bint reported it to Wall, who let it drop with me last evening. I pine until I am husked of my soul. O this cavernous life, full of deep woes in which our unshining flesh lights nothing—a million candles would not shed this gloom from me—this bedroom does stretch a million miles—I am not yet finished with the ploughman—if I were in the land of the Indians I might feel less weary of needles and quills and clocks.

I shuffle my chair from a ruck of the carpet—I know its Persian lions in every claw—I have mapped out its maze until my feet do a jig & kick the wall—my shoe has undone its buckle—I am too fatigued to strap it—I let it fall—I study its silken corpse, 'till the clock strikes me out my dull transport—I straighten, sag—let my head fall upon my arms—emit a sigh that might tatter the ensign of any other lover—sit up once more—scratch my nose—fiddle the ribband at my neck—pick up my pen—let it hang on air until it fall insensible—a lifeless bird, that doth rest its plumage against the far more living wing of an ivory heron—then a knock at my door—a weary 'come'—the maid enters with her smell of the scullery following in a cloud—she does curtsey obligingly—I ignore—she removes my stool under its white cloth—she closes the door soft for she must think me close to slumber—which I am—the clock strikes a quarter, clears its throat, strikes again lest I be in doubt, grates a little—pit-a-pats on—or is that my heart—for I have thought of you!—the long winding road to London betwixt us—the motion of the carriage-wheels—your face at the fore-window—the dust upon your forehead—the passing cots and the stone that says, you are but a handful of miles from your love—but no—he don't alight at the turning—the horses don't stop, he don't signal—he looks backward—a smile in the lips—our glade afar off—this room likewise—'tis cast, a red ribband from the carriage—that flies up in the dust—tumbles to the verge—it does not scruple—it lies on the common highway—to be trampled upon—mangled by hooves & common boots—or ties a pedlar's coat—or be obliterated forever—as the clock strikes again, & his carriage takes the slope—scarce touches the ground—post-haste—away—away—to a nothing—a nought—a silence!—she lifts her head—scratches her nose—doth sigh—doth wait for tea—doth pick up her pen—doth dip it—doth write—so—

ARE YOU FALSE?

I shall strike nothing out today, you perceive.

My aunts wonder I have writ them so much.

I have a spy-glass. It is my brother's, from his school chest left me when he went to sea. A boy's plaything, in brass. I spy through the window. The wood leaps up to me—it is the trick of the glass: I see the garlands woven about the wood—the lark come close—the buttons about the shepherd's garters—I might gaze into the sun till it strike me blind. Last night 'twas full moon—with you also—I oped the window and the spy-glass caught it—my eye was filled—the light was like a maddened horse rearing over me—too white & wild to gaze upon! So all is brought nearer, but what excellent illusions we must live under, that our intelligence and reason does not expire from lack of fancy, and of hope!

Answer me quick.

A.C.

Here is the amount for the carriage. Berate my fancy.

July 20th, '43.

Dear William,—

No post from you. Have you gone? Is this forwarded, or must it linger to be read by a scullion? My cousin Edmund has fallen in the Dutch war. A musket-ball shattered his heart. Fortunate young creature.

They have just now took my spy-glass from me. I could not explicate its presence but as a remembrance of my brother. My husband says it must find its use in the box at theatre. He thinks my brother is a pirate, for being salted on the high seas. Each morning this room stinks of my stool: the heat allows of no air. I forget to beautify myself at my table. I have few visitors. My husband is like the armadillo in my book of animals from Dürer: his hair curls into horns—he rubs too much fat in, then too thick powder. I have told him. He is Armadillo to the line. I have scribbled a cocked hat upon its head. It is my husband.

My fancy runs faster than my reason. I have night terrors. I asked the maid to entertain me—she told me of the legend here, of a shepherd who made love with a witch, and she bore a boy-lamb, that he reared as his own son, till it went among the flock by mishap—and the shepherd, he being old and deaf, don't hear its cries and slew his own son, like Isaac might have done! And the old shepherd haunts the crest still, as apparition, calling out—where, where, where? I fancy I hear him at night, tho' in the morning I think it the owls.

Write me. I cannot be easy 'till you do.

A.C.

Mabberley came across the lawn when I was spying. He winked at me. I saw him thro' the spy-glass. I waved at him. One kind soul in a cavern of cruelties.

A heron flapped along the reach of the river, this early morning, spied thro' my glass. When I returned to my desk, there was not one less—but it had seemed so.

August 16th, 1743.

William,—

I enclose the ribband.

I interpret your silence before your going as all frailty must—with a heavy and vain heart, that my thoughts were ever bent towards you, or that my hopes should dash themselves so repeatedly against such forbidding rock.

Your snuff-box that I gave you, enamelled with a scene of classical love, do not rub it brilliant against the sleeve of the coat that cost you no guineas, I fear, but mine—but cast it into the sea at Naples (I have been studying maps) or let it remain to curse you with my abject spleen.

They harvest beyond my window—I spy them: each row of reapers makes a road into my heart, they flash with grateful weapons, they slice me into ribbands. Our son's eyes render me nothing but hurt.

I got your address off the Squire, who had it off your cook. I throw caution to the wind. Some melancholy cypress might be fitting burial for our kisses.

Do not communicate with me further. My Armadillo sniffs close—I am in confinement still, 'till the apples fall and the air is less feverish, they do tell me. I beat against the door in anger last week—I left trails of my nails, the wood of the door was gashed—I would have beat this warm head upon it, save that I gave myself greater hurt, & my poor dear Phoebe was dashed in the stead, that her face lies in tiny pieces still upon my mantelshelf, lest I forget my pain. They put it down to distraction from excess moisture—purged me—placed my spirits on the right course—rendered me unfit to leave before the autumn. I suspect—tho' my maid reports no ill occurrence between Mabberley & the black—that Armadillo suspects in turn, & must have me hid like in the old fable. I can stand it little longer, without recourse to opiates.

There—I have spilt my coffee upon the paper. Let it spread. Discourse is poison. I shall find a herd of goat, dress in muslin, pipe my hymns to innocence on a thymy slope far from care—& your part of Italy.

I have a blister, where I held my finger above the candle-flame, to see what greater pain is cruel love.

The pain of my son's bringing out—a large-boned baby—was as nothing to his father's cunning.

I write this at dawn upon the window-seat—I have been here most the night, moonlight upon me—owls—then dawn came with song, from the far woods—alas, too far!—the room full now of fragrant harvest—& seeds borne upon the breeze, out the hedgerows—that steal in my little gap—settle on my hair, that is loose about the shoulders—poor silvery things—tiny angels, free to go whither they will, now they have found but useless soil here—one caresses my hand, yet I scarce feel it—blows & rolls to the paper—'tis the seed of wild clymatis, that is named bedwine here, it must grow & tangle these words ere long, or I puff it out again—out the window—there!—it gleams—in the dawn light—high upon the breeze—and higher—& further—whither I don't know, yet it be where I long to follow—'till it be no more, tho' I fancy I glimpse it still—against the glade, the sky—afar off—a gleam—hark!—a lark trills—then nothing—but the scratching of my pen—and the sea—no—'tis the scythes—'tis the scythe that mows down kings, exempts no meaner mortal things—you know the verse—we read it together—all flesh is grass—and the aged man that is Time mows these fields—we loved verses—

Alas.

Adieu.

A.C.

Ulverton Hall.

September 12th, 1743.

To Mr William Sykes:

Received—one snuff-box, & a quantity of clothing, formerly your own, addressed to Elijah Mabberley, Maddle Lane, Ulverton.

This is the last communication shall occur between us. Suffice to say that your folly has reaped its ill reward: the bulky nature of the parcel made concealment beneath Mabberley's shirt impossible. He was thought to be stealing—was followed by Bint—was apprehended in the act of passing the bundle to the black boy, behind the laurel. Both were taken. The black boy don't know anything. Mabberley would not betray me. A simple and loyal soul. He is before the magistrate on Tuesday. I am to be released, at my husband's entreaty—he is full of kindness—to attend the spectacle, if he is to hang. Tho' this won't be likely sooner than October, when I am Out in any case. The black boy Leeward was delivered of a beating by Wall and Bint between them—I heard his screamings—tied up—carried upon the first ship at Portsmouth direct for the West Indies.

The Squire visits tomorrow. I will give him this to forward. I will tell him it is the invitation to the Christening.

I hope you find your stay in Italy pleasing, after your fashion.

Your verse I have burned.

I might fill a page—but let my consolation be—no, 'tis trash—our senses are all deluded—

—save skin upon a candle—

—so—

1775

DISSECTION

Sonday the 20 day of thi incant aug 1775 Surly Ro Ulver

Deer francis

Mr john Pounds tailer du rite this for mee my sone I dont kno how manny thar will Bee of us take pitty on thy mother francis lunnen is a wickit plaic yr father ood bee dropin teeres He sed as you alers hed a wagin tung I bee afeart francis i ent bin to lunnen afore

Mind yr sole

thy evere loving
mother
Sara Shail

Sonday 3 day of this incant sept 1775 Surlyro Ulvoton

My owne son francis,

I ont bare it you mus reply the wagon doo tak this plees replye francis my som

thy evere lovving mother
Sara Chail

Sonday 17 daye of the instan 1775 sept Surley rew Ulv

Deerst sun francis

plees replye a meditly els thy mamy shalt die my son off greeve Mr P tak thi to the wagon God speed itt I praye itt bent be cort when bee the day I shll buck thy weddin shirt & soe as itt hev a ter you mus look trimm thee mus replye

thy loving motther
Sarah Shail

Sundaye 1st dae of thi insant Oct 1775 Surley row Ulvoton

My son francis

thy leter was sh verry shoart the bee poorely shore enohg it were vingern hissop at the mowthe wot thee donne taikin that hat I minds i when thee wer danglin att my duggs they still be teart when i minds I tha thee wer a guzslerer al rite nowe theell be danglin wi all off lunnen lookin upp an lahging alover they faices Mr P hev his shoos on a brickc itt be the wett God hev massy on thee rite emeedittly gie itt to the laddy at the gaite Mr P brothr paye hur he saye Noogait be a terble stink fro the strit

thy lovin mothe
Sara Shail

her bee cow slipp for the cramps

Sunday 15 daye off this insan Oct 1775 surley Rowe Ulvetane

My dear francis my ownly sum,

I hev writ to the King wi Mr Ps hande it shall moov they stoney hartes think on yr sole an pray to God judith saye you hev the tyfoit shee hev thi from john witeacre as hed itt fro a mann on the coche as hev jus lef thy side his naime bee Tom bolt he sais the hev ratts bigern ours an you bee bit an swoln lord hev massy on uss all i ont bare itt wen I thinks on thee innen bee a wickit plaice tha hats blo off temtay shin rite how thee bee I hev a blakk spott on my dugg as be lik fier very sor

thy ever lovein mothr
Sara Shail

Sunday 29th daye of thinsan Oct 1775 Surlyrow Ulverten

My lam

thy leter tinds the fier of my destes I bourn and they dam jintlemen & pasens ooll swing fro al ower heeles sas Mr P the all hev ther tung in the kings ars ower lorde charls be mity chufd at the noose ses judith tha bee yr pochin dayes las weeke he wer blubbrin att all his swanns ther craws wer slitt judith ses the laik wer redd fro they crooel crooel burn thi inn the fier tell thy mammy my lam wen the daye bee theell com back hear arter ward for christern berry ole my son my lam wee be detarmied to fine the shillns uppon my worde

thy loving mother
Sara Shal

her bee clivers leef grind upp for thy tyfoit feavr

Sunday 12th day of this inst Novr 1775 Suleyrowe Ulver

My deer lam francis

wot my son be cutt up inn to ribons wot bee they sur jans jantlemen of the divil too cut upp my owern sun no hand oll toch thee a hare of thy hed els dam my eies an dam this fifly gurnray of engelin for barin my boddy an thine this woreld hev no massy itt makes my blakk spott biggern afore it maks my eies teart it makkes i blas feeme agin God an al His workes it maks i scroop an skweel like ower doore as thee met bee mendin nowe we shll cum onn a waggern by nite wen bee the daye my lam if so bee as thee ent took afore with thy feversweet an fiflth my lam

thy loveng mother
Sara Shail

use this papper atwen the lines

P.S. mark itt bee TRANS POTASHIN for caryin thy cowpse aff I hope ye nkose that john Pounds tailr

Sunday 19th daye o this instan Novr 1775 Surley rowe Ulverton

My lovly lam my son francis

thy mark on the papper came Mr P red itt the numbers i dint paye a penny so the daye be March 31st it bee lik a nale in in my hed Mr Ps brother oll bring thee yr shirte as I hev cleend & lef owt al nite in the moon lite itt maide itt verry wite for thee do you hev a blaide to cutt yr hares & chin you mus be trimm all of lunnen ool be theyar an the famly thy wilfe were heyre yes erdaye shee ses you med hev com bakk wi a sakk o shillns stead of thy cowpse i sed bekky thare ont bee no cowpse hole to berry iff so bee as wee ent at Ti bourne lik yo saye my dov my lam to saiv thee fro them sur jans bluddy dam villions wi their nives & spesely sores i dont heyar swaldld bells francis wiout I heyar thy deth bell tang

lord hav marsy on thee in thy aflition

thy greefing mother
Sara Shail

P.S. hav you frends enouhg to cary it aff els weell be took al so john Pounds tailer

Sundaye 3rd day off this ins Dec 1775 Surly Rowe Ullverton

My deesrt lam Francis

wot bee a mother to du in her destres I mus kape my reaserlusen i bee deturmed thee ooll niver be inn too bluddy ribons them bludy villions dont feear my lam my dov they ont laye a hand onn thee untill the our of djudgemen cometh like a wind an mammon bee strukk down they oll riggle like rabets in thy nette thee soed tha nette weeakes & weeakes by can delelite Mr Ps bro ses a thy hands wer spreethd wi weltin they filfly walls my son thee mawnt be roonin thy hands as mus bee layed on my dugg to heale thy mammy thy swet mus make hole an all so mary oadm for her baren bely thy ded handes mus rub & gie life a noo my sun danglin man danglin man 3 lives fro thee I carste thee forth fro my woom my chitt I gied thee iverry mosel afore my owern mowth you ont bee carste inn too hell fier they had best dokk I all so afor 1 hare on thy hed bournes my dovv rite a meditly & gie itt to hur att the gaite Mr Ps bro gie her a shilln las time Mr P be a bleesin to a poore wido we bee al in extreem destres ther ent a lofe for chirlidern or narn onn us a tall we gates the rine & they gates the leen sartainly dam they euies

thy every loving mothr
sara Shail

P.S. weyar to find 7 shillns for the hang man you aks too much heell taik 7 shilln an likewise fro the sur jans an tye the not tihgt jus the saim I hev seed itt my sealfe aksept thy LOT an praye

john Pounds tailer

Sundaye eve of ower Lords Birthe 1775 Suleyrowe Ulv

My deerst lam francis my owern sun

pleese rite emeeditly I feear you med bee ded we be shramd wi this terbl cawld Mr P hev a terbl hackin caf I dun hev morn 2 stikk to bourne think on thy poore mammy my son as bee ded ripe for diin save shee mus kape her sonn hole for berryal my blakk spot be grawin

thy greefin mothr
Sara Shaill

P.S. gie yr leter to my brothr wen he cums

john Pounds tailr

Sunday 7th daye of this yer of ower lord 1776 Surley rowe Ul

My deesrt owernly francis

Mr Ps bro com heyar for kursmas feste he ses he seed thee in tha fifly stinkin plaice wi no winndoes he hed to spitt els he odd bee feverd he brung the leter dont rite such terbl things I ent afeart of no hawn tings i hev my hor shoo i ent nevar seed the wite shepard on the rode you ont be cutt upp my dov Mr P ses you ont be hawnting & trubling us if they teres thee up spesely iff they sores upp thy hed butt you ont bee wi thy famealy cumin to taik thee dowen afore them bludy villions they sur jans as di sec ses Mr P they ont tuch a hare of my sunns hed as I gied my owern milk too wot wd thy poore dadda saye nowe I mus stop acos Mr P hev bin heyare al arte noon wi his tung stukk out ritin my foyce think on last things & thy sole this noo yeyar ent bee no beter sartin lee I hev coursed they bugers they hares ooll dropp out 1 bye 1

thy loving mammy
Sara Shail

Mr P ooll gie thi to the karrier for 2 peny he bee too kinde

P.S. wot yo esespect our lord sufered & was not saivd by shillns aksept thy LOT ladd & maik pese wi thy maiker yo al wais wer a dail too cokk shore

john Pounds tailer

Sundaye 21st daye othi inst Jany 1776 Surly rowe ulvertone

Deerst my lamfrancis,

I hev wri to the king a gin butt Mr P ses that wer sartainly steelin tha hat as did blo of medbee lord Charls did hev a hande in itt hee du hate thee for pochin his dere my sonn med bee I ooll plede onn my nkees afore his caridge iff it don stop theyars an end for my sealfe wot wd we du at hout Mr P no my sonn he be duin thi for nort save an ol widers lov ther ent nort evill in thatt thee ont be carsting thy loose tung on uss thee alers wer a jumm per francis leefin thy mamy for gone to lunnen an steelin hats they hev hores morn hares on my hed not Mr P as hev hed the pawsley he bee lahgin wot els sav yowelin wen itt be so terbl cawld an hollo the mus praye for uss thee mus praye mend thy wayes in thes las weeakes my lam

thy lovin mather
Sara Shail

P.S. dont rite such tthings agin shee be a fiene ooman by God
john Pounds tailer

Sundaye 4th daye of thi inst Febr 1776 Surley rowe ulver

My deere sonne

if you rite such wordes agin wee ont bee cumin be thee hole in spririt to rite such tthings thee mus be paceant thee mus spectect the wurs if thee dont dangel thee ooll be for trans pottashin like Kristern brin judith ses as you oll bee wontin us to hang on thy heeles arter the kart hev lef thee danglin butt I ses no he wonts uss to cut he dowern afore the sur jans doo she ses that ll bee a grate fite wot do thee think thy mother owern mother her sealf ont be savin her sonne dont rite such tthing francis it bee more teart than my blakk spott tha thy han mus mend thy hans were al wais fine at mendin I stil hev thy net hidd I stroak itt it at nite itt hev thy smel my dovv wot bee a poore wido to du haaf frastid in this winer cawld to gett thee free I praye too the lorde an saye my rimes al nite

thy loving mamy
Sara Shail

P.S. shee bee trwely suffereing els I odd stopp riting dreckly ye be a dying man so mind yr sole youer self ladd

john Pounds Tailer

Sundaye the 18 daye of thisint Febry 1776 Surly row Ulver

Deer francis

thee mus replye thee mawnt fal in too desespare I be verry hungarye I dremed las nite of the apel thee colard for I outer the Manoor orchut thy litel fingars opt an ther wer the apel for thy mammy braive boy it still taist swet on my tung (shee bee weepin nowe john Pounds) I hev soed thy trowsers Mr P gied i the thred wen I smoothd they owt it wer crinlked intoo them shapes ◇ that mean a deth i dont need no sine rite on this papper iff yo dont hev no penies lef medbee that hatt it were coursed a divils hatt to temp thee th wurk howse for I nowe my lam mind yr sole rite a meaditly

thy loving mother
Sara Shail

P.S. you mus hele her blakk spot else itt wil kil hur stark ded hev massy on thy mother ladd wee ent faint hartes as ye saye but we ent fooles neithr

john Pounds tailer

Sundaye the 3rd daye oth instan March 1776 Surly row Ulv

My deerst boy my lam

wot thee be sufferein in thy sole to saye such terbl tthings I bee strukk dum heyar bee wett an stinkin an hollo I hev a caf an Mr P al so I odd cutt aff my dugg for thee I hev no shillns to paye for a coffen or srowd butt thy wilfe saye she hev aksed thee a for but thee hev spend yr monny on bere an gaiming & hev kep nun inn yr poket nowe thee mite du goode a for the lord or the divil taiks thee thy sole med be yowlin danglin owver hell fier wen thy hande med press on my dugg an the Lord sees itt bee good an collers thee for hevn dreckly minut my blakk spott be heled by thy swet thy lipps hev bin a bowt my dugg lang a goe now thee mus mend hur my lam my dovv praye & dont deseper that bee tem tashin wuss tha a fine hatt as blows aff in the strit do thee hev a blaide to shave thy chinn an thy bootes mus be spik or the famealy ont be proude

God bless

fro thy evere loving mothr
Sara Shail

thy wordes were borning firebrans to my hart an Mr P al so he hev spend shillns for thy sak francis

P.S. I hev nott rubd thy mothers dugg with my lipps to maik a spott you mus not slan dere thy mother tthink on djudgement daye thy dam tung wil bourne thee ye mus aproch thy las ower with a clene hart wot I saye be trwe by God hur spott be gurt as a shilln peese an hard ye mus hele itt

john Pounds tailr

Sondaye the 17th daye of thi instan March 1776 surly row ulver

My owernly deerst sun francis

this bee ower las letter a for thy hangin daye judith ses thee be brort owt ope neckd & theyar bee a mos terble ror wind aff that gert bigg river run too the armes of the lord he shalt cuvver thy nekk & holt thy hed hi them as larf ont larf at dums daye heyar be catt ment for thy gritt putt it aneath thy tung dreckly minut they karts thee upp the strit my lam you ont bee blulbrin an maikin i a shamd I shll waive my shorl itt bee the redd wone you mus waive too yr mamy in yr wite finery my buntin abram Web oll mak the coffen thy wilfe hev scrapd shillns for hee ol sam daye wen upp a tree & playd God an frited abram haaf to dearth I hopes thee be lahgin at tha my lam thee odd yowl in the awld dayes my chitt judith shell gie the floures to thee for i shll bee watin att the galowes tree dont shaim uss nowe rite yr las leter but dont rite terbl tthings my dovv

I praye for thy sole an hev sed my rimes wee shll bee 5 I hopes thee hev more theyar to du the job spesely as ucle Rob hev a badd leg God spede my sonne

thy ever loving mothr
Sara Shail

P.S. I hev not red to hur al you rote God forgif thee thy tung asll soon bee lillin oute al rite if thee wernt a doomd felon I odd du a damd deal wuss for thy slandere tha tell thee nowe I hev * thy mother an hev rubbd her duggs with my * for eche leter rit may the divil taik thee as wer niver more tha a ras kel by God wen thee bee slicd upp & throne too the doggs I ool be in heavn al rite with thy mamy soein a fine net in & oute wen thee bee danglin wotch thy cokk it don go upp itt shll al rite but thee ooll be pissin thy sole in too the dust you hev yr jus reward i hev mine al rite

john Pounds tailer

yr mam think this bee a praier soitt bee

Sunday the 7th day of this inst April 1776 Surley Row Ulverton

My dear Francis,

Mr John Bate our Curate writes this for me. The Rector has paid the Coachman 1 shilling to carry it, I have always been a worthy Church attender. We are all very glad at your Pardon. I believe your Prosecutor was moved by God's merciful example to forgive you I hope he has a fine new hat. I have Wept many times for joy, etc. Your mother is exceedingly joyous that you shall be coming home when you have the Money for the coach. Judith also was glad, and your wife also. Mr Pounds trembled with Shock as if he had seen a Ghost. This is the power of Prayer. God be with thee my son. You must not pick up any more fine hats.

Your ever loving Mother,

Sarah Shail

P.S. My black Wen remains very Sore.

1803

RISE

He were a master carpenter, but no master o' men. He didn't allus treat us aright. This were Abraham Webb. His father an granfer were wainwrights, but ater the fire when he were only fourteen there was that much work to do he got down an carved hisself a post in joinery so as he become the finest an most skilled hereabouts. There was that much work to cut, it lasted him years, for them as could pay wanted all manner o' pretty cupboards, an stairs, an mantelshelves. The fire took away, what, a quarter of Ulver, in '45. Bitter sweet for carpenters an suchlike. I were only ten year but I remimbers it. Blizzed away half o' Main Street afore they dowsed him. Melted the rime out to Five Elms. It were a raw winter, but river were warm as a maid.

Aye, Abraham rised on that, for sure. It were his brother did the waggons, though they shared the yard. The brother's son took over now.

I become apprenticed on account of a girl I fancied. She were milkmaid over at Barr's farm, this side o' river. I were jus on fourteen year, speech like turnin a gate on rusty hinges an never stuck up to a girl afore. Meets her early on the way to milkin, luggin her bucket, but it were split awmost atwo an she were that low, bein a pail she'd a-had from when she first begun, that I says to her, 'I'll make thee one afresh, Kath'—thinkin as how that be the shortest way to her heart. So I lops some chestnut an bangs away, an makes such a botch she only laughs when I shows he to her. I had no skills then, he were all square, as I had nowt to bend the timber with—though she be white an soft, chestnut. I vowed then an there to learn myself joinery. How to make wood do for me what my tongue don't.

She buckles to wi' old George Stroude, young tanner down Fogbourne way, soon ater. Reckon as he were workin more'n his straps backerds an forruds, when I were shilly-shallyin. Aye.

Heh.

Though I bint grizzlin, mind. I got down to't afore long. A brace o' nippers. Aye aye.

'That's a Webb,' people'd say, 'that there's a Webb.' They'd point at their cupboards an say it, or in the church where he'd done poppy-heads. It weren't nothin fancy, it weren't fancywork like the stuff up at the Hall, an it weren't hardly ever painted, an gilded, as I sees up at the Hall—but it were solid an agreeable, an still be, for nowt o' Webb's work have ever buckled or cracked. He chosed his timber like a body chooses a woman. For life, an no shilly-shallyin.

He have a-bin in the ground these five year, and I misses him. Winter of '97 he died. Jus afore he hacked his last he'd cock a ear, abed, an hear the dingin in the yard, an he'd know what we were puttin together. He knowed when it were his own coffen. He hears the boards ripped, an sits bolt up in bed, an swears we en't got it seasoned proper. All through the hammerin o' the brads it were shaped beautiful in his own head, an he sweared like fury when he heared one hit off. I says sweared, but it weren't no blasphemy, for he were a church-goer all his days. An that be at the heart o' this story, if you were to cleft it—that, an his hardness. He were pure oak.

Now I don't hold wi' them as says Abraham Webb were the spit of his father in skill. His father stuck to wheels, an had other men do gates an stairs an so forth. No comparin. But I do know as Isaac Webb's father, Jepthah Webb, bein Abraham's granfer, made a wheel poorly so it broke an pitched a man into the next Kingdom. Aye. That were way back, up at Plumm's, the year old dame Anne was made. But by my reckonin, Abraham had soaked up the skill so he were well nigh saturated, an hardly needed to larn in his head. He ud allus have a sweet smell about him, for he were reared in sawdust. You should've seed his hands, hard as a nave an as well nigh chopped, for they'd never been more'n a night away from irons, an allus dark as a gipsy's from oak-juice, he'd felled so many.

Thank 'ee.

Aye. He were right stumpy, he were, an ud allus stand straddle-wise, when he weren't at summat, wi' them hands in his britches, axin nowt o' narn save they get to it, an ud give a bastin to the young-uns if they gives him lip, or shambles in late. I knows, for I feeled it, an it allus drayed blood. But he were patient as the Lord wi' an aggy line, if the boy was eager, an ud allus show us the right way. He were two men.

One treated us aright, t'other not.

Your health, sir.

Aye.

For it weren't so much the beatin, as the hours. We'd be on a job, an he'd have us there afore cock-crow, sayin as how life was for toilin, an to get gumption a body didn't pick it up abed, an then kep us till late a-night. I remimbers them walks—three, four, five mild—athurt the down to some farm or other, pitch dark a-winter, an nowt but a glimmerin in the east o' summertime, an rabbit-scuts we couldn't touch, all our irons an whatnot in our boxes, luggin it all, clatterin along, and then back to our shop an at them floorboards, or doors, or whatever, till well ater candlelight, even o' summer. It weren't jolly, no. There was one lad, name o' Tuck, who didn't ought to have bin apprenticed anyways, but he gets so down in the mouth about it all he throws his box in the river from Saddle Bridge one night, dog-tired, an goes to sea. Abraham be that fretted about the box he gets me to jump in an fish him out, an them poplars were aready turnin leaf. One didn't say no, though. Some o' the tools were gone acause the box were ope when I found he, though it were nowt the worse for the dowsin, an old Abraham wanted me to go back in an fish up them as were fallen out, but I were that shrammed an chatterin I couldn't hear him, an he let me off.

There was a bradawl missin, an a truein plane, an a tenon-saw. That were sad.

Aye.

See these fingers? Rheumatics. Useless.

Couldn't mend a broomstick now. Time was when I were that busy I could've waded through the shavins.

Ah well.

Old Abraham ud say to me, 'Samuel, if thee en't a doer, thee be good as dead.' He were cock-eyed, mind, an this gid him a queer look. But he had the truest line of arn on us. He ud snap that lampblack an saw on it like it were butter, an the grain felled away clean like it were made that way. I could tell his sawin blind. It were music.

One time we gets some work up at the Hall, an not jus the back-stairs, neither. Ladybitch Chalmers wanted her broke bits mended, didn't she? I got a peepful of her stuff, I did. All gilded an carved like it were breathed out an no iron hadn't ever touched it, all leaves an twined in bedwine an ivery door had a-chitted some ivy atop. Smell o' wax, though I don't go along wi' polishin as the fine ones do. Hands on the rails do it, an the boards gets greasy an slippy. They likes the shine, see. Anyways, I gets a bit of a pier-glass, a banger of a glass, twice the size of I, an there was a bit of a wing nicked off a what-d'ye-call, a cupid. I carved this wing out like my life hanged on it, an were right proud at it, all the same, an tapped it on wi' a fillet aback to keep it from topplin off an upsettin her ladyship, though she weren't lackin in cupids, was she, the way she goed on?—an in comes Abraham, an squints at it, an sucks his teeth, an shoves his hands in his britches, an stands straddle-wise, an hums an hahs, an says, 'Samuel, that ben't a wing for a cupid so much as a hawk.' An I says, 'Nay, Mr Webb, not so much a hawk, more a lark.' An he smiles, an says, 'Samuel, best take her down. Thee have got to be handlin on her like thee be smitten.' Wood was allus 'her' to Abraham.

An I did. Still there, I shouldn't wonder. Though they don't deserve it. I'll tell thee on that some other time. She were a crabby old bitch, Lady Chalmers. I seed her picture, from way back, an she were handsome then. Though she still thought she were, the way she beautified herself wi' all that white stuff, an all them red ribbons in her hair. She were not much better nor her son, I'll say that, an that be all but swearin, round here. We don't forget easy. Recallin don't get ramshackle, not round here. No.

See that chap come in now? You ax him about the Chalmers. Atween you an I, he have bagged more deer nor they have. That be his sister wi'n, old Mags Knapp. She was allus broken-mouthed. Lost her teeth ploughin, we say. Green Man reglars, don't know what they be doin in the Never Fear. As you knows as the New Inn, though it en't bin new for a tarnal long time. Had a drop aready. Maybe the law be on 'em. That'll be summat. There en't a mother's son in here as hasn't tried to get what be theirs by right, off o' them Chalmers. Don't tell narn. You be ridin through. Nowt o' yourn, sir.

No.

What Abraham ud allus say to me: 'Thee be adrift, Samuel, an if thee don't get hammerin, thee'll sink.' He was full o' them concoctions, was Abraham. But he were right. My work allus had a weakness about it. Not a big 'un. Jus a kind o' touch about it, that it weren't solid, like his were, all the way from start to finish. It'd start strong, but ud be gnarley, or bungersome, an then strong, an so on. Jus a touch.

Ah well.

Can't all be masters. No.

He could spot a tree as were ready better nor arn other. That was what he had. Dead o' winter, frost cracklin, sap down, first light up in the copses—Baylee mainly, good oak there, middlin tough acause the soil en't thin, an Smithy Copse for elm, an top o' Frum Down for beech, though they've mostly gone now, them as were past Five Elms Farm, on account o' the storms, for they don't root deep, beech, an they were right on brow there, afore sarsens, though there be a fine clump on the estate, agin river, where they put that daft temple, aye, an wych astraddle the river ater Quabb Bottom jus afore old Master Pottinger's mill, goin up, in Grigg's, for we needed a goodish lot o' wych, for the furniture, though

I prefers the Dutch, plenty o' that out Bursop way, an roundabouts, Dutch bein easy on the palm an works wi' you, don't it?—an there he'd be, deep in Baylee, eyein this butt, that butt, an allus better nor his bro for seein the wheel in the crooked uns, ezackerly right, an ud mark 'em, I can see him now, wi' a flick o' the gouge an stride through the old mist, cracklin over the floor—an he'd be fellin the next day, he'd be that quick at hagglin.

They'd crash down all right. He'd have the butts in the bob in no time, up there in the woods. You go to the yard now, see the elm stacked, right hand o' saw-pit, we cut down eight, nine year ago, when we were still gristy. That be my work there, though I won't never fashion it. Could tell you where ivery one of 'em stood, once. All out Bursop way. Ivery one have a tale in her. Like haaf as be fashioned out o' timber in Ulver, I can tell you where it come from, what dern tree. See that old door there? Twenty year old, but it were once up atop Basing's Down, north end o' Swilly Copse, pleasurin its leaves in grawin weather, rustlin in wind. Afore we lopped she, an one day's work got a door out.

Aye. He were more nor sixty then, but he were dashin about like a fox, up there in them copses, wi' his big brown hat an big brown coat. I medn't be able to book-larn, an know letters, but I can read them copses. 'Tis what he gived I.

You ride up to Baylee Copse an see. Other side o' the square here there be Bew's Lane. Go on up there, see, an onto the track an there be Baylee dead ahead. Dead ahead. Best oak roundabouts. Best English oak, save the top end, where the ground be chocky. Wood comes hard out o' that end. Stayin long, then?

Aye. I will. Good an warm.

Aye. It all helps. Kills the worm, don't it, like milk, milk in a milk pail. Them worms fancies chestnut, acause it be white an soft for them little jaws, but they don't like the saturation. That be why the ale be good for thee. Kills the worm.

A good un, but true, if you'll stay for it.

What the rooms be like up there then? Make sure she lays you a fire now. The chill en't out yet. Make sure. That there well side be best. Gets the sun, an not them dingin bells. You a churcher, then? Last time I bin was to lay down my old woman in her tarnal rest, God bless her. Go in there, look at the poppy-heads on the north side. That be my work. Abraham's on the south. You'll know. Never could do as he did. Never could. An the font-lid. That be ourn. I remimbers the tree, up in Baylee. Abraham, he stalks about one mornin, dead o' winter, raw it was, clouds all curdlin, an he were right riled, acause he wanted an oak for the lid that were droxy at the bottom, for the beauty on it, an he couldn't spot un, or more like smell un, an were gettin more an more glowery, till he stopped stock-still anigh a gurt mellow butt, big as a church, an sniffed low, an were pleased as punch, an that be the one. That be atop the font. Nice an streaky, like river-spate ater storms. Two years afore he worked it, mind. Vicar had to wait, didn't he? An Abraham were that vallyble, he did. Atween you an I, though, I can spot a dragon in them patterns. I reckons as how there were a dragon in that tree. He'll avenge hisself one day. 'Tis what oak be. Vengeful. Eh? Heh.

I gets a-dry talkin.

Aye.

It were my hands. Dubby they be, see? Not made for handlin. Not for fine work. Not even afore rheumatics. Though I won't say as I did poor work. But it weren't never admired.

Look. Lay hold o' this here, look. Lay hold o' the haft.

Worked wi'n for nigh on forty year, didn't I? Chiselled my life out, wi' that. Chiselled my life out. Sold the other tools. Couldn't rid me o' that un. Don't sit comfortable in a fine hand. Look. My life in this here haft, see? All worn one side. A pokey kind o' life. But I couldn't rid me o' this. My life in this haft. Nigh worn out.

First job, wi' this un, morticin for the winders in the Vicar's house. Still there, praise the Lord. Them winders have seed a thing or two, I shouldn't wonder. Haven't stuck since, though. Not to my knowledge. That be Webb's work for you. That be Abraham.

Aye.

I en't maunderin, be I? Only had a drop. I en't lush, like. They waters it in here. Even the ale. Look at this table, now. More'n a hundred year old, I reckons. Pegs, see? No brads. Solid oak. That'll be old man Webb's old granfer did this. You can tell from the legs. He allus did a jowl aneath, on ivery one o' his table legs, thought he was makin a gate. That thick ripplin bit, feel it with thy fingers, aneath. See? Aye. Dead as ditch-water, this ale. Watch her next time, when she goes out. Reckons as she flattens it deliberate. Times be like that. All greed an friggin.

Horse round the back, have 'ee? Allus wanted my own horse. Couldn't afford a knacker. Heels touchin workhouse, me. You'll get to Oxford no time, acause it en't rained for days, have it? Thee'll raise the dust, belike, to Oxford. Dry for May. Dry. Though they cows be layin down in Vanners.

Knowed you were a genneman, moment you come down.

Thank 'ee.

Lunnen's a right place, they tells I. All manner o' things goes on in Lunnen. Abraham did a job out there, once. This lady, she wanted a harvest frieze, only she didn't want no city feller doin it. Friend o' the Squire's, weren't she? Old Norcoat. He puts her on to Abraham. He did it. He did the lot. Honeysuckles, flowers, fruits, eggs an tongues, water, raffle, laurel leaves, ribbons, knots, all in best mahogany. 7d a foot run, he cost her. 7d a foot run. Now that be well nigh best carvin, nowt o' your common. She were right happy. He said Lunnen were all bellockin an diddlin an too many strits. Heh. An it stunk more nor Ulver, he said. That be tellin. All manner o' things goes on there, they tells us. An the ladies. They says they be two a penny, in Lunnen.

Tosticated with it. I've forgot as how a woman feels, like. Touch-wood. My pizzle's nowt but touch-wood. Burns but no flame. Ah well.

Firsest job he ever give me—an he weren't much older, mind, nor I were, only seven year, I reckons, atween us, but he were that big, he were a man an I a boy—firsest job he give me, were ladder-spokes. A bit o' shavin. Like this. Shavin 'em for the pole-holes, see. Square the ends. Shave, shave. Fit snug an tight acause, he says, 'Thy work en't over ater job be done. 'Tis jus begun, then. Thee makes a gate, an it begun when the first man swings her ope an shut for the cattle. Thy work goes on till the article be broke up, which if thy work be carried out proper won't be till long ater thee be dead an buried.' 'Tis what he says to I, my firsest day. Never lost that. 'You shaves 'em overmuch, an a man be goin to break his collar.' I reckons as how he was recallin his old granfer, then. The one as did the wheel poorly an broke a man's neck. There be a verse on it in the Chapel yard. Pyke. One o' them Pykes. Can't read it proper now. His stone. Weather don't wear away wood. Timber be stronger nor stone, to my mind, acause it en't as stubborn. It don't jus squat there. Breathes, more like. Moves about. Don't bring the hawthorn into your house acause it breathes ill luck. It knows, see. Beech be good, apple, ash—though I can't abide the smell of ash when I works, when I worked she. Filled the shop, she did, terrible sweet. An beechen copses—ill luck aneath moonlight. Aye.

Muggy in here. Bacco. Never took to pipes myself. Darkens your inside, that smoke. Smokes your heart black. You see what smoke do to timber. Look up there. That there. Hardens and darkens. Never took to it, see.

I reckons the barrel be givin out. Ax her for one afresh, next time. Don't let her stoop it. Nowt but grouts then.

I cut this here mug myself, what, twenty year ago now. Yellow pine. My letters on the side. See? Copied from the parish book. S D *1780.* Samuel. Samuel Daye. Couldn't fit all that on. Jus the letters. One piece o' yellow pine. Fill her slick up from the jug, there's a genneman, an I'll be gettin on with the story.

Aye. Thank 'ee.

We were doin them stairs, weren't we? This were, what, nigh on thretty year ago. Early summer, '75. We were doin them stairs, athurt street at Squire's. Start to finish we laid down them stairs. You wanna knock on his door, jus agin church out there, an ax to see his stairs. Best mahogany. Jamaica mahogany. Nowt o' that deal for the Squire, save on the steps an risers. All as the hand touches, Jamaica mahogany, strong an dark. Best job we ever did, them stairs. Better nor gates, gates an more gates, an mendin. Mint crooked an dark, Squire's place, though not piddlin, an he wanted it fancy, so we puts up a dog-leg stairs, don't we? Abraham hums an hahs, gets out his pencil, draws it all out, fiddles his compass, measures an hums an hahs some more, Squire hoppin from one leg t'other, face all blowzy, bustin his britches, acause he likes his nourishment, don't he?—an Abraham pockets his thoughts an says, 'I'll gets you up there, Squire, like you be on your way to Heaven. Six-inch by ten-inch pitch-board, seven steps, two foot o' landin, winder, six steps, same boot lands as took off down bottom.' That were Abraham's way. Ladder to the Lord, he puts it—knowin, mind, as the Squire was drinkin hisself to it, an have no need of our aid.

So I gets goin on the newels an ballusters, back in our shop, flutin them twelve an eight respective, like, an planin the handrail like it were a lissom gal, that Jamaica mahogany, long clean shavins at my boots, see, mouldin that rail for all them fine hands as the old Squire fancied ud visit him, for he were keen on bibbin wi' the Lords an Ladies, weren't he, the old Squire, God rest him—who rised up on a mahogany staircase, I'll be bound, alightin on the same foot as he set out on, though where ezackerly I'd not put no money on, heh—an the boy (for this were twenty year ater I begun wi' Abraham, an there were others younger) the boy cuts the steps, risers, string-boards, all o' that out o' deal, an over we goes to the Manor, rips the old droxy staircase down, as were well nigh as old as that gurt oak out there, an sets to, hammerin them brads in.

Then Abraham says to I, 'Samuel, thee can try thy hand at the scroll.' That bein what the hand-rail ends on, the scroll, that fancy twirly bit top an bottom, see, an like the hardest part to get true, acause the rail has to find its eye in one turnin of a circle, an that be the trimmest. You gets the scroll wrong, an the whole staircase don't look right. Don't feel right aneath the hand. An you have to turn all them mouldins round into the circle, an scroll it up to the eye like it be water twirlin down a hole. You'd see up at the Hall. What I did be nowt compared wi' that up at the Hall, acause they got Italians, didn't they? Them as did that up at the Hall, they be for Kings an Queens, as don't know a good scroll when they touches it, but they allus pays out for the best, don't they? Aye. We ud knows a good scroll, but we don't have stairs to put 'em on, least I don't, only a ladder with pole-rails, hardly stairs, so no place for fancy work, save in the fancy places, where it gets powder on it, an cream, an all that stuff they plasters on their faces, an no perciation.

All rustlin up them stairs, like they be gods. Aye.

So all be lined up an ship-shape, an up we be goin, an I planes the scroll amiss then true, then cuts t'other, an feels warm an happy, when up comes old man Stiff from farm south side o' Mapleash Down, a good stride up aback the Manor, an says as how all his gates needs shiftin, an new ones doin, an how he needs new doors here an there, an new browsers, an if we can't he'll be goin someplace else, for old Roger Stiff allus wanted things doin afore they be done, like. An we be mumblin through our brads, an white wi' sawdust, an blinkin wi' weariness, acause them stairs takes effort, see, for Squire wants it all grand an no messin, when Abraham claps us on the backs an says, 'Aye aye, old man Stiff needs a goodish few things doin up his way. We'll be endin late, lads.'

He allus called us lads, right up to five year ago, though I were long past thretty year even in '75, when this happened.

That was his way, see.

An we looks at each other, an makes a face all the same, for them stairs weren't all we were at then, no—we were doin stalls for Barr's farm, an nigh on a hundred cogs for the mill, an a fence round what Chalmers'd enclosed (for that were jus begun then, that poor business) an all the littler jobs folk brought in on the chance, like—an here be old Abraham pilin more on, like we were donkeys, past all puttin up with, in our minds.

Now Abraham, we knows, has a patchy temper, so we don't say nothin, but goes on hammerin, an fixin, an smoothin, then ater work the next day it be off to our shop an in there till eleven, makin gates an doors to Abraham's lines, by candlelight, though it were well nigh summer, an off to Stiff's early over Mapleash, an I hangs the big gate into the Gore, as be on the main road just afore turnin off to farm, an there I be fresh up with tom-tit an buntin, a-hangin the big gate, when who should I see but Abraham come. An I turns to the lads an says, 'What he be up to now then, checkin up, like? He looks bucksome enough.' More nor we were, hammerin an stompin the earth hard agin the post fit to bust that early we barely nodded a-nights, an the sun only jus now peeped, an mist all along river, see, down the bottom. Aye aye.

You'll see my gate, off to Oxford, from the saddle, right hand goin out. You'll see her. Biggest gate I ever done. All chamfered for lightness, nice ripplin jowl, brace o' best oak an thick as they come. Swings like the gate o' Heaven for a infant, easy an wide an wi' ne'er a squeal. An old Ben Bowsher hissed out some fancy wings at the forge for that one, for he knowed it were big an special. All splayed they are, an you'll see the twirliest bit of iron ever twisted for the top o' the catch, he were that keen. But a gate be ten hours' work to the hour, an no messin. So where do we find them hours? Not down in the ale-house. Not here. Not a-snug wi' my old woman neither. No. Every night, aye, an we weren't on no spree if we weren't a-home. No. We was in that shop, boots on the cobbles, an no splut from arn on us, acause we were a-feared, I'll be frank, o' that Abraham.

Aye.

He allus called me lad, right to his last breath. An me long past my sixtieth year! Aye. That were his manner. That were his way.

Aye.

I reckons as she oughta be bungin back the spile on this bugger. Air's been at it. I'll have another, though. Make sure she fills it slick to the top, no halves.

Thank 'ee.

I were younger then, surely. When I hangs that gate I be fit an hale, but no lad all the same. Now I be bad in the fingers I be a genneman till my dying day. Like your good self, sir. Nowt to go at, now. Aye. Thy health, sir.

That Abraham.

Listen. He come up to us that mornin an he stands there a-straddle, an sucks at his teeth, an swipes the grass wi' his stick, an nods summat, an he says, 'Lads, thee'll be comin along ship-shape there, I won't deny it. But thee be summat gingerly wi' that old creature of a gate. I'd expected thee to be up an away up to Manor by this hour. Thee'll be havin sup wi' the maids soon, at this rate.' An one o' the lads, a lump of a chap, he be linin up the harr agin the post, readyin it for the hammerin to true, when all on a sudden he stops stock still, an looks upperds, like a hare that's heared summat, and stays so, while I be waitin for him wi' my hammer hangin in the air, see, an the peewits makin a hell on a din, an the other lad stampin his boot down about the post as one ought, for a good hold, when Abraham says, 'What be up wi' thee, Ketchaside'—for that were the big lad's name, one o' the Ketchasides from Maddle Lane—'what be up wi' thee?'

Aye. I can see it all. My memory en't be ramshackle. No.

An this Ketchaside, he stays like that, like a hare that's sniffed summat, till I says, 'Thomas, what thee be up to, then? I can't be lollin about wi' my hammer till the cows come. Hitch that old gal true an let's be gettin up to Manor.'

I was allus behind the master, then.

An the other lad stops his stampin, an we all looks at young Ketchaside, an Abraham bein summat discomfited, like, turns to us an he says, 'What be up with the old boy? He en't goin soft in brain-pan, belike?'

An Ketchaside turns slow, see, an he lets go o' the gate so as it near drops down on my boots, crashin down like, an he says, mortal slow, 'Master, methinks I sees an angel up there.' An Abraham, bein a church-goer, whips his head up an eyes the sky like it were rainin angels, though it be still green wi' dawn, see, an there be I thinkin as how he'd give Ketchaside a good hidin for his cheek—for I knowed Thomas afore, an he'd allus been a original, a rascally kind o' tongue to him—but no, old Abraham acts all gullible like, wi' eyes upperds, but only the peewits be circlin an swoopin, hell on a din, so he looks agin at Ketchaside, half-suspicious like, an says, 'What angel, lad?'

An Ketchaside acts right up, don't he, an spreads his arms like this, an flaps 'em up an down, an says, 'She were mortal big, an all golden, an smiles at I wi' wings wi' a touch o' silver, like they be rimed wi' mornin, master.'

An he plays it up so surely, as Abraham coughs, an spits, an wipes his mouth, an looks upperds agin, agin at Thomas, then at me, an the other boy, an says, 'We'd best be on our knees, then, lads.' An so we all sinks down about the gate, as be a-spraddle on the grass, an offers up our thanks to the Lord, an I be awmost bust from gigglin at the rig, as got the right side o' old Abraham, make no mistake. An he crosses hisself till I thought he'd wrick his wrist, old Abraham.

But we gets to it straight ater, for sure. An stays that night at the Manor, hammerin till eleven, for the Squire be in Bath that week.

That were a ripper, certain sure.

But the next lot were better. This be a deep un. That Sunday, I meets the two lads by luck, like, a-lollin agin the bridge, Bottom Bridge, past Barr's farm, an we walks up Chalky Lane to'ards Plumm Farm, an out atop Ewe Drop Hill, an anigh the Folly Clump, an that daft hut of her Ladybitch's, they call a hermitage, as weren't ramshackle then as 'tis now, an were lived in by Old Surley, as was in the military, an had a head as was agoggle from the wars, see, but she thought him parfit, an a-dressed him in a long white gown, like out o' the Scriptures—daft, weren't it?—an out on the ridge by hatch gate we sat us down on a tuffut, an said as we were jus about slick up to here wi' old Abraham's ways, an kepin us to eleven for the last week, an no sign o' let-up, see.

Now I were summat older nor these two lads. My old woman was allus sayin to me as how I were a slow-worm wi' old Abraham, an didn't say as I ought to him, but bein past thretty it weren't so easy for I to find work else, see, an like I've said I weren't no master, though I could do any joinery you axt of I, an no mistake, but it weren't like Abraham's, it weren't toppermost. No.

I'd bin wi'n for past twenty year by '75, when this went on as I be tellin. An all that time Abraham had never not a snick o' praise for owt I done. Not even for them two scrolls, as I cut for Squire. No. He were mortal near wi' his admiration. He were allus larnin I, right to the last day. That be as how he seed it, by my reckonin. Aye. An I knowed as how I weren't no lean o' the trade, but no fat jobber neither, but summat betwixt the two—on account, as I sees it, of my hands, bein as they are summat dubby, though I allus had the strength, see, in my arms. I could snap a lop a-two the width o' thy thigh, make no mistake. But I never had the touch that he had. An he knowed that, see, to be sure.

Aye.

I will an all.

Thank 'ee.

My old woman, she was onto me, see. As how I never spoke my mind. I was allus behind the master. I felt tart about it some time, his bally-raggin, aye. But I never spoke my mind. Never.

He got my bristles up once or twice, I can tell thee, surely. Aye. That he did.

Heh.

Dead an gone now, all on 'em. Dern it, I never spoke my mind to him. Aye. Now I've had a drop o' two, I don't mind tellin. This en't a grizzle, though. This en't a grizzle. You be a genneman, listenin so long. I be planin through to the heart, make no mistake. Pure oak, this tale. It be a ripper. Don't you go now. Don't you go. You be a-lush as you fancy, you don't have far to rise, up them stairs. Stay wi' me an drain that cask to the grouts, an you won't hear no codger's grizzle out o' me. No. I tells you, there be one or two wenches here as I know ud fancy talkin to a genneman like you, sir. They be a-rampin for a genneman the likes o' you, make no mistake. Fine good clean country wenches, aye. An young an lissom, as ud fancy wrestlin wi' the likes o' you, sir. I knows all about them as be rampin ater decent strangers like you, sir. Hear me out an I'll tell 'em as you be game, sir, to have thy room warmed by a simple wench. Aye.

Make no mistake. You don't want to touch them as be in here. No. They be dampen straw in here. These'd not douse a candle.

Aye.

Heh heh.

See she, like a drownded rat, agin the cask? She ud do it wi' a pig if he paid her. In an out more times nor a nag shot out o' the shafts. Bin whipped at the cart's tail, that un, for thievin wine. Years ago, now. Didn't make her aright, though. Be thievin men from their wives, now. The worsest kind o' men, mind. The worsest kind. Aye. She be lookin our way now. Cotched her one while past, out in the orchut, up to her anticks. Thought it were two lads a picky-back, till I saw it straight. Years ago now. Aye.

I'll bet them ladies as rides up to the Hall, from Lunnen an abouts, I'll bet their limbs be white an smooth as chestnut. Aye. I'll bet.

Aye.

This gettin to be a rigmarole afore I've finished. Abraham allus said I lacked summat. It were allus my thoughts doin the meddlin. I never had his dedication, not to the work in hand. I were allus stuck for that. Mind, I could strip them oaks out their bark quicker nor he, at strippin-time. They'd mount up in the tan-yard thick as the ale-house on pay-night, certain sure. I were out an out the best o' the boys at strippin.

Aye. That I were, certain sure.

He couldn't deny me that.

I don't recall as who first thought on it. Belike it weren't I, but Ketchaside. Out on that down, past Ewe Drop. It were a slappin piece o' mischuf, whoever thought on it. The other boy, name o' Sheppard, he were a mite slippy about it, an wanted nowt to do on it, but when we telled him it were to stop our work bein so tardy, like, he come round to us soon enough, up there on that down. It were deep, that piece o' mischuf. Heh heh.

Poor old Sheppard, the lad thought as how he'd end up at the cart's tail, or worse, transportashin, for goin agin Abraham. It were awmost worth transportashin, the way I seed it. It were deep, an all. Aye.

Heh heh.

Lay the dust in that throat an listen to this. There be a tree, a gurt fine oak, haafway atween Stiff's place an here. It be right agin the road, an all splashed white in the wet, an good'n thick in the leaf, so as thee can hide up there an narn don't ever sees thee. You can be a right King

Charlie up there in that oak. Belike it were the same one as he used. I dunno. Anyways, early next mornin, bein back on the job, like, we comes to the tree, on the way to Stiff's, an shins up it, an sits in all them branches, hearts a pit-a-pat, an we watches the old sun do his bit, an we giggles, an gets sittin easy, like, on them gurt branches, an minds what we've to do, that we've gone over yeserday, an sits tight, waitin.

For Abraham, see.

Now I weren't a lad, but I feeled like one up there in that oak. I used to get pleasure from climbin trees as a lad, if you gets my meanin. I were allus shinnin up an down, as a nipper, an wonderin why I were gettin damp in the britches, like, an it so pleasin. An this, I'll be honest, were the same kind o' pleasure, this piece o' mischuf. I were in great spout, up there in that oak, waitin for Abraham Webb.

For I had the deepest voice, like. It were I as had the job in hand. My heart was a pit-a-pat, I can tell thee, waitin.

Aye. I be dry, thinkin on it. Fill her up.

You'll recall what it be like, up a tree. Thee be king, up there. Thee be master. All spread pokey aneath 'ee, an thee gurt proud, an tall, up there in them branches. Like the old tree be spreadin through thee, growin up through thee, king o' the world, master o' the fields, up there in that tree. Aye. Thee be God, up there.

God.

Aye.

For thee be the one a-rustlin now, with thy gurt proud limbs o' pure oak!

Aye.

A-comin to it. I'll find thee a wench, don't fret. Plenty o' time for that. A clean squishy wench. Give me a spell more an I'll seek one out wi'out a splotch on her. Let I finish.

Gin-trap, see. That be what it were. Gin-trap for master. To be struck by he. Narn else.

So he comes, don't he?—bang on church strikin six he comes over the brow, on his way to Stiff's, checkin up on us. An I cups my hands about my mouth all ready, see, like this, big dubby hands about my mouth, an I sits bolt up, an the other two anigh me sits stock as a hare, an stops their breathin they be so still, an lo behold Abraham's step be comin nearer an nearer, his boots a-clippin them flints like old Bowsher in his forge, see, an my heart be hammerin louder an louder, an all three on us creamy-faced an a-muck with fear, but stock still up that gurt tree like three dead men, only our hearts a-goin, an lo behold Abraham be under us wi' the top of his head an I hears the whistlin through his nose an smells his sweetness an through them leaves I sees him an I sings out, like, I don't blare I sings out, like:

'A-bra-ham . . . !'

Jus like that, see. Heh.

'A-bra-ham . . . !'

Heh.

And he stops bang in his tracks, an he looks up, an I thinks I be for a whippin or worse, I feels so a-feared, but astead o' that I hears him say,

'Yea, my Lord?'

Wi' such a gingerly look on his face I well nigh bust out laughin. For I knew I had done him, then.

It were like the squawk of a hare when the trap strikes. It were tip-top. Aye.

An then I says, all sing-song like, but mortal strong an more bellockin it out this time:

'If thee keepest thy lads at work till eleven,
Thee shalt not enter the kingdom of Heaven!'

An then the two old boys, they gives out a great sigh, like as if God were closin off into the clouds, out of the mortal world full of sin, into His Kingdom, leavin old Abraham starin upperds, up at the sky, as though he have a-had a big crack a-top o' the head.

An he says, all quiet, but wi' a mouth big as a saw-pit:

'Dang un.'

Then he comes to it, like, as though he be on a sudden doushed in cold water, an gets down on his knees, an claps his two hands into one, an makes a gugglin noise out o' his throat, an coughs, an starin upperds he says:

'Lord, dost thou forgive me?'

Aye. An we were quiet as the grave. I tells thee. Sir.

An when he gets up an walks all gawky, like, off, as we thought it, to Stiff's, lookin up now an agin, a mite a-feared, it seemed, o' them old clouds o' early mornin openin wi' a big voice agin, we shins down an runs like the Devil be ater our souls the crow-way across the down to Mapleash Farm—for the road way do a dog-leg, don't it?—an old Abraham, well, we be hid from him by that hedge as were jus about tall enough by then, though it be a mite thicker now, an by the brush as were north o' the road them days.

So we gets a-pantin to Stiff's afore he do, an gets to on the browsins in the cow-stalls, as we were hammerin up afresh, an tryin to clap our mouths up, we were that gleeful, but there be no Abraham that mornin.

An we gets over to the Manor an lays the last three steps, an fixes the ballusters, for the Squire's ascension, like, but no Abraham. An we be a mite worrited now, an when it be time we gets over to the shop, a snick glum-faced, for we be reckonin as how Abraham might've spied us, an be workin his revenge, when eight strikes on the church, an in walks he. An he looks at all on us, an we looks at him as innocent as milk, like, an he says, like the words were skrunged together, an he were pullin 'em a-two wi' his lips:

'Put thy work away, lads. Put thy work away.'

An that be all he says. But spot on eight each day, till the day he kecked his last a-bed, he'd say the same.

'Put thy work away, lads. Put thy work away.'

Like he was a-feared we mightn't, see.

Aye.

A-feared we mightn't.

Heh heh.

That Abraham.

1830

DEPOSITION

I don't know who they were against the ricks. The lanthorn was doused by one of them. There was a great press of the men in the yard and one holloed 'Never mind Harry let us set the blaze off.' Then one I don't know with a brown smock on set his tinderbox to the straw beneath the iron Plough and it were set alight. Then I went with the mob into the Barn & in the middle was the drum of the machine and there were four men including Alfred Dimmick & John Oadam who were breaking the said machine. I don't know the other two men. As they were beating the machine Alfred Dimmick said to Tom Knapp who was standing a few yards from him 'This is a hard job Tom'—and Knapp answered 'Never mind Ally if you are tired I am willing to take your place.' They were smashing the machine with sticks and an axe. Then I saw Farmer Stiff with a lanthorn. He threw a smart little lot of shillings to John Oadam as he came out of the Barn into the yard, very nearly two hundred. I heard Farmer Stiff say as he would mark that d—d ploughman another day (meaning the Prisoner John Oadam). Then we left the Yard by the big gate. I saw about a hundred persons by the light of the burning Plough.

Then we went to the Malt Shovel at the crossroads on the brow and had a pot of beer apiece. The men demanded of the landlord some bread & Cheese. The landlord set candles on the tables as it was not yet light but the men took the candles with them as they left. Some men staid the main of the day there but most of the mob departed at about six o'clock to press more persons. They pressed the occupants of the dwellings on the turnpike into Ulverton. Two carters came up: these carters are James Malt and Harold Tagg. They were willing to come with them on their donkeys. Some of the Mob talked with those in Withy Field & Ley Dean: the said men left their Ploughs in the stitch and joined us: about twenty in all. They carried one stick apiece that were cut from the hedgerows and two had mattocks. One of them was William Bray. He said to me 'Hannah what beest thee doing here?' I replied that I wd not stand aside. We came back into Ulverton to break open the blacksmiths but he (Richard Bowsher) opened it for us: we took the hammers and a sledge-hammer and crow-bars. The horn was blown before the Church and again by the main well. It was not yet light & I was unable to see many Faces I knew: I did not know whether they were willing or unwilling.

Then they went to Barrs Farm and I heard Giles Griffin demand 40s in silver from Farmer Barr for each machine broke. I heard John Oadam say to Farmer Barr that they would be having half a crown after Ladyday or the wind would get the bettermost. This was by the Ricks in the Court. It appeared to me that he meant by this as farmers would have more than their machines broke if no satisfaction in wages was to come. They were about two hundred by then. I should think they staid about twenty minutes in Barrs Farm & were given more bread. Farmer Barr brought out a lanthorn and I saw by that light Edward Pyke and James Malt and Solomon Webb who were against the Door of the Barn. They entered with Farmer Barr and he said he would be glad if they Broke his machines, for they threwed men upon the Parish. They beat and smashed his threshing Machine and chaff-Cutting machine and they drew out his iron Plough and took all of the other pieces out into the Court in a pile. I don't know who the others were as broke the machines. I did not see the £4 given.

The mob left the Court yard and walked across the fields to the Estate (of Ulverton House). They tore up the Fences in the fields named Marridge Butt & Whitesheet Haw, & also in Little Hangy to the crab-apple. I heard many men holloeing that they would have their land back or there would be Blood spilt. Some men carried the fence poles as weapons. Because there was only one lanthorn I do not know who destroyed the fences & I did not recognise any Shout. The lanthorn was bandied about from one to another down the line. The horn was blown several times and the Mob advanced across the meadows as belong to Ulverton Hall (meaning Ulverton House) & they broke down the Hedgerows in several places. I believe John Oadam and Giles Griffin were the leaders. Joseph Scalehorn who is a cripple was carried by two men. This was about seven o'clock. It was first light then. They crossed the river by Bottom Bridge and came up Chalky Lane to Plum Farm (meaning Ulverton House Farm).

When they came to the yard of the said Farm there was Lord Chalmers MP on a horse. The Riot Act was read out from a paper by the said Lord Chalmers. He maintained to the mob that there would be £500 for any man informing against 10 other men. They did not heed him. John Oadam called out that they would be having 2s a day for they wd not starve no more. He went to Lord Chalmers but I did not hear what was said between them. The barn was entered and a threshing machine broke and a Winnowing machine. There were six horses on the said threshing machine and they were unstrapped. I saw them running out of the barn but I did not see the machines smashed. I should think it took thirty minutes to break the machines.

The Mob then proceeded to the Hall (meaning Ulverton House) where there was said to be a great machine also. Myself and the Mob crossed the river again at Bottom Bridge and advanced towards the House through the Park. There was a woman in a black bonnet with a rake. She ran away holloeing and the Yeomanry appeared from behind the Temple: they rode down to meet us at the Lake there. They stopped before they reached us, and pointed their muskets at us. About fifty yards away. The mob called out bread or blood but there were no sticks thrown. Smoke came from a gun. There was a loud noise. I believe from the gun. Saw James Malt falling with a great wound in his face: I believe from a musket-ball. The Mob struck the Yeomanry with Sticks and hammers & crow-bars stones hay-forks and so on.

I was struck by a horse and fell to the ground. I should think they were fighting for thirty minutes. There were many wounds and the Blood was spilling on the ground: I saw John Oadam strike a Yeoman with a hay-fork. Another Yeoman struck the said John Oadam on the shoulder with the butt of his musket. I believe it was Edward Pyke who knocked the said Yeoman down to the ground with a dibble. A horse ran the said Edward Pyke into the Lake. I heard him shout that these d—d villains would boil in their blood for this. Men from both sides fell into the Lake: they were beating the swans away from their persons.

Alfred Dimmick was wearing a white hat: he had a sign on a pole, he told me before it read No Machines. The sign was torn away & he took a blow on his crown. Joseph Scalehorn was carried from the fighting but the yeomen went after them. Some men were running to the House across the Lawn. Tom Ketchaside who is eighty was knocked to the ground & also William Bray.

Lancelot Heddin (Examinant's twin brother) who is a cripple came up to take me away from the Fight. He had no weapon. My dress was torn and I had received a wound on the arm. A yeoman caught my brother by his neck and my brother fell & pulled the Yeoman from his horse. My brother rose & was knocked down by a horse and it appeared to me as he (meaning the Examinant's brother) was Lifeless. Then I ran to fetch assistance, but was apprehended in the Wilderness

you imagine, my dear Emily, the tediousness of this Sessions when in the forefront of my thoughts runs the said matter relating to your health & our Fortune. I have staid in a room without air for three days—'tis in the Squire's aged house, insufferably near the Church. The stench of the labourers vies with the stench of the smoke—we have an ill-built chimney-piece—while I persevere in the translation of but thick grunts into some semblance of Rational discourse. I scribble this between whiles. O for the sweet melody of your name! Quam vellem me nescire literas, as those I face each day, when that gift shuts one up in such a fug as this, far from your person, my dearest. (How fitting a classical reflection, when one learns it came from Nero—in his compassionate youth—about to set his pen upon a writ for the execution of some Malefactor!)

Edward Hobbs, saith that on Monday the 22nd of November instant about two hundred persons were unlawfully and riotously assembled together at Ulverton House in the said county and Examinant saw the Prisoner John Oadam strike Robert Jefferies who was then and there aiding and assisting in suppressing the said Riot. The Prisoner hit the said Robert Jefferies with a hay-fork. I struck him on the back with my musket and he fell to the ground and I then heard him say he would have that d—d Bailiff's blood for posset on the morrow (meaning this Examinant)

I have never insisted anything of the sort. Far be it for me to be adjudged wanting in this matter, for I have ever been solicitous (if you will pardon the play) after your well-being—even before I declared these feelings for you. Indeed, were it not for my appeals to your father, you would not have been released earlier, and so avoided further complexities—as you no doubt have by going North, as it were—to the favour of your uncle and his codicil, however reluctant the climate to shine upon your fair visage, my dearest Emily

Edmund Bunce had a brown Smock.

whereas, if you had but hearkened to my appeals—you were released post-chaise long ago: but be that as it will

Oadam had a crown of bedwine upon his head: of old man's beard. I heard him say that he would be King before tomorrow—this was in jest. Other men had yarrow flowers on their Caps and in their Coats, and I held a flag out of a rag. Most of the Mob departed after thirty minutes but we staid at the Malt Shovel for the remainder of the day. We blew a horn and sang some songs to keep our spirits high. We went to bed early but a Press Gang came round at four o'clock in the night & made us go with them to Bursop & Little Bursop, where we broke up three Machines:

if nothing else, we shall be content at least, with this matrimonial arrangement, that can only be of advantage to all concerned—if one absents from that inclusive gathering your dear father—who cannot be content with a place, as it were, in Heaven. O the Sessions winds on, or down, as my timepiece—regular but slow. We must sweep the floorboards twice a day, as those discharged on their own recognizance to appear in person come for their Examination, it seems, straight from the Field, & those from Prison reek of a cow-byre—which should not surprise, since a cow-byre is indeed their Prison (albeit emptied of the lower beasts)—however, the subsequent foul dunginess means I must hold my handkerchief to my nose nevertheless, or feel giddy. There is no other recourse: the town Gaol being full to its gills, our Lord Chalmers (does your father know him?) has donated his secure cow-house of brick for their incarceration, this being, no doubt, an improvement upon the town lodgings—but meaning I am hardly in the town, where there is a decent theatre on the main road, tho' one's attention is much disturbed by the coaches outside and their infernal clatter, and there are too many pigs in the road, that one must wade through them, if one chooses the wrong morning. Alas, it is always the wrong morning—without your fair white face, my dearest love: I have never, in all my life, seen so many brown Ploughmen as I have seen thro' these last few days—and waggoners, and shepherds, & reapers, and paupers, and Jobbers of every fowl & four-legged beast one might imagine, and Well-diggers, & mealy Mealmen and ruby-cheeked Farmers: it has quite enervated my desire to flee the city's smoke. We are set up in a room of the Manor in the settlement (for so I grace it) named Ulverton—or Ulvers—or Ulverdon—makes no difference—the most dismal place one can imagine—the seat of the Riots in this part of the county—with ditch-mud in the place of road and not a head of thatch without its sprout of moss & weeds. The main Square hardly merits justification of its nomination: but is more a Circle of despondency about a dripping well, whose handle creaks the rope up so loud it forces me to ask for repetition from the Examinants at least ten times of a morning (I exaggerate for effect, for the Manor is some hundred yards along the road, but the church bells shake us each quarter—I feel quite at home as in Bow.) If only you, my dear Emily, had witnessed these Troubles, that you could sit before me and Deposition in the sweetest of tones, while your Examiner gazed upon you from his high table and cross-questioned (but not wiggingly) on the issue of Love—for which there is no Defence. I also have my manly cough returned, tho' the flush

He then saw against the Door twelve or so men by that light. They demanded of him six shillings, or they said they would have him by the scruff and wd threw him into the horse-pond, the bloody bugger, for they had empty bellies enough and so did their Children, & they had not a faggot between them to keep the winter off & to dry their cloathes. He then gave them a purse with the said amount. The Mob soon dispersed, after boasting to his presence that they had broke as many machines

determined on one matter: that we should establish our matrimonial footing on as firm a step as this country will hold—viz., not in London where the powder of ambitious lawyers chokes me in every thoroughfare, but in the calmer pond of some slumberous Country Town, where the bells ring with diffidence over the pompous, and the honest fellow can walk about without an eye ever turned for his rump. We will have a green patch and I shall return promptly for my lunch of kidneys, keeping time by the cathedral spire. If I can tie this up with as strong a ribbon as bundles these briefs for the Prosecution of said wretched Rioters—your father will have to find the sharpest of scissors likewise. If I am thwarted, and forced to breathe more of that pestilent air, I shall grow melancholy as those Greenlanders in Denmark—looking ever north, my dearest!

in Surley Row with my mother and my brother. I was awoken about five o'clock on Sunday the 21st of November last by a horn blowing. I did not get out of bed. I saw several persons at the house opposite and William Dart came to the window of our house and called to us that we must come out. He had on ribands as for the feast of Whitsun & said we must collect shillings & break the machines that do the men's work. I put on my scarf & opened the Door. Old Becky Shail came out of her house with a basket of lardey for all, she said those d—d wretched gentlemen must catch it: she once had a husband hung & cut up in Reding. Giles Griffin said they shall by g—d. My brother was drawn out by the arm. We proceeded down Back Lane, pressing more persons. My brother tied his trousers in the Road for they gave us no time but the Squire is the most insufferable of all: he has ten pairs of tall boots that creak like a coach—& a temper attuned to the weather, that holds his sport in the cup of its hand—a tyranny he will not stand for, but with less elegance in his rhetoric than that famous senator to Vespasian. He brings me cups of warm Port of an evening, settles me before his blazing hearth, and proceeds to vie with the Labouring Classes I have endured all day for bluntness of interest and the complete omission of that essential quality of eloquence that once parted us from the barbarians as flesh of peach from its hairy stone. This is how our rustic gentlemen cross the Rubicon—not with theatre & dancing on the ship but only talk of yields, & the price of corn, & harness, & nags' teeth — & if they grow witty it is like spinning a top with a flail—and if rude—nay not lente but quickly run, you horses of the night! Did I tell you that I knew his son at Winchester? I believe I gave him a welt or two, for he was Junior by three years—a pretty fellow, but a dullard of the first order. He is now in speculation from America

said we did not have number enough to break his machine. He said we did not deserve 2/6d a day for we were paltry fellows who could not turn a Plough without making wind. We left him without abuse because he had stood like a man. We said we would return and went to join the persons that were at Fogbourne. We staid in Fogbourne until one o'clock, breaking there three machines and an iron Plough, & a winnower was already broke by a farmer. We collected £6. We returned to Ulverton where we met the Mob in the Square & we broke the said Farmer Walters's Machine. Then some of us, about fifty persons, went to the Kistle Cross (upon Furzecombe Down) for a meeting where many spoke as we were all one, and a man I do not know in a black hat & Cloak said as we mean to circulate the Gentlemen's blood with the leave of God to make our own blood good. Then over the crest to Effley and beyond

while the Briefs grow into bundles but my hand is sagging—it droops like the houses here, that are all sunk into their mud as if they wish to depart whence they came: for the walls are nothing more than earth and straw, and the roofs likewise—veritable pigsties all—nay, the pigs have better accommodation, & their (meaning the pigs) sour vapours blow less sulphurously past one's nostrils—tho' the desire to expectorate it from one's lungs be equal & said desire quite overcomes those venerable parental injunctions in both cases, alas. There is a noisome mill thankfully distant, & an exceedingly ivied church, & the odd Fine house—in a good red brick, but inhabited by species of country tradesmen only a glove's thickness off those they revile for having hands chapped by their business. These men have daughters shut away like Proserpine in a gloom, awaiting God knows what release by a bachelor with means—once a year, it appears, they ascend to the House where they gaze upon grandiosity and aldermen in equal quantity. Vile is this place of strangled opportunities, and rough fellows not in the least chastened by our proper Oaths and bundles of Terms & brass Ink-pots! Our witnesses creep out from under stones & demand more shillings than we have right to give them—but I give them anyway. So the great weight of the Law descends like some dusty-wigged behemoth in a scarlet stage-coach too small for the ride, and I must look stern and patch up the springs & be forever running to keep up. The dreadful Squire has a plan to carve a Horse on the hillside. All flesh is grass (or in this instance, the reverse

John Stiff, Farmer, saith that on Monday 22nd November instant about one hundred and fifty persons unlawfully entered his Court yard at Mapleash Farm near Ulverton in the said county and Examinant spoke to the Prisoner John Oadam who demanded of him 40s and his machine must be broke and they must have 12s a week in wages after Ladyday or they would bring the Country down like a barn with dry Rot. The Examinant gave the said Prisoner £10 in shillings and said that they must spare any more destruction, for they had already broke his machine. I did not see who broke the Machine, but I believe it was the said Prisoner among them—

not heedful, your father will lose you to his sight—unless you obey his command more peremptorily than good sense will allow, and the heart guide. Does it rain in Matlock?

This vagrant was not given relief. He gave much abuse to the magistrate and was committed to the Cage for a week. The Mob demanded of me the key at six o'clock on the following morning, this being Sunday the 21st of November instant

& it was most amusing. Squire Norcoat placed the flags himself upon the hillside that is South-west of the village, while I looked on in apparent admiration—for I could not see, from my vantage point close by, how this miscellany of fluttering cloth could possibly conform to anything of the remotest resemblance to a horse—save an extremely attenuated hippogriff, with bandy legs, and a neck like an ostrich—

Thereupon they broke ope the door, and drew him (the said vagrant Thomas Durner)

believe it—on both of us mounting the hill a mile away, to the north, with a decent view of Louzy Down (upon which the flags were positioned) this famished Monster began to jostle, and shift, and lose an appendage here and fatten another there—and so, guiding by means of a brass speaking-trumpet, and the breeze advantageous to his bawlings, the Squire had it a Horse within the two hours: those men working gallantly as if under Wellington to move about those flags upon the farthest slope at such distant command.

I did not stop them. The Prisoner Scalehorn who is a cripple was among them & also the Prisoner John Oadam. They were civil to me but I heard Oadam say as they wd be having the good things now

tho' it was a deal too cold for my liking up there: my chest grew tight as a drum with the wind, & I kept my mouth closed or I wd have been taken with a Fit again. It has blown a chill wind here for three days—my throat aches deucedly. Dearest Emily

I told him he could not abuse the Law, for the vagrant had trespassed and used foul language to the Justice. I said that on the Holy day this action (meaning the release of the said vagrant) was blasphemous, and that they shd rest on the Lord's day. He called me a Blackguard, and no man of the cloth, or God, and went into my Kitchen where he took a loaf of bread from the cupboard and stated that if a gallon loaf for each child was not forthcoming bellies would be crying out for justice to Heaven & the Almighty Himself wd weep etc. He waved the loaf in my face as if it was a weapon. Several of the men demanded I should lower my tithes and added—that was the farmers' desire also. I promised then to consider their case, and gave them assurance of this with 3 Sovereigns, for I found it expedient to do so before further abuse was made to my person or Property. They left and I continued with my breakfast. The Mob returned the following afternoon of Monday the 22nd of November tho' much reduced, for many had been taken in the Fight in the early morning of that day instant.

you think we shall marry with or without Consent? If only I had inheritance! Seven hundred a year would do admirably. I dream of this while these fellows are shuffled in, clutching their Caps, and stand mumbling into their beards (tho' I had the Rector Willington come yesterday—insufferably upright). Seven hundred! Surely that avuncular codicil shall be untied soon, my Emily—and my Devotion answered! I have broke a pen this morning—in the middle of Depositioning, as it were, a young Shepherd fellow who is accused of Arson. He cannot be more than fourteen, exceedingly thin-faced but scrofulous, with a tall stovepipe and a spattered smock to his ankles that was no doubt his grandfather's—there are so many of these Wretches they do not clothe them in our dungy prison—he burnt an iron Plough. How extraordinary these actions, that destroy the very Property from whence the means of subsistence are to be supplied. At the very least he will be in Van

Diemen's Land before a twelvemonth is out—he cannot imagine what distance lies between. I mean—between here and that infernal burning place

Edmund Bunce. He had a tinderbox & I saw him put it to the straw

so many of these fellows he might do better to Say Nothing, than mitigate himself into lying. Starvation never loosened the rope, as one might say. Tho' I am not wholly convinced of this hollow-belly wretchedness that The Times is so full of: most of these fellows look apple-cheeked enough to me, tho' slow as oxen (whether from hunger I doubt) and with moist, red eyes—from a combination, I suspect, of wind and ale-house. Some, indeed, have an attenuated look—that have guttered, as it were, into a pool of pauperism, at the base of the Candle. I thought all Ploughmen to be strapping, yet half of these look hardly capable of the said task, with thin shoulders as tho' they have sat at a desk since birth—and with whining, girlish voices that set my teeth on edge. But when I think what I have seen in London—that hardly bears the description of humanity—pestilential—hard by the Inns of

said they had nor warmth nor sufficient bread, and proceeded to abuse the said Edward Hobbs. I heard a gun let off, and saw a man fall. I don't know who fired the gun. I struck the said Giles Griffin with my stick. Griffin kicked my person. Edward Hobbs knocked the said Griffin to the ground & he was trampled upon by diverse persons in the Mob, who were fleeing the horses. Griffin rose and thereupon struck this Examinant with a potato-lifter upon the jaw

digging began yesterday—and this being a most instructive business to witness, as I was able to do in my free hour: the turf is cut into squares—lifted like the peel of an apple—and thus revealing, as it were, the Flesh beneath

in Maddle Lane with my wife & five children. My mother lives with us also. I heard a horn blown & went to the Window. There were many persons outside: they said we are all one & I must go with them & I shd carry a stick. We have no fire so I took a spoon. They said we must collect money as at Whitsun feast.

The effect was dull, for the bared space was not sufficiently lily-white—as your arms are, my Emily—on account of a flintiness, and the sticky boots of the labourers. A quarry has been made for the chalk nearby, that replaces the removed soil, and as I write they are carrying the stone (from which all dark matter has been excised) to the equine place and tipping it & patting it in, this albescence being effected by manual means only—the Squire's efforts are designed for the express purpose of keeping the Devil afar off from otherwise idle hands, and those inflammatory minds certain to see in our carriage of Justice a suitable Pyre for their needs. There has been a pamphlet circulating over the beer-pots that wd drain the bloom from your loveliness

said to him that we have no tatoes nor bread and our children cannot sleep, for they go bedward without sup, only watered milk & sugar, & hardly fire to cook by if we had these things: I said there is hardly ash to sweep into one hand at the end of the day. He answered this will turn to ashes in your mouth, & we must not be tearing the Notices down, for they are good advice. I said, D—n it, these people want money, & they shall have it. He answered that if we wd get money by any means in the open day, we would likewise pay in the open day

& the blacksmith, a great hairy fellow who blows out his cheeks before he speaks, and strikes his knees as tho' they were his anvil (I colour the description somewhat—all tedious here—he is a smallish fellow that reeks of beer-shops and has grey hands) will Hang for certain, as he is down for robbery, Arson, machine-breaking, and extortion. He told me he had robbed only his own shop. He sobbed in the middle point of his Deposition. A fellow sobbing is a most ungainly sight, like seeing a horse limp.

that he has nothing to say.

it aid matters and move your father to be more disposed to this legal fellow who is swollen with love for his daughter more than a Judge with muffins, if this said legal fellow rapt with speechless admiration for a certain countenance was to place his spectacles firmly on his nose—and dip his pen—and commiserate whole-heartedly with said paternal being in his mercantile misfortune?

no answer to this charge.

ing the sole path, as the said legal fellow sees it, out of anguish and sobs and into illumination namely that glittering Paradise of unearthly delights namely betrothal to said counten

hedging in Little Hangy, by the crab-apple. I saw the Mob come over the crest towards me & I thought it was Whitsun, for they were merry & dressed in their best cloathes & wore ribands. They broke the hedge in many places. Some of them came up to me. I asked them why it was Whitsun now, & where was the feast

I merely blackly gloom my days away to an attenuated end—forever yearning—in the Exile, as it were, of love? No more of this. The Horse proceeds upon the hill in all its creamy glory with men about it like flies, tho' this horse cannot flick its mane. There is a frosty glistening to it of a morning and when the mist settles of a late afternoon I almost think it looms like a spectre, like some ideal mount searching for its rider

I read the Riot Act to the assembled Mob. Upon perceiving the riotousness of the said persons to be unabated, I returned immediately to the House, to await the said force of Yeomanry Cavalry. The force came at about eight o'clock. It was fully light by then and the force proceeded to position itself in the woods behind the Doric Temple as it had been ascertained that the Mob were feloniously intent on causing destruction to my own Household,

most tedious supper, announced by a gong, and a gurgle in the throat from the housekeeper, who does not speak, and has a chin mottled in the pattern of a leaf—as if one has fallen thereupon, and sunk in long ago. The Squire, when intoxicated, glares across the dining-table as if intent on finding in one's waistcoat the horizon that might settle him, and his voice has no need of a speaking-trumpet were it to be issuing instructions on a battlefield. He has eyes like a cotter's windows under thatch—suspicious, yet promising warmth that on further exploration—turns to a chill—and grows damper by the long hour, until it altogether hisses into a kind of well, dark and dismal. Yet on the morrow he will be in a crumpled cheerfulness, and all bustle—if the weather allows it. His White Horse has turned him boyish, tho' he powders his head in the fashion of his portraits. Several of the farmers here wear pigtails still. Yesterday I visited the House (a stiff and lofty pile) to Examine (if that term might be used of the discourse) his Lordship Chalmers. His ears are uncommonly large, and his nose looks at you in the place of eyes. He has a thumb-joint that clicks alarmingly in the spaces between words, like a fowling-piece. But I don't think him a bad fellow.

saith: he does not answer the Charge for it will not stand

& we went riding. The rides here are thro' beech. Beech and more beech, and then downland—nay more more & more downland. The whole world might be composed of turf & nibbling sheep, were one to be as these peasants, and not venture forth enough miles to break the downland spell—and see happy clay, and our sweet Thames. There is a dreadful Rollingness to these wretched minds, that need a right-angle sorely to shake them up. I am not a bad rider over gates and hedgerows, tho' I have never taken horse out of London before. I stumbled only once—in an infernal patch of briar and mud that nearly had me threwn headlong. How does Matlock, sweetest Emily? The Special Commission arrives in a fortnight: I must have all the Briefs ready. We hear report that Field Marshal the Duke of W. himself will sit with the Judges, as if their scarlet will not terrify these wretches enough without that great Nose. They shall be dealt with in batches of twenty, or the assize will last till Doomsday—or certainly over Christmas. Alas—still a hundred remain. I must haste them on—they persevere in telling one every twist and turn, as if they are embarked on a yarn of the sea—of marvellous Adventure, such as I would hear from my father as a boy. One has to cut these yards of fustian cloth, as a tailor for a dwarf. A few, I am grateful to report (these the hardest & most guilty) say nothing, and set their jaws (tho' their hands tremble). Sometimes I am in a fog of accent, that is made blinder by the majority of the labourers having severe catarrh, arising (or so I am informed by the Doctor, a bristly young fellow) from the draughts in their dwellings, or the wet straw they reportedly sleep on—but whatever the origin of the Complaint, it causes their accents to sound as tho' slinking past—sunk into themselves, as it were—a quality that makes interpretation a deal more difficult. I have a man beside me, a local fellow of some education (he writes verse)—who lights my way by Translation. So the days pass without you, sweetest Emily.

I do not know who carried the shillings

My regards to your Uncle, & Mrs Hawkes.

Lancelot Heddin of Ulverton labourer aged 27 who was apprehended at Ulverton House on the morning of the 22nd of November and has been discharged on his own recognizance to appear and answer at the Sessions—stated on his Examination on the 5th of December as follows

not a carpet or rug in the place: all is beeswaxed floors and the whole resounds like a perpetual thunderstorm when persons are moving about. The distance the Examinants must cross to stand before my table is a decent one, and I must wait until the echoes of their approach have taken leave of the room (by dint of not finding another wooden surface to bounce off) before I open my mouth at all. It is a very old house, with a groaning flight of stairs too dark—and grim diamond-paned windows—and more beam than is good for the constitution of one's pate. There is a smell of stables throughout. I will soon be munching oats. Please to send more water-colourings—to see the brush of your fair hand in a blue wash of sky is to see Heaven through a sunlit cloud

forced the unwilling. We passed the Gore and into Gumbledons Bush

Horse—who be truly very large—is now complete, barring the eye, which is to be made of smashed glass (Norcoat's servants have been breaking drained Port and Brandy bottles against the walls all morning, an infernal clatter that has set my teeth on edge)—I find the idea vulgar, but appropriately reflective of the progenitor's thirst as much as soul. I had to Examine a beggar this morning, who used foul language against the Squire in his capacity as justice of the Peace, upon which insult our good fellow clapped the bad fellow (who stinks unmercifully) in the Cage, or Blind House—this being a place as small and low as those confined there, off the aforementioned Square—dating from the halcyon days when this settlement was sufficiently swaggering to have its own penal dwelling. The poor fellow being almost blind, I could not draw a word of sense out of him, but only a kind of self-pitying jabber. If he had not been released—he would not now be up for robbery and extortion: he was unlocked by the Rioters. That is an anecdote for your uncle's supper-table, a perfect Exemplum to puff his melancholy. How does his illness fare? If my readings of judicial oratory (I know Lord Erskine almost by heart) has served any purpose, it would be to move your uncle to spill his doubloons out of his codicil as your beauty evidently has not. 'I say by G–d that man is a ruffian who shall, after this, presume to build upon such honest artless conduct as an evidence of guilt.' I have been practising my Lord Erskine in the mirror. I will solicit with the eye and the hand & the voice and woo him from your father. 'Such, my lords, is the case.' I am not very good at tones of thunder, however: my frame buckles frigh

'Why beest thee here, John? What beest thee about?' He answered that it was because they were starving, and that I knew the state of the Poor, who had not enough maintenance to keep a wife and children, and that I must support them and break my machine, that was taking the bread from their mouths, and raise my wages to 2s a day, and half a crown after Ladyday, & they wd have £4 from me. Then Moses Perry came forward & said he was the treasurer, for he was always so for the collection at Whitsun. He had a basket. I took them to the Barn and shewed them as I had already broke my machine, but if the Rector did not lower his tithes, I could not be giving them 2s a

the Eye is in. From afar, it looks quite horrid—it has struck the children here quite dumb with fear. Indeed—this is a quiet place. I am, I must confess, treated without civility: a kind of contemptuous pall of neglect towards betters hangs over the cotters—who seem alarmingly swarthy, as tho' rubbed in charcoal—O for thy fair curls, thy angel's countenance, my Emily! I ope your Locket with abandon. Here is too grim, for so many men have been taken into custody that there is an effect as after war, when the women folk slouch about in shawls and turn their heads as one passes. I do not know how they will deal with the Rioters, my heart. Lord Melbourne at the Home Office was appointed in the middle of all this Trouble, and is more resolute than Peel. I think we shall have some Examples made. But surely not 2,000, which is the full number. Melbourne has made Norcoat furious, for Squire Norcoat cannot sit on the bench—local magistrates are perceived too soft for this, tho' some are harder than flint, & clamour for the rope—for all breakers—without reprieve. I do not feel hard, but I had a stone cast at me last week, & I have had a letter, in a very poor orthography, informing me that my name 'is drawn amongst the Black Harts in the Black Booke', that I am 'a blaggard Enmy of the Peeple', and I must make my Will. Do not fear a moment, my sweet child: these fellows are thoroughly cowed, and this is but the twitch of the dying

bee a hard task, Tom.'

Your father has been written to.

& staid the evening

then to exercise my hand, grown crabbed from the pen and these desultory tales, I walk briskly up the road swinging my arms

said 'That's a good little lot there, Mr Stiff.' He answered that they would be having no less, or there wd be more agitation. He threw it upon the stone of the Court yard. The said John Oadam gathered it up and holloed: he wore a crown of bedwine, that was in beard

uire looks through his telescope at the infernal Horse, tho' he has no need: it struts over us big as a clou

He had some wild Clymatis wound about his head that resembled a Savage's cap of feathers, I believe this was to denote his captainship. I heard one of the Mob refer to him as 'Captain Swing'. He called out we are all one,

capons boiled in their bladders, roasted venison with a marinade of veal, fried ducklings, a complete little cygnet from the Lake, Westphalia ham and a calf's head hashed with larded liver, with ice cream and blancmange as an afterthought. I was the lowliest fellow there, but acted royally. Lady Chalmers referred to me throughout as the Bench: she has a grip like sugar-tongs.

John Oadam saith: that he has nothing to say to these Charges.

but took a coach to Bath. I had to wrest myself from there on the Sunday evening but I staid one night & sipped and ate and Conversed with the civilised. I noted, to my horror, halfway to a theatre, that my waistcoat sported a splash of Chalk upon the breast. It will not remove itself with water. The stagecoach dropped me very late at the turnpike crossing & I walked back without a moon: white to my knees, my cloathes ruined. Infernal country!

I saw the said shepherd Bunce kneel and fire the straw beneath the said iron Plough.

opening ceremony was conducted with appalling seriousness, and All who Matter in the neighbourhood stood about this muddy turf silently cursing its blanched steed, that is taking the field at full stretch—tho' on the grassy lip of its haunches one recognises nothing but a deal of white chalk and the fact one is chilled to the bone. It is attempting to outflank, as it were, the ancient at Uffingdon, to which attaches much superstition: indeed—I have heard it stated that its eye is hollowed by generations of barren females coupling with the moon. I doubt our Squire Norcoat's equestrian challenge to be efficacious in this respect, or to attach to its bony fetlocks and glistening retina anything more than amused indifference. But the fellow is exceedingly puffed up with his creation. I will retain the sight of him bellowing through his Speaking-Trumpet on that far hill for the rest of my years, and shall (I warn you now) regale it to my grandchildren long after all memory of the Law has departed my brain.

doused the candles in the stable. A man with a basket stood against the Door & the carters came out with straw. Some others heaped straw beneath the iron Plough. It was not light enough to see their Faces, tho' I heard one say

round and about again, the identical histories—or histories I must hope are identical, else the mis-match might prolong the Prosecution to a tedious extent. I nudge here and there—for one will have a lanthorn where there has been always a candle—and another a candle where there has been always a tinderbox. Dearest Emily, I have numbed you with my Legal gossip: how does your breathing now, out of the city? And what of Uncle after your father's visit? Does he still smile on us from his ebbing bed? Have you broached the Subject again? A simple stroke of the pen would do it, but can he see? Did your father meddle in his drawer? I am exceeding vexed. My coat is almost out at elbow. Your father cannot have all. How long it takes to weave the cobweb (which is the Will) and how quick to tear it down (which is the Codicil). How, if we are to hang upon your father alas—am I to shift his judgement of me? My letter to him has not been answered. My head swims with all this—round and about—like a whirl-

desperate fellows in the main. They are well-known abouts and are unmarried. They had blackened their faces with soot,

chalked right across the door: 'We have Not yet Dun.' Squire in a heat: thunder on the stairs, & in the pantry. In the Riots, he was conciliatory—says Wellington is a ruffian, for Wellington made suggestion that the magistrates hunt them down for sport with horsewhips and fowling pieces. If Squire were to have his way, there wd be Prison only for these fellows. His own farm has lost three ploughmen and a pig-man, two of whom might hang and all are certain to be transported—if the Briefs do their work. I say to him the Law, in this case, must act as the Example to some, and be merciful to others (we cannot have 2,000 guilty—our prisons are already stuffed with them, and there will be more agitation). He says, that is not our way: he blames all on the machines—and certain 'Radical scoundrels'—& France—and mutters darkly against the tithes—and wd against our local Lord, if he was not enamoured of the dark wine up there, that is served in crystal. Most tedious supper yesterday, at the Doctor's—much of the party & their daughters of the mind that we shd bring the price of Bread lower, & feed these fellows. I said we cannot have robbery, Arson, extortion & machine-breaking without shewing how Diabolical these acts are, or tomorrow our transport ships wd be lower still in the water with the consequence of imaginary grievances—that we must nip in the bud, to save the flower—that Lord C. is for swinging the Mob in toto—that these Horrid acts must spread like a Contagion without hard medicine—and other such ruminations, that impressed the Assembled no end, as all visitors from the Town must, tho' they be cork-brained as the wine. The company included the Archdeacon of Salisbury, a plump fellow by the name of Fisher, & his friend Mr Constable the painter, who then broke out of gloom to strike a somewhat stained fist upon the table, spluttered against various types of dregs—was all for sluicing out the rabble forthwith—that the agitators of Reform were sent by the Devil—that Mechanicks must be kept solitary or their evil dispositions wd be fanned into flame—thus buttressing my argument, but with a degree of passion that almost undid the whole. He is sketching the Cathedral in Salisbury for a great work which shall shew a rainbow over the edifice—this the Ecclesiastical Government according to the Archdeacon, whereupon Mr Constable broke into an exceedingly admirable discourse on opticks, and the lustre of wet grass, and the calm white edges of moving clouds being his soul—or the wet grass was—or both at once—leastways he ended by stating that Paradise was a slimy post in a ditch, or some such, which provoked all present into peals of mirth. Upon returning to the subject of our troubled times, one daughter, of a fierier disposition, stated—looking at me as the chief organ of this illumination—that 'twas hard to call it Extortion, for the like shillings-round was done at Whitsun for the feast, & was an ancient practice in all the villages, & that the labourers were dressed as for this Procession—in ribands & suchlike, & blew horns as on that day. Thereupon there fell a hush, and a clearing of throats—& I kept, as Lord Erskine wd have done, an auspicious silence—that cowed the company quite—until I spoke but these words with a serious demeanour: 'I see no blossom on the trees, madam. Pray excuse me, I did not know it was Whitsun here, & Extortion in London.' This made enough break into laughter, as to patch the threadbare situation. So I hone my rhetoric even at the table. I keep to the road and take a servant with a lanthorn, for I will not be bludgeoned to death in this wretched hole. I am almost finished—the wigs will be huffing and puffing in the

Courthouse next Thursday. The tightness in my chest is gone—I am better with the medicine—tho' this cough hangs

that many were starving. The said Rector Willington answered, that he & his fellows must leave at once, but here is 3 Sovereigns, and he would be seeing to their requests. I staid by the fireplace until the Mob left. As I served the Rector Willington with some kidneys, he said to me that I must not go out this day, and that he hoped the Church wd not be ent

the dregs remain: I stir them to a kind of cloud of comprehensibility, but their minds are slow and stupid, and they slouch, as it were, without a burden on them but one of sloth. My clerk tells me they are weak from hunger—but this cannot be in such provident country, of rich tilth, when the very Hedgerows have been evidently dripping with fruit. But O this wretched winter!—I am feeling pinched and vexed today, from an incident earlier: some children, seated before what I perceived to be a tumbled-down cot—but was on closer inspection teeming with life as a corpse teems with maggots—on the outer edge of the village, whence I was bent on exercising my legs after a crabbed term of duty at my desk—these ragamuffins (all of the most swarthy hue, like sweeps—it appears to me this whole village is inked in dirt) followed me at a distance until I reached the first ridge of the hill, whereupon they stirred themselves to a clamour of the most injudicious calumny against my person, as being knock-kneed—scrawny-necked—the smallest pig in the litter—a 'carroty-pawled cadger' and other descriptions I will not blush you with, all in a dialect so ripe as to be barely comprehended but by those, like myself, forced to become adepts thro' no fault of their own—and upon my waving my walking-cane at them, knob-first, and calling them to be Off, a large fellow joined them, of as Outdoor an appearance as all the labourers here, but somewhat more bent in the back, with filthy black hands—& who stood and watched me for a moment, with a hand upon the shoulders of the Riff-raff about him, as (I thought) a prelude to cajoling and punishment—but who then emitted a chortle that kindled the like in his brood (for I guessed he was the Father) and I was forced to beat an ignominious retreat over the Ridge and out of sight, where I was taken with a small Fit—for I have never been able to withstand Mockery of any sort, but crumble like a Biscuit in hot tea. Such topsy-turviness makes me fear for the Country, as if every weedy word of these inflammatory pamphlets have seeded themselves deep in the fallow hearts of the peasant classes, and by dint of one's mere presence one Ploughs them up willy-nilly to the surface—and thus may be imagined the Harvest to come. Does it rain the like in Matlock? You might paint indoors, if so. Here we tear up turf—these sodden slopes be our canvas—the foamy Horse is shaped so:

I put the straw beneath the Plough. It was not I who put it to the flame. I don't know who did. Then the pieces of the Machines were placed in a heap in the Court & we

down the widest ride yet I fell from the damned beast into

candles on the table. They were took when the Mob departed. About ten men staid the main of the day, demanding of me beer & bread & cheese all the while, until there was none

hurt, bar a laceration upon my arm. My only black-silk coat, with the pearl buttons, is Chalk from collar to tail. I have been baptised, says the good Norcoat, in the veritable sod. But that is little matter when thou, my sweetest love, art in my mind: your letter, that I have kept in my breast pocket, close to my heart, gave me some service this Morning—or rather, the envelope did—as I was taken with a fit of coughing during an Examination—this an effect of the fall, no doubt—and finding my mouth full of Blood, had nowhere to deposit, but bending down behind the desk as if to pick up my pen, that I had knocked to the floor for this purpose—took the letter from my pocket—released it from the envelope—and used that last sweet-scented vessel as my spittoon. The pauper before me was none the wiser through this salvatory Action, tho' almost night then. There was no moon: I could not see who it was knocking on the Door. A horn was blown and a man made a noise like an owl

all night of thick words like cheese to be cut up, then wake in a sweat, cough

banged on the roof with our hay-forks: there is no upstairs. The said Roger Pennell came to the Window and said not to do him any harm & we answered that we would not crush a flower,

O—O my Emily! But to set it down sends my pulse sudden up, & I fear these palpitations—no, I must cease worrying you on the instant—this fearful sight was made hideous by the night's exertions: I had no sleep—I was too tight in the Chest to lay down & coughed the hours away fearfully but not too much Blood—& our sharp north-east of the last days having turned I thought to exercise myself—at dawn—no faintness—nay, I should have stayed within—

were civil. They broke the drum of the machine with a sledge-hammer, and said it was to make better times. I did not know which men they were

muffled from the mist I assure you, my heart. Suffice to say, as I mounted the opposite slope, & the mist clearing, I turned & saw—but the Rooks upon the ridge above, & their infernal clamour, combined with the sight—& made me flushed—& fair giddy—so that I was forced to sit upon a mossy log, until my wits recovered—that I was not mad

about two hundred & fifty of them. They were carrying flags and a horn was blowing: I saw them tear up the fences upon the crest

to anticipate a thing—& to have it dashed!—but I lack sleep, surely—& these wretched papers, that are too thick, & ever roll from my desk to the floor—but to turn & see such a thing, to have one's mind turned inside out, as it were

with a rake. I saw about two hundred persons come up from the river towards me over the Lawn

Black, black as tho' of a sudden cast into deathliness—that mocked the albescence of the frost about it—yet the Eye glittered still! O Emily—'twas a spectre of the most awful hideousness—that leapt up at me—an effect of sleeplessness—& thin light—O the Squire rails & sobs, yet

John Oadam, with a crown of Bedwine (meaning wild Clymatis) wound about his head like feathers & took from the Hedgerows. When I took the said Prisoner into custody I said to him to remove his Crown of bedwine for it was unseemly, and he was no King, not even a Captain

not bombazeen—as you must don soon if our Expectation is correct, my heart—nay, not cloth but soot—common soot—& cinder! Aye—this—awful change but the work of these secret surly creatures, that no doubt hoarded every crumb of charred stuff out their meagre hearths—& scraped their chimneys free of all ancient & inky detritus—then last night like sheep—nay, like wolves—like wolves silently & cunningly—we all unawares, in our rooms—softly mounting that slope—no doubt the whole Mob of them—man, woman & child—all—with bare hands—Donkeys—pails—I can conjecture only—such awful silent cunning—of wolves—and I coughing upon my bed unawares, all the while—they wd have heard—over the night—across the vale—but half a moon—my coughing, & a frost—such stillness—O Emily—scattered about & trampled with ne'er a creak of pail, not a cry!—till that chalky gleam was blinded—doused—to the last—the very last hoof

answering: 'No it bee only plumes of seed that must be planted on the wind

1859

S H U T T E R

Plate XXV

A RIVER-SCENE

Here once more the transient poetry of nature is most eloquently caught, and I am emboldened to suggest that no brush, wielded by whatever genius, could fashion the rushing water about the rocks with so fine a hand as my humble lens. Though recent rains had swollen the course of the Fogbourne to a considerable degree, this day began clear and fine; but in the time it took to set up my apparatus, the clouds (visible to the left) had altered the light considerably. Passing as they did quite slowly across the sun (being early spring, this was not sufficiently low as to be concealed by the foliage upon the left bank) they imparted a most attractive possibility, that reminded me of none other than the painter Herr Friedrich and his stormy effects. The girl upon the bridge is placed to conceive human variety, but I had a deal of difficulty in persuading her to look into the water, and not at my lens!

The bridge is called Saddle Bridge, and is the southern 'gate' into our Village; in rendering a picturesque quality to the subject, its severe state of disrepair serves an ideal purpose, that is naturally lost on those having to clatter across in the dustier world of affairs: indeed, that absent parapet-stone, like a gap in a set of teeth, was reputedly dislodged by nothing heavier than a rook alighting upon it!—causing a coachman a deal of trouble with his reins. The bare poplars upon the right-hand bank assert perspective, and impart a certain grandiosity to the scene, in which the figure of the human might symbolise the fleetingness of our existence. As fleeting, indeed, as the beam of sun that peeped through a slit and silvered the wet rocks in the foreground; an effect one might wait two hours for, and lose in a minute.

Reflections in slow-moving (or still) water, have preoccupied a majority of photographers for quite natural reasons: the beauty of the conception requires merely a stand of trees upon a bank, and favourable light, to succeed—but, it should be cautioned, the result may be as a thousand others. Here, however, the water, upon skipping about the foreground rocks in (as it were) its whitest frocks, takes a tiny plunge and settles, before passing under the darkness of the bridge, into the slow calm that so gratifyingly mirrors, and barely corrugates, that ancient stone arch—to form an O that puts one in mind of gateways, and entrances, and elicits quite other responses from the conventional. And yet, note how the contrary plane of the water surface, highlighted by the glints of leaves and other such matter the river carries upon its bosom, returns the viewer to the strong current of plain reality—which, perhaps, this country girl has averted her gaze from, seeing only fulfilment in the rippling other-world of her fancy!

Plate XXVI

THE PROPOSAL

This may occasion surprise, as I am not given to the artificial posing so beloved of my contemporaries in the field of both plate and canvas. Notice, dear viewer, the abashed and twisted posture of the girl—and the blur that should have been, if ordered circumstances had prevailed, the face of her admirer. No, I did not set up my apparatus with a clatter, then move the limbs of my lovers like so many waxworks, and introduce the boat, whose oars had never before been subject to the young man's sturdy grip. Why otherwise is there that hazy penumbra about the girl's hand, caught in the act of wiping away collected moisture from the summer heat (for you have no doubt noted the elms beyond in full leaf, and the absence of smoke from the distant cottage, and the creamy frock) or the man's foot so ungainly twisted inwards as he leans forward—as if the boat is drifting from the bank and he might lose the touch of his love's fingers, or topple her into the languid water?

On fine summer days of good light, preferably on a Sunday, when the fever of the week's activities ceases, and the drone of the plump bumble-bee is the busiest sound above the sigh of the waters by the mill, the clanking of buckets at the well, and the idle chatter of the population at the wayside (or, alas, upon the tavern benches!), then nothing pleases better than to wrap my machine in brown paper, leaving but a slit for aperture, and wander the Village and its environs for human subjects that may be caught without that formality of response, that considered design and self-conscious air, that the posed picture erstwhile involves. Indeed, in this wise we gentler sex have a distinct advantage, for what better use my otherwise cumbersome crinoline, than as a type of black hood or cover?—if pockets be cut into the material, so that the camera may be held within and remain unseen.

Imagine my pleasure, then, when faint murmurings came to me upon the towpath, and on creeping forward what should I have seen to my astonishment, but the oldest and loveliest of all scenes—two lovers in a boat, in the first and most innocent bloom of love: that first courtship which Shakespeare and all our immortal poets have, at their most exquisite and poignant, immortalised for the world to cherish. May I add my own small reed upon the altar, with this picture, which has as its protagonists not the Illyrian lords and ladies but the rustics of Arden. Or—to be more prosaic and (in the true manner of this art) precise—two of the labouring class, whose vessel is a craft belonging to the butcher and renowned for its leaking qualities, that has soaked the hem of my own dress before now (it serves as the general *factotum* for the Village at a penny a time). With (I might say) only a moment's hesitation, I plucked this bloom in its full glory—or rather (as might be conceived from the girl's attitude) in its 'crumpled bud' phase, for Silvius appeared distinctly unripe in these matters (he is, I later ascertained, the eldest son of the harness maker, and she a horseman's daughter—though whether yet happily bridled is not for me to say).

This part of Ulverton is called of old 'the Vanners'—for what reason I cannot discover. Bottom Bridge is just concealed by the verdant curve; though mediaeval in origin, it is little more than a footbridge, of partly wooden structure, and is soon to be replaced, thus removing the reliance of carriages on the oft-flooded ford beside it. I made several attempts to photograph this bridge, but none was successful. It is said, in the less enlightened corners of our parish, that long ago it was the haunt of a woman, whose love for a man (a departed seaman) went unrequited: until, after many years of waiting upon its boards, she donned widow's weeds, threw herself from the rail, and quickly drowned. My lack of success was no doubt due, in the view of these credulous folk, to the woman's ghostly presence—that blacked out the plates.

Plate XXVII

THE HOUSEHOLD OF SIR HUMPHREY CHALMERS, M.P., AT ULVERTON HOUSE

The posing of large groups should present no special difficulties, if it is remembered by the enthusiastic photographer that heads and hands are forever eager to make their mark and ruin the picture in fuss and needless business, especially where head supports are undesirable. Long exposure is necessary for full detail: it is to be noted here, for instance, that the gold buttons of the footman (fourth from left) are exactly rendered; for the occupation of this gentleman means that the frigidity of good posing presents him with no difficulties, used as he is to 'standing guard'. The plump figure slightly to the front is the steward: his stovepipe has exaggerated the trembling of his head (the result of an injury received, I was informed, as a drummer boy at Waterloo) and I might, if I were (God willing!) to repeat the exercise, request that this good man remove the offending headwear. On the either extremity I have turned the ladies (parlourmaids only) inwards, so that the eye is drawn to the centre of the group, thence to the magnificent copper beeches behind, and so to the house. On the extreme left the edge of the lake might be regarded as a distraction, being heightened by the two swans, but such a picturesque detail could hardly be rejected, and the weighty stature of the house supersedes all else. I do not know what the faint figure in the extreme rear of the picture was doing, for I did not notice him at the time: it must be stressed, that the photographer on this sort of commission must make as sure as possible that the area within the camera's purview is cleared of distractions.

The large laurel hedge to the right, beyond the first beech, is home to a curious, and apparently veracious, legend—though I have heard other versions: a humble shepherd, by the name of William, employee to the Chalmers family in the middle years of the last century, would hide within the said shrubbery in order to view secretly his adored mistress. His distraction eventually forcing him to sea, he ended his days under the lash of an overseer's whip upon a sugar plantation—his visage being so darkened by his downland office, that he was taken for a black in those merciless times. Ulverton House is a fine example of the work of Sir John Vanbrugh, though the Gothic hall on the right is a recent addition. The gardens were laid out by the renowned William Kent, but have undergone numerous minor alterations since that date. A Royal visit, by our own sovereign, was made here a few years past, and it was for that reason the terrace was hung with thirty Venetian-glassed wrought-iron lamps, the fine detail of which is fully visible in this picture, despite the distance from the lens. The foreground distortion of the lawn is, I need hardly explain, owing to the wide angle of the subject.

I might add that the somewhat surly expression of the assembled group (in particular the two stout gardeners with their lawn-mowing machine on the right) may be explained not only by the difficulty of retaining a smile for some minutes, but also by a cold East wind that was blowing at that time across the lawn, lifting up the odd dry leaf, and affecting detrimentally the sharpness of the large dress of the governess (fifth from right) that has billowed alarmingly—a hazard with all outdoor work. Since most domestics are naturally of a surly disposition, at least in this writer's experience, I have once again rendered the facts visibly and honestly, and improved nothing.

Plate XXVIII

A COTTAGE ROOF

The enthusiastic photographer must always be on the watch for Nature's tiny miracles: those effects which urban dwellers lack, and in their smoky habitat grow dulled from, so that the soul remains unmoved by simple glories. Herein is the principal task, then, of the new art of the lens: for what other purpose must we serve but the bettering of humankind, in the bringing to its attention that miraculous system that has its being all about us but that we too easily take for granted: for Time hurries us on, and our needs make us blind.

Here is a simple cottage roof—or rather, a detail from that structure—to illuminate and (if I may be so bold) impart instruction of a spiritual nature. The original is to be discovered down a muddy track known as Surley Row, at the northern extreme of the village, and presents, to the uninitiated observer, a most dilapidated and unattractive prospect. But it is in these areas that the photographic artist wanders with most reward: nothing more profoundly salubrious than an old stone wall, nothing richer than a bedraggled plum-tree, nothing more enticing than a raven's discarded feather, or a dust-filled barn spread with ancient sacks, or a pond wherein the weeds lie dank and idly swaying! For upon these surfaces lies a cornucopia of satisfying differences, that the lens, with its unavailing sincerity, and its unjudging eye, captures upon the plate with a fidelity of draughtsmanship the great Leonardo might have envied. My own soul is moved, not by the ornate sculpture of a great house, or the sighing willows of a great garden—but by the winter branch, the puddled track, a white surf of Shepherd's Purse in a meadow, the silvery plumes of Traveller's Joy upon a hedgerow, the frayed hem of a cotter's shawl. And here, dear viewer, note what riches are to be found if only the eye would seek them out! This is no longer the moss-grown, decaying, vermin-ridden blanket beneath which poverty strives to keep the chill at bay, but a glittering tapestry of loveliness, a source of meticulous meditation, and an assurance that even the humblest and most wretched of abodes is not neglected by the Almighty's brush.

For the frost being severe that January, I noted how, the thick rime on the roofs having melted, the released water ran down to the very tip of each inclined stalk of straw that had been its host—and hung there, as if the simple thatch was unwilling to release its sudden adornment:

when the sun shone, as it did frequently that crisp winter, the whole glittered with a beauty beyond compare, transforming what was sullen and coarse into a sublime perfection. I made several studies of this phenomenon, but I have included here the one which, however inadequately, comes closest to capturing that bejewelled effect—as the Dutch painters once caught the sheen of silk, or the exquisite hint of canker in a peach's bloom, upon their small canvases.

Plate XXIX

ACROSS THE DOWNS

No more suggestive subject than an ancient road, redolent of the past! Here the main highway from our village, where it rises up across Mapleash Down, has served my purpose. If the reader wishes to photograph a road—whether the broad confidence of an old turnpike, or the meddlesome ruts of a track—then choose a day after rain, when the sun is out, but the earth still moist: then see, as here, how the way gleams with a silvery tone, up to the farthest horizon, if the sun be before you, but not so directly in front as to blind. No longer are the pools and brimming ruts a menace to polished shoes, a trial to the scrubbed gig, a curse on the coachman's coat-tails: to the enthusiastic photographer these silver islands are like beacons to a better world, for they lead the eye of the viewer towards the far hills, the distant copse, the shadowy combe: those horizons that speak of sublimities, though the path be hard and long.

On either side, you may notice, the turf of the downland pasture is lacking in details, and dark: but this is quite deliberate, for the road then shines with greater contrast, its curving nature sinuous as the scales of a serpent. Indeed, keeping in mind the very conditions of light essential to the effect, this *chiaroscuro* can hardly be avoided. The great oak upon the right, known popularly as Sam's Throne, its trunk conveniently splashed with the chalk, gives weight and interest to the middle distance, which might otherwise be too sparse—while the glint of the iron catch on the gate in the far distance was, I am content to confess, a happy accident.

You may wonder why it is I have no human interest in this picture—no weary pilgrim leaning against the tree, or plodding his hedge-shadowed way. It is imperative to remember that a human interposition immediately subsumes any sublime feeling in a work; there is a kind of sublime melancholia, I suggest, here present, that arises out of the suggestiveness of a presence just around the corner, or about to come into view—for no road is made for anything other than human passage. If that passage be absent, as here, how pure and clean becomes the metaphor! The spectator is drawn towards his own destiny, in which no one truly shares but our watchful Creator. Only the passing of past generations resounds in all its invisible ghostliness—the tramp of legions, the earls on their palfreys, the peasants bent under their faggots—while those generations to come, the snorting of traction engines and the whip-cracking chaises, lurk in the shadows of destiny.

Plate XXX

THE BLACKSMITH'S SHOP

Here, under the great and cooling shade of the chestnut, Frederic Moon plies his ancient trade. In the long-ago past of pagan mystery, the Evil One passed near Ulverton, and demanded of the smith his service: the smith declined to shoe those terrible hooves, and was turned to stone. The Devil thereupon limped away, leaving his mark in a curious depression on Louzy Down, that the less imaginative say was the quarry for our White Horse (see Plate XV, *ibid.*), that canters (albeit somewhat grey and brambled) upon the same slope. The stone rests, rain-worn, but still (from a north-easterly angle) shaped like a man bent over an anvil, on the brow of a nearby hill, and rare is the villager that dares approach it at full moon, when the forlorn striking of iron on iron is said to echo across the vale.

Happily, in these Christian times, Mr Moon (coincident name!) is asked to cradle nothing more terrible than a nag's leg, as here he is doing. Alas, no amount of cajoling can persuade a horse to keep its head from moving, or tail from swishing, however firm the hand upon the bridle—and Mr Moon's strapping assistant, Master Harry Dimmick, did all in his powers to still the beast. The trestle, grindstone, and other sundry items were purposefully arranged, as in a painter's canvas, to please the eye—much to the amusement of the fellows, who were more used to tossing their tools onto the most convenient spot at hand! Indeed, I requested that the rain-barrel against the wall could be shifted more firmly to the right of the picture, thus counter-weighting the window on the left, but they claimed (in great consternation) that it instantly, and without hesitation, would fall apart, and its precious liquid (this was late summer) be given to the dust.

The older folk, on viewing this operation, were heard to remark how the village was without a smithy for a full year, some thirty-odd years ago. On requesting the reason for this improbable occurrence, I got little satisfaction beyond a few murmurings of 'that trouble', or 'that gurt black day', until one old dame of great spirit informed me that, 'old Dick Bowsher was transported for seven year, an' passed away out yonder, poor soul'—to a silent applause of slow nods and grim faces. Mr Bowsher being the village blacksmith, and accompanied on his sad voyage by several other fine bodies from the locality (their leader, a Mr Oadam, having been dealt with capitally), no replacement was to be had (or, I venture to suggest, desired) and the smithy fell almost into ruins. The crime of said persons? A desire for living wages, and a fear of machinery, that sprang forth in those riots of some thirty years ago, that caused the nation such alarm, but were snuffed out with a ferocity one can only feel belongs to less civilised nations (see Plate XXXIV, *ibid.*), and that has not brought any marked improvement in the lot of our poor John Hodges.

Plate XXXI

AFTER THE HARVEST

Again, I draw the reader's attention to the minute particulars in our surroundings—whether they be rustic or urban—that serve the photographer so efficaciously. This is, indeed, an Example whose title exercises that faculty in the viewer, and once exercised, I venture to hope that the said viewer will depart into the world with a surer eye. For where, you might ask, is the subject? Here is another road (I am partial to roads) and there is a part of a field, and hedgerows, and a clear sky (those sooty black specks are not the outcome of mishandling, but are passing birds—many the image marred by those spirited creatures!) with a farm of picturesque quality in the near distance, sunk under its four great elms (it is known, in the appealing way of country nomenclature, as Five Elms Farm)—but where is the rustling, creaking haywain? Where the dust of the bringing home? Where the rosy-cheeked children riding the stack?

But look more carefully: something has, indeed, passed this way. It is early morning, and the low sun before us lights the track: the track is dry, and absorbs the light. But there is something other, some strewn matter, that does not absorb—that appears to rejoice in the sun; as if its gleam is a welcome, a memory of happier, golden times—before the fall upon dull ruts, or the hook of the eager hawthorn bough! The textural properties of this matter make of it something like precious metal, gathered by passing wheels into the middle part of the road, where it resembles (in actuality) a golden spine, or a long lock of Rapunzel's hair, with its sheen woven into the distance—but likewise immediately puts one in mind of the mental track, with its golden thread of higher effort, that can so easily be blown into disarray by the gusts of fate and bitterness.

This, then, is the only evidence, dear reader, of all the bustling and moisture and thirst and singing that is harvest-time—but how poignant, how much more poignant, this evidence! And for how long will this precious spill—for precious it is indeed, in the thrifty world of the countryside—be allowed to lie in the dust, to be trampled into oblivion by hooves and cart-wheels?

Plate XXXII

DRAWING THE WATER

Banish from your imagination that Biblical scene when Christ approached the woman at the well, in which the young girl no doubt sports a fair complexion, and pretty hands, and a lithe figure—and replace it, I dare suggest, with this image now before you. No pump or well, in this end of the Village (named, appropriate baptising! Back Lane) but a muddy brook beside a rotting gate-post, which surfaces sullenly from its subterranean passage at this point, and several others, along with its cargo of excrement, and drowned rats, and other choice items off the muck-hills, that are regularly heaped up against the cotter's walls.

Replace, then, the young beauty of your illustration with this actual villager (a Mrs Eliza Pyke): for those sturdy buckets on that sturdy yoke are filled to the brim, and may not be transported by pretty hands, and a lithe figure—but by the form you see before you. It is not a want of fellow-feeling has made her taciturn of expression, but the chafing rub of the wood upon her shoulders. It is not indulgence has puffed out her features, but an eternal diet of white bread and weak tea. She has no need of refinement of posture, or of gesture. Lest she stand fair-square and broad—her back would break.

Where is the water bound? It is washing day. The tub will soon be out, the soil-caked garments soaked and scrubbed—but there is no mangle in Back Lane; no mangle but the arms and hands you see before you, soon to be slapping and twisting and pummelling—for do not pretend to yourself, in your mobile imagination, that those heavy garments will steam merrily before a blazing hearth, when it is wet without (as it was that day). In Back Lane, in Ulverton—in the downland heart of our great and glorious Empire—there are no blazing hearths, but only smoke. Alas, that the necessary minute of exposure has blurred those foul billows to a vague, smudged whiteness across the roofs! For this is smoke which would (if the doors were shut fast) choke the occupants to an untimely death, surpassing far the vile air of Manchester or London—and causing one's attention, on passing these miserable hovels, to be caught by the litany of coughing within: the heartbreak treble of the children, or the bass clatter of a father scouring his lungs. For firewood, dear reader—the kind stacked brittle and dry, perhaps, in your orchard (if you are not partial to coal)—firewood does not grow on trees. It must be gathered, or paid for: and few are the places left for gathering, in this Kingdom of the partridge and the hare!

So do not forget, when you next peruse that holy passage, or don your clean silk stocks—do not forget this image, lest vanity take you by the hand, and lead you from heavy-shouldered Truth to the whirling drapery of Illusion.

Plate XXXIII

DUSK IN THE WOODLANDS

A forest of beech in the summer, seen from without, presents a blank wall of leaf, until (if the wood be viewed from the correct compass-point) the ebbing sunlight, from one flank or the other, shafts through the midst, the front wall of trees grows dark in silhouette, and Nature reveals, as in a suddenly pellucid pool, the secret heart of the wood. This effect is more pronounced, perhaps, in winter, when the natural shadows of the wood still render it opaque from the outside, but the absence of leafage allows a startling brilliance of bronze, or copper, or a bloody red, to strike the boles and trunks of the interior, and as it were illuminate the hidden soul, on a fine dying afternoon. Beech woods, of which there are an abundance around our village, favouring as they do the chalk soil, are the true friends of the photographer: their sinuous lengths, unencumbered by ground shrubbery, rise as the pillars of a cathedral to their exultant heights of transpicuous, gauze-thin leafage.

Until the impossible is gained—and the myriad colours of the universe are arrestable likewise on our silvered plates—we must be content with the play of light and shade, the infinitesimal tremble of texture and tone in a moment's grace, the unencumbered beauty of Nature's pen that brings through our lens, as a richly-laden camel through the eye of the needle, her unsurpassable artistry. So this straddling copse, called Bayleaze Wood, of a spring evening, with the breath of night on the air, and the sweet breath of day folding itself onto the forest floor, becomes the entranced glimpse of a better world, where mystery is gilded, and a thousand paths open up where only a screen stood before.

But wait—there is a human figure: poised beside the broad tree on the extreme left, his pale hat chiming with the creamy stroke of the lopped bole on the far right, he stands proudly in his domain—for this is the woodcutter, sharp axe in hand; though he be but a dwarf, but a dab of dark leather, in this gargantuan realm.

Plate XXXIV

PEASANT WOMAN, OR 'FORTITUDE'

The portrait study, with its long ancestry, and its popularity with those who wish their features, at a certain moment in life, to be recalled without the smoothing generosity of the painter's brush, remains the most illustrious, but also the most easily facile, of all photographic subjects. I confess that, for my living, and to keep in servants, I crowd my studio with the good and the great of our fustian county—magistrates, doctors, barristers, professors, divines, and so forth. But now and again I cajole one who would otherwise never set foot in my room, clamp the head of one who would otherwise remain in a fog of others' memories (until the passage of time had eroded even that brief retainment of uniqueness) and etch each wrinkle, each pockmark, each hair, upon a tablet that dares eternity—for there are no flawed elements to the eye of the camera, but only the God-given grace of living appearance, that holds in every line the years endured, and the spirit borne.

This portrait is my most-loved, but not for beauty: Miss Hannah Heddin (now lately deceased) was sixty years of age when this portrait was taken: her mouth shows a severity—she was never known to smile; but her eyes—see how their hooded lids conceal beneath them a natural gaiety, that is not quite quenched! See how the hands, resting upon the hem of her simple (and threadbare) shawl, for all their chapped sturdiness, and arthritic curves, speak of younger days still—in that brass ring about which the skin has folded up, as a field folds up about a boulder. Only the Gainsboroughs amongst the painters can hope to emulate this poignant entrapment of the years—in which the face itself is, as it were, its own artist; and the photographer the humble recorder with his tricks of glass and light.

And do you see, in this grim-faced, wind-ravaged visage, these fingers that have grappled with unyielding flints, and frost-clung roots—do you see something deeper, more unyielding still, than simple endurance of poverty and air? For I have captured for posterity a portrait of the Outcast, an example of Fortitude in the face of scorn and isolation. Owing to some hidden sin effected long ago, involving (as far as I can gather) the deposition of fatal evidence, in the aftermath of 'that trouble' (see Plate XXX, *ibid.*), she has been cast into a realm, as terrible and solitary as if she, too, had been sent to the Antipodes, and suffered its blazing heat and deep loneliness. If I could have recorded the silence she endures, and the spittle of children, whenever she ventures from her outlying cot—how shallowly you would see the spirit of Forgiveness entered into our communities, and how grand the tragedies played on this our tiny stage!

Plate XXXV

THE VILLAGE SCHOOLMASTER

With his brass spectacles, his starched collar, and his general demeanour of youthful authority, Mr Irvine Leslie, B.A., was an unmistakable pillar of our small but robust community, loudly maintaining that those in his charge were as important to him as any Oxford college. Alas! a back room of the rectory is not conducive to learning, and neither is the absence of books (other than tattered exiles from the vestry cupboard), or paper, or slates, or blackboards; or anything more sophisticated for the inculcation of the very rudiments of the intellectual life, than a ruler with which to crack the three Rs, as it were, into the knuckles of the unfortunates under his care—knuckles more used to the gritty chill of stone and earth, than the warmth of a pencil.

If I seem to berate this gentleman before you now, with his curling smile, his smooth skin, his elegant forelock, his gold-ringed fingers and his shiny silk coat (fitting contrast to the previous portrait), then it is not for his inability to surmount these pecunious obstacles to instruction, whether moral, religious, or scholarly, that I do so; for his very appearance ought to have struck admiration out of the rough green shoots in his care, however irregularly they besought themselves to that dingy room which is christened, by some quirk of meagre endowment, the Ulverton National School for Boys and Girls. No, a very Titan of teachers would have lasted no longer than he did (two years), with likewise no more to show for it than a broken ruler, and some inane parroting of portions of the Book of Common Prayer—one book, to be precise, shared out like the loaves and fishes until each torn page grows too black and greasy to be read at all. No, it is not for his failures—which are not his, but Society's—that I adopt the stern manner, but his 'successes'. Fled from a student past of gambling debts and general dissolution, he sought to conceal himself in our pastoral fold, under a respectable wing, and there set about the business of shaking once more that trollop Scandal out of her brief slumber.

Need I say more? Surely not—merely look upon the face my lens has so ruthlessly caught, and see how the corrupt life has slackened the mouth, and watered the eyes, and swollen that handsome nose, yet retained its power to lure the wives of our parish out of their boredoms. Yet as suddenly as he appeared amidst us, reaping his poisonous oats, has he vanished now, not a week after this image was recorded in my studio, not a month prior to my writing these very words—vanished one night after a bout of drinking, vanished like a shadow from our conscience, leaving his belongings, abandoning his conquests, fleeing (no doubt) from that dingy schoolroom, wherein the failure of his moral life must have been daily emblemised in every dusty nook and damp cranny, in every grinding moment of a useless routine, in every bored cough and hideously automatic repetition of our Lord's golden syllables.

Plate XXXVI

THE RECTORY TEA

Far preferable, to my mind, is the human subject when revealed in its natural habitat, than in the studio: how much more possible this is, with the instantaneous brush of the photographer's art, than with the slow dab of the painter's! The Reverend Walter Willington, seen here resting from his spiritual responsibilities in the shrubberied glory of the rectory garden, is a remarkable testimony to the healthy nature of a life devoted to quiet worship and devotion to others: he has been rector in the parish of Ulverton for over fifty years—and now, in his eightieth year, the grandchildren of those he once baptised, are in turn wetted at his hands over the ancient font. When he first came, so lamentably attended to was the church, that on striking the lectern for emphasis during his first sermon, the resultant cloud of dust quite hid him from view. Now the perfume of beeswax prevails, a fine new organ has been installed, and a bag of mint humbugs in the vestry is quite emptied each Sunday, so pressing are the numbers of children that worship.

I choose this picture among many I have taken from the Church brethren amongst us, for its peculiar air of peace: innumerable are the times I have sat as a guest at this very table, in this very same creepered corner of the rectory garden, blooming with lilac, and wished myself to be in no other place but Heaven, were this pouring of the tea to continue for eternity. Only the clamour of the rooks in the graveyard oaks, and the murmur of bees clustering at the foxgloves, and the chimes of crockery—only these tell us we are hurrying on, for the shadow upon the sun-dial fools us it is stilled; while the breeze from the downs ripples through unceasingly, with its hint of grass, and corn, and the faint bells of flocks, moving like flecks of foam upon a green wave.

If higher mortals scoff at my celebration of this parochial encumbrance to novelty and brilliance, to the pursuit of innovation and enterprise, huffing and puffing on its gleaming tracks, then let me say only that life cannot always be moving post-haste until it take our breath away, and fill our eyes with smuts, but that stillness and pause are the essence of struggle, and the pith of sobriety. Let the calm of this humble scene, in which the old stone dial (and its motto) serves as our admonition, be as water that settles the dust upon a highway, and slakes the soul.

And so we bid adieu to our English village, slumbering on in its quiet valley, far from the city and its peculiar wants. Let these twenty-four scenes remain as a portrait faithful to an institution that has grown, not as a railway grows—in dust and curses, in mathematical gauging and ruthless application—but as a nurtured seed, that buds too slow to notice, and yet breaks the frost. That is not sown on the wind, but in the rich tilth of an unrecorded history, plodding on between an English earth and an English sky.

Plate XXXVII

EXCAVATION, EGYPT (GENERAL SCENE)

It was with profound delight and honour that I accepted the invitation last winter, from Mr H. Wallis Dobson, to accompany his team in their excavation of an Egyptian tomb complex, at a site I must refrain from disclosing, lest the riches therein be garlanded by other than the British Museum. The subject of the following ten plates is a site from which no gold has been discovered, but rather the priceless metal of the painted image: scene after scene decorates the walls, as freshly coloured as the day, millenniums past, the hand of the tomb painter applied his brush by the flickering tallow.

It may be of interest to note, how industrious the scene is, with its ladders and spades and earth-spills and boxes, its army of Arabian helpers, stripped to the waist in the blazing sun, its dusty air of application—as if a building was being constructed, or the underground railway of Sir John Fowler were being dug into the sand of Egypt, not the clay of London! This was a surprise to me, who had always imagined excavations to be quiet affairs—of one or two bespectacled scholars, handkerchiefs upon their heads, scraping with a trowel in the studious concentration of a library sojourn. May this plate, then, lighten the ignorance of others, as well as myself, and serve as introduction to the images of the far past these heroic individuals revealed to daylight, after unimaginably lengthy time.

Mr Wallis Dobson may be seen in the middle of the picture, with a paper (it is a map—a magnifying glass, essential for the perusal of plates, reveals this clearly), and the clean-shaven young man to his right is Mr Stephen Quiller, his young assistant—an acknowledged expert in the decoration of ancient tombs.

Plate XXXVIII

TOMB-MOUTH

The peculiarly harsh light of the Middle East presents a challenge to the photographer (I need not mention the problems of fine blown sand in the mechanism, or indeed—I may add with feeling—of cholera) that is only overcome by an equally harsh adjustment of one's prior conclusions, arrived at in the soft, wet light of England. I saw, when perusing this subject, how the glare of the desert, and the deep darkness of the tomb's interior, stood in threatening contrast—so forceful that the image might have vanished completely into mere patterns of light and shade, as unintelligible as newsprint in a foreign country.

I waited, therefore, for the hour before sunset (when the workers were prone upon their prayer-mats) to make this plate, that might remind us of the Tomb of our Risen Lord—with the stone set aside, and the narrow opening; to enter which one is forced to crouch, and walk almost on all fours, before standing upright in the chamber, whose air is so cool upon one's moist cheek, that one immediately shivers. I have included Mr Stephen Quiller for a human scale, that the true size of the opening may be ascertained—although it must be said that he is a tall man, and the smallness of the opening may have been thus exaggerated.

If this image also puts one in mind of the stone burial chamber upon the English downs (see Plate XIII, *ibid.*), then in such coincidences of appearance, a long sea-voyage apart, may lie a secret web of knowledge, that once ascertained and drawn out, could provide a key to all mysteries—and make of the past a well wherein our own thirst might be slaked, and our petty confusions buried.

Plate XXXIX

THE FIRST CHAMBER

Mr Stephen Quiller was considerate enough to allow me a full day within this small room, in order for the apparatus necessary to the recording of its appearance to be set in place: ten lamps in all were required, and the smoke from their explosion almost choked myself and my Egyptian helpers, and Mr Quiller himself. The results are, as you can see, wholly satisfactory, and this method is far less laborious than that of the pencil and paper, though the latter is still more effective when close detail is required, in these difficult conditions: for the effect of the sulphur lamps is to whiten some areas overmuch.

I am intrigued, still, by the small object on the upper left—no doubt, as Mr Quiller surmised, a trick of the light: for it does resemble a bird, such as a rook, or a raven, with spread wings—though no image of that kind (indeed, this first chamber is quite lacking in decoration, save a patterned frieze) is to be discerned upon the walls of this room. This puts me in mind of an instance when, in the developing of a forest subject, I saw (to my evident surprise) what appeared to be an old, white-bearded visage amongst the undergrowth—but on closer inspection, I saw to be the happy conjoining of a grass-stalk, and the leaves of a blackberry bush, and a patch of dappled sunlight.

Imagine my relief—that I had not, after all, captured the Daemon of the forest, or disturbed the Spirit of the woods! Such coincidences of light and dark, inevitable in our art, have given rise to the wildest of speculations, and set bolting out of their lairs the creatures of credulity and superstition, that one might have thought had long gone firmly to ground!

Plates XL to XLIV

THE BURIAL CHAMBER: FIVE VIEWS

Emptied of its material riches by robbers soon after the mummified corpse of the immured personage was sealed from the outside world, the chamber here shown nevertheless lacks nothing in atmosphere, in beauty, and in historical interest. Indeed, I stayed a whole morning in its dark interior without surfacing, so entranced was I by its murals; which are highly coloured, and exquisitely executed. Scenes that my ignorance could not provide an iconography for, rippled upon the plastered surface of the chamber walls: harvest dances, the casting of seed, a wedding procession, a birth, and a journey in a reed boat upon tiny wavelets that seemed almost to shiver in the damp air funnelling into the tomb (and more savage scenes of war, and those I can only describe as indelicate)—these and many others surrounded us upon three levels: a pulsating and ancient tapestry, that for several thousands of years was hid in utter darkness—a blindness wherein nothing moved, no dust collected, and not a sound was heard.

Indeed (I hear myself surmising) was it not until the stone slab stirred again that these paintings had, since the paint was first dry, any kind of existence? Without light of any sort, or eyes to pierce the darkness, did not these works lack being—for thousands of years, even—until Mr Quiller's strong shoulders, and those of his assistants, slid the slab back inch by inch, and sent a pencil-beam of light probing over hands, and eyes, and beaks, and feet? As if breath was stirring within them, and their parts were being touched into swelling fact? Did not the first lamp, and Mr Quiller's astonished eyes behind it, act as vivifiers, the torch of grace upon these lost creatures? And was not that non-being meant to last for eternity—these images merely votive in origin, and left for eyes higher, and stranger, than our own?

Look again, carefully, dear reader, upon these ancient scenes: though the conditions of their recording made detail obscure, you may note the tiny glass vase at the woman's eyes, the wrist-guard upon the warrior's arm, the cushion upon the throne, the sacks of corn within the cart and the carter's whip, the horns upon the plodding oxen, and the great sharp-beaked profile of the bird-god upon his delicate ankles. Sudden illness prevented me from completing the record, alas, but reflect on the ease of your viewing, before you ring for sherry, or for tea: a few weeks after my departure, it was noted (I quote from Mr Quiller's recent letter to me) that 'the colours you thought so fresh (particularly the red) are somewhat dulled, and several areas show signs of severe deterioration—something lifting the paint-surface in flakes, as if a scrubbing-brush had been applied. In our opinion it is the sudden shock of the air, and the evil properties of our own breath, that is causing the damage to the pigment. Thus the removal of the walls is not possible, and, when our detailed drawings are completed, we will perforce seal the opening, and shut this masterpiece once again from the light. I am sorry . . . your sudden ill-health prevented you from completing the photographic record, as this would have been of inestimable advantage to us.' How much more fortunate, then, that my camera's small round eye was at hand to capture at least some of these ancient scenes, before they began to perish.

Plate XLV

THE CROQUET GAME

I have placed this delightful Example deliberately here, not only for chronological accuracy (it is the most recent photograph, from this present hot July of 1859) but also to act as a modern comment upon those strange scenes you have just perused: for if this plate were to be found millenniums hence (as is quite possible) what would our after-generations make of this matter of hoops and mallets? Is the personage with one knee upon the grass (the late—alas!—Mr Stephen Quiller—see previous plates, *ibid.*) in obeisance to some unseen, ruthless deity? Are the long black skirts of the ladies donned as uniform for some violent battle or is this a graveyard, and they in mourning before those memorials of curved wire embedded in the lawn? Is the man in the centre, with his weapon resting on one shoulder (our village Doctor, to be precise), the leader of this ceremony, or the victim of some dreadful rite? And what does the ball there, in its indent of grass beside his feet? Why is his mouth open: is his expression one of joy, or terror? And what does the pale woman (myself!) seated in the wicker Bath-chair before the hedge? Is she alive at all—or is she some waxen idol, the Daemon of the proceedings?

How faint our hold on this hour of life! How weak our grasp on the throbbing vein of ambition! How fleeting these teeming generations, sunlit by the great god Ra, then blessed by a redeeming Creator!

You may be wondering whether it was indeed I who lifted and dropped the shutter upon this scene, seeing my own portrait amongst the group: a strong thread (visible in my right hand) usually suffices, if correctly attached, and tug

1887

gate ope now maunt lope about in Gore patch wi' they crusty bullocks yeeeeeeeeeow bloody pig-stickin them old hooks jus yowlin out for grease haaf rust look yaa that old Stiff all pinch an screw all pinch an bloody screw aye shut he fast now hup ramshackle old bugger see med do with a stoop spikin onto post wi' that hang yaa a deal more years nor Hoppetty have a-had boy eh why Mr Perry why ah well they says as old Tom Ketchaside seed his angel a-whiverin over here when he were a-hangin it an en't no Ulver soul alive as ud take he down an hook a fresh gate like that there clangy newfangled metal bugger over-right to this un hup best foot forrud over road hup yea up stir the dust a bit boy on't want no fancy gig a-runnin us down now hup Walters land this side o' road boy haaf witch an a quarter sheep them Walters hup I on't be tellin thee on that old rag yit awhile now Master Dannul nope see old Freddie Moon's work this oh he did like to bang out fancy like they butterfly wings look top be no more nor a shepherd's crook though hup leave the bugger ope they Walters en't put flock nor herd in here for jus about ten year yea up aye bettermost sunked in buttercup now see like haaf the fields all sour grass all goin to ruin eh heft us up a bit hup yea up whoa about hup stop atop here a breath boy hup whoa haaaaa

aye blackthorn hedge down yonder got no Jack Brinn on her now bloody fussock's furze-bush like my 'tache see hoi there Jo why dost grow thy tache like that Jo tells 'em I gets a second drink out of it a-suckin all the beer frath out aye grass in Little Hangy way down yonder be bang ripe to cut allus have bin forrud see aye got my first refreshments in her boy in Little Hangy boy old Mary Stroude as makes a catkin stand up proud as we lads did say oh one while past now aye a little bruisin o' Walters' corn a touch o' frath out the bottle top wi' old Mary Stroude bubbies thee med git lost atween though she be nowt but a scrunchlin now oh age age you on't know arn o' that yit awhile eh boy though thee'd ax I on it aye thee'd ax I on it yaa they soon git naggin boy they soon git naggin as drays thee to fist thy own refreshments out en't nowt sinful in that nope en't nowt sinful in that no ways yaa dang patch down there agin Hangy ater the crab-apple right to Deedy Lane yonder soggy well nigh fall to fall clung old bitch nigh teared the legs off of I when I were no taller nor thee bist boy a-stitchin her up a-follyin they nags as drayed that plough through too click for a chit like I to kip up wi' save I maunt not nope worser nor a fly in traycle seeeeeeeeeeee that dern loco puffer as don't stop for nowt nor narn hollerin agin nope all they navvie buggers a-cuttin through Long Scarp like it were butter gived I brain fag jus a-watchin they cut dern loco line athurt coomb turf all greasy wi' soot look aye our old May our dame Bunce seed he afore he come when I were still grawin boy law she yowls a gurt monster sorta type o' dragon breathin fire an smoke maw chock full o' folk as don't wait for narn goed straight as a furrer on Gore patch save he don't turn about at the headlans see nope old May squawkin like a hare in a trap anigh church till old Rev Willy Humbug come twitterin out an us knows now as it en't no night mare a-thuddin through coomb nope seeeeeeeeeeeeee firsest time back in '46 I reckoned as it were early bumbledores out afore the last frast then thunder o' Doomsday look drat filthy cloud o' black like Old Gooseberry thrashin all we sinners puff puff puff clicketty clack feel he shake the chaak as minds I on old Jack Brinn hedgin oo he could weave a blackthorn quicker'n cobblin a frock old Jack save narn don't need he now wi' this here drat barb wire see thrift thrift eh lay thy gloves up Jack us gone newfangled now look fifty posties bang bang bang an every one o' they tangs rolled straight athurt Whitesheet Haw yonder nor haaf the day were shot law he says I be no sort nor kind o' use now they've grawed that there tackle aye come the fall he'd allus have a beard full o' bedwine plume hoi dost reckon on a Heaven wi' hedgerows Jack allus a nod back fit to bust wi' clouds in the wind o' bedwine plume aye nips ud go up to he an blow

hup aye yea up aye thee be jus no more nor that now boy a cloud o' bedwine plume yea up hup starboard into Forty Acre tut tut gate ope aready out o' mead look aye God rest thy soul thee'd like a tale or two out of I oh bloody rigmarole more like massy on us casn't disremimber boy old Hoppetty Perry knowed it deep thee shouldn't have never goed off to that scholard shop that Eton toff-shop Hoppetty feeled it deep like a shadder in gut a-hoistin thy trunk up strapped down tight like a coffen wi' thy name on boy could jus about read that Master Dannul eh D. R. HOLLAND big white letters thy face all creamy an teeny atop the collar-starch through the winder then a-rattlin off in that dern carriage till it weren't no more but a plume o' road-dust catched I a bit of a wet eye boy now look you ben't be rollin no hoops athurt no peonies nor strollin athurt no coomb agin wi' Hoppetty save you be a cloud o' bedwine plume as I do catch in the corner o' my optics now an agin aye Dinneford's Magnesia for the heartburn Jonas that's my missus I says bugger thy Dinneford's this en't heartburn woman this en't heartburn well kips the wolf from off of our door it do that bit o' gardenin for thy Mam if so be as it does minds I on thee Master Dannul aye heartbroke aye no Dinneford's bloody Magnesia for that

bloody buggerin hell it do catch I a bit of a wet now kip to the headlan off that barley aye old Forty Acre thee can take her forty-one thee have got to run allus my patch Forty Acre for forty year nowt more nor a haaf inch out stitchin up them furrers boy thee'd ax I why no more nor a haaf inch dost remimber why no more than that Mr Perry never Jo boy never Jo thy Mam puttin in her finger atween us call me Jo call me gramver bloody hell I knowed thee from a sucklin babby boy thee'd crawl ater I an I ud give thee petals off o' the blown roses an black currants as ud turn thee gaamy all over thy face Nurse Puff-Guts crass as a windy sow at thy blotched pinner thee'd hang about I boy thee'd hang about I like as if thee were a bit short o' folk in them days why no more nor a haaf inch out Mr Perry why no more eh a deal straighter nor that dern loco line boy layin the top top furrer well thee hadsn't nowt other choice boy stitchin wi'out a crinkle seein as I were head horseman them days see aye aye head horseman bein as old man Barr were a stickler sherp an tight aye sherp an precious tight at Barr's down yonder thatch an brick there yonder aye we'd call him Barley old man Barr as tied I in aye wonnerful faddy sort o' chap please God face like a windfall yit one copper-fine heart boy aye tips an nails o' my boots Jonas ye be the tips an nails o' my boots on't never disremimber that boy tips an nails o' my boots head horse jus afore my leg goed aneath harrer tines see yonder see no never more nor a haaf inch out else the whole bloody lot were crook an whole blasted field patchy as a peg-rug shuttin-up time acause the rest o' them ploughs ud be follyin thee steady as a mill-pond see ten furrer work then boy nowt o' this newfangled flat-work nope oh hide your head in a bucket full o' piss ater that no sort nor kind o' use at all for nowt ater that aye clit a flint or two oo then them handles didn't haaf dance mind aye a haaf inch out no more an that were bended a haaf inch deal too much so best hold tight athurt the brashy stuff an hum hmmmmmm I allus hummed hmmmmmm see helped I kip all steady aye clit they big flints that en't no laaf on Forty Acre aye yea up doin a nancy boy athurt this hang as were out to diddle thee proper one time all goed kinketty click clack dang it coulter singin like it were jumped-up on anvil agin they horses all a-twitch whoa about waywut whoa waywut steady steady hooit waywut whoa about well clipped a heap o' bogglin skulls boy thretty-two horse skulls eh why horse skulls Mr Perry yaa agin the Evil boy aneath the floorboards see weren't no field o' corn one time that scholard teacher bloke that Mr Quiller as allus smelled o' the rose soap telled I as the plague fever did for the old homes up here jus ater the year dot well I'll be dalled they horse skulls weren't no sort nor kind o' use at all agin that afflishun see shed have gived they a sup o' Bovril apiece boy nope crookt my line astead aye aye toppin a furrer out o' nowt but a decent eye agin o' sight o' that bloody stick in the hedgerow well us never had no specs see age see seed about a hundred white bloody sticks in the laas years an didn't say nowt nope didn't say nowt jus prayed Master Dannul prayed for what they call guidance athurt that there they two cruppers heavin afront an droppin they shits yaa more like us knows 'em better nor He do boy they fields yaa every bloody inch aye awmost smelled it if so be as you was off out a quarter inch thy boots telled thee soon enough nope weren't never Him up there as be hard o' hearin nope knowed them bloody fields better nor I knowed myself hup please God yit mind you a good docit pair o' horses were more nor a haaf on it aye aye a haaf on it were that afore thee med reach the turn wi'out a botch behind thee whoa about there steady steady whoa

hey up an back an up an back agin till all they drat lines rolls past thy sight though you have shut up the lot bunkin off home at the close o' journey like thee be haaf in the corner o' mine Master Dannul massy on us well thinkin it be thy voice then only the barleyoyles astir in the breeze nope thee be ten feet aneath young feller thee on't be nope thee on't be nope nope thee on't be dang an bloody buggerin hell no Dinneford's bloody Magnesia nor no Cockle's bloody Pills nor no patent bloody embocation woman in the whole bloody Empire on't be soothin I oh thy Mam on't have I blubberin don't look right wi' a rake I spect telled her I found his hoop Mrs Holland aneath the rhododendrons like that were a botch then certain sure her shriekin like a hare in a trap Dannul Dannul Dannul deep in the rhododendrons Mrs Holland like he'd only jus now rolled he in tssssssssssssss aye thee'd rub thy hands agin this tsssssss why does barley hiss so Mr Perry like the green sey suckin thy hand a-clippin they ticklin oyles atop blouses more like Master Dannul a thousand ladies' blouses slided off that wind be heartsick for she Mother Nature fattenin up they gals afore the strike o' our hooks I think it is the action of the ears upon each other Mr Perry yaa I tells 'ee summat thee ud never be talkin to the likes of I ater Eton had a-larned thee to be a toff boy no holdin o' my hand athurt field ater that boy nope though it don't make nowt right about that as God did to thee no ways look feather in the hawthorn haafway up like a angel bin through see she throwed out all thy feathers boy thy Mam he were larnin they names Mrs Holland I says she says Mr Perry mind your business all they feathers throwed out jay poker tom-tit jenny-wren buntin peewit mag crow she wi' her pink hankercher pickin they up one by one whoa I was larnin he Mrs Holland look that be heron Mrs Holland whoa I remimbers he findin that one Mrs Holland like it was yeserday pink hankercher like they was dirt that on't be Christern pleased as punch he were wi' the grey heron go away she yowls go away like I were a piece o' clat in her eye a piece o' clat that hurted I I smelled they burn boy I smelled they burn

well we on't be gettin miffy on it aye now thee be a angel upperds one o' they host wi' feathers o' gold flied out o' this sturvin stinkin world boy leastways best to go afore sins clag thee up a-handlin on they bubbies an furrers an thoughts as get thy soul all clammed wi' muck or boozin thy way to Old Gooseberry's throat yowlin every inch o' the road chock-full o' sins no hidin that no chizzlin thy way out o' that nope nope

I en't a-treaded no straight an narrer no ways boy bent as a buckthorn that be why I hobbles an groans see afflishun see hast thou took thy Dr Laville's Jonas I says no doctor's stuff no bloody gout liquor woman be curin I save it be hell's fire we all be monkeys now please God I've heared that haaf monkeys haaf angels well I be ape all through by now an Doomsday on't be worser nor my dang rheumatics Master Dannul drat it I en't hardly able to fetch a breath up some times ater rakin thy Mam's lawn though it do kip the wolf from off of our door I says to the missus it do kip the wolf from off of our door if so be as she yangs at I to stop aye them Bursop maids were allus yangers an chivviers that were my big botch not fetchin breath afore it eh gie out ye mucky bugger wi' that slap as don't mean nowt jus thinkin on her squirted more milk out of I than out her cows now age boy age en't left I nowt o' that but a yangin mouth

aye aye well now best foot forrud kip the pot a-boilin casn't do nowt about it boy casn't disgouge what thee hast aready cut oh I remimbers thee jus here like it were yeserday thy face clammed tight with these here black berries that firsest time boy on't never be black an ripe for thee this year now hup flatulence Mr Perry thy Mam says flatulence an summat wi' a fancy name on the gastrics Mr Perry I says hedgerow fruit be Adam's meat she says blowflies weren't in God's Garden for one Mr Perry for two I says where there be shit there be blowflies Mrs Holland aye she were wonnerful miffy at that nigh lost my bit o' gardenin on account o' that but you on't eat nowt wi'out it come out some place an old Adam ate of every dern tree in the garden it do say wi'out a drop o' Dinneford's bloody Magnesia in sight I says he done his shits he done his proper shits well I do remimbers thee chock-full o' sweetness Master Dannul dang the lot on 'em bloody buggerin Hell it do catch I in throat like a rag in a taypot blind leadin the blind thy Mam'd call it I says Hoppetty en't that bad Mrs Holland poachin eyes see poachin eyes as ud watch she pass in all her best pink toggery years back now eh jus afore she was wedded to that to your Dad Mr Holland oh lovely an jimp aye jimp an fresh an lovely a-holdin onto her bonnet in that old gig as ud pass I by as en't worth a brass farden to she nope yet one time a-broadcastin barley seed like the sight o' she rattlin past towart Church stopped I dead an sended my hands all a-shake like so as I couldn't git my hands in an out o' that seed-lip proper for a bit then come grawin time Jonas old man Barr says what be that rumple in crop atop Whitesheet Haw didst stumble over flint when seedin or beest thee gettin too aged for this kind o' work an back-drappin off a limp wrist eh well old Jonas kep tight smug for I couldn't rightly say as that rumple were a hankerin ater a lady as were makin me maayzy like an thee ud have her eyes an mouth bang in thee sometimes boy then oh I feeled like I did feel like I were strollin on air like I med let they horses dray my plough an have my smoke an no clittin o' no flints atween here an Doomsday look then yaa howsomever some jawlter-head ud lay into I about summat I en't done an lo behold it be all druvved deep agin an low

well now yea up hup best foot forrud down here into beechen copse hup eh eh look look there Red Admirable on that clover look firsest I have seed this year an got a bit teared on the way look aye be needin a fine needle to stitch that little feller up boy aye hup aye cool as a plum at this time o' mornin aneath the beechen trees aye Hoppetty had a cruel fancy on thy old Mam boy down with thy Dad in same parish book as old Jo Perry yit they names be in copperplate an mine be a mark weren't never no scholard boy well bress-ploughin when I were awmost bran new as thee be buggerin hell sunked out o' sight like a gurt stone now what you gone an got thyself that dang flammation on the bellowses for boy didn't they have no meadow-sweet boy they buggers gid they nowt but them pastilles I reckons as thy Mam's breath be ripe wi' them pastilles mint ripe for kissin I says mint ripe for kissin now why bist this here paunchy tree be took right bad atop well fauty wi' rust when old Dick Knapp were took by keeper dodged Dick's knife git rammed to the haft chock in her broke hisself clean atwo now fauty wi' rust aye fauty wi' rust en't right now wi'out thee to finger the hurt boy en't right at all can awmost hear the corn turnin golden in the coombs wi'out thee axin I on this an that that an this this an that it be as if spirit be flied off out o' here an out o' every drat place boy wi'out thee to ax I over agin why that tree aneath withy-wine be fauty wi' rust why that sorrel were ate in the sturvin days why that tixt o' lovin words to old Lizzie Pyke were cut in the bark o' crooked ash yonder one while past save words en't grawed an the old tree have why gurt oak on high road be called Sam's Own as we ud hang from an collar plums wi' a stick shaved sharp out o' Harry Tagg's fruit cart passin aneath hup aye ben't no use at all steppin out wi'out a ear an a eye to stir my old chaak nope en't narn to hear my rigmaroles save in the boozer boy as be only for ale en't narn o' they boozers raaly listenin anyways come come Jonas it be worth a jug o' never fear now worth a jug o' never fear oh forty gallons o' never fear forty gallons o' table beer forty gallons o' worse nor that an forty gallons o' rattle tap yaa allus thought as I'd have a jug out o' thee in the Never Fear as you fine folk knows as New Inn en't bin new for a tarnal long time betwixt thee an I an the gate-post kaaarkok pheasant boy nice fat pheasant whole copse be a-move wi' game yit you collars one whiskut o' beech out o' here they'd pull us up in a jiff them near buggers yaa never had no drop o' milk till I were fourteen save out o' my mam's dugs them close-fisted farmers gid us nowt though it were a-drippin off they noses frozed we were them winters wi'out a stick to rub aye worsest days Master Dannul worsest days an there I goes ploughin on to seventy please God an you as the heron did drop in the moss get sunked when thee be jus about a hobbledehoy what is a hobbledehoy Mr Perry well I never a chap be called a hobbledehoy as be short of a man but more'n a boy thee on't never feel that there gurt sappy feller creep into thy gullet an hinder thy voice an stretch thy limbs summat gawky so as thee on't know where thee begins nor ends all they jimp gals a-splashin an a-squealin in river makin thee a-hanker that bad thee'd want to weep nope on't never git thee out o' that sailor toggery now boy now thee be a-rollin thy hoops over the Awmighty's bestest peonies drat it I were goin to show thee them glass jiggamies wi' the shadders on 'em I telled thee on as I found in old Miss Peep-Hole's attic that Red House it were called then Bew's Lane jus over-right the Chapel an I were axed to clear he out ater she had leaved this world well that were a thing a-sunk into her bath chair anigh I doin the gardenin atween the field jobs then please God plantin her a smacker on the cheek ater she had passed on cold as dewfall boy if you don't kiss the face o' the corpse it do have a knack o' troublin thee afresh aye well I were prunin roses click click oh

Stephen Stephen she do cry all on a sudden them pages o' writin blowed all over lawn oh Mr Quiller well I says he be jus now passed away you knows that ma'am oh Stephen Stephen an she do claps I to her breast though she be that poorly a bag o' bones as twere like bein clapsed by a sparrer oh Stephen Stephen then she do yowl like a hare in a trap as to git the crows an ravens off o' she well I reckoned as she were well nigh to keckin it jus like Mr Quiller as they didn't find nowt wrong wi' jus a kind o' curse they said as come out o' some old king's tomb from the year dot an I says I'll be jus a minut gettin Doc Scott over bein as the maid were out to shop no she cries no a minut be a blur too long too long a minut be a blur too long aye I en't never got rid o' that it have stuck like shit to a blanket a minut be a blur too long then she goes on agin about the birds they crows an ravens an I says there en't no birds save they rooks in the churchyard makin a hell on a din then she do pant an reach deep athin her gurt black skirt as she ud have her camera jiggamy aneath when she were peepin oh I knowed it see I knowed it cotched her one time a-bogglin on old Janey Pocock makin sweet wi' that Mary Stroude's bro his Dad were the top harness-maker round abouts in a boat they was aye aye I seed it all over-right to she stopped dead I were other side o' river jus back from rakin for old man Barr well into her skirt she goed an pulled out a envelope an says when these seeds bloom think on me think on tarnity an how they seeds were older nor a number o' years as made I giddy an how the universe were a ripple on a lake an life were a spuddlin o' the river o' time an whatnot an her hand gid a little jump in mine jus like a rabbet twitchin in snare an lo behold she were dang dead as a nit God rest her soul boy en't never sowed they old black seeds for she med come an trouble I then yit Jo don't mind if thee dost Master Dannul don't mind if thee dost thee can trouble I any old day to show thee them glass jiggamies wi' shadders on 'em clearin out see new chap in her house says take home what you like what don't git throwed in cart Perry my man well I finds they glass jiggamies in attic look an takes they home well nigh fifty on 'em on account o' my teeny-tiny patch as growed my cabbages see aye pushed they on till I had the paunchiest cabbages abouts outside the greenhouse gents knowed for it I was oh knowed for it narn else didn't have no cloches see seed faces in they jiggamies now an agin old Lizzie Pyke wi' a yoke o' water once trees an horses old dame Trason as were chursened Hannah Mary Heddin one time though she were a while dead by then athurt a cabbage one mornin as gid me a fright an a haaf aye jus like old Dick Knapp one day a-bended over my patch as seed a face in there as made him yowl like a pig an turn all creamy-faced so as he had to seat hisself only he never telled I what it were save he were chewin on about a pair o' specs an highty-tighty wives an some Doctor feller puttin he up to it an axin for the Lord's massy afore he claps up well that were different anyways old Dick Knapp axin for the Lord's massy jus on account o' one o' my shadders see like a shadder on his conscience I reckoned aye shifty old bugger old Dick Knapp aye cool as a plum along here boy cool as a plum don't see no faces in they now ater what thretty year don't see no faces now please God

nope I reckons as the smacker on her face wore they hauntins out see never throwed nowt out all my born days see nope smack every one o' my old coats an britches my missus have a-patched into ourn peg-rug boy aye better nor haaf my born days be aneath my heels afront hearth in peg-rug boy well firsest shirt as Buzly Tuck teared off of I one harvest too much booze wantin a picky-back or summat daft that big shirt be cobbled in somewhere there boy Gumbledons aye in Gumbledons old Buzly Tuck as couldn't get a well aye us jus wantin our brencheese see dead beat aye yea up look master rabbin redbreast checkin up on us as we ben't be doin no evil tic-tic nosy little chit look aye well hup brashy piece o' sponge old Gumbledons yit that drat wheat were thick as ever agin the strike well thee'd have to skin thy shirt like a rabbet's fleck off anights them reaper gingins have took that away howsomever them old timers ud maunder on about it aye look look buntin boy aye buntin hup aye them newfangled clackettin dos have took haaf o' the muck an toil away though thee can't sing no filthy chunes no more an so as the hart doth pant hard in the hunt for the brazen elf queen I do dream on her whoa see aye boy you wi' all they stiff-arsed angels I'd better minds me now boy who comes here then hmm hmm TIME O' DAY MISS hmmmmm hm Parkes' daughter aye they gals don't ride side-saddle now see gallopy gallopy gallop pleasurin for a gal see pommel knockin her thatch aneath hill jiggetty jiggetty jig aye Littler my cus Littler Moses acause his old Dad were Moses aready see jus there aneath that beech yonder laas o' the bluebells yonder clanged by a spring-gun in '25 aye bloody cobweb in here with they trippy wires trip bang worser to hang aye off acornin then scat for two day till one o' they keepers brung a waggon out o' Plum Farm Littler in the back aneath a rag sterk dead boy aye sterk bloody dead I remimbers thee'd shiver a bit at that Master Dannul an he were only a nip catched a pound o' shot in his stumps well bled to a husk bettermost haaf the night they reckoned gawpin up on they starries jus yonder agin them there bluebells some on us weaved a cross out o' straw now an agin an leaved it there if we was snarin anyways on't never want to pass away like that boy wi'out narn else to hold thee aye to hold thee an only a nip

dang it bloody buggerin hell this life en't bin no dish o' tay jus about a sop in sour grease it be save thee be one o' they Lordyshits whoa about now you comether an look through here boy you have a peep at palace from the arse-end mind thy soul on this here barb wire don't want to get harled up like a bloody lamb a-fleckin thy sailor toggery off agin they tangs look there see them chaps a-brevettin about the bowlin green they be lookin for a tall blade o' grass as have gone aground aye thee'd chuckle at that Master Dannul tall blade o' grass as have gone aground oh we'd have some laafs boy thy Mam en't never bin one for laafs now she be like Queen Vic boy like she have a gnawin aye everlastinly rustlin black black as the Squire's cream knacker as us old Ulver folk do say now riddle the chaff out o' that boy riddle the chaff out o' that aye all I remimbers be a clink clink o' pails an a scuttlin up scarp an a smell o' burnin gurt glitterin eye aneath moon well haaf asleep I was an only a nip same as thee Master Dannul gettin upsides wi' all they buggers aye you med have bin in there an played the toff afore but you en't never seed it this arsy-versy ways about hast thee now look 'ee yonder awmost to village they silver birch they calls it the Wilderness boy acause it don't have no grass an highty-tighty flowers like a damn carpit well it weren't no bloody wilderness afore nope my gurt-gurt-gramver were born in there no hedge-bit neither nope took they a mornin my gramver telled I to slap they homes down to a plume o' chaak dust an faggots jus for a bit o' garden for they Lordyshits aye an my gramver had it from her own gramver's mouth herself boy aye oh there be us an others here as on't never disremimber that till Doomsday boy won't never disremimber that till the clang o' Doom aye plough an drill an mow atop the chaak aneath en't stirred yaa that gurt lake I remimbers nowt but turf an sheep about she now look a man can't walk straight wi'out doin a nancy boy about they flower beds cotched a swan afore now out o' there splish splish gurt white wings all sooty wi' our mitts blackened up see flit flit stick her in the gullet well that were a doins an a haaf leastways a stop to thy nips howlin wi' hunger for a month yaa have to go to shop for arn dalled thing now here be to all his Lordyshit's jack-rabbets as have biled the pot an kep I off from sturvin well they didn't do nowt for my old Mam boy bag o' bones wi' her givin us young grubs all as she was hern then stone-cartin off Top Field they flints spreethin her mitts I can see they now boy a-strokin us when I were took wi' the scarlet one time a-foldin theyselves an prayin aye I can see they now all welted an crook tallow flame jumpin up her shadder agin the beam an all that mumblin to God as en't never gid us nowt but sour sops aye God shed bloody rest her soul boy if so be as He have one then eh kaaaa kaaaa kaaaa hear they rooks kaaaa kaaaa an haaf a stone o' corn in ivery one o' they nests old Long Togs Long Togs Whiteacre Ralphy Oadam Titchy Ketchaside old Plashy Pottinger as couldn't say owt but plash bein as he didn't hear nowt as a babby but plashin an plashin o' mill-wheel see an my cus Churlet Griffin more a boy wi'out a willum nor a gal an Jonas shinnin the ellums out on Frum Down dinner o' rooks corn fluff in cake-hole while they Chammers-Lavery folk well nigh blawed theyselves at dinner us folk chokin on rook-fluff an they eatin their bloody heads off no folk not even they niggers out Africa way never had to live as us done well one while past some blokes among us did get a mite obstroppelus about it clouted a few gingins all to smash like slitted the grain out like a chicken-throat aye tell me about the Trouble Mr Perry what Master Dannul says I the whole lot over agin oh yes Mr Perry it's topping I think haa yaa thee were allus a bloody good sort boy aye well no better nor ten year I were yit I minds us they men comin out the courthouse like it were yeserday see well my Mam's brother Giley Griffin hollerin don't thee be worrited chit tis only fourteen year then Johnny Cap'n Oadam wavin at us hoi hoi tis danglin for me but it shattent hold gal old Shepherd Bunce's lad as had his flock out Bursop way don't blubber mother tis only life they on't be makin away wi' me an all them fellers come out as were ploughmen an reapers an hedgers an horsemen an shearers an shepherds as you don't git the likes of now well ploughmen as could draw a furrer plum as that horsemen as maunt turn out a team wi'out a bloom as ud blind thee on they flanks aye blind thee on they flanks an my old Mam an Auntie Ruth screamin fit to bust an all on us yowlin knockin our heads an blubberin an the nips blubberin acause they seed their Mams blubberin an squawlin aye their boots didn't never touch no Ulver turf no more nor didn't never squelch up Little Hangy nor go poachin tip-toe in Bayleaze nor get thick nor clamput about the yard nor get thick wi' crossin athurt Mwile Slad nor dusted on the maiden rudge ways handlin their tools o' their occepashins no more nor git poorly in their arn beds an have a stone anigh their heads as nips med pick blooms for an all for nowt boy all for nowt recitin thee on this now boy athout thee don't ezackerly recalls a-lookin on that there fine house an fine garden what they tot-bellies done to kip theyselves blawed galled us with they saddles till the blood come out aye blood come out aye gid us a leg up onto the old cross good an proper boy aye banged they nails in like they were ruttin they highty-tighty wives aye yea up hup best foot forrud Master Dannul lest thee leave a fleck o' thy soul on their drat tangs on't never be a toff now thee on't nope no them buggers on't cotch thee now boy four an twenty Ulver men ne'er hollered in the coomb though morn was come an sun were up twere silent as the tomb aye so climb the hill hi-ho come climb the hill hi-ho we'll gie the lads a milk-white steed that they med gallop home an so forth worth a pot o' bunk an a bit o' twist in the ale-house that patch o' singin as shed be ater you be that dry a-roarin it nope on't never cotch thee an turn thee to a toff now boy thee be old Hoppetty's own now boy old Hoppetty's own as med larn thee all to hisself dang the lot on 'em

a bit o' hush now Jonas hup aye hup pit-a-pat over they leaves first light o' mornin starch-stiff boy poachin this were allus my patch don't fret too bloody old for it now that Ebby Wall yaa knows he backerds never no keeper at this time o' aternoon never changed his beat one step old Ebby Wall Swilly Copse Bayleaze Will's Field Longcroft Clean an Hansome Draggle Ley Six Mild Clump Grigg's Breach Wood back up Dolman's Lane by ten in the mornin bang on as a sun-dial boy his lad do High Ridge Wood he do love a scrap aye best not scrunch about wi' he jus wait for peep o' day that numbed an quiet you feels like couch-grass more'n the image o' God when that damn bunny comes athurt an thee med let fly boy leastways thee don't make no scrunch now Master Dannul thee'd make the toppermost poacher now boy aye reckons you goes plum through they tree-trunks like they be pillars o' mist jus like old Shepherd Willum deep athin this green aye lookin for his lost lamb haaf ram haaf man tuppin wi' a witch one while see tuppin wi' a ewe see what is tuppin Mr Perry aye well what thy Mam an Dad done to get thee together boy leastways I reckons fine folk do it same as we aye well reckons as old Shepherd Willum were jus short of hole aye weren't no witch boy shepherds git poke-starved out on they old downs casn't damn they for it aye don't know as they be arn big folk in Heaven anyways save nips like thee why is this Will's Field Mr Perry it's a jolly thick wood well didn't used to be no copse here jus a scarp bare as thy knuckles save the grass an sheep till one o' they Lordyshits wants to bang away wi' his highty-tighty mates atween trees an sets to a-plantin yit old Shepherd Willum sees nowt but turf and sky look nowt but turf an sky aye rain rain pit-a-pat agin the beechen leaves boy I seed it were gettin all cluttery now thee maunt fret boy thy Mam do make a splut about thee gettin wet didn't never do us no harm oh she did yang about thy constitushun like as if thee en't no more nor a leaf in the wind boy blowed about like that teeny leaf in the wind there now reckons as she thinks as I got thee dowsed laas time deliberate like aye jus afore thee goed off to that scholard shop save she can't rightly say to my head jus gives I the look from the drawin-room winder all creamy-faced an still like aye when I be doin her lawn well us allus reckoned she had coddled thee a deal too much Master Dannul an that old Eton shop jus broke thee atwo nowt to do wi' that laas stroll nope thee runned athurt field in the storm laafin like old King George boy like thee en't never runned wi' the rain a-blowed agin thy face afore tip-top that be in the warm aye coddlin en't never done a soul no good boy en't never done a soul no good my Dad laced I summat terble never did narn no harm Master Dannul a-whackin nips to larn 'em right a bit o' strap aye my Dad didn't never fiddle us though like some on 'em though oh no he didn't never filthy us nips no he never done that nope jus a dustin o' the jacket like

well now hup yea up straight athurt ride here aye towart that edge hup hup aye thy Mam on't abide I now I knows it that en't Christern boy please God on't be doin wi'out that bit o' gardenin like it do kip the wolf from off of our door I says to my missus it do kip the wolf from off of our door hey up best foot forrud Master Dannul aye no dish o' bloody tay eh you make sure he's back at home by luncheon now please Mr Perry well that dang storm didn't haaf dowsh us good an proper boy oh dost remimber that whoa ho we didn't haaf cotch it athurt Louzy not a bloody tree about like a pair o' drownded rats boy don't thee fret I'll tell thy Mam as I have spent haaf my born days a-squelchin about an not a stick for no dern fire in the bad old days boy in from the field wi'out a blink in the hearth boy aye that shrammed an dog-tired thee'd go straight to bed all sogged an nowt but a sobblin o' crust in thy belly boy nips yowlin wi' hunger as thee'd have to snoozle down agin to git warmth they plough lines dancin about in thy head as though thee weren't nowt but a talkin acre o' clag wi' the gripes a-stirred an a-stirred by they drat bitin coulters as ud wake thee click out o' thy dreams an weren't no more'n belly yangin at thee to git poachin like git poachin y'bugger aye nice bangin lot o' wind an a bit o' moon see waitin by the net thee'd stitched in an out out an in in an out a-dreamin on all they fat rabbets as ud shake it dodgin that keeper bang bang bang hup well a decent dog were more nor a haaf on it blowed his brains out they did blowed his brains out old Ketch afront of I well fuck they buggers an fuck the lot on 'em worsest thing they did to I they Lordyshit's blokes an teared my old net up to tatters well aye that ruffled I summat yit had to kip smug like weren't never pulled up boy weren't never cotched in the act like bless my soul hup yea up whoa soft out o' the trees boy don't want narn spottin us bright agin the dark now soft into Ewe Drop whoa about hooit whoa

narn abouts Master Dannul aye fetch our breath a bit agin this here stump here haaaa that river down there ben't be no more nor a trickle out here now dry see dry aye oh thy Mam yanged at I she did dost thee remimber didn't take more nor a jiff for I to knuckle under her like she capped I proper an you all biverin like I be awful sorry Mrs Holland it come clap on us Mrs Holland he'll be all right Mrs Holland jus a lick o' rain an jabberin on like a dicky-bird till the door were shut on I knockin off my hat as rolled athurt the lawn like thy bloody hoop boy now her face through the winder like the face o' death lookin on I gardenin aye a face as I had a hankerin for one while past a-bogglin at I like the creamy face o' doom jus like they say old Agnes Plumm looks out o' that cow-house where she dandled herself up there yonder jus about sees the roofs atop Ewe Drop aye they old timers as were in there ater the Trouble clapped up in chains like a bloody herd o' cows as I have telled thee afore now Master Dannul they old timers says as she did come old Agnes athurt the cow muck tiddy as quaker-grass to gie 'em comfort strokin they brows in the middest night an layin they worrited heads in her lap as weren't death-cold no ways aye all on 'em as come back to their homes they sweared as that were true an old Tom Ketchaside as weren't spared nowt though he were past eighty then boy well he sended us a letter from that Australy Demon's Land as readed as he knowed God's truth as Agnes was raaly there a-treatin they poor buggers like they were her own childern an she looked ezackerly like a angel med look like accardin to him God rest he an my gurt-uncle as was took out wi' old Tom God rest 'em all oh Mr Perry they were felons an vagabonds aye boy aye you kip t'other side o' hedge boy on't be splotched by passin finery there boy oh Mr Perry my mother says you should never spit in public well hawkin boy hawkin out all the hate in us afore it burn I up look don't tell I as fine genneman don't hawk I've feeled it chit afore the toll-house once stone-pickin anigh the highway up by Malt Shovel cross-roads show-off type o' scarlet coach spanks past wi' a young gent on the far end of a glove as have a hackin cough an the winder bein ope out flies this gob as spluts athurt my cheek bright as what you fine folk calls a poppy well don't reckons as he had long to go poor chap yit nowt more to they than summat to hawk on us weren't yaa a thousand acre o' maiden downs won't bolt my hate boy though it burn

I up in hell's fire as they tries to frit thee with them oh oh old Jemps Cullurne be a-comin up the path another queer un boy lie low a tic lie low hmm hmm TIME O' DAY JEMPSY AYE AYE MIDDLIN WEATHER AYE hmmmm hm allus down in the mouth old Jemps Cullurne on account o' tilthin wi' a missus as be mawkier nor a dung cart boy aye hmmmm she have had a babby boy jus now as be chursened Percy Percy well first an laas time a Percy in Ulver I spect yit old Martha Cullurne have allus bin a bit posterin like newfangled ways aye oh old Jempsy rippin wheat one harvest one while back year o' '59 same year as I got hitched up wi' all that marriage lark see aye out Bursop way Bobs Slad wi' the gang anigh the turnpike end when old Jemps he do squeal like a pig an keck up all his brencheese onto the greensard blaaa well why Mr Perry oh thee've heard this norration a good few times afore boy oh I like the fingers part Mr Perry yaa well we scambles through the crop up to Jempsy's line an lo behold a stink an a heap o' flies an when they flies rised off a human face aneath aye jus about stripped o' meat an cut some more abouts an lo behold oh Master Dannul you on't want to be hearin this one agin look Brimstone boy you cotch that little feller an tickle thy mitts wi' the wings oh please Mr Perry go on there's a fellow Mr Perry eh yaa well lo behold that poor bugger were a-layin in the corn like he were slumberin ater booze wi' one mitt aspraal as have two fingers a-missin clean off it an a pair o' brass specs wi' no eyeballs aneath fancy silk coat sterch collar an whatnot see a genneman see well us knowed what it were straight off look though they flies an maggots were in a proper old fizzle a-cleanin he up well at that time there were highway robbers on the big roads athurt downs as ud pop folk on the head an chuck 'em over hedge into corn come summer time so as narn en't findin they till hoi look look down there boy waggon in the river they be tightenin an cleanin her up for the hay load tomorrer I reckons they be cuttin the hay tomorrer aye start o' harvest well Heaven for I boy Heaven be no more for I nor the rattlin o' laas load o' corn home ridin atop that waggon boy well look now lark o' massy if that en't the same bloody waggon out o' Barr's as I remimbers thretty year ago see they letters I medn't read boy yit I knows they letters EDWARD M. BARR ULVERTON clear as daylight EDWARD M. BARR ULVER-

TON though it en't ezackerly right that first name may hap as his son have put his own in what be his bloody name I casn't remimber nowt o' the new names Ernest aye Ernest med be he have took out that Edward bit aye made they buggers like their lives were ridin in 'em look look a-splashin into that water aye that have carted I out the field afore now then bless my heart an soul we do sops our head in ale boy e'en the most close damper of a bloke do get cocked an chirpy never filth an shamin mind never filth an shamin oh no laas shock o' corn throwed up onto that rick well that be another year stitched up see that be another year stitched up an med be as the next year do be aready threddlin its bloody needle but you don't think on that come Harvest Home night nope thee have to souse thy thoughts in ale or thee be too dog-tired to get rollicky at all so drink boys drink an see as 'ee do not spill hup for if 'ee do 'ee shall drink two for that be Master's will aye aye I be jus the old codger in corner now but I do remimbers I a-roarin atop o' table aye throat all roopy from the singin an bellockin aye aye yaa thee dursn't want to hear about Jempsy an the highway robber blokes now boy no aye us all feelin tip-top not out an out lush though no eh oh no eh well they lopped off they two fingers poor bugger for the rings see the gold bloody rings see now boy you on't want to hear all that rigmarole agin aye aye that be the waggon all right us a-whoopin it home oh Heaven boy certain sure an sometimes they wheels groanin out of a field that brashy an thin I have seed they harrers a-blizzy off they tangs athurt it come harrerin time aye on't thee fret about gettin wet boy it be drippin off brim o' my billy cock like a dang waterfall sometimes I don't minds it boy sees my hat we be callin it a billy cock sees my boots we be callin they boots aye atween the two be a belly an a willum one for shes to fill an t'other for to fill 'em hup haa hey up thee on't be gettin too shram an frozed now boy thee'd best run athurt grass there crow's way back or thy Mam'll have my hide boy aye aye it be wettin us proper now boy you on't be gettin too dang cold now eh oh TIME O' DAY YOUNG FELLER AYE NOPE DON'T FRET THYSELF FOR US A LITTLE DAMP NEVER DID NARN NO HARM EH HAA AYE AYE GETTIN THE WAGGONS OUT AYE haa hmm hm old Steve

Trevick's littlest lad as we allus call Marlers for he couldn't never say marbles only marlers dang I be a-dry a-talkin it be jus about shuttin-up time boy you shed run home now run home athurt the wet an I'll be hoppettin ater thee boy shin up Ewe Drop along the scarp then down Chaaky Lane boy Bottom Bridge an home afore thy Mam's dang luncheon-bell be dingin aye git dry aye hup tomorrer I be takin thee off to cunny hump as you fine folk knows as the Barrow Hill why cunny hump Mr Perry well I'll larn thee on that little un some day boy I'll larn thee on that un some day oh bloody buggerin hell Dinneford's bloody Magnesia woman hup hup aye 'ee sees that bloody old sweet chestnut a-wrestlin wi' the ivy in lee agin that daddacky lump o' thatch as was old Aaron Flower's home one while past afore he tumbled into his hearth aye narn heard him blare nor burn poor bugger finest blower o' music round abouts on the old eldern pipe mind us'd walk that brow many a time wi' a rip hook to fields an hear his chunes whiverin doleful over the coomb please God his son have a flock out Fawholt way now well that bloody tree yonder Master Dannul I have stood aneath that Cockle's bloody Pills eh oh a-clapperin the birds off aye aye eh oh a-blubberin wi' cold as a nip longer nor I wants to remimber only I casn't disremimber when I sees owt nope bloody tree never spoke to I only scroop scroop like my dang rheumatics scroop scroop like a blasted gate hinge scroop scroop like mebbe it were sayin summat aye why Mr Perry well mebbe that rag-stabber tailor bogey as be lookin for a needle to cobble he together agin seein as he were claved into more bloody pieces nor be athin ourn peg-rug boy aye a-groanin for a needle see well Poor Pounds Pickle that patch be called where the corn allus have grawed fat on account on it suppin up his red juice accardin to my old gramver as had a heap o' tales boy yaa bloody embocation no bloody embocation oh I en't heared nowt there but wind boy en't feeled nowt but wind pokin in an out o' my hide like it were wantin to sew my shroud out o' myself aye en't never blowed no remimberin off though so who was it then Mr Perry who slew him so cruelly who slashed him up aye well I remimbers old Widder Shail frowsty old fussock ud give I lardy cake an snigger old Becky aye well that'll do that'll do them wood pigeons allus tellin I to clap up that'll do that'll do till tomorrer boy us'll top up that bloody rigmarole tomorrer now yea up don't thee bide in the wet no longer Master Dannul nope nope maunt lope about wi' this here cluttery weather an you lookin all peeky boy hup yea up bloody buggerin hell oh off wi' thee back home dreckly minut boy yea up this here dreckly minut

1914

TREASURE

Looking back on those days, perhaps the most peculiar and haunting instance of this occurred in the opening months of the Great War. Our Squire (he of the skidding motor-car) had taken it into his head to excavate the barrow that lies closest to Ulverton, an impressive mound perched on the rim of the high scarp that falls so gently and lovingly into the Fogbourne's crystal course. How I was roped in to this amateur species of archaeological investigation does not matter here, but it was certainly not all port and cajolery on the part of the Manor.

Ever since my arrival I had felt a restlessness. Grief had settled to a dull and monotonous sense of longing—how tedious this human inability to accept a state of affairs, and plunge into life! I would catch myself, during the first hot days of July, calling out for the punkah-wallah, or searching for the bell to bring Abdul with lemonade on his silver tray; in the severe thunderstorms of that summer I would wonder why the rainfall was so hushed, only to remember that I had but English thatch upon the roof, that took the battering without more than an old gent's mumble of complaint. Come the dawn, and I would wake up startled and address my wife in confused tones. Why was it so blessedly cool? Had Ali (the club-footed one) set my shoes out for the morning? Where were the windows—those three familiar shuttered rectangles of wan grey stripes that, by noon, blazed like Blake's tiger—a fierce chaos of hot light we had dared to frame?

But alas, my wife was not there to answer. Up to the window, then, and draw the curtains: there the soft grey stone of an English church, the elms and the beech, the old gentle roofs, and beyond these, etched by the morning, shrilled by the lark, the high curved brows of our English downland.

As observed earlier, my first winter was deficient in the snow I had clothed my homecoming with, while the first weeks of spring were dreary with day after day of rain. In Chittagong it had, with a baleful simplicity, either blazed or poured: the consolation lay in that very certainty, where the ground at your feet puffed into clouds or splashed one's puttees brown. Days and days of rain during the monsoon season—that was in the order of things. Weeks and weeks of blaze in the dry season—that was decreed in tablets of stone, no doubt the property of the Devil. Inside, in either season, all was shuttered gloom.

In England, all is shifting sands. The weather is mild and muddling. It is not a climate one can hammer a post into, or pin like a butterfly. Because I had expected the spring of the poets—yellow flowers underfoot and blue sky above, et cetera—it rained and rained. The month of March was bedraggled, not crisp. Ah, but then the blossom! Surely that would not disappoint! The cottage has a fine little orchard, with a venerable crab-apple whose delicately tinted flowers I awaited with all the anticipation of a little boy for his birthday; two William pear; a mossed Cox; and that queen of fruits, the damson (three of her). As for the humble whitethorn—how I had dreamed of seeing the lines of lace spread as if by maids for bleaching on the soft green hills, or woven about a small meadow, in which the wild daffodils, the violets, the cuckoo-flowers and the simple daisies are strung by glittering cobwebs each soft morning, that the most jaded and withered soul feels the sap rise, and the presence of the ineffable Oneness breathe all about him!

Alas, no sooner had my little orchard so rejoiced, and the mild spring air fluttered those tiny pale frocks, than Nature undid her finest handiwork with sharp glinting scissors and a malignant sense of timing that makes humanity's efforts look amateurish. My first year home, and England's fruit crops were ruined by the cruellest of late frosts. The slow ripening of apples and pears I had conjured up so often was not to be—certainly not with that glorious abundance one's day-dreams favour under the sluggish fans of Bengal.

How much more was to be withered and changed in that year, and for ever, I could hardly have imagined when we set out up Louzy Hill to the barrow mound that July morning of 1914, the hay-stubble still sopping from the previous night's storm: the Squire striding off in the lead, and we straggled out like Stanley's porters behind. For I had come to involve myself in this local adventure, this delving back into memories safely other than my own, and decidedly older, in a spirit of retreat from more pressing demands on my soul. This is probably true of the majority of our actions, but whether this blights them in some way—well, this is not a work of moral philosophy. Instead, let the episode I am going to relate stand in at this point. Now I am not of Carlyle's opinion, that something known can ever become 'transparent', and so surveyable *in toto*; but the affair of Percy Cullurne, an affair perhaps only achieving its tragic climax much more recently (all in good time, dear reader), continues to exert its uncomfortable presence upon me, like a moral truth struggling to be relieved of its opaque skin.

That first morning, with mist still on the river and dreams hardly banished, we walked slowly up the scarp in single file—and the last of us reached the base of the mound as the church clock rang the quarter of some balefully early hour. The Squire, however, was already clambering up the barrow's side. We remained at the base as instructed, while he stood on the top and ceremonially swung his pick into the wet grass. This decisive action did not have the outcome he had intended. The rain had been of a heavy type that merely rolls away without penetrating parched soil beyond the first inch or so. The Squire's wide frame jolted, and there was a dull thud. A second attack, and this time the fine early-morning air vibrated to a sharp report which elicited a single word, 'flint', from one of the more rueful amongst us. The Squire was dressed in his Homburg hat and a snappy knee-length twill which flapped and muddied itself as he tore at the turf: a sight I will not easily forget, as of some giant underworld God eager to return to his dismal mansion—or of a dwarf scalping and braining some huge submerged Divinity, stuck fast in immemorial sleep.

Its flesh impacted by thousands of generations of grasses and flowers, by the sheer peaceable weight of undisturbed being, it took time for the metal to loosen it sufficiently to dig, but eventually the barrow began to appear on the spade in small chunks bristling with tussocks, irreverently reminding me of the military moustaches sported by colonels in Chittagong. We stood around the base a little sheepishly while the 'Chief' (as I liked to think of him) grunted and groaned, cursing every now and again in his own intimate fashion, and adjusting his pince-nez with a delicacy not suited to the occasion. We were, I have to say, a motley crew, consisting of 'Marlers' Trevick, the strapping head gardener at the Manor; Ernest, the pale schoolteacher; Allun, the chauffeur from Cardiff; Terence Brinn, a small lad with big ears; Tom Sedgwick, the leathery forester; and Dart, the blacksmith's assistant with flared nostrils and decidedly undarting intelligence. One could hope for no better at the approach of harvest.

When the Squire had made sufficient disorder of the smooth grassy crown, he gave us a thumbs-up and the excavation began in earnest. It was very slippery and there was barely room for all of us and our hacking picks and spades. I would go so far as to say it was dangerous—but danger was what I had wanted all along. For a whole morning I thought of nothing but how to avoid flying metal and the discomfort of aching arms. After lunch it began to rain again in slanting gusts across the downs, and it was my duty to hold two umbrellas up, in a feeble attempt to keep the diggers dry. I am not the first to notice how much more difficult it is to hold an umbrella when stationary, than when scurrying across a city.

But loud, dirty Chittagong was far from my thoughts. I was in the midst of a rolling ocean of chalk, the rain had unstoppered all the secreted perfumes of summer, my legs were sodden at the backs of the knees, and I was happy in my task. For task it was. I was as far from any desk and the vile clatter of an office, as from caring whether we flung up gold or rabbits. The point was to work with limbs and an empty mind. Or a mind full only of the great immediacies: the sun and the wind and the earth.

To breathe, to breathe deep of the biscuit scent of rain-swept barley, shuddering reluctantly at every gust! Or of the sweet richness of the vast hay-stack, thatched golden against the shadowy trees! What other sensations more likely to bring a fever of longing to the far-flung servant in some foul and sweaty imperial post, than these reminders of home, and of gentler seasons? For England is so very gentle, compared to the rest of her Empire. That is, the England of forest and stream, of meadow and vale and rolling downland. There her soft breath wafts over us, along with the tinkles of sheep and the high thudding bells of the ancient churches, marking a slower time than that of the outer world of power and striving: a slow pulse which seemed to me then, standing on that high place, eternally beating.

Alas, that we were not more vigilant!

All that week we chopped and sliced, flinging up nothing more enticing than sleek flints of purely natural ancestry. Butterflies, as if dazed by the sudden removal of a favourite haunt, dallied above our heads and Ernest, the schoolteacher, his little moustache wet with exertion, managed to net an Admiral that blazed in his chloroform bottle like a blown coal. The breezes were cool, and the bread and cheese were as fine as the finest dish up there on that scarp, flavoured by hunger and fresh air. I cannot pretend to have contributed much—my arthritis saw to that—but I did my utmost. I think it was that week, or perhaps the week after, that Austria-Hungary declared war on Serbia. Anyway, it did not matter. We had penetrated five feet, the barrow appeared to have sagged in the middle, we had scoured every inch of spill: I was exhausted, but happy. A liveliness had entered my life; the clouds had begun to disperse; I walked, I might say, with the hint of a spring in my step.

In case the reader feels this to be an unwarranted banishment of melancholy, coming as it did on the eve of wider catastrophe, then let me say that I have noticed eves of great things to be often so lineated. We all expected war. The whole village was buzzing with the expectation of it. But it was still not upon us, and none of us had any idea what form it would take. The world demands things of us, it exacts from us its daily toll of fret and grief, but when it takes it upon itself to swagger, to swell into a grander key, to thrust our petty wants aside and make us chorus War, then we sit and wait: we are suspended for a minute; we are unburdened and happy.

And let me say as well that this was the first time since I was a boy that the crack of a book's spine had not interrupted the day's pleasures. Up there on that high mound, I saw nothing but fields and copses stretching away to infinity under the graze of sheep and sun; heard nothing but the murmur of voices, the odd grunt, the wood pigeons purring in the nearby copse, the satisfying splice of the spades keeping their own natural rhythm; felt nothing but the smooth wood handle of my trowel vibrating to the ceaselessly changing resistances of the chalk beneath me. Now I understood that calm certitude the farm-labourer must feel when the job in hand is immediate and clear and devoid of words, that intimate contact with the ancient practices of our race, derided by the city dweller with his insatiable hunger for the new. Never mind that we were seeking treasure, seeking to embody the old village legend of lost riches, searched for still, so it was said, by the ghost of a long-dead shepherd swinging his lantern: for myself, it was a task related to the immemorial tasks of the fields about us, some filled with harvesters and loaded wains, others flecked only with sheep and their lonely flesh-and-blood masters.

No doubt we were microscopic in the great order of things: the soil changed colour on the day the Germans violated Belgian neutrality. It was a sign, apparently, that something, perhaps wooden, had rotted there. The Squire stood and wiped his pince-nez on a bright red 'kerchief, and cautioned us to proceed carefully. He replaced the spectacles on his nose with a great sigh of satisfaction, looking up at the cloudless August sky as if something had been answered from that quarter.

Then a moment of absolute peace ensued, a pause in which everyone present settled into stillness, our trowels and spades motionless, our heads bowed. Over the scarps and vales came the tinkle of sheep-bells, the far shouts of thistle-pulling labourers, the delirious trill of a high lark. The Cabbage Whites and Common Blues fluttered about our heads so close we could almost hear their papery wings. Even Dart, slow, blunt Dart, wiping his nose, appeared aware of the moment's portentousness. Only the odd creak of a leather boot and young Tom Sedgwick's wheezes served to remind us of our corporeal reality.

That evening the Vicar came round (the Rectory dwarfs my cottage) and over a glass of sherry stressed the teleological nature of 'this Slav business', looking upon it as some kind of cod-liver oil for the moral order. He bestowed himself in my old rocking-chair, squeaking it frightfully as he consumed at least a quarter of my sherry, and all but flung himself to the floor at the peak of his oration. It was only on the following morning, joining the others on the barrow, that I heard the inevitable—we started earlier than the newspaper boy, and in those days before the wireless Ulverton was still a refuge from the world of affairs.

It was said jovially that a certain old shepherd by the name of Flower, living in a far-flung hut to the north of the village, and only coming in once a week for his provisions, was the last man in England to know we were at war. I felt envious of the fellow.

That morning, then, there was a curious mixture of the subdued and the excited amongst us. It seemed only fitting that this was the day of the first find. 'Marlers' Trevick suddenly yelped just before dusk in a manner that set the rooks off cawing in the nearby clump of elms. The Squire scrambled down (we had by now a fairly impressive depression) and bent over the spot at which Marlers was jabbing a thick forefinger. A small edge of something glinted in the sun.

Within minutes the Squire had lifted up a small bronze pot in which, as we swiftly discovered, huddled the burnt remains of an ancient Briton. We whooped with delight, and my blisters were forgotten. Ernest made elaborate notes while the rest of us uncorked our water-bottles and drank a rather tepid toast. Allun was despatched to fetch champagne, and when he returned the Squire opened the two bottles without pause, an action which sent frothy jets of Heidsieck's Special Reserve over our sweaty countenances, and only just missed soaking our Bronze-Age friend. As I supped from the bottle, I felt the headiness of victory, and grew momentarily confused as to which great event we were celebrating: the uncovering of the ancient, or the call to arms.

Percy Cullurne was the Manor's under-gardener at the time—between bouts of ploughing and so forth. He had downright refused to take part in the excavation; a mutinous decision which had exercised the Squire's fury. But the man wasn't to be budged, and was too loyal and hard-working a fellow to be dismissed for wishing to tend the estate rather than indulge his master's latest whim.

One afternoon at the end of June, a month before the whim took body, I discovered the reason for this forthright stance. I was walking around the back of the estate, down the path known as the Pightle Way, switching at the defiant yellow splashes of ragwort with my walking stick, and thinking of nothing in particular (which is why, indeed, I walk), when I felt human eyes upon me, and on looking up saw Percy Cullurne staring hard over the barbed-wire fence that, alas, was strung in the stead of a hedge for that stretch of the little meadow.

He nodded, and I stopped. He was holding a scythe and was in the process of sharpening it on a wooden strickle greased with mutton fat. In those days this was a commoner sight, but I was still new enough to the English rural scene that these simple actions held a fascination for me. Although he was then a young man, the ease with which he swept the strickle along the huge curving blade betokened a lifetime of custom. It was, in fact, because of the way even boys looked as if their working skills had been sunk deep into them that I felt a sense of humility before these humble folk. Many of them were (and still are, in this year of 1928) barely literate, yet they could read things other than words—which are paltry specimens before the rich and complex pages of our ancient country. As our roads are tarmacadamed, and the hills littered with our hideous suburban boxes, one can feel this other knowledge wither as a leaf in frost. Ulverton slumbers on (despite the stinking motor-bus and motor-car), huddled about its white dusty roads; for no one has thought it worthwhile, as yet, to lay a smooth black ribbon through here, for the comfort of the pneumatic tyre, and the discomfort of those who wish to dwell in peace.

To return to the scene: after the usual pleasantries between the even rasps of the strickle, I told him that it was a pity he had decided to keep out of the 'treasure-hunt'. He stopped and straightened up. I had used the term in jest (the Squire had insisted on the academic nature of his interest, which explained the presence of Ernest and his notepad), but Cullurne took it literally.

'There be the trouble, sir. En't right, disturbin' the dead for silver.'

I smiled.

'We hope for more than silver. We hope for gold.'

'There. En't right.'

'But my dear man,' I said, a little more seriously, 'our object isn't to plunder. We hope to gain knowledge, and a glimpse of the artistic achievements of our forebears. Necklaces, carved artefacts, or whatever.

And what's more, the sight of someone who lived and breathed thousands of years ago on this very soil.'

His features barely altered.

'An' passed away,' he said.

I smiled again. There was no doubting it: the man was as superstitious as they come, and this provoked in me a certain pleasure that such deeply-rooted instincts still held on in a scientific age.

'Well,' I replied, making ready to go, 'if I see the remotest hint of a haunting, I'll be the first to run blubbering into your cottage. But as it is I am convinced that nothing remains there but the breeze and the grass. I'm in need of the exercise and the change.'

'Aye,' he nodded, 'the master tawld I. It be a gurt loss to you, sir, I 'spect.'

I thanked him for his reflections—the mention of my late wife had cast a pall on the erstwhile subject of our conversation—and continued on down the path until the hiss of the scythe had been obliterated by the summer afternoon's attendant din: bees hummed over the dog-rose that clung to the ancient brick wall of the estate, and a flock of starlings was already raiding what fruit was spared by the frosts in the resplendent orchard that lay half-hidden behind (about which orchard, and its dark future role in this history, more later).

I paused by the dog-rose, remembering how my wife had looked forward to the gentle scent of this loveliest of English flowers. She had never liked India. Her life consisted of boredom and the anticipation of 'coming back' in equal measure. Alas, that the greedy sub-continent had claimed her just a month before I was due to retire! Nature's laws are importunate and harsh. How she would have loathed it, had she known her final resting-place would be the vast cemetery at Chittagong, under the rattling palms—and not in a green and secluded English churchyard.

I wept a little beside the dog-rose, and felt foolish.

I met the Squire the next day. I was on foot, he was in his latest motor-car, whose breeding appeared impeccable—but I confess that I cannot recall the exact stable. It was large and red and curving, with an impressive brass horn which Allun would apply without fail at every corner, serving much the same purpose as the trumpets sounded before the royal train in days of yore. It had a canvas top which, this being a fine day, was fully lowered; we talked, therefore, without impediment, though I have to say that my eyes were uncomfortably full of the dust that the motor-car had churned up in her wake, and which now gently blew down the high street towards us. I had not wanted to talk with the Chief, but my passing had coincided with Allun applying the brakes very hard to avoid a grocer's dray at the corner by the church, and the Squire had hailed me from his temporarily stalled position.

I admired his steed, and so on, but soon enough we were conversing on the approaching enterprise. I had expressed a doubt the previous week about my physical prowess, being a gangly fellow the far side of sixty. I returned to this theme by the church but the Squire once again dismissed my trepidations and stated that my exact mind and quiet presence would fully make up for any muscular defects. He slapped the side of the car with great vigour and brought up the subject of Cullurne. I tip-toed about it, but the Squire's bristly, pale, slightly swollen visage thrust itself towards me; although the dray had clip-clopped off, the road was not yet clear in the Squire's head. There existed a peculiar dependancy in the mind of our village Chief which thralled both us and him; the lowliest member of the community could exert a hold over the Squire by the merest hint of disapproval. This was the burr that snagged him. If the employees of the Manor did not support his various schemes to the hilt, they were the subject of furious enquiry. Four maids were dismissed for making faces at his steam-powered dining-room trolley. It was thrown out soon after—almost certainly because their ridicule had not, nay, could not be assuaged. This is the reason he preferred furious cajolery on his part to outright rejection: knowing this, the village preferred to let him be, and wore two faces.

'Impudence, Fergusson! Damned impudence!'

I replied that, having talked to the guilty party the previous day, there were feelings involved which amounted to a kind of religious dread.

'Absolutely,' he thundered out, causing Allun in front to wipe the windscreen carefully with a rag, 'the man's not only impudent but craven! A lot of bunkum, Fergusson. The man's about as religious as my left ****!'

Knowing the Squire's unfortunate capacity for 'saucy' talk, and feeling this was a prelude to such, I steered away from further considerations of the theological content of his anatomy, and pointed out that his excavating 'team' was quite sufficient in number, given the size of the barrow. But the Squire's concern was not with practicalities, but the deeper realms of our soul, those murky darknesses that others' actions swirl into and slap and clap against: voicing our earliest fears; sounding our profoundest terrors.

'Treasure-hunt!' came the spittle-spumed response. 'That's what they call it, Fergusson. Treasure-hunt! Now where d'you think they got that from, eh? The Vicar and his cronies. Eh? What? Treasure-hunt!'

A great thump on the door of the motor-car, a bark at Allun, and the road swirled once more into clouds, from which tiny chips of granite were expelled towards me—a most suitable afterword. An old man on a bench outside the Green Man inn, by the name of Harry Dimmick, added to the general contamination by expectorating in the direction of what the village termed 'that bloody stink-pot' (showing as little sense of differentiation between the various models as I), and cackling in a manner I found alarming.

A few days after the first of our finds, or a few days after the declaration of war—on whichever hook the reader would prefer to hang that 4th of August—the sound of hammering resounded around the square in Ulverton, small children with hoops (as much in fashion then as now, I seem to recall) gathered in knots about the personage hammering, and some of them shouted out, as best they could, the words RECRUITMENT and MEETING. This meaning nothing to them, they ran to the fields to tell their parents or elder siblings, who—being waist-deep in docks and thistles, et cetera—told them to be gone (if in less delicate and probably unprintable terms), thus returning the children post-haste to the elusive source, whose polysyllabic mysteries were stared at on the basis of the same principle that had the unlettered Charlemagne sleeping with the Bible beneath his pillow: knowledge may be yielded up by sheer proximity.

Thus it was that, returning from the excavation somewhat earlier than usual, owing to a mild attack of heat-stroke, I was accosted by piping voices, and explained as best I could to the gathered throng of dirty knees and faces and dirtier skirts (the recent habit of dressing little boys in boys' garments was not yet taken up in 1914) the meaning of RECRUITMENT; while the elders of the village, some of whom must have been familiar with the King's shilling, looked on with their customary suspicion at the newcomer's lofty cognisance of things beyond the Fogbourne vale.

Suffice to say that explaining to those little scruffy beings the principles of our conduct of war, which necessitates the calling forth of suicidal impulses, and the separation of husband from wife, son from mother, brother from sister, but most especially alarming in their eyes, father from child, was not the easiest task allotted to me, and quite surpassed the stickiest situation ever encountered in India. One charming little fellow, by the name of Stephen Bunce, hand in hand with his minuscule sister, stared up at me with such a profound look of innocence on his wee face that tears all but sprang to my eyes as I talked. That this onerous task was given to me at all is still to be regretted, for ever since (I feel) those same children have looked upon me as some kings in ancient plays look upon the Messenger: as somehow culpable of the havoc he brings news of. Though they are now (even the innocent little Stephen) all large and lusty and grown-up, it is not just my outsider complex that causes me to feel a chill, a little shiver of hatred and blame, as one of them passes me in the lane. Now imagine that sense increased tenfold, twentyfold, in the friable mind of the Squire—but the reader will perceive I am jumping ahead.

In the days before the meeting, only one urn and a small food vessel were uncovered from the newly-exposed layers of the barrow, but anticipation, and the hypnotic rhythm of the trowels, somehow made talk of the war superfluous. The last was a general blur of excitement and dread; this was a carefully delineated reality. Indeed, I would sleep at night with the same patch of chalky earth revolving before my eyes in vivid proximity and detail, with the mournful calls of peewits still sounding in my ears. It was at least an improvement on shakily bobbing fans and the bloated corpses of dogs.

The meeting, taking place just before harvest, was attended by the whole village. In those days, as now, long evenings in cramped cottages (or on its back-door step in the summer) were eagerly broken. The piano's wrong notes grow increasingly intrusive, the gramophone loses its appeal with its frozen repertoire, and the crystal set had not yet appeared to while away useless hours upon, fiddling with a cat's whisker! The same greasy cards snap dully on the same dark tables, the same brass ring swoops to clink against the same worn horn, while the clay-pipes and the gallon jugs have to be filled in the proverbial sweat of hay-prickled brows—and the songs and recitations cannot always be paying. Come the end of the summer months the whole village (though now there are rumours of electrification) crouches in a paraffin-flickering tedium—for books have not yet dispensed their eternal treasures in the majority of our homes. Staring into the fire links us, surely, with our primitive ancestors, for no other occupation was then, or is now, so heavily resorted to.

A small podium had been erected in the middle of the square, with a bleached Union Jack (our Women's Institute has it now) draped across the front. Three chairs and a table occupied most of the dais, and when the Squire, the Vicar, and a militarily-uniformed gentleman stepped up together, there was a brief toppling of furniture. The local photographer was hopping about attempting to keep a space in front of him clear of the crowd, and the local constable was ingratiating himself with a second uniformed gentleman. Three rows of chairs were positioned at one side for the higher echelons of the village, rather like boxes in the theatre, and perceiving myself to be one of this division I sat down. Children were tugging at skirts, hoops were clattering, a group of men in smocks were guffawing, and the church bell proceeded to join in with the quarter. The elders were gathered on benches before the New Inn, and they nodded and talked all the way through the booming nonsense of the first uniformed gentleman; while the crowd, I am sorry to say, gawped most impressively.

Feeling a thirst come on in the warm dusk, I glanced towards the inn as if a mere glance would appease, and saw, with an unwarranted jolt of the soul, the Manor's under-gardener leaning against the oak that grows outside that establishment, and shelters it, with a jug in one hand and a tankard in the other. Something about him puzzled me, and when the Vicar rose in turn and declaimed his own piping version of nonsense, I realised what it was: Percy Cullurne was watching, not the contents of the podium, but something above and beyond it. Turning surreptitiously about in my chair, I saw what it was: a house-martin busy in its nest in the eaves of the Post Office, flashing that tell-tale white patch as it swooped and scurried. I fancied I saw a smile upon the face of Percy Cullurne, but he was just too far the other side of the square for me to be absolutely certain.

When the Vicar had sat down to desultory applause, the Squire stood up and I forced myself to listen. I was keen to know how the Chief would handle his mission. During the week or so of the excavation, I had grown quite fond of him. One cannot help but grow fond of men with whom one is in physical concord, with whom a simple labour is being undertaken, an end met, and with whom few words serve. This is the other side of that useless and ghastly custom called War: companionship forged harder than iron in the heat of battle, in the slow fire of wounds and deprivation. I fancy, too, that those old men outside the ale-house, in almost permanent agonies from various rheumatic complaints brought on by their lifelong exposure to cold and wet, some crippled by the sheer weight of the work they had endured and mastered, had an unspoken bond amongst themselves, that thrilled more to silence than words, and might be recalled next time the reader enters an ale-house in the country, and thinks himself in the company of dumb idiots.

The Squire was sporting a white blazer and trousers, with a gold watch hanging lustrously from his white waistcoat. The crowd were mostly in their Sunday best, so that the scene resembled an old sombre painting of, say, St Michael before a host of sinners. Nothing about the Squire betokened a military demeanour: his shape was that of a William pear, his pince-nez sported a red silk ribbon, his hair was mounted above his head in two polished waves either side of a deep trough, each wave ending in a small curl over the forehead. His hands were small and his feet likewise, but they were the only dapper parts: there was a general air of dissipation about him, most especially in the creamy pallor of his face, which blurred the edge of neatness and admonished his attempts at moral heartiness. His vigorous fury spluttered with an element of indignation, lacking the cool deadliness of the true autocrat. He struggled against himself as much as his perceived enemies, but without that essential intelligence that might have allowed him to grow in stature and self-knowledge. In short, he was the model of an English country gentleman of those pre-war years—and he was (almost) never hateful.

The first part of his speech was a comfortable rug woven from the fleece of that familiar flock, consisting of Native Spot, Bosom of the Hills, Lord Nelson, Rich and Happy England, and Admiral Rodney—the last mainly on account of some blood shared with the weaver. The second part of the speech began to snap and flap a little, holding aloft Valour, Enterprise, Sacrifice, Boadicea, Heroic Zeal, and sundry other gilded sentiments, taking their shine from their proximity to Barbarous Foe, Tyrannical Ambition, and The Hun. The Destruction of Frederikshald was slowly unrolled as anecdote, at which point some of the listeners evidently grew weary of defences being staunch and resistances being vigorous—the fate of a Norwegian town in 1716 holding no immediate interest for them—and began to talk amongst themselves. The Squire saw this, and two small spots of red rose in his cheeks. Frederikshald was abandoned mid-cannon, there was a splutter and an adjustment of the pince-nez, but the foolhardy few—particularly the group of fellows in smocks, from whom a guffaw was to be heard now and again—continued to brandish their lucifers above the exceedingly dry tinder of the Squire's wrath.

The Vicar coughed, the Major scowled, I lowered my head, a louder guffaw sounded, there was a brief silence. Having head thus lowered, and eyes fixed firmly on the ground, with all the comfort of a chap sheltering beneath an ammunition lorry, I was mightily surprised to hear, instead of an explosion, a long 'Ooooo' from all about me, rather as if a flock of giant doves had winged happily into the square, and nested amongst us. Looking up, I saw a most remarkable sight: the Squire was holding aloft a large curved sword, polished to a mirror, which flashed the evening sun across our eyes and caused me to blink hurriedly. In the other hand he was holding its tasselled crimson scabbard, from which it had evidently just been drawn. Where this magnificent weapon (identified by the frumpy lady on my right as a cavalryman's sabre) had emerged from I cannot say, but it transformed the Squire thoroughly, as if its magical properties of Valour, Enterprise, Sacrifice, and Heroic Zeal had trickled down into his arm, and then his chest, and so on, and filled his whole otherwise unremarkable frame.

He then opened his mouth and delivered a single sentence, which had neither the Valours nor the Zeals about it, but was memorable for its simple earnestness. In its own small way it could have jostled in some Heavenly Mausoleum for Oratory with Queen Elizabeth's speech at Tilbury ('I know I have the body but of a weak and feeble woman . . .' et cetera), which were it not for dusty schoolrooms I would now probably find as invigorating as the oaken-hearted soldiery were reported to have done. The secret of the Squire's earnestness, however, was in its straightforward childishness—perhaps boyishness would be a kinder term. He transformed the essential boyishness of all these abstract sentiments into something touchable and felt. He caught the nursery mood of the country in this microcosm of place, and moved our hearts; for we saw the little boy in him and so felt the little boy in us; each small hand enclosed in a firm grasp that was History bidding us from above to come.

'My grandfather,' cried he, 'bore this sword at Waterloo!'

Another 'Oooo' extended the final syllable, and the Major and the Vicar smiled at each other. The sword's magical properties increased. It flashed back at us the golden dazzling moments of British victories. Its needle-sharp point proclaimed our freedoms. Its sleek curve was as perpetual as the spumed steely coastline of our island. The Squire swung it through the evening air, and its high hiss was the civilised thrum of the great Empire, quietly valiant, subduing only the primitive and bloody places of the world, erecting Industry in its stead.

Yes, dear reader, all these moth-eaten images spun through my mind, and allowed me for a moment (the sentiment was short-lived) to comprehend the effect, to be buoyed up, as it were, on the swell, and not sink in spluttering condemnation.

The Union Jack draped over the front of the podium swelled slightly in the evening breeze, that carried on its bosom the scent of golden fields awaiting the reapers' blades; and the Squire lowered the sword and touched the front edge of the podium, so that all eyes followed its line to the heart of their flag.

'Once again we are called. Once again the foe knocks at our gates. Once again our young men, our hearts of oak, have the opportunity to join this great march, to wield this same sword, to follow this same flag. The flag that says we are free forever. No Napoleon, no Hun, no barbarous tyrant will ever tear it from us.'

The effect, as I have said, was short-lived on me, once the usual threadbare patches had returned. But for the humble folk gathered in the square, whose lives were generally field-hedged, or scullery-encompassed, whose intellects then (even more than now) resembled their living rooms—shut up and musty, turned into parlours for the odd Sunday or the once-a-year guest, the odd jolt in an unchanging routine; and whose concerns therefore barely rose above the washing-tub or the driving coulter or the pennies in the sugar-tin—for these people the Squire's speech somehow unbarred the bolts and blew open the doors: some featureless excitement was emerging; something to harass boredom out of its hole, to arrest the mangle in its squealing, eternal revolutions.

There was one exception to this depressing phenomenon: the under-gardener of the Manor remained transfixed not by the venerable sabre that had slashed flesh at Waterloo, but by the house-martin. Whether his interest was real or otherwise, I did not, and still do not, know; the several conversations on matters botanical and ornithological I had had with him made me pretty certain of his deep knowledge. But I fancy the house-martin was a kind of point of meditation, whose real purpose was to deflect that hypnotic flash. I felt ashamed of my own brief thrill, and there arose in me a corresponding defiance—even a sense of disgust at the emotions unleashed across this still summer's evening in rural England. But the Squire was now at the climax of his oratorical symphony: this was the point of the meeting, and an injection of the lowest element of that 'radical Fire' which binds love and wrath, and is called Envy.

'The Major has asked me to tell you that any man here who is willing to defend our country, to fight for freedom, in the name of God, may step forward and declare himself. Yesterday, the village of Bursop gave to the cause thirty of its young vigorous men. Thirty! And, I hear someone call out—harvest is only a week away! But the women and children of Bursop are doughty enough, apparently, to gather the corn, and free their menfolk for an even nobler harvest. Shall Ulverton be bested by Bursop? Shall Bursop be the name that rings down the annals of history, as the village that stepped forward when the hour called, and laid itself upon the, ah . . .'

There was a brief pause, as the Squire's grasp of metaphorical nicety gave out, and the choices had evidently narrowed to a morbid few, reeking of pagan rather than Christian virtues, and being altogether too passive (I assume 'pyre' and 'altar' were prime candidates) for the occasion. In retrospect, how fitting would that metaphor have been! This hitch in the proceedings was saved by a shout from one of the smocks, to the effect (I paraphrase) that Bursop folk were ineffectual layabouts, and we could do better—whereupon the whole crowd roared to a man, or shrieked to a woman. Such behaviour would not have seemed so hateful had they been picking teams for their annual cricket match, but memories of my nephew's facial injuries in the South African war loomed before me, and refused to evaporate. I began to feel nauseous, and spun a mental thread between myself and Percy Cullurne, who remained unsettlingly oblivious to the proceedings.

The Squire grinned and adjusted his pince-nez, and my fondness for him was as the melting snow. Suffice to say that a few more shovelfuls of the poorest quality coal, and the blaze was undousable. Another great roar, a shifting and shoving about, and suddenly there they were—the spoils of eloquence: thirty-two strapping fellows (well, most of them were strapping) in a neat line between the people and the podium. They shifted from foot to foot, they tossed pebbles from one hand to the other, they scratched their noses, they grinned ostentatiously at loved ones. I thought of Carlyle's dictum, that 'there is nothing in the world you can conceive so difficult, as that of getting a set of men gathered together as soldiers'. I reflected: here are a group of agricultural labourers, or whatever, in their Sunday best, which was not saying a great deal, who would no more 'walk into the cannon's mouth' for one man as they would wipe their dirty boots on entering the scullery—and yet in a few months or so, that is exactly what they will be doing. I remain with 'cannon's mouth', for my notions of war were then as outmoded, dear reader, as the flashing sabre was—and if you were to conquer the temporal flux, and return as you are to that square, and stand beside me and whisper of all that you now know—of spitting machine-guns and lumbering metal monsters, of men cut down like fairground toys, of hideous waste in a universe of sucking mud, of gas and shrieks and drowning horses—I should think of you as utterly mad!

For did not the poignancy of that moment clutch even at my cynical heart? India and my wife's death had not quite corroded all my softer faculties, I fear: a faint tinge of pride, that my newly-adopted home had pipped Bursop by two runs, as it were, crept into my visage. My mouth found itself curving into a satisfied smile, my head nodded at the frumpy lady to my right, and the cantankerous gent to my left, and for a moment I was sealed in tight with the lot of them.

It was at that moment that I realised, with an unwarranted jump to the heart, that Trevick and the other 'diggers' were absent. This thought was all but instantaneous with a sudden concern that all our barrow 'team' would be despatched forthwith to Flanders. There was a flurry, a straightening of backs, a darting in and out from under a black cloth, a shuffling of the three Important Persons into a group beside the Sacrificial Lambs, and the flashlight exploded like a tiny bomb, making the Vicar jump a little, which explains why his face is a thankful blur, his deadly role forgotten to history (I have the photograph before me now). I fretted at the absence of my companions on the barrow. An awful truth began to dawn upon me. And as this livid light rose in my mind, I saw Percy Cullurne leaning against the water-pump that dribbled into its trough between the podium and the New Inn, and is still tenaciously known as 'The Well'; he was cupping a handful of water to his mouth. The line of men were having their hands shaken by the Major, and the crowd were waiting for the next stage in the proceedings. The Major stepped onto the podium for a final address. There was quiet. Then as he opened his mouth there was a squeak from the water-pump, then another: it had (and still has) an infernal squeak. Percy Cullurne had a hot face, and was bathing it, snorting and shaking his great wide head. I was reminded of the baptism of our Lord, for some reason. Anyway, there was a hint of purification about the action.

The Major turned; the Squire turned. Up to that point the Squire had not noticed Percy Cullurne. Now all eyes were turned on Percy Cullurne. Percy Cullurne stood upright and saw us watching him. He scanned our eyes and shook his hands free of water, as he had done on that very spot thousands of times before, I am sure. He sniffed. He spat, though not in anger: it was a practical, working-man's expectoration. He sniffed again and passed a hand across his mouth. Every action of his had become entrancing. One almost expected him to start dancing and singing, as in the music-hall, or produce a rabbit from his cloth-cap (needless to say, Percy Cullurne was not in his Sunday best). But then he fell still, and merely stared us back. It was our turn to move.

'Ah!' came from the Major. The Major thought that enough, evidently.

The Squire had no choice. Anyway, his Furies were at him. His moment of personal glory was crumbling before his very eyes. He cleared his throat. He could, with a great effort of will, have turned his back, and said nothing. 'The greatest events,' as Fielding puts it, 'are produced by a nice train of little circumstances.' How different things might have been then!

'Ah!' came from the Squire.

Percy Cullurne cocked his head slightly, like a faithful dog who has just received an unfamiliar command.

'Cullurne,' said the Squire. He lifted his chin up, and placed his small hands behind his back, and rocked to and fro on his heels. His hair-oil gleamed in a decent imitation of St Michael's helmet.

'There's a place at the end, Cullurne. Make it thirty-three.'

The crowd murmured its approval, along with one or two shouts from smocks, to the effect that Percy could stop a regiment with two fingers, if he could find them—which from the laughter that followed was clearly not meant to be complimentary; but its probable vulgar import, hidden in the multiple folds of village irony, was wholly lost on me. Percy Cullurne rested an elbow against the pump and continued to stare at us with nothing but puzzlement showing across his features. The frumpy old lady to my right leaned across in front of me to the cantankerous gent on my left and whispered, 'Village idiot!' To my shame, I did not flick her hat off, but merely wrinkled my nose at the stench of naphthalene, and emphatically cleared my throat.

Small beads of perspiration began to run down the Squire's nose. He compressed his lips and puckered them in and out, like a child about to cry ('bivering'—as the local dialect rather charmingly has it). He looked anxiously about him for what I could only imagine was an escape route. Fury was grappling with a sense of absolute funk. This was extraordinary. His fingers locked themselves behind his back, then writhed. I believe to this day that he knew he was defeated. Percy Cullurne had probably terrified him for years, though he was twice Cullurne's age, and of course immeasurably superior in social position. I know men of impeccable breeding who live in abject fear of a particular domestic servant (often the butler). It is, I think, a need, a profound desire, acting within them. Percy Cullurne has never grappled with himself. He is, in one way, as insentient to his own soul as a plant or a tree because he has never felt a need to query that inner self. His soul is commensurate with desire: his desire is his soul, and the soul remains content merely to be.

'Come on man,' said the Squire, 'come on.'

Cullurne passed a big hand across his big face, which appeared to wipe away the puzzlement, pushed himself off from the pump and began to walk towards us. It was a space of only some thirty yards, but his slow, shambling gait, the ease of his great limbs, the utter silence that surrounded the strike of his iron-shod heels against the hard ground, the sudden shattering of a big dry whorl of horse-dung by an oblivious boot, his long shadow dancing over the stony earth—all this made his progress as slow as a Titan's, as if a figure from some Homeric bronze-hammered past had loomed, had risen again into our midst. I can't honestly say now whether I knew what he was about to do: perhaps all of us thought he would shuffle onto the end of the line, to a cheer no doubt, and the meeting would have been accounted a great success. Whatever Cullurne was or was not to do, we knew we would never forget that slow, methodical advance towards us, transfixing time itself; bespeaking slow, hard hours in the field, or in the dusty barn, or in the great lavish garden of the Manor; and arresting, for a long minute, our madness.

Whatever we were thinking, two Important Persons were in no doubt of his intentions: the Vicar, his head on one side, his palms together, was ready to grant his blessing; the Major had come down from the podium and was standing with an equally ready hand extended from a crisp cuff; the Squire, however, was rigid from head to toe. The Sacrificial Lambs watched Cullurne from the corner of their eyes, until Cullurne came to a stop two paces from them, and from the Squire. The crowd were eerily quiet. The whole square appeared suspended in a great silence, into which Cullurne's voice broke—I was tempted to say like the blows of a blacksmith's hammer, but it wasn't like that at all. It was not violent, it was not thrust from him: it seemed to branch as naturally from him, in those soft syllables, as a tree from the earth. I cannot put it into words. Suffice to say that he spoke quietly, as if only to the Squire—but there was not a man or woman in that wide square who did not hear him.

'I'd rather,' he said, 'bide at home.'

The Squire swallowed. His fingers writhed.

'Stay at home, man?'

The man nodded slowly. There were a few titters in the crowd, and a smock snorted. The cantankerous gent on my left tut-tutted violently.

The Squire lifted his chin still higher.

'Duty, Cullurne. I would be proud for one of my servants to answer the call of the hour. His country in need. And so on. Duty, Cullurne. Duty.'

The Major's hand drooped, but did not fall. The Vicar's mouth puckered into a mew of distaste. My heart, I have to say, was hammering wildly. There was a curious taste of metal in my mouth. The church rang the quarter, thudding its fleet hooves across our temporal defiance. As the echoes washed away, the under-gardener spoke again.

'I'd rather bide at home, sir. That's all.'

The crowd's titters grew into chuckles. The young men in the line shifted from foot to foot, grinning.

'I see,' said the Squire. He looked about him, as if for aid. People averted their eyes—myself included. He began to glower. He was grappling with himself; it was painful to watch. It was, in some profound way, embarrassing.

'Yes. I see. He would rather stay at home. Yes. I see. What? Well, if a man would rather stay at home, then who are we to stop him, what? What? Thank you, Cullurne.'

Bare reportage cannot convey the deep hatred sometimes evinced between men through the simplest address. The words of the Squire were more spat out than spoken. The crowd murmured. Cullurne turned and walked away, and every eye followed his long strides, every heart beat to his steady rhythm—until each step became no more than a faint echo, dwindling to silence through the empty lanes.

Activity broke out again in the square: the crowd began to disperse into small knots, the young men gave their names to a dapper clerk who had suddenly appeared from the side of the crowd, the hoops rattled and a green-liveried automobile roared to a stop outside the Post Office and diverted everyone's attention. It was the Major's. When I looked above it, at the eaves, I saw nothing. The house-martin had gone.

It was not I who chose Ulverton as the 'happy spot' for my final innings; it was the skein of family connections that pulled me to this place. My wife's second cousin, Mrs Mary Holland, had lived in the village for almost all her married life; although her husband was long dead by the time I settled here, she was so enamoured of the place in which she had brought up her family, that she had vowed to stay on and not retire, as was the wont then, to a widow's decline in Weymouth. Our friendship began through tragedy: having lost her darling son, Daniel, to influenza in his first term at Eton in the same year as my own brother was appointed housemaster there, in 1886, relationships were established more closely than would otherwise have been the case, for the stricken mother needed all the support we could give her; mine being of the post-marked variety, until my leave gave us the opportunity to visit her in 1893. I well remember the carriage mounting that last hill north of Ulverton, cresting the bare, nibbled flanks of Frum Down, and giving us all of a sudden that enchanted view of the verdant river, the clustering trees, the black thatch of ancient roofs and the simple grey stone of the church, that bespoke all our exiled dreams, and seemed to embody all our fairest fancies! Apart from the odd straggling copse, and the neat lushness of Ulverton House, all about was naked and desolate, even repellent (how ignorant I was then of the springy exhilaration of our bare downland!)—but this only served to heighten the charms of this remote village. We were stricken by love, and vowed to make this 'our' England on the final return from India. Alas, our plans were only half-realised, as it were: dashed by dysentery and death—and sometimes I find the association dreadful in my solitude; Mrs Holland too now lying beside her husband and her son near the Saxon yew of our secluded churchyard, their tombstone recording their allotted spans only a little less mutely than the grassy mounds of the labouring generations, whose stones are as bereft of art as their lives.

When I am depressed in spirits I play Chopin. I am famous for this: my cottage being on the main street, facing the high flint wall of the churchyard, the open windows of summer mean that any passing souls are vexed by my missed notes, or stirred by my harmonies. On that day, that August day fourteen years ago, as the thirty-two young men of Ulverton clambered aboard the bus and waved their proud farewells, and were trotted out of sight, to some distant and unimaginable vista, each dressed as if for a church outing, or a visit to town with their beloveds, I played my heart out. Mrs Holland sat by the window and listened, tears welling in her eyes through the B minor Sonata, as the cries of the young men sounded in the street, their younger siblings shrieked and whistled, their mothers and fathers waved and kissed and blew their noses, and the bus momentarily darkened the room as it passed.

'It will only be a small affair,' said Mrs Holland. 'My dear husband used to play this.'

I said nothing and played on.

Ulverton had more volunteers than any other village on the downs. The rhetorical flourish with the sabre had played its part, for everyone said how 'the Squire hev done us proud, then.' I continued to work shoulder to shoulder with the men he had forbidden to attend the meeting. At least, that is how I interpreted their absence. In the way of things here, no one questioned this privilege, because no one saw it as such; believe it or not, those lucky few with their noses to the chalk were seen as exhibiting extreme unselfishness. They were making their sacrifice for the sake of knowledge and discovery. The talk of treasure-hunts dwindled in the tap-rooms of Ulverton. That healthy air of ruefulness which I had so valued in the English countryman and countrywoman evaporated in those early months of the war: loins were girded, and spines stiffened, and the deadlier face of patriotism shown, in a way I found thoroughly alarming.

There was only one pariah, one Untouchable, in our pastoral haven—and that was Percy Cullurne. 'Craven' was the least insulting, and the most printable, of the many qualifications made upon his good name that summer and autumn. He, in his turn, lapsed into near silence, seeming not to feel the sting of the verbal sticks and stones, and the odd scrawled contribution to fellow-feeling upon his cottage door, and the various small missiles aimed at him by the dwarf regiments, goaded on by their zealous parents. It might have turned out otherwise: a hundred years earlier, he would no doubt have been the hero of the hour, carried shoulder-high around a burning rick. But the vans of Socialism, odious though they were, had only trundled ineffectually through our village by 1914: perhaps owing to the memories of the older folk, still vivid, of the terrible results of rebellion, and a general relieving of hardship and poverty, there was little connection made between the ranting from the vans and the famous last words of John Oadam [alias 'Captain Bedwine' of the ballads—see *The Book of Downland Songs*, 1923]; little attempt to relate the tenets of the placarded strangers with the fenced-off woods and the touched cap, that deference as ingrained as the soil in the furrows of their hands.

Not that the members of the 'team' were happy with this arrangement—I mean, their enforced sacrifice. I don't want to give the impression that they were burning to be off into foreign parts, and slaughter the Hun: no, it was far more owing to an uncomfortable sense of exclusiveness; a coat that carries well in Pall Mall, but not amongst the labouring brethren of rural England. Exclusiveness, or difference, without material satisfaction—that is too close to the outsider complex. Every aside in the Half Moon, or the Malt Shovel, or the Green Man, or the New Inn; every little silence at their leaving; every knowing smile or wink in the lane; each military or patriotic reference in the Harvest Home songs of that summer's end; every slow, laborious reading-out of the newspaper before the assembled family or the tap-room company became a jab, a prod, not just to the conscience but to that feeling of belonging so essential to the otherwise lonely human animal. Our village was more full of eccentrics then than now, but even the most awry of minds was inextricably woven into the common fabric, just as the trees in the wood grow more individual the more familiar one becomes with the mass. Matters have changed: our great roads are thronged with motor-cars and lorries, the wireless tinkles, the telephone connects us with far-away towns. Ulverton is slowly losing its sense of remoteness; each day brings the world nearer, darkening my room with its passing, pruning us of our odder growths, blowing away the strong rich scents that come of stagnation. The nearest high scarp is no longer the edge of the world, and heads barely turn when the toot of a motor-car sounds at Church Corner. Is this to be regretted? Time, dear reader, shall arbitrate upon that question—not I.

Let us remain with that group of men huddled upon the high hills of chalky England in the late summer of 1914: let us try to imagine their position, and feel their discomfort: let us equate it with our own moments in life, when someone has done something that reflects a light back upon us, in which we are uncomfortably exposed to our conscience, and to the imagined grievances of others. Then in the penultimate week of August the bell tolled a death-knell; and slow and dull and remorseless it sounded across the downs. Each man cocked an ear, paused in his delicate work. A far shout from a stubbled field, and a cart rocking with its corn-load stopped. Two great whirring reapers in a field below us plodded on, their magnificent harnessed teams oblivious to human misfortunes—but the drivers turned in their seats to look down at the village, and the women paused by their stooks, lifting their bonnets to gaze. Tiny figures were to be seen hurtling up various tracks, childish shrills sounded, the harvesters in the fields came together in knots and dispersed, and soon enough Sidney Bint, the baker's small boy, came panting up the side of the mound, and the name of Jimmy Tuck resounded shrilly over our little scooped world. A pale lad with a stutter who had done me some service by mending the stone outhouse roof at the bottom of my garden—making of it a study wherein I sit now, in the scent of buddleia, just as I did then through those golden evenings—Jimmy Tuck died at Mauberge on August 21st, blown apart by an artillery shell.

We all turned to the Squire as the lad stood there, panting, apparently exhilarated by the effect his words had had. Another boy popped up beside him, swore softly at being beaten to it, put his hand on his friend's shoulder, and looked down at us with equal anticipation. I felt for a moment as though I was on a stage, in an ancient theatre, where ritual grief sounded after ritual murder. We were looking to the Squire as if he were the salvatory King, as if he might raise his arms, and open his throat, and wail for all of us. Instead, he reached into his waistcoat pocket and took out two pennies, flicked them to the boys (who scampered off down Louzy Hill, shrieking at their good fortune), scratched his forehead, and indicated with his trowel that we should continue—and nothing more was said for the rest of the day, bar the odd 'poor bugger' murmured into the chalk. I felt now as if I were at a tea-party where a guest had loudly broken wind; where some rule had been broken and custom breached by the unforeseen—and no one was quite sure what to do about it.

So it was not unexpected when Marlers stood up at the end of a day's excavation and announced that this was to be his last week. His leggings were white with chalk; his face was streaked like a clown's. He said that

Jimmy Tuck's mother looked at him funny, that the nips looked at him funny, that the whole universe, in effect, was looking at 'awld Marlers funny'. I had indeed looked at him, I must say, with a wry internal grin since our first encounter, when he had come to advise on the contents of my greenhouse, and I had displayed the newcomer's unerring ability to try too hard. 'Ah, good morning Mr Marlow, come in,' said I. 'My name en't Marlow,' came the lugubrious reply, 'it be Trevick.' Why 'Marlers' I have not been able to discover. Not that it matters now: how many bright appendages are lost, how many quirks and tics that make up the human sum of personality slip beneath the earth, when faceless Death strikes!

Back on the barrow, the Squire blanched a little at this news. 'It's your decision,' he said. He could have said little else, in the circumstances. Ernest, whom he was consulting at that minute, sucked on a pencil.

'Duty,' said Marlers, glancing at the others, who were wiping their trowels on the soft tussocks. 'You talked of duty at the meetin', so we understand. That's why all our young lads have gone. You an' your sword from Waterloo, sir.'

'Yes,' said the Squire, looking down. 'Of course. Duty.'

Ernest began to flick through his drawings. Urns, shards, an iron hair-pin, yesterday's broken beaker impressed with a comb in crude diamond-shaped patterns. Nothing of significance or value.

'Yes. Of course. Duty.'

Marlers, Allun the chauffeur, Terence Brinn, and wheezy but no doubt formidable Tom Sedgwick—all left at the end of the week. Ernest stayed, of course—as well as Dart, nostrils quivering like a horse, content with his stupidity. The Squire was devastated, and consoled himself by shooting pigeons for a week in Bailey's Wood—while the barrow was left under canvas wraps. A month of disappointing finds had taken its toll, and now war had interrupted his long-held ambition (this is how I now interpreted it) to take possession of an ancient treasure.

Sometime during this week of idleness, Ernest called round and (in between taking sips of tea with his tongue-tip protruded, like a cat at its milk) explained to me the various stages through which the barrow had passed before resting content with tussocks and butterflies and the odd rustic rump for four thousand or so years. His enthusiasm was tempered by the possibility that our Chief had lost interest. This was, he claimed, a sign of the amateur.

'Though, of course, I cannot, um, blame him. Of course.'

I nodded. His moustache was wiped free of tea and malt biscuit and he spread out a diagram on the table between us.

'Here,' he said, pointing to a large oblong ringing the welter of circles and crosses; 'here is the latest burial-phase. A ditch dug around the mound in which, um, we have found evidence of burial by cremation. The discoloration of the soil is probably due to the rotting of wooden stakes surrounding the most recent, um, mound phase.'

He paused. I was impressed.

'From previous expeditions which I have been party to I predict that, um, an earlier phase will yield something much more exciting.'

'Why should it?'

He smiled.

'The initial justification for such a sizeable mound,' he replied, in a triumphant tone befitting the Assistant Secretary of our county's Archaeological Society. His moustache quivered at my quizzical look. 'Our finds up to now, um, these recent finds—they were simply additions. And cremation is, I believe, associated with later centuries. If we continue, I confidently predict that, um, we will uncover a rich burial, uncremated, with grave-goods to match. It might take many weeks, but I am sure it will be, um, worth it.'

I sat back and pondered his assertions while he lapped his tea. In actual fact, I was hardly bothered one way or another. With such recent memories of my wife's last illness, I was growing averse to finding anything at all, if it meant uncovering something so manifestly morbid. To reveal the dead is not to release them.

'I see. But with whom? Dart? He's more a liability than a help. He still believes the trowel is his hammer and the chalk the anvil, if I'm not mistaken. He would smash the skull before we saw it. I say we should enlist some female support, but the Chief is dead agin it, needless to say.'

Ernest laughed—giggled would be a better description. The Chief's misogyny was the best known fact about him—the oft-given explanation of his bachelor state, accompanied with an apparent unconcern at the inevitable withering of the Norcoat-Wells tree.

'Yes, there's the problem. Um, I've often wondered why the under-gardener hasn't joined us. He's, um, very strong.'

'Percy Cullurne?'

'Yes.'

I sighed. 'That man has strong opinions of his own. As you saw—or rather, would have seen, at the meeting.'

'I heard, yes,' he said, flushing a little at this somewhat oblique reproval. 'But what are these opinions? Concerning the excavation, I mean.' He coughed and blew his nose, in case I had forgotten about his weakly constitution. 'He never,' he added, 'says very much.'

'That's partly because the Squire has forbidden him to do so. Button your lip, he was told, apparently. Too much talk of treasure. So that is what Cullurne has done, *in toto*. I have had several most fruitful discussions with him on ornithological and botanical matters, as well as other more general concerns, such as the survival of the soul after death. Now it is exceedingly difficult to extract the shortest of sentences from him, unless you are talking of the weather, or the crops, or such like. And that in an almost impenetrable dialect, which was not the case before.'

'Ah,' Ernest nodded, and wiped his moustache with the corner of his handkerchief. 'Then we will have to work slowly. Or recruit others. Older men. A pity, a pity. Um, yourself excused, of course. The new chauffeur looks very, um, frail. And the harvest is at its height. Pray for a fine autumn.'

After the Battle of the Marne, which raged through the first and second week of September, and in which our county regiment was not involved, the Germans dug in at the Aisne and trench warfare began. It was around then that my depressions returned. That week of enforced inaction through a spell of unusually hot weather, joined with a certain emptiness about the village heart, and the sight of a small girl outside the village shop weeping for her father 'as goed off to fight on my birthday, an' med never come back!'—these played on my nerves, already as much frayed as my skin was by the many years of tropical sun. A colonial servant is instantly recognisable by his bleached and desiccated hair, his prematurely lined face, the hand-shake from repeated bouts of fever, and frequently (not, I am happy to add, in my case) the redolence of alcoholic addiction. His wife will be a mirror image, if wispier throughout, and with eyes dazed by monsoon-boredom and the company of dolts. Dark moods are an occupational hazard, even more so when these husks return to their mother-country, and find her erring on the side of dampness rather than coolness, as well as changed for the worse—always changed for the worse. The great wheels of the Empire, though in my opinion faltering now, grind her servants as effectively as they do her coffee-beans, but with far less substance to the end product. They are somehow emptied of anything but a kind of bitter regret, as if true happiness had only just eluded them in the middle of blinding squares or on the netted verandahs. How much happier that man who remains in his birthplace, and does not take the horizon as his gate to contentment!

My dreams around this time were all of skeletons, turning their heads in the chalk and grinning at me with my wife's face; not the face I married and loved but the late phantasmagoric countenance of advanced dysentery. When the excavations resumed in the middle of the month with Dart, Ernest, the Squire, the new chauffeur Dick Lock, a white-stubbled handyman named Davey Purdue who was almost my age, and Robert Rose—an unpleasantly supercilious young northerner, who had been a footman up at Ulverton House until the loss of the last Chalmers-Lavery in the Titanic disaster—I had half a mind to give the whole thing up. But I persisted, partly for the sake of the exercise and the fresh air, and partly, curious as it may sound, for the sake of our Chief, whose pale complexion now bore small vein-marks of anxiety across the cheeks, but whom Ernest had persuaded nevertheless to continue with the enterprise. My weakness and my strength had always been an abiding sense of loyalty—even to those whom I could otherwise condemn. And as each scrape of the trowel rang off the flints and was taken by the breeze, a new sense of excitement hovered, despite my nostalgia for Marlers's quiet quips, and Tom's wheeze, and Terence Brinn's silly laugh, and Allun's nonchalant handling of the Squire's moods. Stumpy Dick Lock was amiable enough, but Rose's affected superiority and coarse humour cast a blight on those days, so that the golden presence of the Ineffable rarely stirred and rustled.

About a week after harvest I was walking that same back-path that comes out behind the brick wall of the Manor estate and its effulgent dog-rose, when I glimpsed Cullurne pouring feed into a tin trough. The sheep—an unusual spiral-horned breed the Squire was keen on promulgating—were running towards him and pressed quite happily about his knees as he shook the sack out. The dust hazed him in a copper-coloured aureole as the autumn sun levelled itself through the leaves of the small wood behind. He saw me, and raised his hand in greeting. I thought how clear and simple that life was, how like the ancient shepherds on the slopes of Attica he must look! I walked to the gate, and he came over and leaned on the iron. Flecks of bran nestled in his hair and in his stubble; his jacket was buttonless. He rested a boot on the lower cross-piece. His repose was one of energy held in check, his big arms the calmer for the exertion they were used to.

'Middlin' weather,' he said. He sucked on a tooth with a most impressive squeal.

'Very decent weather, I thought,' said I, putting his caution down to the usual tendency of rural folk to underplay good fortune.

'Drought,' he replied, without a hint of superciliousness. 'Ben't be goin' to rain agin till November, by my finger.'

'Ah, drought,' said I, feeling once more the unbridgeable gulf between myself and my surroundings on anything other than aesthetic terms. 'Of course. Drought.'

'Put the harvest in your pipe an' smoke her. Malt-rashed. Atermath ben't hardly wuth gallin the herse-collar vor. Put her in your pipe too. Cheaper nor twist.'

This being a particularly opaque piece of information, I merely nodded my head, and vowed to join the English Dialect Society forthwith—as I usually vowed when talking to the recently uncompromising Percy Cullurne, or any other provincially-immured inhabitant.

Then I remembered a local saying taught me by Marlers, and tried it out, feeling the proverbial coals-to-Newcastle effect, but not willing to let such an extraordinarily suitable slot go unfilled—even though the phrase had struck me as odd, having all the riddling quality of so many rural saws.

'Yes indeed,' I ventured. 'Ahem. What be bad for the hay be good for the termites.'

The effect was unexpected. Cullurne paused a moment, then burst into most uncharacteristic fits of laughter; tears poured from his eyes, and made admirable inroads through the dust and dirt on his cheeks. He slapped the gate, then his knees, and shook his head as the attack subsided, much as he had shaken water from his face in the square. Far from being mortified, I too was affected, and snorted into my fist, my chest heaving in a manner I had not known for months, even years. Eventually I managed to ask him what had been so amiss in my use of local wisdom. Another peal, several repetitions of the saying, each followed by further peals, then a wiping of eyes, a blowing of nose into a greasy rag, a shaking of his head, a brief apology, then the illumination:

'Turmuts! What be good vor the haay be bad vor the turmuts!'

Inevitably the merriment was resumed, at my picturing of a termite as somehow inextricably countering hay, instead of the common and water-loving turnip, and by the end of this session I was feeling quite weak, but astoundingly well, as if I had walked the downs twice over without a break in my stride.

'It was Marlers who taught me that,' I said. 'I evidently misheard him. Well I do miss him, you know. I miss all of them. Don't you?'

Cullurne wiped his eyes and grunted. He sucked on his tooth. He sniffed.

'Silly buggers,' was all he murmured.

We did not notice the horse even when it had rounded the corner for, as the gate was well tucked into the hedgerow, it had remained half-hidden by the tall bobbing splash-red of mallow and knapweed along the wayside. I was halfway through an observation upon the sterling qualities of young Jimmy Tuck, and the apparent mental collapse of his widowed mother subsequent to his death, when I looked up and saw the bristly face of the Squire just as he was pulling on the reins to stop. I felt a cloud of dust settle grittily in my open mouth, and shut it. He glared at me for a moment then glanced not at Cullurne but at a point about two feet above his head.

'See about the fence at the bottom of Brambleberry Piece,' he snapped. (Not quite a true reportage: the name of the field was codified by familiarity into 'Bram's', but I have over the years since joined the two nomenclatures of our village—the official and the non-official—and must take the opportunity to show off my research.)

The Squire then looked back at me with what I can only describe as small eyes, switched at the horse with his crop as though he rather wished my flank were under it, and left us once more in a swirl of dust, thudding into a gallop as the track meandered onto the open downland. Bluebottles clamped themselves without a moment's hesitation on the fresh dung. Cullurne shrugged at my raised eyebrows.

'Best see 'bout ut then,' he said.

'Well, he was to the point.' Cullurne nodded and walked off, touching his brow. I watched him for a moment, then turned and left that spot myself; left the foolish nuzzling of the sheep in their feed, the finches scrabbling about the hedgerow, the gold disc of the sun filtering through a thousand leaves as it sank—left that particular place enjoined on that particular evening, in which two forces came together for a moment, bristled, and departed; as if all that is irreconcilable lay not in the far-off thump and whistle and wet of the Aisne, but there, in that golden, English dusk, that glimpse of Attica!

It was, I think, at the beginning of the following week, when I had shoved a ladder into the branches of my apple-tree and was twirling the russets easily off their stems of an evening, that Lock, assigned to a corner of the (by now) vast digging area, clambered up the stepped side of the site and thrust something at Ernest, who almost fell off his canvas stool in fright, for the object in question was a dagger. The Squire, relieving himself against a nearby elm, had scarcely buttoned himself back into decency when Ernest's excited shriek brought him hurtling back. Lock's eyes were wide in his small face as he pointed out the exact spot in which the dagger had lain. It was, Ernest stated, of bronze or copper, with a simple triangular blade and a pointed tang to which a wooden hilt would have been tied by twine.

We were each assigned a tiny area and given a brush, of the sort used in watercolour painting—except for Dart, who was told to wield his trowel as far as possible from the rest of us. It was a tedious business, especially as it had rained unexpectedly (though Cullurne's prediction was to come true) and the soil was wet, gathering into small clods with each stroke. Ernest joined us and it was he, fortunately, who first revealed the hump which stroke by stroke, hour by hour, turned inexorably into the cranium of a buried ancient. I fancied we were painting it into life, and had difficulty in grasping the extraordinary truth of that long sleep—though but a moment in comparison with the aeons of buried Time those rolling chalk hills were witness to, the millions and millions of submerged years my feet compressed each time I walked that turf, the unimaginably lengthy accumulations of centuries that saw the slow sinking of microscopic sea-creatures and the slow rising of their bodily memorial: the same that marked my knees bone-white as I kneeled to my task within the opened barrow. The ancient White Horse, which lay then shrouded in a tangle of bramble on the scarp below us, was but a second old in comparison with the flesh it had once been cut from. The tesserae of the past—Bronze-Age, Roman, mediaeval—thrown up by the coulter are as infant toys to the booming venerableness of the chalk that cradles them. And we—who are we to flail and clamour, to batter and slay, when all that surrounds us tells us of our insignificance, of our infinitesimal capacities, of our inevitable anonymity in the eternal reaches of Time?

But there in our barrow the present peeled back into sufficient ancientness to make every man around me thrill to the sight. The Squire bent down with his mouth open, his pince-nez crooked, his hair stuck upright—the almost comic embodiment of boyish excitement—as the brushes unveiled the eye-sockets, then the nose cavity, and finally the grin of those broken teeth and their slung jaw: as if the face of some horror had broken a calm sea's surface and rested there. Within a week the outline of the complete skeleton had been sketched, as it were, into view—my own contribution being the right hand and the knees upon which the scattered knuckles rested. From the rim of the barrow, a man's height above it, the body resembled that of a foetus, legs tucked up towards the chin—except that the head was curiously swivelled round, staring up at the indifferent passage of the clouds.

Walking home one evening that same week, I saw a group of children running excitedly to the low wall that fronted one part of the square, and which penned in a few pigs belonging to several of the villagers—one of whom was Percy Cullurne. I heard the children's chant before I saw the object of their mockery, and with a shock unravelled the uneven chorus into its component parts:

> 'Bid-at-ome, bid-at-ome, bid-at-ome Yeller!
> His body en't o' steel
> But o' pigeon's muck an' feather!'

I was already aware that 'Yeller' referred to Percy Cullurne, but the appended verse, repeated vociferously, was new to me. A study should be made of the genesis of these types of incidental or topical verses, as indicating a remarkable degree of creative unanimity, since the progenitor is never to be tracked down, for he almost certainly doesn't exist. Scraps of popular local rhymes, deeply sunk into every village child's otherwise unbookish mind, are often found in these new-fashioned and temporary verses, suggesting that the core is adapted and re-used again and again—raided virtually spontaneously. In the above example, the imagery has strong echoes of our Christmas-Tide 'Mummers' play about it—'muck' having been substituted for 'milk'—although if they had been familiar with their Shakespeare they might have kept with the latter! Recently, with the increased use of our great poets in even the village schools, fragments of Kipling and Walter de la Mare have been spotted, though in a context our educators would no doubt look upon in an unfavourable light.

Here, however, in the still-remote country, these town-bred educators might see, all about them, old things put to new and unlikely uses: each summer I have seen the children make their camps beside the river out of old iron bedsteads threaded with reeds, and sods piled on the top and sides, and an old iron pot glowing through the night, so that sometimes I have felt back in the days when our ancient warrior was flesh and blood, polishing his sword before a smoking hut. I have seen a waggon wheel become a merry-go-round (of sorts) twirled on its hub, while a rusty plough-wheel has served as a champion hoop, kicking up the dust down the Fogbourne Road for a good half-mile before burying itself in the hedgerow not three feet from me, shedding clouds of Old Man's Beard upon my own. I have stood upon many a peg-rug woven from a lifetime's worn-out garments, warming my hands in as pleasant a fug of reminiscence and tobacco as any London drawing-room might provide. And as for the bits and pieces to be found reincarnated in the humble cottage garden!—digression's confined space dictates I must mention only the most memorable (and perhaps tragic) instance, in which I discovered over fifty irreplaceable glass-plate negatives nestling amongst the weeds of a neighbour's ragged patch. Apparently the previous occupant, an old labourer named Jo Perry (a rather tiresome, rambling fellow according to Mrs Holland, who employed him in his latter years as a handyman and gardener, and who was left the sum of his worldly goods) had used them as cloches for his cabbages. Sadly, most of them were ruined, scoured clean by unnumbered seasons. The few that survived include a fine study of our former blacksmith's shop (now a garage for motor-car repairs); a remarkable portrait of an old peasant woman of the last century; and a candid study of the village schoolmaster of some seventy years ago, which sparked memories and thereby spawned a book [*No Dead Men, No Tales,* 1919] for which I was accused of libel by our local doctor—but that little episode must await its proper turn. Suffice to say that each negative, once developed, showed the degree of loss occasioned by this otherwise resourceful adaptation—though none could say with certainty who the masterly progenitor was (see also Chapter VII).

To return to the scene, on that mild October day of 1914: there in the pig-pen, as I had surmised, stood Percy Cullurne, indifferent to the metrical taunt of the village urchins. He was scattering straw across the churned, stinking mud, and when I shouted at the children and made for them with my doughty Indian walking cane, he looked up only for a moment, returning to his sows as the chanters scattered in squeals and giggles. One of them threw a pebble vaguely in my direction, but the force of gravity sufficiently enfeebled it to close its parabola with a 'ping' on the handle of the village pump. I felt a sudden darkness of mood close over me, and felt quite incapable of conversation. Or perhaps I was embarrassed, somehow, by the humiliation of the man. I walked away without a word or a glance. Hardly had I returned to my cottage and slumped into my chair when a feeling of shame rose within me: Cullurne had felt neither humiliation nor oppression, I was sure. That is the true power: to recognise that it is one's beholders that impose these things upon one, and that the soul remains uncorrupted, untouched.

Perhaps there was some deep connection working, for 'Wipers' had begun a day previously, and Mrs Trevick received the news soon after that her husband had been killed in action. I have done some research since then: it was at about the same time as I was crossing the square that a burst of machine-gun fire cut Marlers Trevick in two, almost upon enemy lines. His unit was all but wiped out in those few, terrible minutes. It was from roughly that day that Percy Cullurne's nickname changed from 'Yeller' to 'Bidatome'. I never heard the chant again. 'Bidatome' he bears still, if somewhat worn by use and laziness to 'Bid'm'. But even 'Bid'm' reminds us of its origin, much as an old coin reminds us of some great monarch, though the head be almost smoothed away.

As Ypres claimed man after man who had stood shoulder to shoulder on that August evening, and November came in cold and wet, a terrible nightmarish atmosphere descended upon Ulverton—so that it seemed, at times, as if I never truly woke up out of my own night horrors, but walked the streets of the damned. Few of those young men would be returning after all, to seed the land and bring the next harvest in, to hand on their qualities, to keep the heart of the village pumping strong. Cullurne kept a silence that even I could not break. Up on the downs, brushing without a word at the burial site, we would hear the bell tolling in long, slow arcs of sound, and the Squire would whiten as we paused, wondering again—who?

One afternoon young Sidney Bint came running up the track towards us, soon after we had heard the bell once more. He panted upon the rim.

'Well?' snapped the Squire. His eyes, I noticed, were full of fear.

The lad took a deep breath.

'It's Mr Allun, sir.'

'Allun?'

'He's back.'

'They've sent him back? Was that the tolling?'

'Reverend axt as to make an apology, sir. 'E's not dead, sir.'

The Squire closed his eyes.

'Thank God,' he sighed. 'I'll go and see him.'

The boy shifted from foot to foot. I asked him if there was anything else he wanted to say. He stared for a moment at the skeleton, although he had seen it some days before, when he had brought the news of Herbert Daye's death (the young man who had made my bookshelves too small) from 'injuries received' and so forth. The Squire was climbing the ladder, and Lock was looking slightly piqued, as if Allun was likely to slip on his chauffeur's gloves immediately.

I think I had guessed what the boy was going to say.

' 'E's got no arms, sir.'

The Squire paused on the rim, feet still resting on the ladder, hands ready to push him onto the level. I remember his back against the sky, his drooping shoulders, his bowed head. He looked colossal, the very figure of utter and deep weariness. Dart laughed.

Allun put a brave face on it. He had been handling a grenade, a German stick type, attempting to pick the thing up and hurl it back. He lost one arm immediately and, as he put it, 'thought as how it would miss the gear-stick, look you'. His other arm developed gangrene in the flesh-wound. He was terribly thin, stranded amongst his automobile mementoes in the estate cottage, his wooden prostheses lying weirdly across the table while his stumps 'took a bit of a rest, look you'.

Soon afterwards we spent our last afternoon on the downs: the weather was blowing cold and the soil was hardening with the sharp night frosts of late November. We had dug right round the skeleton, and it was lifted by means of a pulley and our hands onto the side. Wrapped in canvas, the body of the ancient was placed on cushions in a cart, and then, at a nod from the Squire, taken slowly down the track, the great iron-tyred rims circling through the ruts and over flints so cautiously we could count the spokes . . . eight, nine, ten, eleven, twelve. Twelve. The number the war eventually claimed from our village. The Squire followed the bier down like a mourner.

As I watched them go, preparing to clear the site of our implements, Ernest came up with the wooden box in which he had placed the smaller finds. I asked to see them, perhaps for the last time, before they were assigned to some dusty glass case. Like a boy with his stone collection, he handed them to me one by one: the bronze dagger, and the iron hair-pin; a polished greenstone wrist-guard (or so we guessed), with nine holes at each end capped with sheet-gold, and broken—probably as part of a ritual; and a bone pendant, stained by the corroding dagger, found beside the ribs, carved into the form of a leaping animal (a hare?) and painfully crude. Hardly a treasure. But each, as it lay in my hand, had an extra weight; of silence perhaps, 'deep as Eternity', and the value of silence, that had lain unstirred under tussocks and cloud for four thousand years, until the Squire smote through the turf with his blade.

1953

W I N G

MAGNETIC RECORDING No. 24 (Transcript)
File under Broadcasts/Way of Life (B/WL)

BBC Home Service (West) 'That Was My Day: Cartoonist Herbert Bradman talks about a very special day last month.' 10.10 p.m. March 6th 1953

(*Note*: first five-and-a-half minutes lost due to magnetic tape snapping.)

[. . .] bangs the tray with his small hammer and the toffee cracks. Then comes the tattoo. Well, the crumbs bounce up and down as if electrified. Now I have no idea why Mr Bint must perform this tattoo with his little hammer. It makes the tray clatter frightfully. Perhaps it is in order to release the cracked toffee from the grease paper. Perhaps it is in order to make a very loud noise. One day, I will ask him. But not today. No, not today. For today is a very special day. Isn't it, Sidney? But Mr Bint just snaps a paper bag off a hook with many other paper bags upon it, and whistles a single bar from the opening of Chopin's B minor Sonata. At least, that is what it sounds like. And he is always whistling it. One day, I will ask him. Not today. No, not today. Meanwhile, I will continue to—well, marvel. Now come on, I hear you say, what exactly are you marvelling at? Well, dear listener, at the great strides we have made in communication by means of the wireless. Even our shopkeepers bend an ear to the Third Programme.

Mr Bint slips the dark toffee into the paper bag. He knows I cannot bear to have my fingers stickied. Who can, but grubby little creatures, as don't know better? Talking of these, there are quite a few strung out behind me. Oh dear, I think they are rather impatient today. Well, I have never seen Bint's Bakery so full. And that applies to the shelves, too.

'A quarter of liquorice pomfret cakes, please, Sidney. And four acid drops.' Do I hear a groan behind me? Someone drops their penny.

MT 24 B/wl p. 2

Consternation. And today of all days. Do not worry, she has got it. She is called Marjorie. She has just got over the chicken-pox. But did I not see her in the Village Stores? Of course, her parents have the shop. 'But it don't sell sweets, sir. Just bleach.' Just bleach? Well, that is a shame. Just bleach.

Goodness me, I have been quite distracted by little Marjorie. The liquorice pomfret cakes have tumbled into the scale-pan. What a satisfying rattle! And the smaller boys and girls think so, too. They press forward a little. A tiny grubby face pops up beside me. 'Hurry up, mister!' That is too much for Mr Bint. His shop is neat as any pin. It is not made for them young grubs, fresh from ditch and road, from farm and misty orchard. But he has to make a living, just like all of us. Out, all out! In a trice they are exactly that. Well, they know the ropes. But I would not wager on his windows staying clean for long. Yes, I am right. He looks at the faces smudged against the glass, then he looks at me. His look says: today, one has to make allowances. Today, it is only proper. Yes, that is the spirit, Mr Bint. That is the spirit that will see us through this anxious age, if anything will. Tolerance, I think they call it. Alive and well it is too, in our little village. Now can I have my acid drops, please?

Yes, indeed. Today, we are going to go the whole hog. I take out—well, you have guessed it: my ration book. I place it on the polished wooden counter, just as I do every time. But today, Mr Bint smiles. He knows. The liquorice pomfret cakes slide off the scale-pan into a second paper bag. What a satisfying rustle! Now I hope he does not mind me saying this, I really do, but Mr Bint has a rather impressive wart on his forehead. And at this juncture, I usually glance towards it. I usually think: well, how surprising, this inability of many people to take advantage of the considerable medical advances made in our time. To burn out a wart, or lance a carbuncle, is the least of the challenges facing medical science, under the benign auspices of our National Health Service and the many technical instruments at its command. And so on. You know the type of thing. But today is different. Today we have quite other thoughts in the head. Quite other, as Mr Bint spins the

MT 24 B/wl p. 3

paper bag round and round to close it, and the mingling aromas of confectionary, and fleed cakes, and bags of flour, and cottage loaves, and jam doughnuts, and goodness knows what else one finds in an English country bakery seem to spin *me* round and round, too.

Now for the other jar. The one crammed with yellow acid drops, of course. Oh dear—the lid has been split slightly, in its long and busy career. The lid is made of Bakelite. I do not wish to cast aspersions. Oh no. But I have to say this: I do feel a sense of relief when the plastic lid is off—and most especially today. Mr Bint's plump, floury hand squeezes through the neck. Down it goes. Viewed through the blueish glass, those fingers do resemble something rather nasty moving along the sea-bed, do they not? No, not today. Today, there is nothing nasty about it. All is glowing, all is happy. Let us rather say, it is like watching the Derby on my twelve-inch television. That is the spirit. And out those fingers come, with four acid drops . . . well, clawed, I have to admit it, off the congealed honeycomb. Always four. Nothing nasty about that, either.

Now comes the third paper bag, and in they go. Thud thud. Thud thud. I say, you are calling out over your cocoa, what's all this thudding about? Ah yes. You see, Mr Bint always lets the acid drops fall from a rather extravagant height into their little paper bag. Videlicet, dear listener, if you don't mind a bit of Latin—the full vertical stretch of his long right arm. That crisp blue cuff of his baker's coat gets caught at the elbow, so high does he stretch up. What strange characters, you are thinking to yourself—what strange characters there are in our villages! Well, it is all for my benefit, of course: those crisp thuds send a flutter through my (I have to say) ample frame. Likewise, the faces pressed against the door flutter [. . .]* open under the weight. Little creatures spill onto the floor. Mr Bint sweeps them out. The door tinkles shut. We are quite alone. As should be. Never mind the faces smudged against the glass: the hour has come. The moment beckons. For the first time in our transaction, Mr Bint speaks. 'Let's take it from here then, Mr Bradman,'

* (five seconds lost due to electrical interference)

MT 24 B/wl p. 4

he says, in what I understand to be a Jimmy Edwards voice. At least, that is what a little fellow told me last week. Last week: how far away that seems today, how dismal, how colourless, how empty of the vital! Hey, look out—is the hour not coming, and the moment beckoning, and so forth? I pick up my ration book and tear out several stamps. No prizes for guessing which ones, now.

'Well, Sidney, old fellow, at least we have come through.' I tear up those stamps into tiny pieces. I lean over the counter and scatter them over his head like confetti, standing on my toes to do so. If I were a poetic sort of chap, I'd say they fell upon his hair as the snow falls upon a glistening tilth, or some such. But as I am not, I shall stick with confetti. Mr Bint did not quite stop smiling. He saw the joke. Of course he did. As did the youngsters outside, from the sound of it. After all, I did thereupon purchase, in celebration of this memorable day for all we sweet-toothed folk, a dozen more acid drops and as many aniseed balls, one pound weight of liquorice allsorts, one shilling's worth extra of Mrs Dorothy Bint's luscious dark toffee, a clutch of barley-sugar sticks, a giant bag of mint humbugs, and an elegant box of a certain well-known store's aptly-named 'Regal' milk chocolates. And I am quite sure that there was enough left for the little ones outside. Quite sure. But I do not suppose he remembered to pick out that confetti from his hair before he let the hordes in with that familiar merry tinkle of the door. Never mind. This has been a happy day. A very happy chewing, and sucking, and munching, and tearing-up-of-stamps sort of day. Indeed it has. Not for you? Look, I have two mint humbugs left. Oh, come on then: you can have one, too.

END OF BROADCAST

Sat. 7th March 1953
Cold, sleety. Dumplings.

Filing & collating a.m. Typing up Herbert's broadcast p.m. A bit sniffly today. H. miffed at being called 'cartoonist' in Radio T., but all smiles about broadcast last night. Said what did I think of his 'masses' voice? I said if I'm one of the masses, then you've certainly scored a hit with me, Mr B. But a different sort of hit, I'm afraid, with Mr Sidney Bint. Oh, really? The wart, Mr B. What about the wart, Violet my dear? Only reporting Mrs Bint who had a little word, as you might say, outside the Post Office this morning, Mr B. Well, said Herbert, perhaps he'll get it burnt out now it's famous. (Oo ouch, as Mother wd say.) Both listened to magnetic tape recording of broadcast in study at 6.30 + transcript. Herbert rather snarly about lost start. I said I couldn't quite get hang of it (magnetic tape recorder). It just snapped, Mr B. He lent me a book—'Magnetic Recording' by Dr S. J. Begun. Must keep abreast, Violet my dear.

Sun. 8th March 1953
Cold, sleety. Roast.

Holy Communion. Sermon on fasting. Stiff in joints & bit feverish. Big dose of Fenning's made me a bit 'squiffy'. Walter de la Mare on wireless reading own poems. That brought it all back. H. silent over luncheon. Went down to my room earlier than usual. Plum tapping on bathroom window in gusts again. Must lop it. Bed by 8 p.m.

Mon. 9th March 1953
Cold, gusty. Bovril.

Indexing a.m. Still bit feverish. Onto my throat. Appt at Moon's Garage: said Lanchester needs new clutch & suggested Mr B. purchase a Hillman Minx ('Just happen to have one here, Miss Nightingale'). Old

Dick (Mr Lock) passing, said Hillmans 'load of old bolts' (I think that's what he said). Mr Moon said Hillman Minx won London to Cape Town last year. Old Dick said who wants to drive from London to Cape Town? Got rather chilled while they were arguing. Thought of King George bidding farewell to Princess Eliz. at London Airport without scarf or hat in biting wind this time last year. Dead a week later. Over lunch H. fixed date of Burial: night of Coronation (June 2nd). I said that's going to be a rush, Mr B. He said come on, my dear, that's not how we won the war. In bed by 7 p.m. Low.

Tues. & Wed.: down with 'flu.

Thurs. 12th March 1953
Cold, drizzly. Tomato soup.

Up and about at last. H. rather unsympathetic. Slow Mrs Dart broke Hoover but at least she brought me hot milk each day. Greatness has no time for ailments, I reflect. BURIAL date fixed publicly—letter for local paper. Repository blueprint passed by factory, but steel supplies a bit so-so, Mr Bradman. Like Mother wd say: a bit so-so this week are we, Violet? H. so good on 'phone—used his clipped, civilisation-at-stake voice, and loud man on other end quite cowed. My Mosley tone, Violet. Always gets results out of the vulgus. Typing a.m. and p.m. Glass of sherry (Dry Fly? Fly Dry? anyway, prefer sweeter) with H. at 6.30 after combing session. H. ventured I shd contribute something OF MY OWN MAKING to Project. Oh surely not, Mr B.! A sort of short 'impression' of my thirteen years with Herbert E. Bradman. To be STRICTLY honest. PROMISE not to read it, my dear. YOU MUST NOT SAY NO. Little chance of that when Herbert's got brace between teeth, as nasty Lionel Maddocks used to say about me. To my face. Like having a gate in your mouth. Did some good, I suppose. In the end. Still feeling weak. Used up three bottles of Fenning's @ 1/9d each! H. to buy Hillman in instalments. Which end first, I joked. Big thump on my bathroom window just before tea. Almost broke it. Rugby ball from Manor School. Such an ugly dirty heavy leather thing. Had to fish it out of the thuya by hand. Reminded me of raising Father's head up in his last days. It'll be cricket balls next.

Fri. 13th March 1953
V. cold, grey. Cod.

Typing. Didn't venture out. Harriet Barlow fell under wheel of articulated lorry outside Sale Lido on a Friday 13th—A.F.C. Gala Dance Night, mind you. We did have some times. Bed early to start The Nanking Road. Scalded my midriff with cocoa, for my indulgence.

Sat. 14th March 1953
Muggy, overcast. Spam fritters.

Typing. Feeling blue. Don Carlos & his Samba Orchestra on wireless saved my day over supper once again. Gets my toes tapping. Close my eyes, can almost see the Astoria. Kenneth on the clarinet, bless him. Pranged on ops, how Gordon put it. Wd always send a card on my birthday. Shd really have gone back for the funeral. Old times. Maybe if I'd stayed up North, etc. Like a fish out of water here. Not that he had a penny to rub, just a load of charm. Went a bit far that time, though. Artificial knickers, Violet my love? Best off, I'd say. Best off. Funny lip from blowing clarinet. Feel it now. Poor Kenneth. Cd have been a widow, I could. And her mite. Children. In loving memory of our dear husband and father, F/O Kenneth Lingham (33 Squadron) killed on operations June 9th, 1944. Loving Wife Violet, and Your Son & Daughter . . . What a thought. Hope it didn't burn, that's all, like that poor chap who came down near Mapleash Farm. Right over our heads, Mrs Stiff said, and into Gore Field luckily, so he didn't smash the crops. (Ruined the orchids, though.) So low we could see his gloves trying to do something, said Mr Stiff. Same year I think. Might have been

Kenneth, except it was German. I couldn't go and have a look. Smelling it was enough. Filthy black smoke. Didn't hear a thing, though, that's the funny part. Always asked after me, acc. to Gordon, did Kenneth. Herbert rather snarly over lunch. Meat-paste doesn't agree with him, he says. I said it's lifting up all those boxes. Suggested Doan's. Must catch ruptures early.

Sun. 15th March 1953
Overcast. Roast, ice-cream.

Holy Communion. Sermon on refugees crisis, needless to say: 70,000,000 without homes as result of wars! What with this & world hunger & rising prices & chill, felt rather hopeless. Jesus hardly comes into them (sermons) these days. Sort of tacked on at end. Period started early over tea with H. in middle of one of his 'lectures'. Difficult to find space between sentences to excuse oneself. Miss Enid Walwyn also present. I pretended to have coughing fit and ran out. Caught a glimpse of Herbert looking astonished. Went to drawer in my room but no Tampax. Suspect H. has been rifling it for Material ('Health & Hygiene?'). Felt my blood boiling. Have to approach him. Used flannel instead. Most unsatisfactory. Pains. (Feeling so-so are we, Violet? Yes, Mother.) Returned to H., who looked peeved. He had lost thread. Miss W. had departed in interim. I do apologise, Mr B.: a moth in the oesophagus, as my father used to say. Herbert spent next forty-five minutes extolling virtues (intellectual & physical) of Miss Enid you-know-who. I said Miss Willington much missed all the same. Miss Willington? Miss Walwyn's predecessor at the village school, Mr B. Was that deliberate, Violet? Deliberate, Mr B.? (Awful headache by now.) To drag in that rotting stuck-up old bag when the subject is Miss Walwyn must have been deliberate, Violet. There was nothing slatternly about Miss Willington, Mr B. Are you suggesting that Miss Walwyn is a slattern, Violet? Not at all, Mr B.; I am referring to your unfortunate term of abuse, for I am quite sure that Miss Walwyn is a clean-living young lady, as every schoolteacher ought to be, at least where I come from. H. just glowered then. 'What's My Line' night, so he let me watch in living room, as promised. Freezing. All the way through felt guilty at taking on so with Herbert. Eamonn Andrews has a nice voice.

Mon. 16th March 1953: my birthday! 42!
Cold, sleety. Spam.

Typing. Uncle Eric sent bottle of Cherry Heering: somehow leaked in post and parcel stuck up. Auntie Pamela sent usual stockings. Cousin Roy forty Gold Flake. Shirley Leatherbarrow Aertex corset plus six Lavender Bathjoys. She is a funny sort. Vernon Crawshaw 1 red rose (crumpled) & 1 gramophone record (Ivor Novello: 'Weave Your Spell Soft Melody'). I don't know. He knows I only have the wireless. Disappointing. Nothing from Mother. Had a little weep over Kenneth, which surprised me. He wd always remember. Those cheeky cards from Germany. Got 'bus to Odeon: 'It Always Rains On Sunday'. Saw it several years ago but penny dropped too late. Ghastly cough next to me, loads of sputum—rays from projector lit it up. Makes you realise how far it (sputum) sprays normally, like with cigarette smoke—thick in light shafts, hardly visible otherwise. Looked like cinema was on fire. As also with dust in sunlight. The country's full of floating matter. Miracle we can breathe at all. Got back late, no lights on, but cd have sworn heard front door put to soon after. Feel a bit nauseous from 'bus. All those twisty bends. Rocking. And pitch black either side over those downs. Cd have been at sea. At least in war you had the camps. Who was it saw a Roman in his headlights? Lots of little fires flickering in the valley where it should have been electrics. And this Roman with a spear. And rather unshaven, he said. Who was it? Never think of Romans as being anything but clean. Funny Mr Vic Tuck the postman, probably. Bed around midnight on glass of Cherry Heering. Page all sticky now. (Chin up, Violet. Chin up.) Awful spoonerism that time on 'phone. With Mr Vic Tuck. Happens all the time, Miss Nightingale. Does it now? Feel like giggling. Old times. Whirling about. Too much Cherry Heering. Cheery Herring. Herry Cheering. Bappy Hirthday Violet! Oh golly

Tues. 17th March 1953
Clear. Pork Chop. Canned peas tasted off.

Typing & collating all day. Headachc. H. has decided to re-do his adolescence ('too miserable, got to jolly it all up') so that's more transcripts. Oh dear, Mr B., if you don't mind my saying so, I do find the Soundmirror irksome (that's the word) to operate. Irksome, Violet? Irksome, Mr B. You do realise what you're saying, Violet, don't you? You're saying that £69 10s worth of the latest in magnetic tape recorders ought to be chucked up because you're too damned fool to learn it. Now where's my doughnut? At least I'm not working for Mr Evelyn Waugh, I always tell myself, after what Gladys Unsworth passed on that time. Pure poison, she said. 10 p.m., & he's still recording: comes down through floorboards of study. Like a tummy rumble. Amazing that he can find so much to talk about. I couldn't.

Wed. 18th March 1953
Clear a.m., overcast p.m. Toad-in-the-hole.

Card-indexing & filing a.m. Cross-referencing p.m. (where does one draw the line? Cd go on forever!) Went with H. to meeting of Ulverton Coronation Committee, 6.30 p.m. Wasted ten minutes struggling with stove. Herbert wants to tie in Burial with Festivities. Newspaper out tomorrow, took copy of letter. Philis Punter-Wall in Chair, so arrived at A.O.B. swiftly. H. spoke after reading out letter. Mr Donald Jefferies said it was barmy, and what the heck does quotidian mean? I did warn H. about quotidian. Much too fancy. Herbert glowered. I took the reins. Said one had to think in bigger terms than our Sovereign's Coronation: what with atomic and hydrogen bombs, the Reds, 70,000,000 homeless, refugees, world hunger and so forth, we could do our bit. What bit? (Mr Donald Jefferies.) For civilisation. At stake etc. Supposing it all goes up in smoke. Then what? Mr Norman Stroude said I haven't the foggiest, I won't be around. Laughter. Mr Donald Jefferies said it was still barmy. Nice Mr Stewart Daye said he liked it. Mr Sidney Bint glowered at

Herbert & scratched wart menacingly. It really is unpleasant. Hygiene. Tiny pieces of it in our bread, most like. Perish the thought. What you'd see if you could would stop you eating anything, I'm sure. Ignorance is bliss when it comes to the microscopic, as Vernon Crawshaw would always say. He's a funny one. Red rose my foot. Wouldn't hurt a fly, though. Just not my sort. Always smelt of that stuff they bottle dead things in, that was the trouble. Mr Norman Stroude put his arm on my shoulder & squeezed. Breath beery. Said what do you want to know about my daily life, Miss Nightingale? All contributions welcome, I said, looking straight out. Miss Enid Walwyn said it was a super idea and clapped her hands. Herbert smiled. Miss Walwyn has a way with words. Rather high voice. Dr Scott-Parkes said in his capacity as a local man whose family had tended the sick for three generations etc., he felt it tended to the morbid, and had no place in the Age of Hope. Herbert said the Age of Neuroses, rather boomingly. Dr Scott-Parkes took off spectacles and blinked slowly at him, like in surgery. There's some odd little tale about the Scott-Parkes, but I can't remember what. Dark cupboards. Will have to ask Mrs Dart. Except she always goes on so and expects a cup of tea and a digestive at the end of it and nothing gets done. Can't watch her when she's having her tea-break. Sip like a bath going out. Digestive dunked to soften it. She ought to get teeth, at least. It really is very chill in the Village Hall. Mr Sidney Bint said what's going into it—ten pounds of aniseed balls? H. said we didn't quite catch that Sidney old man. Urn making queer noises so break for tea. New lavender-coloured cups, very nice, result of Horticultural Society Square Dance Raffle. Hortic's property therefore, but all welcome to use. What about breakages? Ah, said Mrs Whiteacre, that's a question for the committee. Which one, pray? She wasn't sure. All these fuzzy edges, it's a wonder things go on. People break things and don't report them, said Mr Bint. In a queer voice. Discussion resumes. H. reads out letter again. Lots of nods. Motion carried by majority of 1. Mr Donald Jefferies suggests it happens after bonfire. Bonfire? Biggest ever, to be made out of waggons. Waggons? Splendidly combustible. A new Elizabethan era. Ties in with Mr Bradman's do. Burying the past and all that. Passing of horse and cart in favour of tractor & trailer. H. says

I'm not burying the past. Mr Bint says aniseed balls again. H. says what? Mr Jefferies says it all ties in. He and Scouts to scour the parish for all sorts. Waggons, carts, ploughs, old farming tools etc. Biggest bonfire ever. Beacon. Beacons to be lit from Land's End to John O'Groats. Ulverton's to be the biggest and brightest, etc. Mrs Whiteacre says do you realise she'll be same age as first one? Our Sovereign. Motion carried, none against, 1 abstention (Miss W., who is fond of waggons needless to say) and Meeting breaks up amicably. Herbert spent evening, after combing session, hopping about floor of living room and spilling his whisky on rug. I was very satisfied with my contribution. H. pecked me on forehead when I gave him his nightcap. Bristly, like Kenneth. Nearly mentioned Tampax matter, but balked at last moment. Chill tonight. Orchard House rather draughty with easterly. Whistles. Plum flicking again. Brand's Essence definitely buoying appetite. Bit worn out, actually. What with

Thurs. 19th March 1953
Clear, windy. V. cold. Hard frost. Luncheon meat.

Typing & collating a.m., 'phoning p.m. Mrs Iris Webb popped round tea-time. Gave us all her support. Had read the newspaper letter. Could her little daughter Susan show us her needlepoint? H. said needlepoint wasn't on the list. But you asked in your letter for local contributions. Representative is the word, said Herbert. (Why does greatness have to be so gruff sometimes?) Mrs Webb leaves in bit of a huff. H. turns to me: what is bloody needlepoint? Bell rings. Mrs Maud Oadam. She has brought along her grandfather Ralph's animal traps. Horrid. H. says that's for the bonfire. Mrs Oadam leaves in a bigger huff than Mrs Webb. I meant THE bonfire, H. shouts. Bell rings. Mr Horace Rose holding a footman's jacket. His father's. Rather fine. Nice gold buttons. Used to serve up at the big house. Serve up what? Serve, says Mr Rose, with a sniff. H. says, politely, I am concerned with the present, not the past. Modern times! 1953! Mirro Modern Cleanser. Deaf Aids. Auto-changer gramophones. Projection television. Oxo cubes. Coloured magazines. Plastic switches. Phensic tablets. Tampax internal sanitary protection (aha). Magnetic tape recorders. Silvifix Hair Cream. And so on. Do you see? A single example of anything modern that will fit. Not a footman's jacket, Mr Rose. Go and see Mr Jefferies. That is his department. Mr Rose told H. that he was an ungrateful bugger and why doesn't he bury himself too while he's about it? Left in a bigger huff than Mrs Oadam. Not a good start. Left notice on gate: 'All Contributions For Posterity, Please Bring Sat. May 2nd or Sun. May 3rd.' H. retired early, so took opportunity to search Deposit Room for missing personal item. Not in 'Health & Hygiene' boxes. Nearly gave up. Clock ticking made me nervous. Chill. Switched on new electric fire though rather loud click might wake H. in room above, I feared. Did not consider 'Domestic Comforts' as already indexed it, but only to F with 'Medical Advances'. Searched without success in unpleasant material (rupture girdles, stethoscope, hypodermic syringes etc.). Then noticed them (Tampax) clear as day tucked into 'Vogues & Luxuries' box along with sunglasses, powder compact, lipstick, electric mop etc. Vogues & Luxuries! Greatness does have its oversights. Am quite irritated. Have to have a word. Fuzzy edges. Where does one Section end and the next begin, I ask myself. Scald still tender.

Whoops—left electric fire on. Have to go up. Drat.

Fri. 20th March 1953
Mild, damp. Kippers.

Typing all day. H. in London. Sneaked into living room and watched dance programme—Jack Parnell etc. Put the Ivor Novello and one of Herbert's (Tommy Kinsman & his Dance Orchestra—rather good) on Autochanger & got it to work. Danced around room till giddy. Knocked over vase & chipped off lip. One of the Chinese pair H. says looted from Peking palace in Mr Mao's revolution. Priceless. Tried to stick it back on, but wdn't hold. Blame Mrs Dart? Don't want H. to think I go in living room as matter of course. He's funny about that.

Sat. 21st March 1953
Mild, damp. Pork pie.

Indexing a.m. & p.m. 'Medical Advances' rather unpleasant. Makes me feel morbid. Keep seeing Joan Lowe's husband sunk in chair. Sick-room. Disinfectant worse than what it was getting out. Broke her, really. Lucky Father went when he did, perhaps. In prime. Bang. Walked to clear head. Up to White Horse. They ought to scour it, or whatever. Daffs in beech clump near barrow. Friendly robin. Shoes held up well in mulch. Thought how difficult to tree-spot without leafage. Herbert's drawings always v. accurate: said once he kept file of tree sketches so all his pictures have same trees in background. Shd I start on about Tampax? Got them back, at least. He might not notice. H. getting more & more short as day draws nearer. Ticked me off tonight for not stirring powder in cocoa. Floating about on top. Makes me giddy, he said. Well I never. And how's YOUR contribution going, my dear? Very well, thank you, Mr B. (MUST start it TOMORROW.) Just found half-sucked acid drop stuck on dressing-room table. Feel like Miss Marple, sometimes.

LIFE UNDER HERBERT E. BRADMAN.
by Violet Nightingale

(File . . . ?)

Introduction

I first started with

I came to the country the countryside to the village of Ulv

On the eve of war, when

I walked up the gravel drive of Orchard House that summer's day with

I scrunched

Being Mr Bradman's personal secretary (he prefers the term 'assistant', but the post was advertised using the former title), I was always seen by him as being an integral part of the 'Project', if only to collate the relevant data, type

With his half-moon spectacles and ill-cut jacket, Mr Bradman struck me at first sight as one of those employers who would forever need 'tidying up'—even to the extent of supplying my wages now and

Knowing Herbert E. Bradman to have been one of the leading artists on 'Punch' for many years (see 'Collected Works' and magazine samples) I expected that diffidence to worldly matters that goes hand-in-hand with the artistic life. I was thoroughly prepared to find umbrellas in the refrigerator (see 'Domestic Comforts') and the chicken hanging in the hall, as you might say! So I was surprised, on that July day of 1939, scrunching up the drive, to find a man to open the door on the door opening wholly in command of himself, punctilious in the extreme, and courteous. He was dressed in a Harris Tweed jacket, which although rather well-used, was cert and slightly burnt on the sleeve, was certainly of top quality. He received me in the main sitting room of his house: this being a generous pile construction of a somewhat mediaeval look, though built (according to the inlaid stone) as recently as 1929, on the former site of the Manor orchard—several ancient pear trees, three apple-trees, and one dwindling plum scraping my bathroom window to attest attesting to that fact, and the old brick wall, of course. He shook my hand warmly, and showed me his 'studio', a perfectly charming converted garage with a huge skylight facing North. Our problems with our battles to keep this clear of a Virginia creeper which he refuses to uproot have given rise to many of his famous 'Gardener In A Sweat' cartoo humorous drawings, and furnished our professional relationship with the kind of laughter discovered one finds on only at on the tops of precarious ladders. Although

Although I had, like many others, confused Mr Herbert E. Bradman with Mr H. E. Bateman (they happen they unfortunately share the same initials—see 'Minor Rivals' section of 'Commentary on the Collected Works'), Herbert (or Mr B., as I like to call him) jocularly) has no singular trade-mark like Mr Bateman's characters, whose horrified popping eyes leave me disg more repelled than amused. Neither, indeed, is he equipped with a regular sinecure like Mr Arth Alb like Mr Bestall's 'Rupert the Bear' strip in the 'Daily Express', or Mr A. B. Payne's famous trio in the 'Daily Mirror' (I myself attended the 1928 rally of 'Gugnuncs' at the Royal Albert Hall!) Instead, Herbert strives to capture the modern way of life and its peculiar idiosyncrasies in a careful, almost painstaking line. Enthusiasts of his work (and there are still a fair number) have taken pleasure in identifying the makes of car in his 'Modern Motoring Mania' series, or the species of flower in his 'Irene Rambler' strip for the 'Schoolgirl's Own Annual', in which her highly amusing muddy adventures ran from 1924 to 1927. The manner in which he can sum up whole personalities with a few deft strokes of his pen has earned him many admirers: as he has famously said—'get the nose right, and the rest follows!' I have come to love to cherish his grand scenes of modern bustle and confusion, from which there always seems to be a policeman's frantic arm emerging; or those well-known farmyard scenes of pretty milkmaids and ruddy yokels scattering cocks an cockerels hens a their poultry and or and those society galas with their slim ladies and monocled young men, all about to meet with disa catastrophe.

Sun. 22nd March 1953
Mild, damp. Chicken, prunes & custard.

Matins. Sermon rather dull on Contrition or something. Always reminds me of a car part, Contrition. Young Rev. Appleton has nice voice, a waste. Church cd do with electric heaters, stinks of paraffin. H. chatty over lunch. Hasn't noticed chipped lip? Will plead ignorance if does, for sake of Project. Walked up to Plum Farm to check on wood dog violet behind. Mr Desmond Dimmick in yard, cutting down that nice big tree. Hailed me to come over unfortunately & had to enter. Dung everywhere. Stink still on shoes. Wanted to show me his implements: went into big old barn. Funny-looking plough, harrow, manure knife (!), something beginning with D (dribble?) and sheep-bells etc. all in heap under cobwebs. Had read our letter and so forth. I said my bit about present, not past. Said he'd give us fertiliser bag. What we needed was lots of fertiliser spread about & grass dug up like in war. That or starvation. Then the usual if my old grandad Harry etc. Always blamed you Northerners and all yr smoke, Miss Nightingale. And that Squire! Barn full of dust, got right into my tubes. Sudden shaft of sun showed it all up, like searchlight. I don't think agricultural matters will ever be my cup of gladness, as Father wd say. You Northerners my foot. Showed me swallows' nest, though. Come back every year and as old as the barn (1713 on the lintel!) but they always say that. Started 'contribution' after tea—bad start but picked up after a bit. Queer putting down yr own life. Though it's more Herbert's really of course. Wood dog violet out, anyway.

Mon. 23rd March 1953
Cold, sunny. Spam.

Typing all day. H.'s new transcripts completely different version of his teenage years. Same person? Woman's Hour had nice thing on widows. Made me cry, thinking of Kenneth. Daft. H. took my hand after combing session and said I was his staff. Hip back again. Asked Mrs Dart about the Scott-Parkes story. Well, I never. Long time ago, though.

Tues. 24th March 1953
Cold, overcast. Lamb chop.

Typing & 'phoning. Nice postcard of Florence from Shirley Leatherbarrow. She does get about. Miss Walwyn round after school. Loads of giggling up there. Stamping shook plaster off. Don't remember room being this chill and damp. Basements are the devil to get warm. Bit off-colour. At least office is warm, being above living room. What a queer, higgledy-piggledy house this is! All these bits of stairs. My bathroom that bit warmer cos that bit higher. Pity window is tinted in bathroom cos nice view of garden otherwise. Mind you, who knows who or what might peer in if it wasn't. Never feel quite private on lavatory as it is. That plum branch gives me the frits sometimes. Have to have big lop & burn session. Hillman Minx brought round by Mr Moon's son Ted of the gummy forelock, Lanchester part-exchanged. Quite sad to see it go. Been a part of life here all along. Had nice comfortable smell, like the vestry at St Catherine's. I do worry about Herbert's driving. It's not the same, I tell him, you do have to keep on the right side of the road these days, even in the country. Road through village busier and busier since they let the petrol go. Always tell the articulated lorries by my tooth-glass.

Wed. 25th March 1953
Cold, grey. Kidneys.

Cross-referencing and labelling. Off-colour. Coronation Committee Meeting at 6.30 p.m.: they spent twenty minutes trying to get that stove to light. Lucky I'd got the long johns on, given my circulation problems.

Wanted to have map of Burial Site. Herbert said it's part of tennis-court at end of garden. Mr Bint said you haven't got a tennis-court. H. said it was turned to vegetables at opening of war, but I still call it the tennis-court Sidney. Cd have sworn H. said 'wart' instead of 'war'. It's so easy. Like 'Mr Short' for little Mr Long at Salford Motor Engineers. Those were times. Mrs Whiteacre said that's what our late Sovereign did with the flower beds. H. said his bit about donating Burial Site to parish: legally common land in perpetuity etc. with cypress hedge about & access from Pightle Lane cos it's after wall ends. That means we'll have to maintain it said Mr Donald Jefferies. H. said you only have to keep Location Stone clean of weeds that's not much to ask when you consider what's at stake. What on earth is at stake? (Mrs Whiteacre). Civilisation. Oh I didn't know civilisation was at stake (Mrs Whiteacre). We had all this last time (Mr Norman Stroude). That's a turn-up for the books having common land give back instead of having it took away (nice Mr Stewart Daye). Let's not go all political now (Mrs Philis Punter-Wall). Who's going to pay for it then? (Mr Donald Jefferies). Quite a big bill after three thousand years eh? (Mr Norman Stroude). General laughter. Volunteers I'm sure (Mrs Philis Punter-Wall) but this is a Parish Council matter next item please. H. said it's all been cleared with the P.C. Committee and did his flared nostrils thing. Dr Scott-Parkes said could I get a word in now please there's a serious bunting problem cos of paper supplies. I can't look at Dr Scott-Parkes in quite the same way after what Mrs Dart told me. Will try and order book from library. Although I'd better not carry it about in case he sees me with it. Never know what he might do. Sins of the fathers and so forth. Might have been handed down to him, in the blood, etc. He has got funny eyes. Jealousy! Best keep out of it. I felt like strangling Rita Smelt that time. She and poor Kenneth. Well she did go on so. Triumphant. In the back row, Violet! Those were times. Can't see a picture of Shirley Temple without feeling nasty. Mr Stroude said use toilet paper, winked at Miss Walwyn. Rev. Appleton present this time said he's got so much junk in vestry must be some bunting somewhere. Junk? He does like to appear broad-minded. Philis Punter-Wall twitched, but she doesn't give a lot away. Mrs Whiteacre said W.I. had lots from '35 Silver Jubilee, but had '25' on every flag goodness me wasn't that a lot of stitching. Mr Jefferies said at least we'll have biggest bonfire ever. Mr Daye said seems like yesterday. I said there's rolls and rolls of canvas left by Ministry of Works up at the big house. Can see it from the woods behind. Volunteered to investigate. Thank you, Miss Nightingale. N.B.: how does Mr Bint know we haven't got tennis-court? That's what I mean about sitting on the lavatory.

Thurs. 26th March 1953
Heavy rain. Cheese potato.

Labelling. Missed Mrs D.'s Diary. Not that it seems to matter. Miss Walwyn round again. Soaked through, dribbled on hall parquet. It'll come up, I said. She didn't offer to wipe it, of course. Down on my hands and knees. I let her see and why not? Pride's not in it. As Father wd say: the only skivvies I've ever donned are my vest and underpants! Tea-time I went into living room as usual with tray, no one there, gas-fire full up, nasty fug, steam rising like nobody's business off clothes flung (that's the word) onto settee, identified Miss W.'s briefs and bra, pink, probably hand-knitted. Cream blouse a bit scorched. Located her by giggle: in studio with Herbert. Rapped on door. Opened. Ah, said Herbert, she's brought the tea. Violet is my staff. So I can see, said Miss W., with a small giggle. Wrapped up in Herbert's dressing-gown, my present to him Xmas of '42, the purple one, not seen it for years I must say, and not even bothering to use the cord not that I mind a nipple or two, we've had plenty of those in the drawing classes in the old days, but it was the attitude. H.'s hair standing on end, quite comic. Enid is the perfect model, said Herbert, doesn't move a muscle. Do you like Marie? said I. Who's Marie? said Miss Walwyn. Biscuit, said I. Your blouse is scorched.

Fri. 27th March 1953
Clearing, nice light (Constable). Large plaice.

Collating & indexing all day. Brisk walk after tea, getting dark, big clouds shooting over me on scarp, felt giddy looking up, like about to go with them, bright & dark at same time, nice fresh breeze straight off sea all those miles away, felt Barrow could open up and contents walk out any minute. Pity he's been taken out already. Or perhaps not. Came back with torch. Last of light showing in big puddles all silvery. Wish I could paint. Don't think the Kodak would catch it. Lying in bed all aglow. Miss W. chattering above. MUST get on with 'essay' over weekend. Camomile lotion works a treat on scald.

MY LIFE UNDER HERBERT E. BRADMAN (cont.)

Part I

The War Years

Being deep in the
Only one bomb fe one stick of bom
The first time

Mr Bradman first mooted his 'Project' to me in the middle of a 'blackout' in the late September of 1940—Britain's darkest and yet finest hour (see Cine Reel 14B). We would sit together (I had then a ba, I had then, and still have, a 'basement' flat in Orchard House—really the converted scullery and pantry) in his 'Anderson'-type shelter at the bottom of the garden, waiting for the 'All Clear' to sound in a rather beastly stink comprised of Mr Bradman's pipe and my Gold Flake. He finally broke the monotonous silence with a sneeze a cough, proceeded by a great snort which vibrated the thick moustache which then (as now) sprouted generously from his upper lip. The single electric light-bulb that illuminated us (he had 'rigged up' the system himself) lent a lugubrious look to his face, as it was positioned directly above his head. Once, when the stick of bombs that cracked the plaster in the church (fortuitously revealing some crude medi but charming mediaeval wall-paintings of angels, ships and suchlike, as well as blowing part of a Saxon drinking-horn through Mrs Hilda Blumlein's front window!) dropped dow thudd shattered the quiet of the village (see red asterisks on Topography Sheet 27C) this bulb swung alarmingly and made those shadows shift in quite horr terrifying ways across his over his eyes and mouth. In fact, this reminded me of his 'Chemical Experiments That Went Wrong' series, which appeared briefly in 'The Sketch' in 193 , and were perhaps the most morbid of Herbert Bradman's creations (for these and all other works see 'Collected Works').

There was a further silence following the snort, broken by my enquiry as to what Mr Bradman might be snorting about? He gruffly acknowledged my observation, and then squee he then leant acr he then placed uncharacteristically put his hand upon my thi left knee, leaning across to do so.

'Violet,' he said, 'I think we are all lost.'

'Come come, Mr Bradman,' I replied, 'we got through the last lot.' He sla

He patted my knee in a friendly fashion and leaned back to his spot his position under the electric light-bulb. Closing his eyes, he took a great suck on his pipe, rattling the phlegm caught inside, and blew out three rings which exactly circled the electric light before breaking up against the corrugated-iron roof. of our shelter.

'No, Violet my lovely,' he said (that's that particular term of endearment not being unu not being usual to him), 'I think we are all doomed.'

It was then, at that late hour of the evening, that Mr Bradman outlined his 'Project', which needs no further comment here. Used as I was to eccentric employees in the past, I had never encountered anything mad and madcap or odd about Mr Bradman.—save for his hab except for our daily 'combing' session, merely a hangover from our evacuees period. though I haven't found an infestation for several years. (remove?)

At first I was dismayed to find someone I regarded as an eminently sane person suffering from the 'blues', and that this had produced in him some curious ideas—rather as if the genius the bit of his genius that had created those painstaking illustrations of chaos and disa catastrophe had begun to take over him over. I likened it at first to a tumour, and would attempt to 'operate' at tea-time, trying to jolly him up in front of the gas fire in the main living room (Orchard House is one of those dwellings rarely without a chill). But after several sleepless nights in the 'shelter' during the worst days of the Blitz on London (Cine Reels 13A & B), I for one became quite enthusiastic about the whole thing. Little more was said, however, after the tide began to turn against Hitler and his henchm minions, and Herbert was preoccupied with what he called his 'propaganda' work for several local councils, and a series of delightful 'pepping-up' strips for troop magazines. I had all but forgotten our rather heated discussions in the fug of the Anderson on those warm September nights, until that fateful summer's day almost eight years ago, when over my wireless came the news that the atomic bomb had been dropped onto Hir from a great height onto a Japanese city, with frightful results (Cine Reel 15A).

With the subsequent bursting of atomic bombs on land and underwater off Bikini Atoll (Cine Reel 15B), Herbert's rather dusty Project once again became the our main topic of conversation. This was all at about the same time as British rationing (see 'How We Live', under 'Diet') spread, quite literally, to one's daily bread—a real nuis a rather parlous state of affairs it seemed! Herbert had also just been given 'the push' by the editor of 'Punch': there is little room for a Herbert Bradman amongst the 'jazzy', scribbled, American-style humorous drawings that now appeal to the masses—interested only in 'getting a kick' out of things. Following this setback, Herbert would sit for hours on the bench in our in his garden at Ulv in sleepy little Ulverton, just gazing at the begonias, as if he had been switched off by some careless hand. It was on one of these occasions that I brought to him an envelope I had found while sorting through his drawers: it appeared, from its rattling sound, to have nothing more inside it than a lot of seeds, but was marked in an old-fashioned script, 'First Chamber, December 9th, 1858'—so I had not thrown it away directly. A light almost immediately spread across his face, his eyebrows shot up, and within moments he was standing upon the bench shouting unintelligibly at the top of his voice. Somewhat perturbed at this reaction, I got up and went for a glass of his favourite summer 'quench'.

When I returned from the kitchen with a tall glass of chilled lemon barley water, I had no sooner stepped into the garden than I realised Mr Bradman had gone. It was a beautiful August day in 1946, and the smell of the harvest from the fields beyond the church was quite heady, particularly with the rather high odour of the tractor fumes (see 'Men On the Land', Chap. 19) wafting over the wall every now and then. I had taken to wearing sunglasses (see 'Facial Wear' section of 'Vogues and Luxuries') for health reasons, and had taken them off to go indoors, as the house is rather somb on the dark side. Putting them back on, the glare of the garden was reduced, and I was able to see Mr Bradman's form entangled in the shrubbery behind the bench. He had, it seemed, tumbled in his excitement into my newly-planted dwarf conifers, breaking not a few of the prize azaleas etc. on the way. On crossing the lawn as quickly as a full glass of lemon barley water allows one to, I was relieved to find him un not quite to discover him undeterred, muttering to himself with what I thought was a serious gash on his cheek, but turned out to be a crimson petal off my lobelia! He wouldn't be budged, and my attempts at pulling him out ended in ignominious failure, with lemon barley water sticking down my front and my straw sun-hat rather the worse for wear beside him. and myself on my bottom. on my behind

Seeing that he had not actually harmed himself, and that my struggles were useless, I set about repairing some of the damage with secateurs (see 'Men on the Land', Appendix) and pea-sticks as best I could. During this operation, I could quite clearly hear Herbert discussing with himself his grandiose plans, for the envelope contained seeds extracted from a Pharaoh's tomb, and 'the symbolic parallel was not lost on me' (as he later put it). Even now, when I water that shrubbery (we no longer emply a full-time gardener, of course), I think of its verdant nest as being the real birth-place of the 'Project' and all our subsequent effrt over the last six years.

I do hope that you forgive the vagaries of the rather ancient typewriter (see 'Mechanical Inventions') with which I am proceeding: the ribbon has a tendency to slip down which explains the red bits now and again! while the 'o' key has now decided to stick every so often—most trying! One is, I reflect, so dependent on mechanical devices or 'gadgets' these days: when one considers how complicated a typewriter is, let alone a modern passenger aircraft of some thousands of horse-power and enormous tonnage, the miracle is that we are not all deluged in wires and steel frm one day to the next. If my 'o' key were to stick completely—as the dusty 'z' appears to have done—I would have to resort to a fountain pen. This would break Mr Bradman's cardinal rule of absolute clarity and the need for an 'objectivity' or 'purity' in presentation. This is not at all the same thing as his belief in 'the vital', or as he puts it or what he terms 'the fiery essence of concentrated personal being', which is why samples of handwriting and voices recorded on a magnetic tape recording machine have been included—as well, of course, as the 'Collected Works' of Mr Bradman himself. These (as you will see) include several pen-and-ink riginals from the Twenties, and a chalk drawing which was the basis for his 'Bournville' illustration of 1940. This rather splendid work was to be displayed on giant hoardings outside Birmingham and Coventry Central Stations, but the wood-pulp crisis (stemming from the German invasion of Norway in that year, see Cine Reel 11F) forced the Bournville Company to 'hold back' for the common good. The original painting was (alas!) destroyed in the bombing of Coventry on the night of the 14th November, 1940—a blow which caused Herbert to lose his taste for large-scale, highly prestigious commissins.

Sat. 28th March 1953
Mild, fitful sun. Dumplings.

Typing a.m., then essay until 8.30! Got up to H.'s shrubbery tumble. Missed out the bicycle-saddle incident. Thought it best all round.

Sun. 29th March 1953
Mild, sunny. Chicken, semolina.

Matins. Sermon on world hunger. Rather depressing. Walked briskly after lunch. Medium-length new one: northerly direction up main road, left thru gate just after big thick pollarded oak you can see faces in, that Mrs Dart calls 'Samson' (rather appropriate I suppose), straight across fields above Five Elms Farm, thru beech wood behind Ulverton Hall (a few primroses, but park still an awful mess thru trees), down to river, over wobbly plank, up Ewe Drop (nice name), along scarp all way to Barrow, down Louzy Hill (not nice name) and home to great big steaming mug of Brooke Bond's. Best walk for years. Marked it orange on Ordnance Survey. Felt cd almost take off on top. Dampened by Miss W. nattering on about Mr T. S. Eliot & I said oh yes I mean to read the Four Quintets. They both howled (that's the word). Then H. said they had planted the Cupressocyparis leylandii (I've looked it up) around the Burial Site, thinking to fox me I suppose, but I said very straight I thought Cupressus lawsoniana wd have been better for the density. Get as good as you give, as Father wd say. Miss Walwyn's big dark eyes flashed at that, all right. She's got some Jewish in her I'm sure. Poor things.

Mon. 30th March 1953
Mild, gusty. Spam fritters.

Mummy seeds have COME UP!! Herbert hugged me, but pipe singed my hair—awful smell. Amazing really to think those tiny green shoots, that tender & with dew on them, have been dormant for 3,000 years!! A miracle pure and simple. Makes you think. Went to Webb's Yard to see about wood for Sample Compartments (cherry, they say) & mentioned miracle. Old Mr Webb said he remembers a Mr George Fergusson, used to live opp. church in Miss Walwyn's little cottage, saying something about curse. Ah yes, I said, it was Mr Fergusson gave the mummy seeds to Mr Bradman in 1931, just before Mr Fergusson passed on. They wd walk together. Forgotten till I came across the envelope just after the war. (What's this, Mr B.? Goodness gracious, Violet, we shall see them bloom!) No, old Mr Webb rather thought something to do with Squire digging up cunnyump. Cunnyump? Barrow, Miss Nightingale. I said probably more the Egyptological angle. Blank look from Mr Webb. Asks in funny voice have I ever seed him. Blank look from Miss Nightingale. Seeded who, pray? The Squire, Miss Nightingale. Ah, seen. I have never seen the Squire, Mr Webb. He took his own life, I believe, in 1923. Aye, with a Martini Henry under the plum-tree. That's why they sold her off. Her? The orchard, Miss Nightingale. Your Mr Bradman's orchard. Aye, under the plum-tree, in the mouth, no face poor bugger. That'll be all, Mr Webb. Order to be ready by May 15th. Exit Miss Nightingale. Lying in bed. Won't sleep. Like Wuthering Heights, near the beginning. Knuckles on the window pane. Let me in, let me in! Awful. Wonder what drove him to it? Sometimes think H. cd, when in a gloom. Mother used to say it, but not the type. Widowhood. She just soldiers on & lucky to have Gordon now she's doolally. Funny neither of us ever did the normal. Poor Jean Lowe so proud of her ring. Lost its colour after Fred died. She saw it as sign, but only 9-carat Utility. Mind you, 22 carat under £5 now they've lifted controls, I noticed in town last month. Gustier than ever tonight. Flicking away at window. Knock knock, knock knock. Saw Wuthering H. with Kenneth, Shirley and lame little Ivor Gilchrist that time. Could have blown me over with a feather after. Six inches off the ground, I felt. Not cos of Olivier of course, no. Kenneth. Storm scene, music bashing out, rain pouring off their hair, load of shouting & kissing, then felt hand on my knee. Moved up sideways like a crab. Started snapping my suspenders. Thought the whole row wd hear. Snap snap. Snap snap. Those were times. Didn't touch anything more though. He wasn't that sort. Not that time. Wonder if Squire had one? A wife. Can't bear to think on it. Children. That face, all over the plums I spose. Tiny bits of it still in bark, quite likely. Hope the pane holds. Oh God. I'd just die, just like that. Snap snap. Snap snap. Oh Kenneth.

Tues. 31st March 1953
Mild, windy. Sausage.

Labelling Material till lunch. Sneaked out 2.00 and lopped plum as best I could given the implement (big rusty saw from shed, got it caught in the tennis-net, took a tumble yanking it & distemper stain from old tin on skirt now, drat it. MUST clear the thing out. Felt like I was in an H. E. Bradman cartoon!) His nibs in London with Miss You-know-who. Please himself. Some of us have work to get on with. Last time Violet in London was when Gordon came down for that big model train do. '47! Time's more than a twin-prop, as Father wd say.

Midnight. No sight nor sound of Herbert. Terrible if anything's happened to him. Wanted him to take train. That Hillman! Take the train, Mr B. No, said H., I'm taking my Minx. Big giggle from Miss W. I went all hot in face, I'm afraid to say. Don't think she's prepared to recognise Herbert's greatness. She paints too. Little watercolours. Rather browny. Golly it's quiet. Almost miss that branch knocking. Perhaps a tree has fallen onto car. Sausage repeating. Nothing real in them. Artificial. Never seen a pig, probably. Come on, Herbert. Not like you. This is what I mean. Big dark eyes flashing. I'll have to have a word. Not going to let Project slip away at last moment. Herbert's Second Coming, she calls it. There's still respect. Don't like the way she calls him Josef whenever he gets short, either. Just the same moustache, Violet! Miss Nightingale, until further notice, Miss Walwyn. Jocularly, but meant. Is it different up North, Miss Nightingale? Cheek. Anyway he's dead now. That horrible man. We can all breathe easier. Though H. doesn't think so. We're all doomed, Violet. Oh thank God that's him. Them.

1.30 a.m. Bits of plaster on me. What a racket. Stamping. Stamping. Coming down like confetti, awful. Must see to it. I do think it's a bit much in the small hours. Really. Stamping about like that.

Wed. April 1st 1953
Cool, snow up in Buxton as usual. Potato soup.

Typing all day. Frayed (that's the word) after last night: front door banged 4.30 a.m.! H. slept in till 11.15. Unfortunate, as had usual April Fool boiled egg joke up my sleeve. Sat there for ages, waiting. Something about that spoon going straight through always makes my year. Falls for it every time, Herbert does. Superstitious about that sort of thing not coming off. Took a tumble on the Dry Fly bottle on rug, completely empty. Nearly brained myself against the mahogany drop-side table—that antique claw-footed one Mrs Dart left her mark on, as you might say. Somebody has to hold the fort. That's how that man died when I was at Mather & Platt's on the shorthand. Slippery floor. Went flying. Caught the edge of something. Mr Ryland, I think. Mr Ryland. Looks right. Or was that that dreadful Works Accountant at Jackson Heywood's? Never let me alone. Awful George Formby imitations. Put rubber bands around his teeth or something like that. From his teeth to the top of his head, that was it. Awful. Looked a bit like Herbert did this morning. In a bit of a rumple this morning are we? as Mother used to say. Lunch-time kept my mouth shut. It pays. Tea-time was just cups and gas fire popping till I brought up the Tampax issue. I think I ought to mention that I believe you have been borrowing certain items from my intimate drawers, Mr B. You only had to ask. Growl from Herbert: not now, Violet. Told him I had to say it or burst. You only had to ask. Herbert suddenly leaps out of sofa. Ask did you say? Ask? Ask Violet Nightingale for a pack of bloody sanitary towels? You didn't have to be so explicit, Mr B. Exactly, Violet, exactly! My God, I've not realised a damn thing! What thing, Mr B.? Oh, never mind! Go to the pictures! Go to the bloody pictures! I was not planning on visiting the cinema tonight, Mr B., but if that is your wish, then so be it. Looking straight out. Exit Herbert with a large snort. Only sound in living room my tea-cup trembling in its saucer. And gas fire of course. I can see it. Six years of work heading for the gutter. Sliding off. Horrible. Horrible.

Thurs. April 2nd 1953
Cold, grey. Kidneys.

Shopping a.m. Mrs Hobbs said her Marjorie has complete set Brooke Bond butterfly cards. Wd like to donate it to Project. I said that wd be too great a sacrifice for a little girl. Mrs Hobbs insistent. Cd go into 'Hobbies & Pastimes' I spose. Or 'Wild Life'. That's the trouble. Fuzzy edges. Indexing p.m. Postcard from Mother: Bexhill-on-Sea with Manchester Spiritualists Social Club. 'I've heard from Father.' Why can't folk leave past alone?

Fri. April 3rd 1953
Cold, grey. Haddock.

Typing & collating all day. Fingers hurt. Lumbago?

Sat. April 4th 1953
Cold, showery. Poached egg.

Typing all day. Second ribbon in a week. Some bits of Herbert's teenage years every bit as bad as Mr D. H. Lawrence's works. Quite unnecessary, but greatness knows no bounds, as Gladys Unsworth wd say. Too busy supporting Mother & Gordon to get up to that sort of nonsense. Except for that time with Kenneth and Gordon's cat. On the settee at home. Mother opposite. You make a nice cup of tea, Violet, when you do. Thank you Mother. Gordon's big fat tabby on my lap, though I didn't like it a bit. Esmerelda I think its name was. Smelt. Kenneth stroking it. Stroking it on the back, pressing it down on my lap, flattening it almost. I hear you're in dye-stuffs, Kenneth. That's right Mrs Nightingale. Pressing it down but it seemed to like it. Purring fit to kill. Then a finger around the ears, so they flicked. Violet's second cousin is at Trafford Park in the labs there, isn't he Violet? Our Vernon. But I don't think it's dye-stuffs. Do take a biscuit. Thank you very much, Mrs Nightingale, I think I will. Then back about the neck (of the cat of course) which they like, cats do. Heart thumping away and room getting hotter. I thought my face wd catch fire. He was in the East Lancashire Tuberculosis Colony at Barrowmore before that of course, as a lab assistant, our Vernon. Wasn't he Violet? Though they've never been close. (Always that line, always that.) Was he really, Mrs Nightingale? Then hand suddenly under, tickling the tummy. Just tickling its tummy on my lap. Just tickling its tummy. Knuckles rippling in and out, in and out. Big knuckles, had Kenneth. Big strong knuckles. In and out. I'm glad to see you like cats, Kenneth. Our Violet prefers birds. Oh I've always liked cats, Mrs Nightingale. But his hand came out slowly oh it did. Room so hot. All blurred. Birds. Isn't that right, Violet? Mother's voice all echoey and then the cat jumps off. Like stripping almost. All cold suddenly. I don't suppose Kenneth ever realised

Herbert all gloom. No sign of Miss W. Ought to go up to mansion tomorrow for that canvas. Or they'll be on at me. Queer without that knocking

Oh Kenneth

Sun. April 5th 1953
Damp, bright intervals. Packed lunch (meat-paste, Marmite). Cod, roly-poly.

Holy Communion. Sermon lost me. Palm Sunday used to be simple. Young Rev. Appleton much too smart & most likely lefty so will empty church soon. Not that Bew's Lane Chapel looks up to much. Spotted a cobweb across door the other week. Got back to find note from H.: Gone Out for Day. Love Herbert. First time 'Love'. Decided to make Ulverton Hse visit into proper outing. Wore wellies in case. Mistake: rubbed bunions almost raw. Sloes in bloom already up Deedy Lane. I'm still only halfway thru last year's brew! Got to big iron gate, pushed it, got stuck in gravel, pushed it again & Ministry of Works sign fell off catching little toe. Poor mite. Ever so painful. Cut across park to mansion. Mistake: covered with rubbish and tore skirt on nail from collapsed Nissen hut. Will be forest of nettles in summer. So-called lake stinks to heaven. Used to drive the tanks straight through it, I remember. Saw them many a time thru trees at back: big roar and splash, little chaps wobbling on top, heck of a din they made. Got all the birds going. Had to practise somewhere I suppose. Fell over big boot (Size 12) probably off big German P.O.W. Reminded me of Herbert's classic 'Stamp Him Out' cartoon in '41: tiny Adolf trampling Europe map in shadow of enormous Allied boot. That was greatness all right, said so much. And so painstaking. Stone steps only a bit chipped, but loads of green glass bits all over terrace, & burnt patches. Never believe they've been gone three years. And almost ten since those Yanks! Time's more than a twin-prop, as Father wd say. Young Doris Ketchaside's no doubt counting every day, with those twins of hers. Some cheeky chappie put 'Colour courtesy of the 101st Airborne Division' on her pram one time, acc. to Mrs Dart. The father might have fallen on the Normandy beaches, I said, never mind his skin. It always takes two, as Mother wd say. Maybe tramps camp in the House now. Thought made me shiver. Had a sip of coffee from thermos & that helped: kept my innards warm at least. Such a lovely classical front, despite all: sun broke through &

beautiful tall golden stone columns soared all glowing—Palladian? Like huge sad temple. Doors had dreadful creak, like horror film. Gloomy inside: practically every window covered in plywood, nasty slivers of glass. That's Ulverton youth for you: no respect. Even had a stone thrown at me once, just for ticking off bad language. Need a flick on the ear-hole from P.C. Trevick, I said. Went into very long room (dining room originally?), absolutely running with damp. Cd almost mangle the air, as Grandma used to say on fog days. Smelt of urine. But electric torch showed rather attractive ornate ceiling (plasterwork, of course). Cricked neck slightly, looking. Lilies, ivy, wild clematis and I think a pelargonium but rest too chipped. Pity somebody had lit fire in one corner—big black scorch marks above, carved oak (?) panelling all buckled & paint bubbled off. Lovely old fireplace taller than me with pink and white roses inlaid in middle, once I'd wiped away filth with my hankie. Very good detail on the roses. Heavy shower suddenly outside: water dripped into fireplace! Peckish, so ate lunch on one remaining wobbly chair next to portable wash-stand bang in middle of room chock-a-block with cigarette stubs. Soldiers so careless. Echoes of my thermos flask each time I placed it on floor made me feel rather too far away from everyone for my liking, for some reason. Room too big. Must have been magnificent (no other word) one time—big mirrors, chandeliers, footmen, crystal decanters etc. Mr Rose serving up. Declined, everything has. Herbert's quite right. Sinking ship. Had to go upstairs, of course: huge marble staircase. Pretended I had long silk dress rustling up behind me. Lord Kenneth in bow-tie at top. Turned left (South Wing, one time). Corridors pitch-black, thank goodness for torch. No electrics at all that worked. All rooms locked! Mice scuttling behind. Come on, Violet! Bet Ministry of Works locked up just out of habit. Torch revealed filthy graffiti, unfortunately, all over walls. Though a little pencilled 'Mutti' which I think means Mother in German, which was rather touching, next to the light switch. And rather snarly griffins (?) on ceiling in landing. Rest ruined. Went into North Wing and one door at end slightly open, cd see streak of light. Peeped in & sun just sneaking thru windows where plywood had come off. Three metal beds, torn-out magazine pages (females without a stitch, needless to say) on wall, electric light-bulb on long wire in middle. High ceiling with v. chubby cherubs flying all about & cheeky smiles, rather worse for wear, paint a bit flaky like my pastry. One with a Hitler moustache which is just vandalism really. Amazing to think this was once ever so posh bedroom. Nice view of that beech wood behind, Mr Dimmick's farm, downs etc. Gaudy wallpaper but soldier must have attacked it with knife—hanging off in long strips as if grated. Crimson colour underneath. A bit like meat at the butcher's. Crimson colour actually silk. Still smooth. Knife had cut silk to ribbons in one place—no respect—dull brown underneath. Original layer I spose. Reminded me of my own room in Mortlake, after the flood: bottom layer bright red poppies or something. Distempered the lot pale violet (of course!). Just putting a finger on the silk when heard creak like bed-springs behind. Heart in mouth. Neck prickling. Turned round eventually: not a soul, as you might say. Then saw big lump under Army blanket on middle bed. Don't know why, prodded it first with the umbrella. Soft. Ugh. Reminded me of bodies after bombing raid on Newbury. '43. Tea with vicar of St John's. Shudder, boom. Plaster on hair. Went out. Church completely flattened thru smoke. Vicar (can't remember his name—Simpson?) just broke out in huge sobs. Stood there like about to start a running race, arms dangling, great loud sobs coming out of him & a rather tall thin man. Wd have put my arm round him then but had very full cup of tea & didn't want to put it down in middle of road, understandably. Left cup & saucer on nearest low wall but he'd gone to wreckage of nearby houses by the time I was back. Always regretted not putting arm round him. Bodies brought out & all soft but stiff also. Horrible. Anyway, prodded blanket again with my finger, felt sick, ran STRAIGHT out of bedroom, DOWN stairs & into marbly entrance hall quick as a flash. Cd have sworn heard Miss W.'s giggle at some point, maybe at beginning, but mustn't start imagining things. Dark flashy eyes might have sort of deep influence, as Mother wd put it. BUT just about to go out of front door when saw big white bundle in corner: huge long roll of bandage. Cdn't bear to go round the back to check the canvas, anyway, given my state. White muslin bandage perfect for bunting: can dye it all colours of rainbow if they want. Got a bit soggy on way back in shower. Meat-paste repeating. H. got in at 8.15. Said how was the mansion? I said pleasant, thank you. Don't remember telling him I was going. Big smile from Herbert. How was your day, Mr B.? Oh, satisfying, Violet, very satisfying. Another big twinkly smile. His face completely changes when he smiles. Said nothing more. He was rather wet, hadn't taken the Hillman, had faintly familiar musty smell about him. Well, I don't like to probe.

Mon. April 6th 1953
Cold, blustery. Pork pie.

Typing all day, back where I left off before on 'The Life As Lived': no more teenage years, I said to H. over lunch. You can only have seven, you know. He didn't even chuckle: a world of his own. His memory is amazing, though. I spose the inner life of the great visionary (and H. *is* that, whatever people say) as important as the outer, but I would like to know when he eats now and again! Magnetic tape recorder holding up. Feel I know Herbert better than myself, sometimes.

Tues. April 7th 1953
Milder, showery. Lamb chop.

Typing all day. Fagged out!

Wed. April 8th 1953
Mild, showery. Cheese potato.

Typing all day. Stiff. Hip again. Mr Sedgwick the stonemason over from Fawholt. He was the one did last lot on war memorial and missed the 'b' on Cecil Scablehorne's, acc. to Mrs Dart. Typed out Location Stone lettering in block caps, just in case. Nice man. Asthmatic, like Gordon.

Thurs. April 9th 1953
Nice & sunny. Yorkshire pud.

Typing 'The Life As Lived' all day. Up to p. 1530 (1938). Butterflies about it, but I am looking forward to 'my' years. Can be hard on folk, mind you. Just as well his father's passed on, in a way. Though no one alive will ever read it. Presume they'll still have scholars about, in 3,000 years, to translate it all! His Mother wd be pleased. Butter obviously cdn't melt in his mouth. Hip eased a bit with the extra cushion.

Fri. April 10th 1953
Damp, overcast. Cod.

Typing all day. Mummy seed shoots appear to be sweet peas. House-martins back, scrabbling away above the study. Wonder where they've been?!

Sat. April 11th 1953
Damp, cloudy. Boiled egg.

Typing a.m., H. out all day. Shopping p.m. Much more in shops than a year ago, I realise. Mrs Hobbs onto me about those butterfly cards again. Sniffily. Very stiff. Quick walk up to Bayley's Wood. Primroses lovely. First wood anemones in usual spot. Oxlips! Wood lark. Fox? MUST get on with essay, though fingers agony. Don't know whether shd mention 'naughties'!? (You must be completely honest, my dear, for the sake of posterity. For the sake of truth.) Naturally, Mr B.

Part 3

The Project Years

For the last six years I have dedicated myself to the 'Project' on a daily basis—much of my work involving 'phone calls to public lending libraries (especially the British Museum Library), experts in all fields, inexpensive hotels and so on; card-indexing, filing and cross-referencing; collating and binding; and typing the material as it comes. I have left the 'creative' work, of course, to Mr Bradman. The merry tap-dance (see 'Mass Entertainments') of these keys have kept many an unwanted knife-grinder (or whoever) kicking his heels at the tradesman's entrance, while in his 'studio' Mr Bradman has drawn and written until the smoke metaphorically comes out of his ears!

Given the task in hand, it is not surprising that Mr Bradman has neglected his professional career, and many believe that he has di has either passed away or has retired completely from the pages of the 'shinies' and the children's annuals. If they could only come to little Ulverton, and watch him burn the 'midnight oil' in a fog of pipe-tobacco, their assumptions would quickly be dashed. I should really

I really ought

Mr Bradman is not a 'la

Although

I ought to say at this point that our professional relationship, while clo intimate, has never impinged on our private domains. I am quite I am well aware of the 'Freudian' implications of an employer and his female 'assistant' living toge living under the same roof, but apart from our Sunday 'roast' and sandwiches at lunch-time, meals are taken quite separately. I have my own gas-supplied kitchen in the flat, and a separate entrance behind a small fence. Now and again questions are there are prying typ inevitably the lo I do find the 'locals' rather trying, espec most parti although Miss Enid Walwyn, the young teacher at our village school, has a way with words that Herbert, for one, finds alluring. She is well versed in English literature, and many is the time we have argued the respective merits of Mr Edmund Blunden and Mr T. S. Eliot over a jam doughnut. or two. Herbert Bradman's unique qualities are such that many find his comp He does have a way with I must say, there is however still however despite there is no one else who knows Herbert E. Bradman as well as myself.

At this poin

Something of his

Opening a drawer one day, I was rather star

I think I've already mentioned that Herbert drew illustrations for 'glossies' like 'The Tatler'. They especially liked his abilitics in the human torso direction; no one could rival Herbert in that line. Flicking through those magnificent colured pages of the Twenties and early Thirties, it is quite obvious to me that Herbert's double-spreads exceed all his rivals. 'Cleopatra's Bath-House' or 'The Nymphs Laughed At Their Reflections' (not in a pool but in the bumper of a white Lagonda motor-car!) rival Mr Bestall's more languid creations. The female frm, in Herbert's hands, looks so light and slim (whether clad or no) that one might almost believe it is truly angelic. Apart from anything else, of course, his drawings undoubtedly promoted our very light, hygienic clothing that did away with the clumsy garments of yesteryear, and that are, in the opinion of the Ministry of Health, highly beneficial to health to general well-being. But like Mr D. H. Lawr

But there are

Sun. April 12th 1953
V. dark, spitting. Chicken & stewed apple.

Easter service odd with it being so gloomy outside. Angel on wall of church subject of sermon. Has big dark eyes like Miss W.'s, unfortunately. Philis Punter-Wall says its wings are grey heron if you know what you're looking for. She does like to show off her expertise. I said I thought angels were above all that. Used to nest on the river in my grandfather's day, she said, all sniffy. Chill. Old Bidem (don't know his real name!) rather eloquent on flowers in churchyard, or wd have been if I had understood the half (thick accent). Got onto fruit. I said was it true about the Squire under plum-tree? Said wrong thing, evidently: he went all silent & big brown face twitched all over. Never know what you're touching sometimes. Well, I said (to save the situation), at least he enjoyed a last drink, acc. to Mr Webb. That Martini. Sheila Stiff's baby looks definitely mongoloid. Doesn't move a muscle and it's nearly five months. The obvious joke came into my head just as I was taking the wine (she'd brought him up to be blessed) and I felt so evil. On Easter Sunday too. Sometimes Communion makes me feel strong all over though. I think it's the taste apart from anything else of course. The bread and wine in your mouth, and you can smell it off the others back in the pew, all part of the same thing. I don't know. Herbert thinks it's all rubbish of course. But he won't dissuade me. Miss W. still goes, at least. His eyes rather sparkly at moment—new lease of life, but doesn't mention Project very much. Has just about finished illustrations to last chapter of 'The Life As Lived', he told me over lunch. I'll interleave them with the typescript myself, Violet, when you've finished it. Oh, I think I can manage that, Mr B.! No no, Violet, leave it to me, leave it to me. Rather sternly. I mentioned how much I was looking forward to typing out next instalment. Blank look from Herbert. Didn't say any more. Struggled with my 'essay' all afternoon but hopeless. Gardened. Looked at the Pharaoh's sweet peas & suddenly felt tearful & small. Nice talk on old waggons on wireless at moment by a Mr Ewart Evans. Quite poetic. Never knew harness was so complicated.

Mon. April 13th 1953
Clearing. Spam fritters.

Miss W. back from her holiday somewhere: loads of giggling above now needless to say. Squealing. Typed 'The Life As Lived' all day, up to August 1939. Not a hint of my interview in July. He does get his dates a bit out sometimes. Comes of not keeping strict diary. Tempted to hear on but that's never been my way. I type what I have to type, & hear what I like to hear. The Nanking Road rather good. Took in cocoa tray and Miss W. had got there first. Felt like that time Gordon brought Father's slippers down while I was on the toilet & I was only about seven. Betrayed. Miss W. in easy chair said oh here's Violet now can you help us. Herbert thinks the name 'Ulverton' is because they used to have wolves but I say it's either owls or Canute. Canute of the waves? I enquired, coolly. Yes, she said. Then something about Canute and his bodyguards and their manners. Well, I'm not one of her pupils. So what do you think, my dear? from Herbert. I said History's not my subject, Mr B., and I have more important things on my mind than nomenclature (that was the word, uttered straight out). Then H. did his vulgar bit. The valley's shape and all that. Just to make me flush, no doubt. Who the devil lopped off the V, etc. Gives out big roar of laughter. Miss W. tut-tutted I'll give her that. Sometimes I wonder whether Herbert ever quite got over his teenage years, as they say about Mozart I believe. Miss Walwyn is rather full of herself, that's the trouble. Up too many pegs, as Father always snapped about Kenneth, poor soul. Though only a quarter Jewish, in the end.

Tues. April 14th 1953
Mild, v. bright sun. Bovril.

Typed 'The L. As L.' up to December 1939. Nothing. That is, nothing on myself. I think he must have got his years wrong. That doesn't bode well for whole, does it? No appetite—funny butterflies feeling in stomach. Dull play about talking pigs on wireless. Light only has Accordion Band on. Third just thumpy Beethoven. Have to drown giggles somehow. I'm very worried, actually. A Daisy Powder or I'll not get off at all, though the packet's rather old (got it after V.E. Day for obvious reasons!). Finished Cherry Heering, talking of that. Meant to offer some to Herbert. Never seems to be free of an evening to come down, these days.

Wed. April 15th 1953
Mild, sunny. Bovril.

Up to August 1940. Nothing! Only: 'I gave the papers to my secretary and drove immediately off, exultant with a newfound feeling of liberation from all the daily dross of this scheming, sick world.' No appetite. Awful caved-in feeling in stomach. Doan's haven't helped. Mother used to swear by Cockle's for nervous indigestion. That awful giggling. Squealing. Like Mr Oadam's pigs. Coronation Committee Meeting 6.30: Mr Donald Jefferies said he's got every waggon in the parish & lots of implements for the bonfire. I said did he hear that interesting programme on Sunday? He said obsolete equine carriages have nothing to do with our new Elizabethan era of streamlined speed & efficiency. Dr Scott-Parkes took off his spectacles and mentioned possibility of national famine if we didn't increase productivity. Like he tells you to eat plenty of greens or else. Mr Daye said we must increase crop yields by something or other. Mr Stroude said what happened to the ploughing-up policy and chortled (that's the word). Then they all went on and on. Mouths moving, arms waving. Subsidies. Phosphates. Batteries. Fifty per cent something. Hill farming obsolete. Policy at half-cock. Artificial inseminating vital (I think that's what my Minutes say). On and on. Lots of nodding. Felt such a fool about the waggons, like I was simple. Low tonight. Secretary! Want to read on but never been my way.

Oh Herbert

Thurs. April 16th 1953
Warm, clear intervals. Potato soup.

Up to end of 1940. Nothing. 'My secretary opened the door & Mr Alfred Bestall entered.' Alfred, of course. Nice man. Herbert nearly got Rupert in 1932. He just couldn't get the face right. Very good on Nutwood & surrounds, though. That lovely valley.

Fri. April 17th 1953
Warm, sunny. Bread & dripping.

Up to August '41. Nothing. 'The feeling that my energies were at their peak was a potent one, and only when my secretary came in with a cup of cocoa (O the reins of routine!) did that flowing current of creative electricity cease.' I'd thought he'd have brought me in when the Project idea was floated. That time in the shelter. Walked the river up to Grigg's Wood and back. Clear my head. Lovely still day. Everything a bit like glass. Thought of those singers who can shatter it (glass). Made attempt (no one about) on Saddle Bridge leaning over but came out a funny squeak. Fancy if I had and the world suddenly went with a pop. Could almost imagine it, it all looked so fragile and leaves sticky & translucent, like Shirley's first in the hospital. Its eyelids. Sunlit trees and water and whatnot. Felt just like a little girl again, on the bridge. Looking into the water. Making my squeak. Yes yes.

Sat. April 18th 1953
Warm, gusty. Bovril.

End of '41. 'It was leafing through a book on fossils in the shade of the pear-tree, and seeing a photograph of a prehistoric fly caught in amber, that re-awoke that long-buried dream, and only when my secretary interrupted my reverie with some lemon barley water, did I descend from that glorious, potent mountain!'

Interrupted

Sun. April 19th 1953
Cool, raining.

Holy Communion. Felt dizzy, left before sermon. Thought angel was about to fall on top of me. Suffocating. In bed. Excused presence at lunch. V. low. Nothing in me. Glass of milk helped.

Oh Herbert

Mon. April 20th 1953
Mild, squalls.

Typed. Summer of '42. Nothing. Nothing at all. Those spool things make me giddy, going round and round like that.

Tues. April 21st 1953
Mild, grey. Tomato soup.

Typed. End of '42. Nothing. 'Well, I suppose you have felt this power, this desire to change the world. Come on now, have you not? I have! My secretary has not. My baker has not. Your linoleum salesman has not. But we have!' Letter from Museum (only took them eight months): 'The item you retrieved from the River Fogbourne is not, as you thought, a Saxon dagger but a bradawl, probably eighteenth century.' A non-spiral boring-tool, apparently. Might have known.

Wed. April 22nd 1953
Mild, sunny. Boiled egg.

Typed. Middle of '43. Nothing. 'Only the tapping keys of the distant typewriter came between me and a sort of glowing Nirvana as my pen flowed across the white page.' House-martin poisoned. Too much noise, said Herbert. So looking forward to those tiny mouths yearning.

Thurs. April 23rd 1953
Fresh, sunny. Marie biscuits.

December '43. 'My secretary went down to her room, leaving me to enjoy that delicious solitude of the self-seeker before the roaring fire. What a Xmas, truly, for the ripe soul!' Up to Barrow. Greater celandine out. Common blue. Corn bunting on telegraph wire. Peewits.

Fri. April 24th 1953
Cool, sunny intervals. Thin Arrowroot biscuits.

Mr Bradman in London. Up to September '44. 'The bombs rained down upon Europe, but I was elsewhere in my soul. I drew deliriously, obsessively, ended only by cocoa brought on a tray, the powder still circling slowly upon the top, like the Milky Way, like the spiral of the ancients, like the Vital Desire itself!' Letter from Gordon. Mother's a turn for the worse. I'll have to go up I spose.

Sat. April 25th 1953
Chill, snow in Buxton. Vegetable soup.

Miss W. upstairs. Spring '45. Nothing. Nothing at all.

Wrote to Gordon. Will be coming up. Took in cocoa and music blasting away on gramophone. Miss W. and H. in easy chairs with eyes shut. Thought they were asleep. Turned it right down. Your cocoa, Mr B., and I think I'll be turning in now. You'd think I'd kicked them. That supreme moment, Violet, and you shattered it! Supreme moment,

Mr B.? Gerontius meeting the angel! Face to face at last! Oh the dross and trivia of this world, obscene, obscene!

Sometimes I feel like having a good weep

Sun. April 26th 1953
Cold. Soup.

H. Communion. Walk to White Horse. Mr Stephen Bunce found me. Brought horse & cart, took me down. Gave me brandy in his council house in Vanners Crescent. Smelt of dogs. Kind folk. Never been in one before. You looks very creamy, Miss Nightingale. Thank you. Thank you. Thank you.

Oh Violet

Mon. April 27th to Fri. May 1st 1953: incapacitated. Panic overhead. Furniture moved about like thunder. Mrs Dart said saw robin tap my window which means a death. Sorry to disappoint, I said.

Sat. May 2nd 1953
Warm, sunny. Dumplings.

Contributions weekend. Certainly 'quotidian'. H. kept out of way. No more HP Sauce bottles tomorrow, and that's flat. Headache from smiling. Some of the clothes smell. Well

Sun. Apr

Tues. May

Mon. May 18th 1953
Warm, overcast. Yorkshire pudding.

'The Life As Lived' finished. Nothing. Last paragraph. Spring 1953. 'Enid and I walked up that day to the ruined mansion, her eyes flashing hope, mine only adoration. "April is the cruellest month", she whispered, as we climbed to the terrace hand in hand. Within, where England's old order had crumbled to dripping ceilings and scrawled walls, where perhaps you, the reader, are now cropping your sheep, or landing your space rockets, we found a bed. Here the seed was planted anew, as I had planted those ancient seeds. Just as I now plant this great steel seed filled with the dross of our so-called "civilisation", and the struggle of one to free himself, as an angel must from the material shards of a lesser world, through the agency of the female essence, from that trivial and clogging stuff we call "daily life", that you see before you in all its reality. And even there, the world invaded, poked us, did not let us be (see illustration). Only in death may that joy be everlasting, may that seed flower, just as this seed before you now has flowered in your eyes, like the golden flower of Homer. Pick it, and rejoice! May it give you hope! May it give you life! May it give you, too, O posterity, that vital fire of love!'

Handed it all over. Apple-pie order. Illustrations coming on, Mr B.? All done, Violet. Goodness gracious, you are a marvel, my dear. Look at this! So neat and tidy! Well I was thoroughly trained, Mr B. May I have a glance at the illustrations? Oh no my dear. There are some things that even you cannot view. Only posterity has that privilege, my dear!

Seems to have forgotten about my written contribution. Just as well. No stomach for it.

Tues. May

Wed. May 20th 1953

Mild. Coronation Committee Meeting: no more bunting needed, Miss N. You shd have brought it earlier! Ill, I know. But thank you anyway on behalf of the etc. Maybe the cottage hospital wd be interested? You're looking better, I'll say that. Have you checked yr garden for bonfire stuff? It's rather wild at back, Miss N. Found two waggons already & a threshing machine in old barn on Barr's Farm—hid under collapsed roof for 25 years, can you imagine? Gardened. Herbert distant. Biggest bonfire ever. Red Admiral. Chiff-chaff behind shed. No waggons.

Thu

Sun. May 24th 1953

Missed church. Hiked (that's the word) up to Kisser Cross. Blowy. Wind right through me. Buffeting. So open up there, that's the trouble. Let it push me off, almost. Like flying. Or as if nothing in way of it (i.e. the wind). Skylark on fence-post. Prefer it up high, funny scruffy brown thing down here. THINK I SAW STONE CURLEW!! Need stronger binoculars.

Elgar blasting away again. Her present to him, I believe.

Mon. May 25th 1953

Repository arrived on back of lorry. Only a week late. Like big bomb. Shiny steel. Makes me look wide. Mr Webb put cherrywood compartments inside. Fit to a T, look, Mr Bradman. Packing the Material. I don't say much.

Tue.

Thurs. May 28th 1953

Packing the Material. Location Stone delivered. 'Posterity' spelt with an 'e' on the end. At least he got the 4953 date right, and Percy Bysshe Shelley. 'Of bitter prophecy' a bit too crowded, I thought, but then I'm always a stickler. H. displeased, but I didn't tell him about the wrong celandine on Wordsworth's. Why should I? Don't have

Fri. May 29th 1953

Packing. Herbert like little boy. Bisto in with the Oxo cubes now, Violet!

Don't have the stomach, but I do it.

Sat. May 30th

Mummy sweet pea's first flower. Rather small, but bright yellow. Picked it before a soul was up, just like that. In jam-jar on my window-sill. Waited 3,000 years and only felt early morning sun & a bit of a breeze on its petals. Better than nothing. Like a bird's-foot trefoil, that golden

Sun. May 31st '53

Walked up to scarp at dawn. Back along river. Whinchat. Bit of white campion by stile. Viper's bugloss in usual place (early). Ragged robin out at last in Quabb B. Heron by ruined mill? Repository all ready for Burial (Planting, he calls it now. Well, it's a bit late for me to change). Tripped over bunting on way to church. Bunting everywhere. Miss W.

got children at school to make them, needless to say. All colours of rainbow. Gold and silver even, like wings. Rather windy. Bit of sun. Bonfire or whatever by Saddle Bridge half-built already. Big. Waggons & carts one on top of another like they've dropped from sky. Thump thump. Loads of axes swinging away at lots of things. Big sweaty men grinning, tossing on wooden bits, swinging their axes. Nice old hay-wain straight out of Constable went in two minutes. Splinters flying they'd better watch their eyes. Two men holding either end of plough, looked just like Mr Dimmick's. One two three & on it goes. Little boy rolling barrel up. Waggons looked bigger all piled up. Like a pile of elephants out of that book on Africa. Gone without a struggle, as Joan Lowe said of her Eric. Little by Little, as Kenneth said, rather cruelly. Scribbled down the names on Gordon's envelope. Habit. Have to have a name, don't we? They've all got a bit of flaky paint & a name. Like on war memorial. Poppy day. Blast on the trumpet. JOHN STIFF, MAPLEASH FARM ULVERTON 1833. LORD CHARLES H. CHALMERS ULVERTON HOUSE FARM, ULVERTON. ERNEST M. BARR ULVERTON 1887. JACOB SWIF . . . (rest indecipherable—greasy patch on Gordon's envelope). Funny poem on wireless full of names. Like lullaby spinning round and round. Gordon's good on names. Missed 'What's My Line'. Thought it best all round. Hardly seen him. It sounds a bit religious, this. Will send me to sleep I hope. Nice voices

Mon. June 1st 1953

Big hole in garden. Instructions deposited in the bank vault. Officially. Repository to be opened 4953 (June 2nd I suppose). Don't have faith that bank vaults will survive but still. Big mechanical digger thing snorting away. Tore up lawn in two minutes, azaleas with it of course. Small crane coming tomorrow to lift it in. Six years' work. More, really. Meat-paste repeating. Nerves. Everything packed. He's going about waving his hands like little boy. Another mummy sweet pea out. Just in time for his speech. Whole village gone a bit mad, really. With Coronation, not our do, of course. Scouts came & put canvas wrap over it cos it's set to pour. Our Sovereign will get soaked says Mrs Whiteacre. Took the roll of bandage up to bonfire or whatever. Taller than the trees now, just waiting. Like the back of Ray Leatherbarrow when Shirley was late to the altar. She and her pink roses. River gurgling past. Hooked bandage on waggon shaft & walked round and round, only circled twice before it (bandage) gave out. Tucked end into cart-wheel. Little boy watching with nose problem. What's your name? Clive Walters Miss, what you up to, Miss? I'm wrapping it all up, Master Walters. You're bonkers, Miss. Bonkers! Runs off. Bonkers!

Miss W. squealing. Stamping. Plaster coming down like confetti.

4 a.m.: went out to garden with torch. Had to. Cool in nightie. Slippers soaked. Fiddled with toggles on canvas wrap for half an hour (Scout knots). Got it open. Lifted lid with a bit of an effort. Had to have a peep at the illustrations. 'The Life As Lived' on top. I've every right. Owl. Heart thumping. Painstaking work. Miss W. naked. Well, I'd thought as much. Cd hardly hold the torch straight. Last picture. Woman in wellington boots. Thick coat. Those buttons. A few deft ink strokes etc. Currant-bun face. Raisin for a mouth. Big frown. He's always been good at frowns. Teeth. Adapted (could spot this a mile off) from his Matron McOgre strip in 'The Schoolgirl's Own Annual' 1928 to 1931. Prods a bed with an umbrella. Cherubs on the ceiling. Naked foot protruding from blanket. Well, I might have known. Nice trees thru window. Caught it to a T, Violet. Caught it to a T. Rip it out, stumble over lawn, stop, go back, take out 'The Life As Lived', stumble over lawn, big folder suddenly bursts open like Father vomiting that time I bore him to the toilet, told him they were all show those artificial leather ones, paper, paper everywhere, all soggy with dew, taste salt on my lip suddenly and oh Violet you're not snivelling again are you oh yes

oh yes

On my knees, probably catch my death & then the moon comes out, like snow all over the lawn that paper. Had to pick it up. Owl. Definitely screech. That's something. Matron McOgre. Well, I'd started hadn't I & all starts have to finish as Father wd say. Go back, take out next folder. Take out all the folders. Six years & a folder for each. Reach right up to my chin hold yr head high Violet. Walk back slowly over lawn. Here we are. Well done Violet. Well, she's got Grandad's bones, Kenneth. Oh Mother. Two old cases from wardrobe. Three folders in each. Spread them out. Have to go back to shut it. Pause a bit by big dark steel shape. Didn't I? Owl. That's something. Lots of wild bits at the back. Take out 'Collected Works'. That's a big artist's file type of thing and it's all in there. Bournville. Paxo Stuffing series. Hitler. Cheek by jowl with the others. All those spirals and flames I never took to much. My inner workings Violet. I don't know if I have any of those, Mr B. Moon comes out like a searchlight. You cd see them probing. Those times. Nice. All neatly packed. Television looking up like a little pond with the moon in it. Bisto with the Oxo. Lucozade with the Victory V lozenges. Hoover a bit of a squeeze. That Soundmirror. Not going round & round now, is it? Gilbey's gin half empty, I noticed. Big film canisters. Shd keep them busy hence. Savages, probably. Or big round heads like in that film. Lid back on. Dark. You don't need the light, Violet. Canvas wrap. 'Collected Works' in Father's big old suitcase. Never went anywhere with it, in the end. Go upstairs to check he wasn't awake. Snoring like thunder. In bed. Cocoa.

They think they've reached the top, on the wireless. That'd be fitting.

oh Violet what is it now

Tues. June 2nd 1953

BURIAL DAY (I stick with tradition)

Watched Coronation with him in living room. He was holding forth unfortunately so missed the Queen Is Crowned shout. Wiped away a tear during National Anthem. All those crowds in the pouring rain. Wd have liked to have hummed along but he was at his peak. Suddenly stopped & said I looked bleached with a piercing stare. Bleached, Mr B.? Tea in village hall after. Miss W. doing her bit. Parish pageant. Sweets tossed. Buckets of rain, freezing wind for June. Didn't have umbrella, understandably. Axe from Charles I's Execution float fell off & nearly took little Peter Jefferies' head with it. Tug-of-war between Bursop men & Ulv. men won by Bursop, like most yrs. Came out of river sopping, poor things, though land workers are used to it I spose. 7.30 p.m.: Home Service, 'The Kingdom Dances'. The Jolly Waggoners wired up off wireless. Loudspeakers howling in the square & everyone tripping up & giggling. Whirling about. Squealing, giggling. Beacons to be lit foll. Queen's Broadcast, Ulv. will await signal from Bursop. Jeers. We won't wait for them sloppies etc. Then whirling about again. Squealing & giggling. Avoided the drink then. I know what I have to do. Someone sick outside 'The New Inn'. Little boys up in oak tree whistling & throwing streamers. Howling stops in middle: groans. Crackle crackle. Big voice, ever so familiar. Historic day. Seed for the future. A record of our times. Planting to be at 10.30 p.m. following Lighting of Beacon. Grounds of Orchard Hse. Champagne served. I wanted to weep, but didn't. Contrition, Violet. Contrition's a car part. Minx. Cheers & claps. Miss W.'s face suddenly: aren't you thrilled, Violet? I didn't say anything. Howling again. Rose from my canvas stool & retired swiftly to the garden. Peace. Fetch wheelbarrow out of shed. Howling in distance, like wolves. Almost dark. Rain stopped, at least. Rooks. Bump (that's the word with its wobbly wheel) barrow over grass to my entrance. Place the suitcases in. Put door to. Bump off suitcases to bonfire. Bleached, feeling very bleached. Wait. Bandage slipped a bit. Tuck it up. Moon pops out, makes it gleam all white like ribbon round present. Shirley Leatherbarrow's cake. Those times. That's pretty, Miss Nightingale! Snorts, titters. People looming up from bridge. Wait. More people looming up, torches, lights, a lantern. Everyone present & correct for Sovereign's Broadcast. All over Empire they wait, I think. In the hot places, the cold. Everyone in big circle round big dark lump like dormant volcano I spose. Splendidly combustible. All of a sudden Queen's nice tone. Hush. Heart thumping. Queasy. Shd have placed cases on before but wanted to be sure. No one's asked me yet. Can't see him or Miss W. Broadcast gives pop & dies in middle. Groan, like wounded animal. Father groaned in his last hours like that, like he was only being jocular. Starts up again. God bless you all. Cheers. Wipe away little tear. Well, it can't be helped. Big man empties can of paraffin onto pile & whips away his foot from last few drops. Bit of ballet, really. Laughs. Speech. New Eliz. era etc. On & on. Donald Jefferies on stool. Tipsy. Loses paper. Biggest beacon of them all etc. Light new from old (like Father's chain-smoking) then suddenly feel urge & push barrow forward like in a dream, Rev. Appleton starting long thing on world hunger & world hope, defender of our faith etc. & reach pile with barrow & look up. Feel giddy. Light way to better world etc. Big wheel just in front of me. Shouts from behind of course. What's in those then Miss Nightingale? Eh Violet? Got yr knickers in those eh—sssshh Norman really! Clapping. Wait. I'm not going to rush things. Bleached. Moon pops out again & makes me giddy watching it rush past thru clouds. Mr Barr as Parish C. Chairman picks mediaeval-looking torch up. Come on, Burslops! Flare goes up, cheers. Big torch ignited, Mr Barr holds it out in front of him, whiffs of paraffin, Mr Jefferies recites little poem but Mr Barr already there prodding flaming torch in & looking serious. Nothing. Whiffs of smoke. Mr Barr laughs & says something then flames. Big flames. Mr Barr steps back & everyone's face looks like Hallowe'en. Waggon name starts to bubble. Watch out there! Turn around & like oven on my ear. Miss W.'s face leaping up & down, with him, next to him, his face leaping up & down, whole crowd's face moving up & down as one, mouths open, big dark mouths going up & down just like those foundry men at Hulme Steel Works where I did that dull book-keeping for a month, turn back to it, ERNEST M. BARR (grandfather?) settling with a whoosh & sparks bit of hair-singe, watch out Miss! Retreat, pick up first suitcase hear him behind with a what's in there Violet but I don't answer just throw it on.

oh Violet. oh

just throw it on then the other two
you need a rap over the knuckles my girl
oh Mother she's only little

have another glass Violet smuggled down a bottle go on you've a right

then the other two Violet what's in those look at his face spasms all over his face or is it the firelight big wheel rolls down on fire screams settles in the grass burning like that Catherine wheel that time Father took us to the Municipal do look Gordon & violet look whizz whizz & Guy Fawkes with those bangers in his mouth exploding into flaming straw his face was all spasms I'll say that oh Violet

white bits falling down into our hair I cd see the firelight in his eyes when I looked & that terrible face that man who burned over Germany & limped back Gordon knew him vaguely knew Kenneth he did oh they do remarkable things now what if he'd lived our Kenneth they've put the wheel out a bit of a danger always goes down well what's in those then my dear tugging & tugging at my sleeve he must have guessed but he wdn't have believed preferred not to know I spose just bury it what's in those then my dear old letters dead past yes I know the feeling! guffaws & turns to the fire oh his big nose sweaty & gleaming & the cases they've gone now no there's the last one buckling & burning oh I hope it doesn't open

oh it does the heat or something.

It did.

bang & the lid's up & look a bit of paper curling up shoots out & up & up

tiny little white thing above the flames.

he hasn't seen, arm round Miss Walwyn mouth open like little boy

up it goes tiny little white thing drawing maybe up & up into the night & over those lovely poplars gusting away because there's quite a gust tonight Violet away from all the fire & tiny white thing like that seagull at Cleethorpes

that last time with Kenneth

I cd have stayed
little white thing over the sea
sitting on the cliff
over all that sea
too much champagne
putting it in at last & stamping down earth I thought the crane wd topple over

oh it's so demeaning being sick
Philis P-W swore she heard a long-eared didn't tell her of the stone curlew why shd I don't have the stomach it's the bubbles
clapping wolf-whistling from Manor School dormitories that's what I mean about sitting on the lavatory the type little Ivor Gilchrist used to do better than any wolf-whistles I mean & little speech from him clapping in it goes stone pulled over by big burly men stamping down earth stamping
I'm off tomorrow Mr B. Here's yr cocoa. You are a funny old stick, Violet my dear
oh fuck off
Violet my dear?
Miss W. pulling him away
oh fuck off as Father wd not ever say no
oh fuck off

oh Violet

1988

H E R E

VIPER'S BUGLOSS
PRODUCTIONS

A YEAR IN THE LIFE:
'Clive's Seasons'

POST-PRODUCTION SCRIPT

Generic title sequence
Title on screen: 'A Year in the Life'

Ext. day:
Wide-shot tumulus with sun rising behind it
Long-shot rooks circling trees

Dawn chorus

Wipe
Long-s road thru downs:
Distant car approaching

Mid-s thru side window:
Tracking on passing countryside

Pop music—car radio

Close-up Clive Walters driving, nodding head to music

Wide-s thru windscreen on Ulverton village approach: church tower above roofs

Long-s panorama of village from church tower

Cut music:
Dawn sounds

Pan & pick up on Clive's car entering village, pan following car through Main Street, zoom in on car moving between roofs & trees etc.

Fade in Vivaldi 'Spring' (Allegro—Spring's Awakening)

Programme title supered: 'Clive's Seasons'

Tilt slow up to downland horizon & sunrise

Mid-s car approaching down farm track

Close-up Clive in car pulling on hand-brake

Music faint

Mid-s Clive getting out of car

Pull back to long-s as Clive walks to field site: farm, hills etc. in background

Mid close-up from below of Clive surveying field around him

CLIVE VOICE-OVER:
My family came from round here.

Pan field: Clive's point of view

I've come back. At least er, that's how I—I like to think of it.

Wide-s hedge, woods etc.

When I look at a site, I don't think, you know, there's a load of money. Hey, there's so many grand.

Long-s Five Elms Farm

What I—I er, first think of is, that's beautiful and there's a history. That's what I—it's what I always think.

Close-up Clive gazing

That's who I am. Sentimental I suppose! *(Laughs)* Yep.

Crawler caption: *'Year/life 5—Clive Walters, property developer'*		*Build up Vivaldi*
Close-up blossom on bough, sunlight behind *Pull back to long-s tractor spraying* *Mid-s cows with misty breath*		
Int. day: *Mid-s Clive shutting door of his office in barn*		*Cut Vivaldi on door*
Mid-s Clive with fag at his desk *Interview sync.*	CLIVE: Well er, when I saw the site, when it came up, that was it. I wanted it. Bad.	
Close-up site map, Clive's finger taps it	That's the baby. *(Coughs)* That's the beaut.	
Mid-s Clive	I like to think of myself as the er, the enabler. The developer em, how shall I put it . . . enables. Yup. *(Coughs)* Yup. Put it like so. From the second my shoes touch that bloody field, I enable er, er, *it* to happen. Come hell or high water. As the case may be. *(Laughs)*	
Still: Snapshot of Clive as boy	I wanted to be a, a helicopter pilot. Er, that didn't work. Scared of bloody heights. I followed my father into the em, the—into building, the trade.	

Still: Clive's father	He was a, oh he was, he was a great bloke. Same big er, jaw—as you might say. The Walters er, jaw-line.
Mid-s Clive	We're stubborn buggers y'know. Have to be. In this trade. Yep.
Ext. day: *Pan Clive walking up street to estate agents, tilt up to name: 'Jeffreys & Jeffreys'*	
Int. day: *Clive entering estate agents*	
Mid-s Clive & Padmore in office shaking hands	PADMORE: Hallo, er, Clive . . .
	CLIVE: All right . . . ?
Mid-s Padmore seated behind desk, nodding	CLIVE V/O: I think we'd er, when all's said and done er, Brian, when you think of the potential it's—we're not—I'm not happy, Brian, with this at all—
Mid-s Clive seated	—for a starters it's bloody ridiculous. No, it is. I'm sat here with the necessaries Brian and he's—if he's—if he is serious he's got to get his arse of his right into gear, Brian.
Mid-s Padmore	PADMORE: Clive I think, to me the main
Crawler caption: 'Brian Padmore, estate agent'	problem, as we see it, er, here em, is that—look at it this way then. It's

Grade 2 and 3 agricultural, roughly 50 percent er, sub-grade 3a, and certainly in our view, as there's going to be no leaning whatsoever from the Council on er, on this one, the owner does feel he can go for the absolute top drawer. He—

Mid-s Clive

CLIVE:
Okay. If I—listen Brian. 280K. And that is stretched, as it were.

PADMORE:
I'll put that one er, to him.

CLIVE:
Let's hope he don't er fart about—

Mid-s Padmore

PADMORE:
I can only er, put it to him Clive.

Mid-s Clive

CLIVE:
And what's more, Brian, I am—I do feel in my bones, that this is a damn good site. However, Brian, I'm a little bit cautious, I'll be frank—a little bit er, concerned, as you well know—

PADMORE:
Drainage?—

CLIVE:
Well it could be a problem Brian. And if we have to go to, to er, resort to pumping and piling—because I don't really know what's down there, do we?

Wide-s Clive & Padmore

PADMORE:
That limits your margins.

CLIVE:
Either that, or I go for the extended er, site option and run into er, get strung up by God knows what on permissions. Because I'm right in thinking that Site B has not got outline but is an infill potential er, in the Local Structure Plan, is that correct?

PADMORE:
As far as these things go Clive, yes.

Mid-s Clive

CLIVE:
Thank you Brian.

Mid-s Padmore nodding

Ext. day:
Tracking shot across downland
Tracking shot of feet jogging along lane
Pull back to Clive jogging
Mid-s staying with him

CLIVE:
Haa . . . it's . . . phoo . . . you've got to . . . trim, keep on the ball, and phoo . . . all that, this . . . ha . . . good country air . . . hahh . . . in the old bellows . . . keeps it . . . keeps up the . . . concentration . . . phoo . . . blimey . . . ha! for the job . . . attack . . . haa . . . see you later . . . as it were . . .

Long-s Clive jogging off up lane
Tilt up to overhead trees flashing sunlight

Mid-close-up road sign: 'Ulverton 2 miles'
Pull back to pan Clive jogging past, turning to give thumbs-up

Freeze (sign/Clive)
Fade out colour to sepia

Shepherd's pipe music

Sequence of old sepia photos of Ulverton tossed onto freeze-still

Int. day:
Mid-s Duckett looking at photos, then tossing each onto dining-table

Fade music

Close-up Duckett looking at photos, smiling

DUCKETT V/O:
I suppose, what one of the—one of the real beauties *is* its quietness. Of the village. Its tranquillity.

Mid-s Duckett at window, looking out

Crawler caption: 'Raymond Duckett, local historian'

DUCKETT V/O:
And if anyone was to—to have told me that, well, quite frankly that the quiet of village life—as we know it, you see, was to—is to be threatened, then there's no benefit to anyone is there? And the history too. That's all going.

Ext. day:
Mid-s Duckett looking up at thatched cottage

DUCKETT:
This is one of the oldest you see. In Ulverton village itself. Er, this is—this street or lane rather, this is Surley Row, where I'm standing at the end of the lane now—and it was as a matter of fact, the poorest, would you believe, part of the village!

Pan to cottage porch & house name: 'Serenity'

Wide-s Volvo car parked in front of cottage
Close-up bird on cottage lawn pulling worm

DUCKETT V/O:
Conditions were, one has to say er, they were truly shocking. When one considers—when one takes it all into account, the damp and filth and of course er, certainly the er, hunger. That is history, to my mind. Of the village itself.

Long-s Duckett standing at end of lane & cottages etc.

Ext. day:
Mid-s village hall off square
Zoom in on sign: 'Ulverton Village Hall'

Int. day:
Parish Council meeting
Tracking-shot councillors including Duckett to close-up Barker at head of table

BARKER:
. . . access would be from Deedy

Lane. Now what he's saying, the developer Mr er, Walters, is that unless we go—go ahead and approve this, this extra ah, development, then quids on there'll be no—nothing at all of low-cost housing, these er, starter homes I think they call 'em—

Crawler caption: 'Wing-Commander Barker, Parish Council Chairman'

Close-up Rose

ROSE:
I think, Chairman, surely we—the village has very—has sufficient shops to support this—we want more houses surely and I for one, while I know it's—it's—it looks like the whole thing's getting out of hand, we'll lose those small em, houses outright—

Crawler caption: 'Marjorie Rose, owner of Ulverton village stores'

Track across members

BARKER:
Taken. Any further comments?

Close-up Duckett

DUCKETT:
I—it is fifteen houses in the open countryside Mr Chairman, when all's said and done, and there we are. When's it—where's it all going to end? Do we er, really want all—every field to be put under tarmac, surely not—

Wide-s members

BARKER:
Taken. Any—

Close-up Rose

ROSE:
Have the NT—have the National Trust said anything at all because I

mean Deedy Lane is the main way into er, into the—the House and Park—

Ext. day:
Long-s Ulverton House from lawn thru trees

Music: Vivaldi 'Spring' (Largo—The Sleeping Goatherd)

Wide-s Clive walking around lake

Close-up swan on lake
Pull back to wide-s Clive gazing at swan

Mid-close-up Clive seated on rustic bench by lake & turning to camera

Fade music

CLIVE:

Well, it's through. With the er, Parish bods. Bloody marvellous. I'm feeling great. I got the extended er, the extra field at er, discount, accessway via Deedy Lane and another er, fifteen units. So that er, I gets to build some low-cost er, homes and we're just up the—we're actually in sight, up the bloody road, of this, as it were. That is prestige. Natural—National Trust property. Now that's beautiful really, isn't it? I'm feeling . . . yep. Great. First stage over. Spring is er, well and truly in. *(Laughs)*

Vivaldi up

Long-s Clive on bench;
mansion etc. in background

Fade out
Vivaldi

Close-up cottage sign: 'The Old Smithy'
Pull back to wide-s cottage & budding chestnut tree

Int. day:
Mid-s Barker in study
Interview sync.

BARKER:

Goodness me, it's tough. Now on the one hand—desire to er, preserve. Keep distinct. Er, distinctive and traditional and er, and so on. On the other side—

Pan across room: silver, paintings etc.

need to, how shall one put it erm . . . hmmm . . . develop. New blood. This—this village is awfully steep, for your ordinary chap. Too many weekenders, you see. So, yes. I'm certainly for er, for sensitive

Mid-s Barker

development within er, within of course, the overall plan of the—of the District Council fellers. Oh yes. Oh yes.

Definitely.

Ext. day:
Close-up Clive's Wellies stepping into shot on muddy field site
Tilt up to show Clive making notes on pad

BARKER V/O:

It's all a question, when it comes

Long-s Clive tiny in huge field

er, down to the nitty-gritty, of never letting the chap, be he er, developer, or whatever, er, out of your sights. Not for a second. And we are on AONB, of course. Oh yes.

Int. day:
Mid-s Barker
interview sync.

BARKER:

Oh yes. And being AONB puts the old brakes on a little. Cramps er, their style a trifle! Ho yes.

Ext. day:
Panorama of Ulverton nestling in downs with view of White Horse
Crawler caption: 'Designated as an area of outstanding natural beauty, or AONB.
Pinpointed in local report as having tourist & recreation potential'

Shepherd's pipe music

Mid-s lorries, cars etc. thundering past on motorway

Zoom-shot sun-dial in Vicar's garden, leaves etc.
Glimpse of motorway in far distance

Long-s from bridge of busy motorway, tilt to follow Clive's car

Cut music

Close-up Clive in car driving along motorway
Interview sync.

CLIVE:

Now it's the District Council. I'm er, *reasonably* confident. That . . . they'll er, they will . . . pass it. The Parish bods loved it. Absolutely loved it. You could have knocked me over with a feather. Lovely. Yep. Very supportive. Yep. Bloody hell I thought er, what's he gonna say, the er, Chairman of the Parish Council. You could have knocked me over with a feather. Yep.

Mid-s thru car window of motorway traffic etc.

Close-up Clive driving Interview sync.

CLIVE:

My application for Site A was er, passed by the District Council in er, December of last year. The Parish bods have accepted my er, my detailed proposals for both sites in fact. So I'm reasonably confident, on this one. Look. This . . . let's be straight about this. This motorway is a godsend to the local community. The potential's bloody magnificent. Two thousand er, years ago it was the whatsit—the Ridgeway. Now it's this. Heart of the countryside with all modern er, convenience. All business and leisure and you name it er, facilities locally. And er, London, Bristol, Oxford and of course Southampton even—one hour. Journey time. On a good day. Godsend. Isn't it? Not too many cones today. Eh?

Mid-s of landscape zipping past thru side window

All my ancestors were . . . er, what you might call shepherds. The Walters clan. From round er, round here. Yep. I've er, myself have got a small flock, little do, side-line hobby sort of thing. Ten Hampshire Down ewes. Local breed. Superb. Nice tight fleece, Hampshires. Good and *(Coughs)* nice and heavy in the, you know, shoulder and so on. Good strong necks. What, how they like it, you see. How they like it. Meaty. Quickest-growing lambs, in fact, in the er, business. Carcass weight out of it, out of a lamb in er, three months of er, 18 kilos. Average. Yep. And small farmers. You know. A hedger and thatcher. Sawyer. Er, bookhawker, one of 'em. Turned their hand to anything in those days. Eh? Look at that idiot. Mainly farming folk, though. All round here. My ancestors. Bloody awful life. Bloody awful. Can't er, can't go back to all that now can we? *(Laughs)*

Close-up Clive driving

Mid-s from bridge of Clive's car passing below, tilt up to long & follow it

Pop music—car radio

Cut music

Wide-s council chamber
Crawler caption: 'April 23rd: Meeting of Fogbourne District Council Planning B Sub-committee'

Pan on audience to close-up

Clive writing notes

Wide-s councillors

Close-up Dixon

DIXON:

—And according to the local Plan Consultative Draft this site is firmly outside the physical limits of the village as delineated in the plan and er, as the previous site A was not, er—being seen to be visually, as

Crawler caption: 'Graham Dixon, chief planning officer'

you can see from the screen, part of the linear development north of the village whereas we are basically in a situation here we have er, come over—come across before, which is one in which an extension into high-quality open countryside is justified by the applicant saying he would—it would be then be economic, economical for me to go ahead with some low-cost housing in the original scheme whereas in fact he has met the er, residential value within—of that land, within the overall cost of that land and by and for his first scheme, as far as we understand it, in the surveys and options report, which to put it bluntly—to grant this a permission would be a clear case of er, urban encroachment into an area designated AONB and clearly er, contrary to the Structure Plan.

Close-up Chairman

Comments from the local member?

Close-up Rose	Well I must say it's er, it's quite a tough one to chew but yes, I can see the reasons underlined Mr. Chairman . . .
Close-up Clive in audience, hand over face	
Mid-s thru car window of landscape zipping past	
Close-up Clive driving	CLIVE: A downer. Make no bones about it. I er, I'll reserve my comments. It's bloody ridiculous. Know why the er, the locals are for it? Slurry. Stink. Stank the bloody place out. Bad neighbour use. So they were all screaming. That's er, that's Site B that the . . . they've just refused. Bloody ridiculous. You can't move . . . But er, try and try again. Yep. Pressure on. Blood from a stone. Comes eventually. Bloody ridiculous.
Wide-s motorway & Clive's car passing, pull back & pan L over grass to stone cross on hummock Zoom in on faded inscription: 'God hath answered the cry of my soul'	
Long-s Bradman striding on far crest of hill *Mid-s Bradman wiping her feet at door of old chapel & entering*	

Mid-s Bradman in easy chair with cat *Interview sync.* *Crawler caption: 'Enid Bradman, Secretary, Ulverton Preservation Society'*	BRADMAN: We succeeded last time. That was the er, the er, er . . . when we managed to have the motorway diverted would you believe. Yes, that was a damn fine moment! *(Leans forward & laughs)* Wasn't it Milton? Animals understand—you do don't you? Oh, that was our . . . most er, triumphant day in the village. When they er, diverted that er, horrible motorway! Just enough. The er, a rather special monument. The Kisser Cross, as we call it. Quaker you see. Yes indeed. We never wanted it you see. I've lived here er, nearly forty years! In the village, in various er, in three different houses now. My bit of England forever part of me. D'you see? It's . . . oh it's real love.
Pan across Bradman's paintings on wall of local scenes *Mid-s Bradman*	BRADMAN: And I show that er, that love as best I can, in my art. D'you see? I used to be a teacher, yes, before my late er, husband grew poorly. Oh the rolling hills and trees and the light here you know, it's very special. I try to . . . capture its very special er, tea-brown quality. Bracken-brown would perhaps be better, yes. A very clear, d'you see, brackeny quality to the light. There's . . . you see, there's nothing

really but rolling downs from here, between here and the sea. Is there

Close-up photo of Bradman with husband in wheelchair

Milton? I—I would take my late husband right up to the top of the hill er, oh yes. Every afternoon, you see. He had such love for the place.

Close-up cartoon of farmyard by husband

Herbert Bradman the er, artist and er, thinker. Oh yes. Push him right up. My eternal hills, he would say. Wouldn't he Milton? I—it's a very

Mid-s Bradman

real, a very deep love d'you see? Oh dear yes. *(Leans forward & laughs)*

Fade in Vivaldi 'Spring' (Allegro—Country Dance)

Aerial panorama sequence: Over rolling downs, then over Ulverton village, over rolling downs north up to kink in motorway

Crawler caption: '1972: Route three miles north of Ulverton altered by village protest . . .'

Circle round stone monument in kink of motorway & zoom in on it

Crawler caption: '. . . to save the so-called Kisser Cross, now designated site of special historical significance'

Music up

<table>
<tr><td>1972 library footage:
Protesters rally, crowd around stone, placards etc., tussles with police etc.</td><td>Fade music</td></tr>
<tr><td>Int. evening:
Close-up ticking grandfather clock</td><td></td></tr>
<tr><td>Mid-s group of five around table in Bradman's converted chapel</td><td></td></tr>
<tr><td>Zoom in on tablet above door: 'Erected in Brick 1712 Ye Shall Receive'</td><td></td></tr>
<tr><td>Close-up Bradman nodding</td><td>DUCKETT V/O:
I do think, personally, we really must avoid the—the same mistake again—</td></tr>
<tr><td></td><td>BRADMAN:
—oh yes—</td></tr>
<tr><td>Close-up Duckett</td><td>DUCKETT:
—and if I may say so, em, I think this development is the em, thin end of the edge, erm—if only because these plans keep being changed and—</td></tr>
<tr><td>Wide-s group members listening</td><td>DUCKETT:
—quite honestly, I came here for peace and yes, and tranquillity, and it's all been rather out of the frying pan into the er, fire—</td></tr>
<tr><td>Close-up Bradman</td><td>BRADMAN:
He—this Walters man has been</td></tr>
</table>

refused, of course, to go any er, further aren't I right in saying but er, but I presume the appeal and whatnot once the—the man's got the bit between his teeth d'you see. And we'll be like—we'll have to be like hawks over the streetlamps, surely. Adam dear?

Crawler caption: 'May 2nd: Meeting of Ulverton Preservation Society'

Pan across to close-up Thorpe

THORPE:

Well what I wanted to say is—is that er, he's a difficult character, he's—he's a toughie, basically, and em, I think it's . . . (*Sighs*) I mean look at that, er, estate up at er—in Bursop. Saddle Stone Yard. Now he won er, on that one. Got away with absolute murder. All er, big er, executive stuff. We're just going to have to be very tough. And we're going to have to be absolutely sure that that second, er, field isn't er—isn't developed. Otherwise it's just going to be open door to—to everyone. He just mustn't develop that open er—that other field. And apparently Martin . . . Oadam wants—wants to get right out of Five Elms Farm, so that'll be the next one to—to go.

Crawler caption: 'Adam Thorpe, local author & performer'

Close-up cat on settee

BRADMAN V/O:

Yes, goodness gracious no, another one. Oh that'll be light-industrial thingummies again er, units. Hm?

So if the appeal, d'you see, goes through, my worry is . . .

Close-up clock ticking over murmur of voices
Fade image/sound

Ext. day:
Mid-close-up excavator teeth slamming into earth & rising up with load

Mid-s man in helmet watching

Close-up excavator driver

Wide-s rooks rising from trees

Mid-s smoke in sky, tilt down to site bonfire & man tossing branches on

Mid-s Clive in helmet discussing with man in helmet over sheets of plans

Long-s site from farm thru dead elm

Mid-s Clive sitting on sewage pipe
Interview sync. above excavator noise

CLIVE:
This is it, as you might say. D Day. So far, no problems! *(Laughs)* My architect's happy, er, I'm happy, and my crew are taking out the er, stripping the top soil now, and er, grading it out to the correct er, levels. Problem is, this field has got a helluva ripple in it and a er, a bit

of a funny dip as well as a—as you can see, quite a little hang to it so er, we are, in fact, doing a—doing a quite a bit of er, filling as well here, yes. But basically, er—yep. We've got started today, on the first site. Come hell or high water, as it were! And if we get the other site, over there, on er, when we er—having appealed, that shall be great. We'll have to wait and see, as you might say! *(Laughs)*

Long-s of site from hillcrest other side of road

Int. day:
Wide-s Dixon walking down corridor, pan L as he enters office & door swings shut

DIXON V/O:
As the Chief Planning Officer, my concern is for the scenic quality of the county to be er, conserved. But of course—and this is a very

Close-up plan of country placed on table
Wide-s Dixon & colleagues looking at plan
Close-up Dixon

attractive district—there's also the competing pressures of er, employment, and er, promotional activities providing—to provide that employment, and er, the need, quite simply, to er, to—for our housing needs. Our policy in this district is to try to maximise

Close-up plan, zoom in to show 'Ulverton' & red boundary, tapped by finger

potential land use er, while retaining the essential er, fabric of the villages and the surrounding landscape.

Mid-s Dixon seated in office
Interview sync.

DIXON:
Because this er, landscape is of a

somewhat undulating topography, as is very easily seen, er—realised when you drive through, indeed, it is somewhat vulnerable, especially when and where there's a er, lack of broad-leaved or otherwise er, woodland. So my job, as I see it, is to weigh—to weigh up, indeed, the . . . frequently conflicting pressures between needs within, er the overall countryside envelope. And let me tell you er—you can't, as they say, please all of them all of the time. No way. So I do get a bit of a stick from all sides!

Close-up Dixon on phone	DIXON: —I see, he is appealing—has appealed—right Mrs Bradman . . . yes . . . yes . . . Well I mean I'm, I am well aware of the situation and will be monitoring it closely Mrs Bradman . . . yes . . . Okay . . . thank you very—yes—goodbye.
Mid-s Dixon putting phone down & addressing camera	DIXON: Well there you are he's appealed. Against our decision. That of course is his right and it may er, well be that good—the good offices of the Secretary of State decide we were er, wrong. Which will be a bit of a blow er, but it won't be the first time! No. There is er, a certain design criticism to be actioned on in that eventuality but er, but I'm

sure that will be forthcoming from Mr Walters. And we will of course press for low-cost units to be incorporated should it be that er, that the permission is granted in the final er . . . given that situation. We do want a relatively static population in these villages er—of mothers with young children and so on, for the diminishing er, in order to retain a particular level of er, facilities. Primary school, food shop, post office and so on. Otherwise we are going to have on our hands a lot of dying villages. If we don't er, press for low-cost units.

So. We wait and see on this one.

Music: Vivaldi 'Summer' (Allegro—Languor)

Mid-s corn field & poppies

Close-up bumblebee

Mid-s leafy oak-tree

Slow-motion wide-s kids pouring out of Ulverton primary school

Cut music

Mid-s Clive to camera on site

CLIVE:

Here goes!

Construction sequence
Computer animation:
Mid-s excavator
Mid-s sewage pipe lowered & tilt to trench
Close-up man in helmet waving arms
Close-up cement mixer
Close-up concrete pouring into trench
Mid-s Clive nodding
Close-up building regs officer frowning
Wide-s site & farm beyond site plan supered

Music: Vivaldi 'Summer' (Allegro—various winds)

Cut music

Ext. day:
Close-up pub sign 'The New Inn'

Int. day:
Mid-s Clive & crew in corner of pub

CLIVE:
—no, no, that slab on unit 5 Mike, it's got a er, a decent pitch but he was thinking the finish weren't wood float for the stoop but I er, I got that sorted out and then it was, then he was on at me er, what he was really hassling me on like ninepins was on the, the fact that he—he er didn't reckon we'd filled tight enough under the sills on er, on unit 6—

BUILDER:
—come on!—

CLIVE:
—any road, I got that one sorted

Close-up builder drinking	out but you know if we—it's gonna be a bugger with the Westminsters at the back if we have to pile er, I mean that stepping came out a bit bloody long, didn't it Ted?
Mid-s group	TED: Well you know what I think I think we didn't have to step.
	CLIVE: What you think mate don't matter, it's the regs officer mate. Now we'll have a go at stripping for the—at the back for the Westies but er, but that's next week and now I er, I've got to have that bloody lot down now parged and mopped by Saturday or we'll be arse out of gear okay? Same again Mike.
Wide-s pub	
Ext. evening: *Long-s pub, pan round square onto flowers around old pump in middle*	
Ext. day: *Wide-s Clive walking into Plum Farm Business Park across gravel drive*	
Mid-s Clive greeting Curtis in shirtsleeves by the 'Barn'	
Close-up Curtis	CURTIS: Yes I will be honest with you Clive

we're very very happy with the whole set-up.

CLIVE:
That's fine.

CURTIS:
Yes. This environment is er, I can only say wonderful, being the kind of enterprise we are, Clive, is ideally suited to—to this kind of environment—and the girls for one are happy with the view! *(Laughs)* No, I feel definitely happier with my work situation and let's be absolutely honest about this—who would honestly want to swap er, this work environment for the previous? No—no I am really and truly er—I am convinced, Clive, like your good self, that this is the—the future as far as we know it for em, for the kind of businesses that now are in the main, Clive, free to go where the hell they want. And only, to be honest, a wally would er, wouldn't want to take the—the pleasant-environment option. The countryside is very very good for the business I'll be honest, absolutely honest with you Clive and I don't mind er, being absolutely up-front about it. We are happy yes.

Crawler caption: 'Graham Curtis, Plum Communications'

Close-up Clive nodding

Close-up Curtis

Mid-s Clive & Curtis

CLIVE:
I'm very pleased to hear that,

Graham. Now you've heard about my little option on the field site down there, now er, I'm asking you in your opinion do you feel this village will benefit from the kind of development on that extended er, site that I—I am having in mind. Namely, traditional cottage-style as ever, of course, but I am considering now a barn-style unit with studio flats that I would have thought might well er, suit the kind of employees Plum Communications, for a start-off, not to mention the er, the other firms currently here er, er, located. Might well suit your type of trainees. Being young trainees.

Close-up Curtis

CURTIS:
Absolutely. Plus being the type of building that pleases the eye, Clive. I think, to be absolutely frank er, Clive, is that the fact you didn't really alter or play around very much with the exteriors of, say, our unit here, behind me, being as you

Mid-s barn
Zoom in to 1713 above door

can see the previous barn of the er, of the old farm in what really is a most attractive albeit wholesome I would say, er, brick, that is a very large part of the attraction of this

Pan round yard

site. Plus being able to drive up in about two minutes ten seconds at a rough estimate! *(Laughs)*

Close-up Curtis	CLIVE: A satisfied customer I er, I do believe! And you find the—the barn conversion suitable for housing your er—
Close-up Curtis holding up floppy disc	CURTIS: —our type of components being mainly, er in the main computer hardware for training purposes and in many instances producing er, commercial software packages, yes. No, I would say quite definitely Clive that this environment in general, that is about us now, including the village itself of Ulverton, is the best marketing tool we could possibly have. It says, quite honestly er, that you are quality, a quality firm producing a quality product.
Mid-s Clive & Curtis	CLIVE: The green surrounds and the fresh air.
	CURTIS: Yes. But they might do—they might improve the pubs Clive! If that's not speaking out of turn.
	CLIVE: Well, Graham, the New Inn is out on tender, as it were. And it's er, it's just about due for a revamp in my opinion too, yes.

CURTIS:

After a couple of hundred years I should think yes! Judging from the floor-mats! *(Laughs)*

CLIVE:

Yes. Do they still make Capstan cigarettes? *(Laughs to camera)*

Int. day:
Close-up hand on beer pump
Close-up beer being jetted out of pump into glass
Tilt to follow pint being handed over bar & man drinking
Pull back to show public bar (beams, benches etc.) of The New Inn

Close-up men talking
Close-up dart thudding into dartboard

Mid-s group of old men at table
Interviews sync.

CULLURNE:

Well that's it, innit? If you let—if you have too many houses, see, then what's going to—what's going to happen see—

ROSE:

Village life is disappearing in my view.

KETCHASIDE (middle-aged man):

You've gotta have houses.

ROSE:

Ye-es, but not—not what he

wants—what they want. It's all money money innit? These days. True. It's—

Crawler caption: 'Reg Cullurne, resident'

CULLURNE:
You've gotta have money mate. Them old boys doing up them houses they've got more money than I ever had. We was eleven. In one—eleven in one cottage. In the twenties. Forever coming and going. Get your feet under someone else's table, that's what she'd say, my old mother—

BUNCE:
£3 a week. In the thirties. Building. 18-shilling cycling allowance, if, let me make it clear, you went to Head Office first—

ROSE:
And the old tortoise stoves—remember them?

CULLURNE:
Paraffin lamps. The old Aladdins. With a little mantle.

KETCHASIDE:
Here they go.

ROSE:
They knew how to make things in those days. Look at that table there. That's more than two hundred years old I'll bet. Oak.

Crawler caption: 'Steve Bunce, resident'

BUNCE:
Oh yes we'd all—all have a table. Peg-rugs on the floor weren't it? And this was after the first caper in France—I'm not that bloody old! *(Laughs)*

KETCHASIDE:
Don't believe a word—

CULLURNE:
Rubbish them houses in't they? Bloody rubbish *(coughs)* them new houses. Putting up on Little Hangy. Bloody rubbish. Bloody sardines.

KETCHASIDE:
200 thou apiece.

CULLURNE:
Rubbish. That's what I think.

KETCHASIDE:
We've gotta have bloody houses. Haven't we?

BUNCE:
But what—

Crawler caption: 'Clark Ketchaside, resident'

KETCHASIDE:
No, we have. I mean live in, for living in. Not—no weekenders, types. You know. Here today gone tomorrow. Eh? Don't go li-listening to this lot! *(Laughs)*

BUNCE:
Well . . . who's talking then eh? Yankee-doodle an whatnot. *(To*

camera) You won't be understanding that! *(Laughs)*

KETCHASIDE:
Let's talk about them deer then shall we? *(General laughter)*

Close-up gnarled hand on table
Close-up mouth grinning & drinking

Mid-s group

Crawler caption: 'Horace Rose, resident'

ROSE:
Well this used to be a real village, wasn't it? You only went where it was very adjacent, when I was a nip. Walked. Walked everywhere.

BUNCE:
I remember—remember ploughing Little Hangy oh yes. Bugger to cut too. With nags. Oh aye—horses. Till just after the war. Got rid of all them—the sheep, didn't they? In the first do. Out of a job. All to cereals.

ROSE:
Yep.

BUNCE:
End up in the brick kiln. Piece work. Oh yes. Lovely red brick. Closed. *(Coughs)*

CULLURNE:
Like everything—

BUNCE:

Horses till just after the er,
the—that second big do. Oh yes.
Eh? Didn't we?

KETCHASIDE:

Here they go.

ROSE:

I used to work up at Plum Farm
y'know. Like me mum. What
they—what they gone and got up
there now then? Bloody
co—computers or whatnot is it?
Some old nonsense.

BUNCE:

Something that earns them a packet
for doing bugger all. In my view.

CULLURNE:

Farming's finished though, innit?
Well that's true innit? Finished—

KETCHASIDE:

Still gotta eat—

ROSE:

French rubbish, New Zealand.
Daughter-in-law's shop. Full of it.

BUNCE:

Bloody Common Mar—

ROSE:

Not what I—we went out for, was
it? Eh? Old Hitler. And that—the
big Hall. That used to be private.

My dad worked up there. Oh yes. Grand. Really grand. Wasn't it? *(Coughs)* Open to any bugger, ennit? Now.

CULLURNE:
My dad did what was right. Stayed at home. The first do. That's what he did.

ROSE:
Don't know about that now—

KETCHASIDE:
Here we go—

CULLURNE:
Listen. He wasn't a white-feather man. He—he didn't think he—it was bloody worth it. And he was bloody right.

ROSE:
Mine went and he was bloody killed—

KETCHASIDE:
We're er, supposed to be talking about Mr Walters's houses I do—

Zoom in on Cullurne

CULLURNE:
Now what? That's village pride. Innit? You ax about my dad. Percy. Mr Cullurne. You won't li—you won't hear a word spoken agin him—

ROSE:
All right, Reg, all right—

CULLURNE:
And that's—that's pride. We belong—this is the real village in this—in here—

KETCHASIDE:
How about another real jar then—

Mid-s group laughing

Ext. day:
Wide-s corn-dolly class in old barn
Mid-s teacher (Caird), helping student
Close-up straw being plaited
Pan close-up corn dollies hung in row
Mid-s cottage garden with flowers etc.

Mid-s Caird & kids on grass
Interview sync.

CAIRD:
We're not against, em, new houses. My kids go to the village school—

CHILD:
Megan's my best friend!

Crawler caption: 'Sally Caird, founder member of the Downland Workshop'

CAIRD:
She's not at the school, is she? *(Pause)* Want to go on the swing? *(Pause)* No, what we're against is the . . . it's more the kind of people. It attracts. Em . . . they don't really join in the community. Go and play with Sam, Bryony.

That's right. I mean, it's so different here. *(Pause)* It's so erm, healthy. You can't bring other . . . what, rhythms in. Other energies. It's a way of life, this way, and you bring in more cars, and more gadgets, and the whole urban thing, you know? It's sad. Feed the rabbits, Sam. *(Pause)* It's a very ancient and old er . . . erm, landscape here. It's a very deep, very deep. Barrows, stone circles and I—I don't know if you know but there are really beautiful strange patterns in the corn, made. And the old people. The old skills. That's what we're trying to keep going. And er . . . *(sighs)* I think you have got to . . . to—to find it. This was an—a revelation to us. After London. Space. *(Pause)* Let's keep it.

Fade

Pan files etc. in Clive's office

Mid-s Clive in office

Interview sync.

CLIVE:

Well I've got the concrete blocks for—up for five of the units, and all parged to a tee, nice bricks coming over next week, and we'll er, we'll be digging at the back for the Westies. That's the er, that's the toffy—the big houses, the Westminsters. Four beds, en suite, detached, Victorian con—

Victorian-style conservatory, all that sort of . . . very nice. No news, as yet, on the er, on the appeal. But I don't see why not, given there is a housing need in this area, and the lower bit of Deedy Lane was er, earmarked for infill on the Local Structure Plan. Density could be er, a problem, but you see the Parish want that low-cost housing and er, my barn-style unit should be a winner. That went into—on my detailed application to the Secretary of er, of State. So I am, yes, reasonably confident, as it were. The thing is as I see things, is that it's all balance. And that's not the way er, all abouts here, certain folk see it. Is it? Certain folk who shall be nameless. *(Laughs)* And the thing is, you won't see a weekender, as they—these same people do go on about all the time—you won't see a single one on this development. Oh no. So I can't see what they want, actually! But I must say so far, cross fingers the er, the weather's on our side. Look at my—Clive's tan! *(Laughs)* And I have got my eye on a certain er, business property in the village so I think I will have—go and partake of a little refreshment down there. Yes.

Ext. day:
Pan Clive entering The New Inn saloon bar

Music: 'John Barleycorn'

Int. day:
Close-up Clive drinking lager at bar
Mid-s landlord nodding & Clive talking

Ext. day:
Pan Clive leaving pub, turning to camera & winking with a thumbs-up

Freeze

Cut music

Crawler caption: 'August 2nd—appeal successful. Permission granted for ten houses & one multi-unit on Site B. August 4th—New Inn contract signed'

Mid-s combine harvester looming up over corn

Long-s through bales onto Site A: brick houses, scaffolding etc.
Mid-s man laying bricks

CLIVE V/O:
Well pleased, yep. We're getting there. You know, we developers have er, a little bit of a bad name. But when you look—look at the kind of dwellings we're now, at—at present—constructing—trying to incorporate it all with the

Wide-s wrapped stack of bricks
Zoom in on name across polythene: 'Redland Olde English'

Pan over new roof tiles

Mid-s man laying tiles

Wide-s Clive nodding & foreman talking

Mid-close-up Clive talking to foreman

surrounds—well, I mean there's no sense in that kind of feeling, is there? We are wholly traditional in—in design, actually. Now I'm parish born and bred, so I'm not talking er, out of line here.

CLIVE:

—Romany Spartan, yep. For the en suite. And Greensward for the lower toilet and Crinkle Tan for the upstairs. Yes. And you might er, tell him to get his arse in gear a bit. Don't let him tell him—tell you he hasn't got any Greensward *(coughs)* that Grey Heron rubbish he's always trying to get—

FOREMAN:

Porcelain door handles.

CLIVE:

What about them?

FOREMAN:

They're a bugger to get the right size. You know they sent the—

CLIVE:

Christ. Are we weather-tight on the Balmorals yet, Ted?

FOREMAN:

We are.

CLIVE:

What idiot put the wallboard on the grass?

FOREMAN:
We did lose the bottom—er, the buggers delivered it early didn't they—

CLIVE:
That's not what I asked Ted, I said it—who put it—them on the damp—

FOREMAN:
Roger.

CLIVE:
Well tell Roger he can see me tonight. All right? Now get the finish floor in before—

Long-s Clive & foreman over hay in barn, pull back focus onto beams

Close-up book on desk: Firkins and Felloes: A Parish History *by Raymond F. Duckett*

Shepherd's pipe music

Pan across books on shelf: rural history, customs etc.
Zoom in on last book & pan down spine: Up in Arms: The True Story of Cap'n Bedwine *(by) R. F. Duckett*

Mid-close-up Duckett at typewriter

Fade music

Mid-s Duckett at desk
Interview sync.

DUCKETT:
Well—well we are disappointed. That goes without saying, doesn't

it? Erm, but we do—we must fight on of course. It is a fact that Mr Walters is, unfortunately em, the er—the tip of an iceberg. Now do you know that fifty years ago the A-road, the very busy Fogbourne–Swindon road, was unmetalled? Oh yes. All the green fields had their em, their own names you know. The Gore. Gumbledon Acres. Apple Dean. Whitesheet Haw. Brambleberry Piece. Top and er, Bottom Field. Little Hangy. That's the one Mr Walters is er, on. Old word for sticky. Not hanging. A whole—whole way of life. Knowledge. Yes. That's what Mr Walters and . . . and his ilk, our way of—our urban, suburban, whatever you like to put a name to it—that's what is under threat. That old knowledge. Apart from the tranquillity. A sort of wisdom, I would go as so far as to say. Yes. Fight on!

Thunder

Wide-s wind in ripe corn
Close-up branch swaying
Wide-s dark clouds passing

Thunder clap, into Vivaldi 'Summer'

Mid-s rain hammering on plastic covers on site
Wide-s rain on a completed

Balmoral house
Close-up puddle in mud

(Presto—Summer Storm)

Wide-s site houses foreground, pan to church etc. beyond, zoom in on clock on tower thru rain spotting lens
Wide-s people hurrying from church in rain

Int. day:
Long-s Bradman alone in church, on knees in pew

Fade music

Close-up Bradman profile

BRADMAN:
I don't know if er, if—if it makes any difference, no. But you see the church is—is where it er, it all happens d'you see. Birth, baptism, marriage. Death of course. And I do ask God if he shall, if He will help us of course. Just a little

Pan across old frescoes: Adam, Noah's Ark, wing of angel

teeny-tiny bit of help, muscle or what—oh yes. Every Sunday, d'you see? And I do recall my pupils getting a penny for singing in the choir. Oh yes. Or a Mackintosh toffee bar. Now isn't that funny? Clear as a bell. Oh yes. Man with a

Pan choir stall, tilt up on pulpit

monocle. *(Laughs)* I was a bit of a convert, really. Things happen. *(Pause)* Well, there is evil in the world, isn't there? Everything

Close-up Bradman

changes so—so fast these days, d'you see? So fast. Well it's—it's all these men! *(Laughs to camera)*

Thunder

Mid-s Clive in door of site hut, sheltering

CLIVE:
Rain stops play as the Bishop said! Business and er, pleasure now! See you down there!

Pan on Clive running to car

Close-up wheel scrunching to stop, tilt up to show The New Inn in background

Int. day:
Wide-s empty saloon bar, pan onto Clive & Knapp at table poring over plan

KNAPP:
. . . without partitions of any sort. Right? And er . . . if we can retain the door there—

CLIVE:
On this sort of job, Geoff, what we're basically looking for is er, is style. You wanna strip out the dowdy kinda stuff, and you wanna make it er, amicable. But what we don't, is er—what we don't require is sort of throwing out the baby with the bathwater as it were. That's what slightly, if you don't mind me saying, worries me about the false er, the trellis ceiling with the repro er, geraniums—

KNAPP:
Vines.

CLIVE:
What—right. What—what I think you want, is the open plan yes, but

instead of—if you want to be rid of these oak tables and so on—

Crawler caption: 'Geoff Knapp, publican'

KNAPP:
Too bloody big Clive. You can't move.

CLIVE:
But in retaining the rustic look, with the . . . how about this. Twenty repro sewing tables, cast iron, bentwood seating, a nice distressed medieval sort of thing, settle, you know the high . . . thing—and I've seen *(coughs)* 'scuse me—I have—the warehouse does have some very nice hunting prints

Close-up Knapp nodding

with brass spots all but thrown in, and er, and you want some local er, shots er, I've got a nice one with all the chaps lined up in the square, you know, off to war and so forth, all the ladies in those—those queer bo-bonnets-type things, y'know, quite classy actually. And er, that blacksmith's, nice old blacksmith's one, you know, shoeing the old horse and whatnot . . . er, Brian had a copy I think of his advert—

Close-up sepia photo on wall of old peasant woman

KNAPP:
Give the old girl a good dust.

CLIVE:
Yes that one, yes, nice frame and you're away Geoff, or you can blow

Close-up Clive

it right up like the waggon one in er, whatsit—

KNAPP:
'Half Moon' up at Fawholt?

Mid-s Clive & Knapp

CLIVE:
That's right. Lovely. Do a nice Stilton ploughman's up there too, by the way, Geoff. That nice er, Diane up there. And a chili con carne that you will know about a couple of days after but er, anyway—that'll do as my old grandad used to say! About er, half the price of that bloody Mill House too, 'scuse my French. Erm, so you've got your—you've opened it all up, a bit of air and light, a bit of pine, your conservatory at the back for—for your posh do's—a

Close-up Clive

nice ambience, elegant-style fittings all over the shop, and you've retained your rustic feel—because you're going to get—

KNAPP
—well if—

CLIVE:
—no listen, Geoff. You're gonna get your real-ale types, aren't you?

Wide-s Clive & Knapp

KNAPP:
Yeah—

CLIVE:
But you don't want to lose—you

want—you would like to sort of market yourself for the office-lunch type do in the country, as well. Right? As well as your country-and-whatsit-Western evenings. Now as I see it you've—we've got all that in a barrel this way. Before you show it to the int des bods who you've got to watch costwise like a bloody eagle. We did a pub—you know it—'Malt Shovel' up er, by the flyover—bloody great ornamental pew from—beautiful piece—from some cathedral or other. Could we get him in? For the bar—could we get the bugger in? Paid a bob or two for that er, that one. So you've got to know er, what you want Geoff.

KNAPP:
Well I mean we're not a church for a start-off are we? *(Laughs)*

Mid-s Clive & Knapp laughing to camera

Long-s downs, pan to pick up fox-hunters

Vivaldi 'Autumn' (Allegro—The Hunt)

Pan across yellowing leaves of wood to hunters zipping past & away

Mid-s horse jumping hedge over camera, tilt up & cut into

close-up excavator above lifting earth

Mid-s excavator stopped
Wide-s Clive & men studying trench

Close-up foreman wiping his face

Fade out music

Mid-s Clive by trench

CLIVE:
Well, we've got a problem.
Look down there.

Tilt to trench, zoom in on skull & armbones part exposed

This was er, Phase 2 of the er, of Tedder's Mede, as we are now named. Foundations for. But the Westminsters are held up by that little chap. Known of any murders round here recently? What's more,

Close-up eye socket

the—this ground is like a bloody sponge. We're going to have to pile it. So i-it's not my bloody day. Clive is not er, happy. No.

Wide-s thru hut window of Clive on phone

Shepherd's pipe music

Crawler caption: 'September 28th: Clive contacts police. Local archaeologists alerted'

POLICEWOMAN ON PHONE V/O:
Hallo, is that the Archaeological Society? Hallo . . . We've got a little something for you we think . . .

Mid-s farm sign: 'Keep Out. Minimal Disease Area'
Pan onto site glimpsed between silo & pig batteries, zoom in on new houses

ARCHAEOLOGIST ON PHONE V/O:
. . . David? Hallo. It's Mike here. We've got ourselves some bones to play with. Yes. Over at Ulverton. Yes. Probably Civil—

Wide-s group in trench digging around skeleton, pull back to Clive on edge shaking his head		*Music fainter*
Mid-s builder *Interview sync.*	BUILDER: Quite a shock, yeah. Bit tight up against the er, unit there so I—I was hand-stripping. Yeah. Quite a shock. Broke his old skull a bit. Dream about it I spect!	
Mid-close-up Thorpe & Caird squatting down by trench		
Close-up skull, pan down whole body to feet-bones	CLIVE V/O ON PHONE: . . . bloody nuisance . . . yeah . . . well I don't know . . . yep . . . quite a hold-up yep, may have been foul play as it were . . .	
		Cut music
Mid-s archaeologists, with anorak hoods up, chatting by trench *Pan archaeols.' faces*	1ST ARCHAEOLOGIST: . . . no skirmish here nothing. OS ref er, bom bom 464750. Hm. I think it, if we take the gold coin to be a—to be plunder—	
	2ND ARCHAEOLOGIST: Not necessarily.	
Close-up skeleton's hand	1ST ARCHAEOLOGIST: We've—I think we can safely say, soldier. Probably Crom—	
Close-up remains of boots	3RD ARCHAEOLOGIST: Best example I've seen locally of leather preservation incidentally . . .	

1ST ARCHAEOLOGIST:
Yes—and a bit of er, what looks like, I think we can safely say, silk. Ribbon? In his hand er, I think we—

Close-up 2nd Archaeol.

2ND ARCHAEOLOGIST:
But he has been bonked on the head—

Close-up of cranium

3RD ARCHAEOLOGIST:
The cranial damage from the builder's spade is quite distinct from the, what was probably, em . . .

2ND ARCHAEOLOGIST:
The fatal blow, yes.

Mid-s 3rd Archaeol.

3RD ARCHAEOLOGIST:
Yes.

1ST ARCHAEOLOGIST:
Well he may have been pursued from the . . . battle site itself—

Close-up of coins in between vertebrae etc.

3RD ARCHAEOLOGIST:
Odd that the coins haven't been—weren't taken . . .

1ST ARCHAEOLOGIST:
From their position near the colon it may be they were er, swallowed, of course—

Close-up 2nd Archaeol.

2ND ARCHAEOLOGIST:
Oo, painful . . . ! *(Laughter)*

Long-s archaeologists through

excavator teeth
Skeleton sequence
Computer animation:
Close-ups Clive & new houses supered on—

Vivaldi 'Autumn' (Allegro—Dance & Song of Country Folk)

Wide-s above of skeleton being lifted out in foam packing
Mid-s skeleton package being loaded into van, doors closed, pan to follow van out of site

Zoom in on still of coins

Wide-s Bradman, Duckett, Thorpe & Caird by farm gate

BRADMAN:
Oh very exciting. Aren't we, Adam? Oh—

THORPE:
Fascinating. Love it.

DUCKETT:
Well it's history again, isn't it? That's the point. Isn't it?

THORPE:
It's—

CAIRD:
Isn't it every . . . that almost every field has it own—has its tale, really—

BRADMAN:
Every field!

Mid-s of bricks, tilt up to show 'Walters Homes: A Prestige Development . . .' on sign, pan up to company flag flapping in wind

Music ends (close of movement)

Fade

Int. day:
Mid-s Dixon on phone

DIXON:
Prior to commencement, Mr Walters, of Site B, I would just like to confirm receipt of your amended site plan . . . yes . . . good. On the question of soft landscaping, er you know our policy is for a mixture of evergreen and deciduous and er, shrub cover I expect to be somewhat denser against the open farmland er, bordering the west—yes . . . That's right. Yes. Now the barn-style unit is, as I understand it, to be er—that is the driveway I'm referring to er—will be covered in red-top tarmac, because there was some—not shingle, no. Right Mr Walters. Fine. Well that's clear in my mind now and—right yes er, I'll be writing to confirm our points then Mr Walters . . .

Close-up Dixon off phone
Interview sync.

DIXON:
We do, in our area, require really a very high er, level of spatial form and character—and we'd get a load of stick if we did otherwise—for

the—for this kind of—particularly this kind of shared surface accessway er, layout. Where it is, in fact, contributing to what is already an extremely attractive and of course historic village situated as it is, on the downland itself. In this particular er, instance. But of course there are many others. As you can see from my desk! *(Chuckles)* Yes. We lost on this one. But I'm happy with er, with Mr Walters's er, planned design as it stands. Let's hope he doesn't find any more skeletons in the cupboard—as you might say! *(Chuckles)*

Close-up local newspaper headline: 'Whoops! Dem Old Bones!'

Mid-s Clive holding newspaper Interview sync.

CLIVE:

Bloody awful. Disastrous to be frank. Bloody awful. It's a turn-off isn't it? We've just got the showhouse open, tomorrow's champers day, open house as it were, and we've got this bugger landed on our doorstep. Bad image, you see. Skeletons and so forth. You'd be very surprised how many people are overcome by superstition on the—the matter of buying, or choosing, houses. Ghosts. Curses. That sort of nonsense. Never bothered me. Like that er, Orchard House. In the village. By the Manor School, where my youngest goes. Revamped the whole lot top to toe what, ten years ago.

Photo of house with scaffolding etc.

CLIVE V/O:

Right out. Yep. When I was still just a er, a builder and decorator. On that one. And at the end of the garden there's a er, poetic er . . .

Mid-close-up stone tablet

stone tablet. Trees all round it. Where the previous owner, a sort of artist chappie, had buried his works. Eccentric type. Oh yes.

Slow-motion shot Enid Bradman walking on downs

Better be careful 'cos i-it's his widow who's not going along with my plans, as you might say. But it—not that it was a part of the property in fact er, but it—it sold him. Never mind the graffiti it er, it was a little bit of a story. Added a

Close-up window thru nodding branches

few thou, yep. Except of course that the old Squire chappie knocks on the windows so they say. Who did himself in. Years ago. Didn't mention the knocking I'll be honest! But then some of the

Library footage:
Close-up owl in tree

punters, they er—they go and take a house like a shot that has—with that sort of er, bloody history. Dennis Nilsen's up in London. Snapped up. *(Laughs)*

Mid-s Clive

CLIVE:

Character. All depends on er, how

you handle it. But er, I'll be living this one down for some time to come. Bad smell. Media, you er—they get hold of it, well. Bloody awful. It's a soldier or something wasn't it? Bloody unfortunate, actually. Oh well. There's always something isn't there? To wipe the grin off your smile, as my old er, dad used to say as it were.

Ext. day:
Mid-s Five Elms Farm
Pan Oadam climbing down off grain silo

OADAM:

Mid-s Oadam in front of silo
Interview sync.

I heard about it, yes. Doesn't make no difference to me. Er . . . isn't my field any more is it? Good luck to 'em then. Got the harvest in just in the nick didn't I? Oh yes all the land round here, it's hardly worth it is it? Well I mean farming you know, isn't what it used to be. We haven't got the support. Golf courses isn't it now? I could try that. You've got to diversify. Well I mean. You've—we've got to diversify. Nothing else to it. My son, he's er, he's going—gone into deliveries. Nappies. His own business. Makes more carting round nappies than I do farming. Isn't it? *(Snorts)* Can't do anything right, I mean. Chemicals. What? Load of

Crawler caption: 'Martin Oadam, farmer'

	fuss about water and so on. Carp carp. No. No future in all this. And we've been—we've been farmers two hundred years mate. I don't know I don't. Isn't it? Ridiculous.
Ext. morning: *Long-s Clive's house thru flock of sheep*	
Int. morning: *Wide-s Clive & wife at breakfast table, TV behind*	TV VOICE: . . . first reports say that the shootings were probably the work of the Hizbollah. Calm has descended on the city, but . . . *(Continues under conversation)*
Mid-s Clive with newspaper, sipping tea	CLIVE: Half a one of those 75ers each. Of champers. I got five cases.
Mid-s Mrs Walters pouring tea	MRS WALTERS: How many?
Pan to Clive	CLIVE: Should be enough.
	MRS WALTERS: How many then?
	CLIVE: Er, not a clue.
Wide-s both	MRS WALTERS: Well should be.
	CLIVE: Bloody jokes about skeletons I presume. The usual Made in Taiwan er, rib-ticklers.

MRS. WALTERS:
Can you pick up er, Gary tonight? Honey.

CLIVE:
Eh?

Mid-s Mrs Walters with knife

MRS WALTERS:
Gary. Honey please.

CLIVE:
No. Basically.

MRS WALTERS:
Mrs Turner's poorly. Thanks.

Mid-s Clive

CLIVE:
Oh.

MRS WALTERS:
Well who's going to—

CLIVE:
What time?

Wide-s both

MRS WALTERS:
American football night—

CLIVE:
Bloody hell.

Close-up Clive biting toast to camera

Close-up cork popping
Close-up mouth at champagne glass, zoom in on lips breaking into laugh
Close-up scissors cutting red ribbon
Mid-s Clive holding up two ends

Vivaldi 'Autumn' (Allegro—Dance & Song of Country Folk)

of ribbon & laughing
Wide-s people studying fitted
kitchen units
Close-up Clive chatting, tilt down
to his hand stroking bathroom
tiles
Mid-s woman struggling to open
window-latch
Mid-s Clive shaking hands in hall
Close-up sales consultant
displaying door handle
Close-up woman struggling with
window-latch
Mid-s man feeling bath, pan &
zoom in on brass tap being
turned on by woman
Close-up champagne being
poured into glass
Wide-s group gazing at open
fireplace
Mid-s woman struggling with
window-latch
Close-up finger rubbing moulded
architrave
Close-up mouth laughing
Close-up woman's hand still
struggling with latch
Mid-s sales consultant adjusting
her skirt
Wide-s group gazing at
thermostat
Mid-s front door opening to two
more couples
Mid-s sales office desk &
brochures

Pan close-up across brochure:
'Luxury homes in an exceptional
countryside location,' tilt down to
photo of autumn leaves,
pull back focus to blur

Ext. day:
Wide-s showhouse & people in
front, tilt up & zoom in on woman
flinging open window with
surprised look

Cut music on
first
crescendo

Mid-s Clive in sales office

CLIVE:
Sold seven plots. Well, to be er, precise, as best I may, we've had seven deposits of 500 quid apiece. Six weeks to exchange, price guaranteed. So er, we've had a couple of Balmorals, one er, haven't we?—one Windsor gone, and a Westie. If my memory serves me correctly, befuddled as it is with the er, bubbles. And no rib—

Mid-s sales consultant

SALES CONSULTANT:
That's correct—

Wide-s both

CLIVE:
Thank you Liz! Thank you! She's my right-hand whatsit as it were, Liz.

Close-up Liz giggling

Have some more—

Ext day:
Mid-s couple & kids in front of patch of earth on Site B
Interview sync.

MAN:
We liked it, yes.

WOMAN:
We did want to live in the countryside—

MAN:
Actually, we—we were quite impressed initially, I think, by the location more than the er, actual homes!

WOMAN:
Well, it's very er, important we think and for the children too, we believe. To have that kind of—

MAN:
Well, to have that country life.

WOMAN:
We liked this plot, didn't we Greg?

MAN:
I've always been a dreamer.

Mid-s sign stuck in earth: 'Plot 12'
Fast sequence close-ups of 'Sold' stickers
Cut to mid-s Clive toasting with glass to camera outside showhouse

Long-s over large tree-stump of Caird & Duckett walking up to

gate & opening it *Wide-s thru passing cars of Caird & Duckett leaning on gate with cows beyond* *Mid-close-up of both talking over road noise etc.*	
	CAIRD: This was always known as the Gore, apparently.
	DUCKETT: That's right Sally. This field was known as the Gore. Gore meaning, Sally, a level rather low-lying land—piece of land. As this is, of course, is er, low.
	CAIRD: And this gate. You found a er—something interesting out about this, even this old metal gate, didn't you, Ray?
Close-up Duckett's hand on cross-bar	DUCKETT: That's right Sally. A lovely little story—*(Pause for plane passing overhead)* . . . As you may notice it is a lovely piece of Edwardian, I would say, ironwork. Made in the er, local blacksmith's shop. Excellent craftsmanship. Now this would have been one of the first metal gates—
Mid-s Caird & Duckett	CAIRD: All of wood before. Oak?
	DUCKETT: Yes—

CAIRD:
Could you tell us the er, story about this gate?

DUCKETT:
Oh marvellous. A certain young fellow, a shepherd I believe, or in certain versions a er, a schoolmaster—

CAIRD:
And in one a German . . . erm, pilot?

DUCKETT:
Well I think that's a rather more modern version, I'd say—

CAIRD:
—an up-date.

DUCKETT:
As you might well put it, yes! Well this fellow, let's assume a shepherd, was sitting on this er, very gate Sally. Now this gate was wooden then, of course. Like all the gates round here then. Beautiful work, of course, in those days, all works of—well art, really . . .

CAIRD:
And he was bumped off isn't that right? By person or persons unknown.

DUCKETT:
Well yes. That's right. And of

course folk began to see him sitting on the gate just where he was slain so cruelly by a passing vagabond. For a few pennies. Because of course in those days—

CAIRD:

And no one dared mend the gate when it em fi—eventually started to fall off its er, hinges.

DUCKETT:

That's right Sally. Until eventually some clever chap did put this lovely iron gate in its place that we er, are—have right here, and of course—

CAIRD:

It was too cold to sit on.

DUCKETT:

That's right. No ghost! *(Both laugh)*

CAIRD:

That's great. Every er, spot has its own em, kind of er—

DUCKETT:

Oh yes. Now I wonder what that skeleton, for instance, was doing there, Sally.

Pan R from their faces to pollarded oak, pull back to long-s Five Elms Farm over road & fields Zoom in on roofs of development just visible beyond

Mid-s piles on Site A, tilt up as shaft rams down

Close-up leaves falling off branch
Close-up bedraggled 'old man's beard' in hedge
Close-up foam in river
Crawler caption: 'November—pumping & piling continues. Only 50% of plots on both sites sold'

Wide-s group of youths outside bus shelter in square, zoom in on motorbike wheel

Mid-s youths
Interview sync.

1ST YOUTH:
Eh? Well. We've gotta have houses.

2ND YOUTH:
Jobs innit?

1ST YOUTH:
Well I mean it in't—

3RD YOUTH:
Dump round here—

2ND YOUTH:
Shuddup, Mandy. It's all right.

1ST YOUTH:
There in't a lot to do is there?

Crawler caption: 'Jason Scablehorne'

4TH YOUTH:
Self-motivation. No, tha-that's what it is, you've gotta have. Well I mean we en't gonna save the world and all the dolphins and weather and suchlike just by standing around—

3RD YOUTH:
Shuddup Jason—*(Giggles)*

2ND YOUTH:
Shuddup Mandy—

4TH YOUTH:
Well that's what I think. You go and build houses everywhere you in't gonna—there isn't gonna be any world left is there?

2ND YOUTH:
All gonna go anyway. Innit? En't nothing we can do about it—

1ST YOUTH:
Da-ancing!

3RD YOUTH:
Boogie-boogie—

2ND YOUTH:
Shuddup Mandy—

5TH YOUTH:
They should abolish politicians for a start. I hate politicians.

3RD YOUTH:
You gotta—

Crawler caption: 'Hazel Griffin'

2ND YOUTH:
It's all right here I mean we're not all starving like all the Africans and so on are we I mean I gave—we gave—we did a fast like for them didn't we? And we got, what was it—

4TH YOUTH:
Fifty-eight pounds and 50 pence.

2ND YOUTH:
Yeah I mean—

5TH YOUTH:
All the politicians straight in their pockets that would—

Crawler caption: 'Leon Pyke'

1ST YOUTH:
Anyway he can't sell. Them new houses, can he? I've seen all the signs he hasn't sold much has he? My dad says—

3RD YOUTH:
I'm a skeleton—woooo!

2ND YOUTH:
Shuddup Mandy—

1ST YOUTH:
Curse of Five Elms Farm innit?
(General giggling)

Int. day:
Mid-s Clive on phone

CLIVE:
Hallo. Webb's Timber Yard? Hallo. Clive Walters of Walters New Homes Ltd. Got a problem here. Hallo, Mike yes. A little bit sticky here. That Novaply board you got for us at such er, in double-quick time—for the interior trim that's right—well the stuff be a little bit swollen. Yeah. That's the three-ply. On arrival, yep. And I'm running nose up against schedule at present. Yep.

Mid-s Clive at desk
Interview sync.

Not all hunky-dory, no. Er, no I have to be er, I have to be straightforward about it and say that it's on the bumpy stretch at present, yes. I er—I—one does expect this, of course, but this feller does seem to be having its fair er, share of hassle, yes. Yep. The er, negative publicity didn't help. No. This bloody curse or something. I do have enemies abouts, of course. The Preservation lot. Misinformation. And the general economic downturn. And the er, the bloody weather needless to say. Clive is not, at present, a happy chap. No. No. Definitely not.

Ext. day:
Long-s bare wood on crest
Mid-s tractor ploughing
Mid-close-up sticker on window—'For Sale'

Vivaldi 'Winter' (Largo—Rain)

Music faint

Mid-s couple & kids outside Balmoral house
Interview sync.

WOMAN:
Very nice, isn't it Tony?

MAN:
We're very pleased.

WOMAN:
It's all a bit of a mess and a—a bit noisy but—

MAN:
We are living on a building-site

when it comes down to it. But er, we're very pleased. A very nice general all-round finish to the place, we think.

WOMAN:
And I lit a fire in the fireplace, haven't we Tony? *(Laughs)* That was a story and a half! *(Laughs)*

MAN:
We're very pleased, yes.

Int. evening:
Mid-s Clive smoking at desk, zoom in on fag & trembling fingers
Wide-s thru window, rain spotting glass

Music up

Int. day:
Wide-s Clive with Padmore in his office

PADMORE:
. . . not moving at all, Clive. But we do expect a bit of an upswing in the—come the spring actually—

CLIVE:
I'm going to blow a load of money on this little lot if it's er, doesn't do so Brian fairly urgently—

PADMORE:
Well we're fairly confident Clive. And the conversion going okay as a matter of interest is it?

Mid-close-up hammer smashing inner wall
Close-up Knapp pointing

Music—'John Barleycorn'

Ext. day:
Tracking shot of old tables &
benches etc. piled up outside in
square car-park

Close-up inn sign being
unhooked

Close-up drilling into outside wall
Wide-s conservatory parts being
assembled
Mid-s Clive with folded arms
watching
Mid-s waggon wheel being hung
on outside wall
Mid-s new sign being put up,
zoom in on new name—'The
Never Fear'

Int. day:
Wide-s Clive & Knapp etc.
clicking glasses in new large
interior
Close-up ribbon being cut
Wide-s people cheering
Close-up pint at mouth
Close-up sepia photo on wall of
men lined up in square
Zoom in on grinning face — *Fade music*

Ext. night:
Wide-s Ulverton Council Estate

Int. night:
Wide-s Bunce on settee watching
TV
Mid-close-up Bunce — BUNCE:
Interview sync. — Load of old rubbish, innit? None

of us lot well, we don't go now. Not since they've gone and er . . . made a pig's ear out with it. Have we? Cheaper to stay in here at home. Wife don't like it. Rather be—have me out under her feet. True! *(Laughs)* Yaa, load of old rubbish. Can't go calling it the 'Never Fear' can you? That was what we used to say. Eh? Come down for a pint a Never Fear then? Then it was, what, table beer. Then worse nor that. Then the old rattle-tap. Piss-water, that was. *(Laughs, into coughing)* Oh aye. Thruppence a pint. Yeh. Big hunk a cheese on the er, on the bar. Eh? All have knives on you then. And er, ha'penny for a clay-pipe, free if you was er, if you was in with old Jimmy Herring. That was it. Penny-ha'penny for shag-bacco. See you through the night. Oh yeh. Well it's never the same, is it? Let's go and have a bunk. Or a never fear. That's right. Burn er, burn him down we should. Burn the bugger down pardon my tongue. *(Coughs)* It's all changing. For the bloody worse. Oh yeh. Just as well look, I won't be round too long to see it all. In't that so? *(Laughs)* Least I don't come half-cut though, does I? Back home? Eh? *(Laughs)* Now? Eh? No. And the 'Green

Close-up fingers crooked on lap

Close-up Bunce

Man', that's all music, music. Videos.

Mid-s Bunce watching TV
Close-up TV, zoom in on game-show host

Ext. day:
Long-s snow falling across down

Vivaldi 'Winter' faint (Allegro non molto—frozen, shivering etc.)

Wide-s snow falling on Site B—bricks, plastic covers, excavator etc.
Pan to Site A
Long-s new houses in snow

CLIVE V/O ON PHONE:
I see, yep. No joy from them then. Right. Well I'm paying dearly for it. Oh yes. Bloody local magazine. Doing a series on er, curses. What? Well sort of . . . yep. Yeah. Legends, yep. This bloke Thorpe. Alan Thorpe. Author. In er, *Wessex*, *The Wessex Nave. Nave.* Yeah. Last week. Yep. They did one on er, it was Five Elms bloody Farm. I think it's all—eh? How do I know what the bloody circulation is? The principle of it Brian. It's a—it's an A-one *(coughs)* an, a top-notch bloody scandal actually Brian. Graham's written—Graham Curtis up at Plum Communications—he's written in about it. Bloody furious. Invented the whole bloody lot if

Close-up barbed wire with torn plastic bag blowing

Close-up crow in snow

you ask me. My name. Got a Walters nasty in with a bloody great jaw. As far as I can see it's all but libel Brian. Yeah. Well read it then. Here, er, listen to this. *(Reading)* 'He was a big man with a big nose and drank.' It's not bloody funny er, Brian. Eh? We are not amused at all, seriously. This er, character Walters does away with this bloke and it's the same bloke er, is implied as such, as our bony friend

Close-up frozen glove in snow

what we unfortunately dug up Brian, yeah. First anyone's heard about it. Totally invented. Total fiction Brian. Martin Oadam's hopping mad. Yeah. Well it's his bloody farm isn't it? Already got some weirdos with a crystal whatsit

Long-s site under snow from hill

bloody ball come along. I know. Metal detectors next, all over the bloody shop. Yep. Right Brian. Yep. Bloody furious actually, as it were . . .

Vivaldi up, then cut

Int. day:
Close-up Thorpe's story in The Wessex Nave, *zoom in on illustration of shepherd holding lantern, fade into close-up real lantern hanging from beam*

Mid-s Thorpe in chair by word processor

THORPE:
Yes, I've heard that Mr Walters

Interview sync.

isn't very pleased—I've received a . . . letter from him, saying so, in no uncertain terms. But er, I don't regret using his name, it's a—Walters is a local name. The oldest stone in—in the graveyard here, that's legible. 1689. That's where I er, took it from. Er, I'm er, doing a whole series of stories on shepherds. I've done a lot of research, a lot of local research, and cr, all my stories are based on fact and er, using local legends and so on. I don't think it's—I think it's rather Mr Walters's reading. I think it's . . . it's up to him. If he wishes to read it in that way, then . . . let him do so. But I certainly don't take anything back.

Ext. day:
Tracking shot of downland
Crawler caption: 'February—slump in house sales deepens. Work on Site B postponed until April'

Vivaldi 'Winter' (Allegro—Crossing the Ice)

Music faint

Close-up Clive in car
Interview sync.

CLIVE:

I've blown a load of money. 250 grand in fact. Pulled the prices right down. Buyers are laughing. Getting right out of it—clean out of multiples. Fingers burnt to a cinder actually, as it were. Win some lose some. You want—people want to have houses, don't they? And what do you get in the—when you build folk—when you put the buggers up, the actual houses they want? Kick after kick. Bang bang. Bloody scandal, isn't it? No, bloody awful year. Speaking personally. Bloody terrible. For Clive. But there'll be another. Eh? Ups and downs. Another year. Yep. That's how, what you got—have to think. Another year. There's always that. Another year.

Ext. day: *Mid-s car zipping past, pan to follow thru downland until out of sight over crest of hill*	*Music up*
Pan round & down to village & zoom in on new development *Hold*	*Fade music*
End credits supered on—	*Shepherd's pipe music*
Long-s sun setting behind tumulus	

Acknowledgements

Among the numerous books and articles that have been of invaluable help and inspiration to me, I would especially like to mention the following: Edward Lisle's Observations in Husbandry (London, 1757), Major B. Lowsley's A Glossary of Berkshire Words & Phrases (London, 1888), and the Treasury Solicitors' briefs concerning the labourers' rising of 1830 (Public Record Office), certain phrases of which I have incorporated in 'Deposition'.

Among the many people who have wittingly or unwittingly contributed to the making of this book, I am particularly indebted to the following for their help and advice, for which I thank them: Ray Bulpit, William and Dorothy Pierpoint, Jean and Mauricette Robard, Eric Shinwell, Sheila and Barney Thorpe, and my editor, Robin Robertson. I would also like to thank my wife, Jo, for her unstinting support and unerring judgement. 'Treasure' is dedicated to the late Tom Iremonger, whose story it was.